PRAISE FOR
BEN KANE

'**Brilliantly entertaining**. In Matthew Carrey, Ben Kane has created a wonderfully flawed but human hero, a man who, often unwittingly and many times entirely through his own errors of judgement, finds himself caught up in one desperate escapade after another, and which, like the very best historical adventures, see him cross seas and travel continents and, along the way, meet an array of acutely observed characters from villains to femme fatales and to Napoleon himself. Ben Kane's **attention to historical detail is also second-to-none** – in *Napoleon's Spy* he has brought Napoleon's calamitous Russian campaign vividly and compelling to life in **one of the most enjoyable and compelling historical romps** I've read in a very long time'

James Holland, historian, writer and broadcaster

'*Napoleon's Spy* is a **tour de force on an epic scale** that immerses the reader in the scent of cannon smoke and the whistle of grapeshot. You can almost taste the fear. The 1812 campaign is a story of immense sacrifice, enormous courage and a man who never knew when to take a step back until it was too late for those who revered him. **Ben Kane is one of our finest historical novelists** and his passion for his subject shines through on every page'

Douglas Jackson, author of *Hero of Rome*

'As soon as I read the first few pages of a Ben Kane novel, I'm all in. It was no different with *Napoleon's Spy*. **Kane's historical detail is as intriguing and fascinating as his characters are compelling. His prose is lively, economical and intimate**, so that this story reads like a first hand account, but with the Kane master storyteller treatment. In fact, *Napoleon's Spy* is an **exemplar of a Ben Kane novel; exciting, immersive, well researched and great fun**. The author's very name has long been a seal of quality, and here he is at the top of his (or anybody's) game. What I love about this book, and his others too, is that it feels nostalgic. It reminds me of those classic, epic Hollywood movies of the 1950s and 1960s, which fired my imagination as a child and, in many ways, shaped me. **We have a flawed hero on a mission, thwarted by colourful villains and beset by every danger, all set against an epic backdrop of nation-defining war. What's not to love? Bravo, Ben Kane, you've done it again**'

Giles Kristian, author of *Lancelot*

'With intrigue, espionage and duels, this is a great adventure story set against the epic background of Napoleon's doomed invasion of Russia'

Adrian Goldsworthy, bestselling historian

'Ben Kane pivots from ancient Rome and medieval England to the Napoleonic Wars, and **delivers up a rip-roaring tale full of both swashbuckling and pathos**. Half-English, half-French Matthieu Carrey battles a weakness for cards and wine which frequently lands him in hot water, finding himself strong-armed into the reluctant position of Imperial messenger for Napoleon and clandestine spy for the English. Matthieu makes an **appealingly flawed hero**, fighting not only illicit duels and Cossack lances on the Grand Armee's campaign through Russia, but his own worst impulses. **It looks like the adventures of *Napoleon's Spy* may continue for future books - I for one will be first in line!**'

Kate Quinn, author of *Blood Sisters*

'**An epic tale** that never loses sight of the raw experience of the hero. **I loved *Napoleon's Spy***'

Simon Scarrow, author of the *Eagles of the Empire* series

'The first half of *Napoleon's Spy* is fun – a picturesque tale of duels, love affairs and gambling dens. The second is a searing, vivid account of Napoleon's terrible retreat from Moscow'

Antonia Senior, *The Times*

'Richard the Lionheart's name echoes down the centuries as one of history's greatest warriors, and **this book will immortalise him** even more. **A rip-roaring epic**, filled with arrows and spattered with blood. **Gird yourself with mail when you start**'

Paul Finch, author of *Strangers*

'Kane's virtues as a writer of historical adventures – **lively prose, thorough research, colourful action** – are again apparent'

Nick Rennison, *The Sunday Times*

'*Lionheart* has plenty of **betrayal, bloodshed and rich historical detail**'

Martin Chilton, *Independent*

'Plenty of **action, blood, scheming, hatred, stealth and politics** here, if that's what you want in your read – **and you know it is!**'

Sunday Sport

'To read one of Ben Kane's **astonishingly well-researched**, bestselling novels is to know that you are, historically speaking, in safe hands'

Elizabeth Buchan, *Daily Mail*

'This is a **stunningly visual and powerful** read: Kane's power of description is **second to none** . . . Perfect for anyone who is suffering from *Game of Thrones* withdrawal symptoms'

Helena Gumley-Mason, *The Lady*

'**Fans of battle-heavy historical fiction will, justly, adore *Clash of Empires*.** With its rounded historical characters and **fascinating** historical setting, it deserves a wider audience'

Antonia Senior, *The Times*

'**Grabs you from the start and never lets go.** Thrilling action combines with historical authenticity to summon up a whole world in a sweeping tale of politics and war. **A triumph!**'

Harry Sidebottom, author of the *The Last Hour*

'**Exceptional**. Kane's excelled once again in capturing the terror and the glory . . . of the ancient battlefield, and this story is one that's been begging for an expert hand for a long time'

Anthony Riches, author of the Empire series

'**Carried off with panache** and Kane's expansive, engaging, action-packed style. A complex, **fraught, moving and passionate** slice of history **from one of our generation's most ambitious and engaging writers**' Manda Scott, author of the Boudica series

'It's a broad canvas Kane is painting on, but he does it with **vivid** colours and, like the Romans themselves, he can show great admiration for a Greek enemy and still kick them in the balls'

Robert Low, author of the Oathsworn series

'Ben Kane manages to marry broad narrative invention with detailed historical research . . . in taut, authoritative prose . . . **his passion for the past, and for the craft of story-telling, shines from every page**'

Toby Clements, author of the Kingmaker series

'This **thrilling** series opener delivers every cough, spit, curse and gush of blood to set up the mighty clash of the title. Can't really fault this one' Jon Wise, *Weekend Sport*

'Ben Kane's new series **explores the bloody final clash between ancient Greece and upstart Rome**, focusing on soldiers and leaders from both worlds and **telling the story of a bloody war with style**'

Charlotte Heathcote, *Sunday Express S Magazine*

'**A thumping good read.** You can feel the earth tremble from the great battle scenes and feel the desperation of those caught up in the conflict. Kane's brilliant research weaves its way lightly throughout'

David Gilman, author of the Master of War series

BEN KANE is one of the most hard-working and successful historical writers in the industry. His third book, *The Road to Rome*, was a *Sunday Times* number four bestseller, and almost every title since has been a top ten bestseller. Born in Kenya, Kane moved to Ireland at the age of seven. After qualifying as a veterinarian, he worked in small animal practice and during the terrible Foot and Mouth Disease outbreak in 2001. Despite his veterinary career, he retained a deep love of history; this led him to begin writing.

His first novel, *The Forgotten Legion*, was published in 2008; since then he has written five series of Roman novels, a trilogy about Richard the Lionheart, and a collection of short stories. Kane lives in Somerset with his two children.

Also by Ben Kane

The Forgotten Legion Chronicles
The Forgotten Legion
The Silver Eagle
The Road to Rome

Hannibal
Enemy of Rome
Fields of Blood
Clouds of War

Eagles of Rome
Eagles at War
Hunting the Eagles
Eagles in the Storm

Clash of Empires
Clash of Empires
The Falling Sword

Spartacus
The Gladiator
Rebellion

Lionheart
Lionheart
Crusader
King

Standalone Novels
Napoleon's Spy

Short Story Collections
Sands of the Arena

STORMCROW

BEN KANE

ORION

First published in Great Britain in 2024 by Orion Fiction,
an imprint of The Orion Publishing Group Ltd,
Carmelite House, 50 Victoria Embankment
London EC4Y 0DZ

An Hachette UK company

1 3 5 7 9 10 8 6 4 2

A CIP catalogue record for this book
is available from the British Library.

ISBN (Hardback) 978 1 3987 1460 1
ISBN (Export Trade Paperback) 978 1 3987 1461 8
ISBN (eBook) 978 1 3987 1463 2

Typeset by Input Data Services Ltd, Bridgwater, Somerset

Printed and bound in Great Britain by Clays Ltd, Elcograf S.p.A.

MIX
Paper from
responsible sources
FSC® C104740
FSC
www.fsc.org

www.orionbooks.co.uk

For Andy Farrell, with massive thanks and huge respect.
Your work with the Irish men's rugby team has been quite remarkable.
It will never be forgotten. Thank you, sir!

Putting a note at the start of my novel is becoming something of a habit. As with *Napoleon's Spy*, I feel the need from the outset to explain details found in the book, because they may be unfamiliar to some readers.

A quick explanation: The Norse were a people who lived in modern-day Denmark, Sweden and Norway from the eighth to the early eleventh century A D. They were seafarers, traders, settlers and farmers. Vikings were a specific group of Norsemen, part-time warriors who served jarls, and sometimes went raiding. In other words, all Vikings were Norse, but most Norsemen were not Vikings.

In medieval Norse culture the main performers of *seiðr*, sorcery, were women. The men who practised it were effeminate and existed in a 'sexually charged state of dishonour', to quote Professor Neil Price, author of *The Viking Way*. They were regarded as unmanly, and by implication, assumed to adopt the female role in sex. Interestingly, being gay was acceptable among the Irish.

In 2017 the revisiting of a grave find from Birka in Sweden changed interpretation of Norse culture forever. A skeleton buried with the accoutrements of a warrior: an axe, quiver of arrows, spears and a sword, had originally been determined as male. When re-examined by archaeologist Anna Kjellström, it was found, remarkably, to be that of a woman. A woman, buried with war gear. The debate since has been endless, but one thing is clear – this woman was a warrior.

The find is not perhaps as unique as it might first seem. There are recorded instances of women serving in the Royal Navy in the Napoleonic conflict, as well as in the armies of the American Civil War. Their motivation remains unclear, but it is reasonable to put forward possible explanations. They may have been following their husbands or lovers into military service. They may have simply been seeking adventure. Fleeing domestic abuse. Or they may have been transgender.

In the tenth and eleventh centuries, Dublin had one of the largest slave markets in Europe. The sale of black slaves there is also in the historical record. Racism may have existed then as now, but there is no evidence in Norse culture of negative attitude towards people of colour.

These, then, are the historical bases for some of the characters you will read about in *Stormcrow* – not demented figments of my 'woke' imagination, but people who really could have existed.

ÉRIU

LOCHLANN

Ulfreksfjord

Man

CONNACHTA

ULAIDH

Caírlinn

Inis Mon

Cluain
Mhic
Nóis

Loch
Ainninn

MIDHE

Bóinn

LAIGHIN

Dubhlinn

Sionainn

Ruirthech

Gleann Máma

Luimnech

OSRAIGHE

BRETLAND

MUMHAN

Siúr

Waesfjord

Vedrarfjord

Dun Corcaighe

Saint
Petroc's Stowe

WEST-
BRETLAND

Cambronn

Gower

There were dozens of small
kingdoms in Ireland of the
late 10th/early 11th century.
Only the main ones are shown.

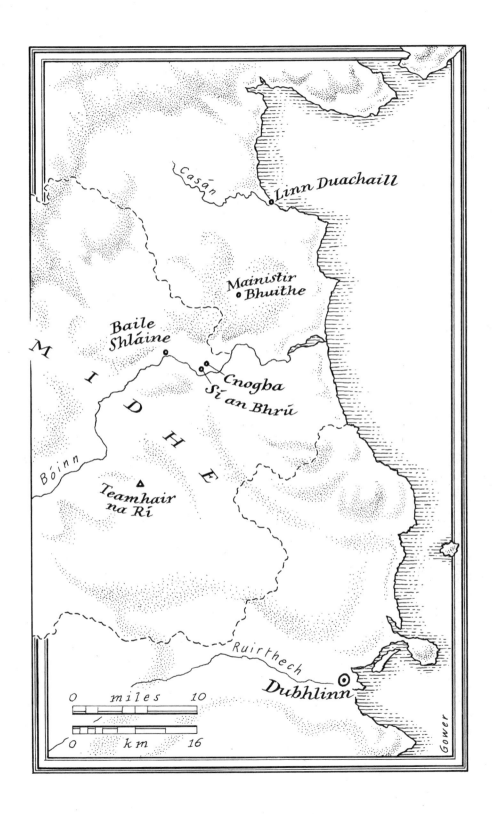

Casán

Linn Duachaill

Mainistir
Bhuithe

Baile
Shláine

M I D H E

Cnogba
Sí an Bhrú

Bóinn

Teamhair
na Rí

Ruirthech

Dubhlinn

Gower

0   miles   10

0   k m   16

PROLOGUE

M esmerised, I stared at the dark shape on the muddy sand.
Just ordered by my mother to see what the previous night's
storm might have sent ashore, I had disgruntledly spooned down the
last of my barley porridge, thrown on my cloak and left the longhouse.
There would be sea wrack, I had decided, lots of it, hard to work
through for flotsam and jetsam. There would be dog whelks too, on the
rocks. If my luck was in, there might be timber. Every so often, ship's
cargo washed up; that too would be cause for celebration.

What I had not anticipated this gusty spring morning was a corpse.

The man lay on his back some fifty paces away, where the receding
tide had left him. I wove a path in his direction, staying on the drier
patches of sand, all the while my attention returning to the body. What
flesh I could see was wrinkled and pale, the effects of time in the water.
Bearded, fully clothed in tunic and leggings, he looked to be a Norseman, like my father Thorgil.

It could not be my father, however, because I had seen him already,
sooty-faced, hard at work in his forge. It could not be my father, because this man wore a silver arm ring, and there was a scabbarded
sword attached to his belt. Only the wealthy afforded such jewellery
and weapons.

Fascinated, for I was not allowed to handle the few swords that my
father made, I went closer. I was only a little scared. Death, of animals
and people, was an everyday occurrence. Not every newborn lamb survived; every autumn, we slaughtered a pig. People died too, like Rodrek
the thrall, taken by a fever two years before, or our nearest neighbour,
Old Inga, whom I had found dead in bed some months since. This
corpse was very different. Half the top of its head was missing, sliced
away by the look of it. This man had not drowned, I thought, but been
slain.

Alarmed, my gaze went seaward. The water was choppy, white horses capping the waves to the horizon, but of longships there was not a sign. Relief filled me. It was not raiding season, yet stranger things had happened. I wondered uneasily if anyone would come looking for this dead man. It was unlikely, I decided. His comrades would have no idea that his body had ended up on the strand at Linn Duachaill.

Krrruk. A flutter of black wings, and a raven landed a dozen steps away. It cocked a beady eye at me, and hopped towards the corpse.

The sudden cold I felt had nothing to do with the wind.

Ravens were sacred to the god Oðin. Two of them he had, Huginn and Muninn, Thought and Memory. Flying hither and thither over the world, they returned each evening to perch on his shoulders, bringing news.

Only now did I notice the absence of gulls. Expert scavengers, they should have been here in numbers, feasting on the dead man's flesh. There were none. 'Because Oðin's bird is here,' I whispered.

If my mother had heard me, she would have boxed my ears. Irish and a devout Christian, she reviled the Norse gods. My father, though, still held faith with the beliefs of his ancestors. I did too, finding little to admire in the Christ worshippers' turn-the-other-cheek behaviour.

Krrruk. The raven hopped onto the dead man's belly. To my amazement, it did not make for his face, but the hilt of the sword. *Mine*, the gesture said. That was very plain, even to my thirteen-year-old eyes.

'Finn!'

We had few neighbours; the voice could not have been that of many people, but I would have known Vekel's voice anywhere. The same age as me, near enough, he was the only other boy in the immediate area. Tall, gangling, womanish, he was my best friend.

'Finn!'

'What?' I did not turn my head, but watched the raven. In between pecks at the yellow-white hilt, it appeared to be studying me. I was not sure where the courage came from to stare back, yet I did.

'Did he drown?'

'No. Someone took off the top of his head.'

'And now Oðin's raven is on him? Finn, come away!' There was an unusual nervousness in Vekel's voice.

I saw the sword first, I thought stubbornly, and took a step towards the corpse.

'Finn! *Finn!*'

I hesitated. I had always been fierce-tempered, and loved rough-and-tumble horseplay. When the chance came to battle another boy, I took it every time. Fighting came naturally to me, I did not know why. I had regular dreams of being a warrior, a painter of the wolf's tooth. In all likelihood, though, I would train as a smith like my father. Vekel was very different. Living with his grandmother, both parents dead, he was, most agreed, destined for a *seiðr* life, an existence entwined with magic. It wasn't just his uncanny ability with horses, or his feminine behaviour; he liked darkness, tales of Ragnarök, anything to do with the spirit world. When his father died, he had crept unseen from his bed and sat out all night by the grave, so, he proudly revealed afterwards, he could better commune with the shade.

The mere thought loosened my bowels. Why then, I wondered, did I not feel the same fear about possibly depriving a god's chosen bird of its prize?

Two more steps. Now I eyed the sword with naked greed. It was magnificent. The hilt seemed to be ivory, and the silver-chased scabbard ran down to an elaborately carved chape. I wanted it, more than anything in my life before.

Another step.

The raven let out a croak, and stayed where it was.

'Finn! Are you mad?'

'I saw the sword first,' I told the raven.

'What did you say?' Vekel shouted.

The bird's head cocked this way and that. Its beak clacked.

A raven could not carry a sword away, I thought. Maybe Oðin himself would come to claim it, but I doubted that. Sightings of gods were rare as hen's teeth. After the raven had eaten its fill, it would fly off, and whoever next came upon the body would take the princely blade. It might as well be mine, I decided.

Another two steps, within touching distance of corpse and bird.

Incredibly, the raven did not move.

'Let me have the sword,' I said, the words rising unbidden to my lips, 'and I swear to serve Oðin the length of my days.'

Time slowed. Vekel's cries and questions dimmed in my ears. My focus narrowed. All I saw was the raven's glossy black head, beak slightly agape. Its flint-black eyes bored into me.

3

My mouth dried. A pulse beat in my throat.

'Is this truly your oath?' the raven seemed to ask.

'Strike me down if I lie.' My voice, not quite broken, cracked on the last word. 'From this moment, I am Oðin's servant.'

Krrruk. Krrruk. The raven hopped off the corpse, as if to let me approach. Its head bobbed up and down; it did not fly away.

Something made me glance over my shoulder. Vekel was watching from a short distance away, and his mouth was hanging open. That reaction, from my magic-loving friend, was a spur to the last of my indecision.

'With your permission,' I said gravely to the raven, and reached down to slip off the dead man's baldric.

A little while later, I was walking the strand. The baldric was not adjustable, so the sword, by my side, reached almost to my left foot. I did not care. A quick look had revealed the blade to be every bit as magnificent as the scabbard. I felt like a giant. I did not know how long my jubilation would last, however. I suspected that upon my return my father would take the sword from me. Therefore, I decided, my search of the beach would be slow.

Vekel had not challenged the raven as I had. After a wary look at the corpse, after asking if I truly wanted the blade – my reply had been a vehement 'yes' – he had come with me. He demanded every last detail. There wasn't much to tell, I told him, laying out my story. Repeating the oath to Oðin, however, the magnitude of what I had done drove home.

'You did what?' Vekel's expression was again a picture.

'In return for the sword, I dedicated myself to Oðin.' My cheeks were warming; said aloud now, it sounded childish. Stupid.

Vekel walked on in silence.

I glanced sidelong at my friend, expecting him to chide, or even make fun of me, but he was deep in thought. I concentrated on looking for timber, or anything of value that the tide might have delivered. I could not resist a peek over my shoulder either. The raven was gone. Gulls were quarrelling over the corpse. More circled overhead. The air of mystery had vanished.

'Of course!'

'What?' To myself, I said, *do not let him tell me that Oðin will curse me unless I put the sword back.*

'It's so obvious I didn't see it at first.' Vekel's thin face had lit up.

'Tell me!'

'The raven knew you were going to be there.'

'It did?'

He buffeted me with an arm. 'Oðin told him!'

All I could do was stare. There was something guarded about his last words, almost as if he'd held back information, but my hopes of keeping the blade soaring, I paid no heed.

'Oðin wanted you to have the sword, so he sent the raven,' Vekel said. 'Huginn, it was.'

How he ascertained the god's purpose, I had no idea, still less how he knew which raven it had been. But Vekel's words held the ring of conviction, and I believed them. My father would too. My friend's manner, his behaviour, meant that many people regarded him as spirit-touched. I think it helped that there was no *vitki* in the area, no one else associated with seiðr. Few would have the conviction to deny what Vekel said.

'Look.' Vekel's arm pointed into the freshening breeze.

Great banks of cloud, black and thunderous, had gathered far out to sea.

'Another storm is coming,' I said.

'Oðin again. He has interceded with Thor to mark the occasion.'

I gave him an uneasy smile. It was incredible enough for a god to give me a sword; quite another for two deities to be involved.

'There can be only one name for you now.' Vekel's expression was solemn.

I dared not speak my mind: *Sword-stealer. Corpse-thief.*

'Stormcrow.'

PART ONE
AD 994

CHAPTER ONE

No one ever came looking for the corpse or his sword, and over the next four years, many things happened. The first and most significant occurrence was my mother's death in labour, birthing a third child she, narrow-hipped, should never have borne. It was a kindness that the babe, a girl, did not live out the day of its arrival in this world. The family shrank, leaving me, my younger sister Ashild, and my father. Ashild, strong-willed and capable, took over the running of the house. It was as well, for my father's heart had been broken. Despite his Norse background and my mother's Irish one, they had made a good match, and largely been content with one another.

During this time I grew, mostly upwards, but I also filled out. By seventeen, I was stocky, broad-chested and the same height as my father, who was taller than most. I was cocky with it, not least because daily work in the smithy had seen me muscled like an ox. I was able to use an axe and shield, thanks to my father. He had long given up war, but as a young man sailed with the Dyflin Norse, his kin, raiding down the coastline and around to the kingdom of Mumhan. He rarely spoke of it, and was at first reluctant for me to learn weaponcraft. 'Better to work iron,' he would growl. 'It's safer.' I ground him down, though, with a mixture of flattery and outright begging.

He was too busy to train me as much as I wanted, though. War is not pretty, he would sometimes say in his cups. Better to have soot stain your hands than blood. Imagining myself a hero in one of the sagas, I did not listen. Long after our occasional sessions ended, I would practise the moves he taught me outside our longhouse. A training partner would have been good, but the only boys of my own age in the settlement were a neighbour's son Berghard, dim-witted since being kicked in the head by a bull, and Vekel. The latter had an aversion to weapons.

9

It was rare indeed that I could persuade him to pick up axe and shield and stand against me.

Despite my dreams, I was no battle-ready warrior, but at least my father had not taken the sword from me, as I had first worried. I think he might have, but Vekel's account of how I had found it changed his mind. He would *not* teach me how to use it. Better learn from a master, or not at all, he said, adding, especially when the blade came from a god. It was hard logic, but I accepted it. I lived in hope that Vekel had been correct about the raven, and that because of it, my time would come one day. Whether it was because of these hopes, or just an innate wanderlust, I had long been eager to spread my wings and leave Linn Duachaill.

Few people except Vekel called me 'Stormcrow', but everyone had heard the story of the sword. The tale had grown with the years. There had been two ravens, one of which had guided me to it, while the other had picked up and offered part of the baldric to me. Thunder had rumbled overhead when I took hold of the weapon. Enjoying the untruths, I made no effort to dispel them.

Vekel was my constant companion during that time, but an occasion when he was not bears mention. It was perhaps a year after my discovery of the sword, one of those spring days when for the first time in what seems an age, the sunshine is warm. When every plant is growing, every tree branch budding and verdant. When the birdsong has a joyous tone evident to all, and male hares box for supremacy in the paddocks.

Linn Duachaill was humming with excitement. It didn't take much. A Norse trader, Egil the Fat, had called in on his way up the coast. It was a yearly, much looked forward to event. Once Egil's broad-bellied knarr was safely moored in the best landing spot, which lay around the first two bends of the river, his thralls unloaded merchandise. Most of the people in the settlement were there to watch, me included. I hoped that Vekel, who had gone for a walk on his own, would soon arrive.

Egil's son Olvir, a corpulent, surly youth about a year older than Vekel and I, had come on the voyage too. He was a contrast to his jovial father, and never offered a greeting to us. As Egil waxed lyrical about the exotic origins of his goods: Valland, Miklagard, Serkland and Groenland, Olvir, who had probably heard it a hundred times before, rolled his eyes and wandered off. I didn't care.

As well as the costly and out-of-the-ordinary, Egil had staples every-one needed. The women gathered around the bales of coloured wool and rolls of off-white linen, touching, and muttering together about the price. There were glass beads and ring-headed dress pins from Jorvik, pieces of jet, amber from Lochlann. I had never seen the like of the woman's headdress, fashioned from a wondrously smooth fabric called silk. He had spindle whorls, loom weights, glass smoothers, fine bone needles and skates made from pig bones. Hjaltland honing stones lay beside pottery and metalworking crucibles from northern Britain, and quernstones fashioned from a porous, honeycombed type of rock that Egil said came from a fire-mountain.

I was drawn to the most expensive and rare objects for sale. These ones Egil stood over, his keen eyes moving between them and the watching audience to them every now and again. There were bear claws, and even a whole pelt, *tafl* pieces of ivory and whalebone, and the tusk of a fantastical but real beast called a *hrossvalr*. Much larger than a seal, and dangerous, Egil said, it lived in Groenland. I spotted a silver disc brooch fashioned like a large coin and covered in mysterious script, and wondered if Ashild would like it. I dared to ask the price, which was so high I gasped. Egil, the master, immedi-ately halved what he'd asked, and suggested I take the brooch off his hands. I coloured, and replied that it was still far more than I could afford.

Egil, who like as not had been aware, took my reply good-humouredly.

Something else caught my eye, and I was brought back to the beach, the corpse, the sword and the raven. Reaching out, I wondered how it had escaped my notice. A silver amulet, it was the length of my thumb from the tip to the first knuckle, and less than half that across. Intri-cate, interwoven lines formed the wings, the body, the tail, the head of a bird. The breath caught in my chest. It was a raven, no question, one of Oðin's.

Egil had seen my interest. 'A nice piece, is it not?'

'Finn!'

I turned with a smile. 'Come and look, Ashild.'

'Not now, Finn!' Her face was pinched, and not at all happy.

Alarm stirring, the amulet forgotten, I stepped away from the on-lookers. 'What is it?'

'Vekel is hurt.'

'While he was out walking?' That was odd, I thought. The flat land-scape around Linn Duachaill offered little in the way of danger.

She lowered her voice. 'No, it's Olvir. He's beating Vekel for no reason.'

We began to run, my sister leading the way.

'I heard the shouts and cries,' said Ashild, 'and when I got there, told Olvir to stop. He laughed, and said I was a straw-footed slattern, good for nothing but breeding brats.'

I was even more angry now. 'Where is he?'

'Just the other side of the rampart.'

Where no one would hear or see, I thought, fresh urgency driving me on.

I outstripped Ashild, and came haring through the cart-wide en-trance at top speed. Olvir was standing over a prone Vekel. I heard him say, 'What's wrong, you *ragr-nithing*? *Ergi*!' He kicked my friend, who cried out.

Rage pulsing behind my eyes – the words he'd used were derogatory in the extreme – and frantic to help Vekel, I gave no consideration to the fact that Olvir was bigger by some margin, and heavier built. He heard me, but didn't have time to react. I hit him in the middle of the back with my shoulder, sending him flying forward. He went down in a sprawl of limbs, just managing to stop his face hitting the ground. I came in fast, kicking him in the midriff. He *oof*ed, but he didn't give in. A meaty hand grabbed my leg. Then he sprang up, wrapping his arms round me, and took us both to the dirt. He was on top, a fight-winning position, and stars exploded in my head as he clattered me one, two.

I was incandescent, though, that he had attacked my friend. With pain as my fuel, I punched him in the pit of his belly, and when he gasped, I did it again. He collapsed sideways, and wriggling like an eel, I freed myself and stood. Ashild swooped in like a *valkyrja*. Armed with a length of branch, she began to beat Olvir. He tried to grab it, to grab her, but she was too quick and too angry. She stopped when the branch broke, by which point Olvir's face and defensively raised arms were cut and bleeding.

Panting, she glanced at Vekel, who was looking on in astonishment. 'Are you all right?'

'I am.' Wiping his tear-streaked cheeks, he approached Olvir, who cowered. 'No means no,' said Vekel.

'What did he do?' I demanded.

'He wanted to lie with you,' said Ashild, woman-sharp.

'Something like that,' said Vekel, a long-nailed forefinger circling his lips.

Understanding and revulsion crashed in. 'And when you refused, he attacked you?'

A nod.

Perplexed that a man who preferred men would assault one of his own kind, I kicked Olvir again several times. He did not defend himself. 'Touch my friend again,' I told him, 'and I'll cut your throat.' Murderous words from a youth who had never drawn blood, but I was in deadly earnest.

'Before he does that,' said Ashild, kicking him herself, 'I will cut off your prick and shove it down your throat.'

We left him there, the nithing. He didn't dare follow, at least until we had gone back inside the settlement.

'He'll tell his father lies,' Vekel said. 'That I tried to seduce him.'

'It doesn't matter,' I said stoutly. 'We found him beating you senseless. You're half his size. He got what was coming to him.'

'Father will support us,' said Ashild.

Vekel looked at each of us in turn. 'You're good friends. Thank you.'

When I went back to Egil's spot, there was no sign of Olvir. I haggled hard, and bought the raven amulet. I slipped it onto a thong, and hung it around my neck. By all the gods, it felt good. I felt stronger, as if Oðin were watching me.

There was no further trouble, and Egil departed later that day without a word of complaint. My opinion on the matter, and the others agreed, was that Olvir hadn't said anything, probably because he was terrified Vekel would tell the truth of what had happened. As the saying went, throw shit at a wall, and some of it will stick. Olvir did not want even the whiff of a suggestion that he had ragr tendencies. Among the Irish, it was acceptable, but not among the Norse.

Vekel had always been interested in the spirit world, and things mystical, but I think the incident with Olvir helped him to choose his path in life. He didn't speak of it to me, but not long after, he left with a vitki who passed through Linn Duachaill from time to time. He came back three years later, a changed person. Where he had been different, he was now strange. His femininity was even more pronounced; he wore eyeliner, women's necklaces and a silver bracelet from which hung tiny silver chairs; he spoke in a high, lilting tone. Tellingly, few said a mocking word or joked about his appearance. One look at his iron staff, the mark of a seer, was enough to terrify most. And the next time Olvir came back with Egil, he gave Vekel a very wide berth indeed.

I regarded Vekel with a degree of wariness, but he was still my friend. After all, I had known him since we were snot-nosed brats. Whether it was stealing fresh-baked bread, digging trap trenches in the sand to catch fish when the tide went out, gorging on blackberries and apples, we had done it together. True, there were times we did not share – such as when he wanted to sit near graves to commune with the dead, or when I was off chasing girls – but that did not stop us being closer than kin. I had missed him sorely when he was gone, and now he had returned, his oddness was not going to stand between us. Vekel did not admit to any regrets, but even he could not hide the pleasure in his eyes the first time we met. He sought me out each day as well, gladdening my heart further.

Another detail that stood out brightly from the humdrum of everyday life came one autumn, when the evenings were really drawing in. The last blackberries dew-glistened in the brambles, the cattle were growing winter-shaggy, and the rooks chattered and gossiped with each other in the still-leafy treetops. I had been for a wander along the beach, and finding little, was returning, chilled, to the settlement. Thinking of the forge's baking heat, I headed there rather than the longhouse. Rather than find my father hard at work as I might have expected, I entered to find him quiet upon his old, three-legged stool.

He said nothing.

I went close to the forge-fire, and spread out my hands, enjoying the radiating warmth. 'Did you hit your thumb?'

I almost missed the single shake of his head.

This was not right, I thought. 'Are you taken ill, Father?'

Another slow shake.

I stared, and shock-realised that his shoulders were juddering: he was weeping. A solid, quiet man, I had only seen tears on his face once, as we buried my mother. The cold in my bones forgotten, I crossed the space between us. All I needed to do was reach out and touch him.

The distance seemed as far as the stars.

'Finn?' A grief-wracked croak.

'I'm here, Father.' My hand went out, hovered over his shoulder, but I could not bring it down. My father was the strong one, the bastion upon which our family was built. This weakness unsettled, shook me to my core. 'I'm here,' I managed, but no more.

'Father?' Ashild's voice, calling from the longhouse.

He did not answer.

My arm dropped, yet I was still by his side when she came in. One look, and she was crouched in front of our father, one hand on his knee, the other touching his face.

'Are you ill?'

'No,' he whispered.

'You are crying.' Then, more sharply, 'You've been drinking too.'

Silence.

I looked at Ashild, gave her questioning expression an I-have-no-idea shrug.

She stroked Father's shoulder. 'We're here.'

Another silence, which felt as long as the seemingly never-ending winter did each year. I did not say a word. I could not. I wanted Ashild to speak, to make it better the way our mother always had when there was something wrong.

'It was an autumn day like this that Mother went into labour.' Ashild's voice reverberated with sadness.

Father began to cry silently again.

It was so obvious I wanted to slap myself.

'If only I could have done something . . .' Father's voice died away.

'A midwife could have done nothing either. The babe was stuck fast.' Ashild's tone was firm, adult-like.

I remembered peering inside the longhouse and seeing, past the broad back of our neighbour Ragnfrid, who was helping, my mother's contorted, sweat-drenched features. That was before Ashild, scolding, had shut the door in my face. I had never seen my mother alive again. The scab came off the old grief. Tears pricked my eyes, but I could not deal with this, or my father's state.

Ashild saw. Knew. 'The broth needs stirring, Finn.'

I gave her a grateful look, and stumbled from the forge.

She and my father came in some time later; he seemed more at ease.

We ate in silence, and the incident was never mentioned again.

CHAPTER TWO

O ne bright morning late the following spring, I was preparing to
go and check on our cattle. In winter we kept them close to
home, where it was easy to see when one sickened, or wolves were after
the calves, but in summertime we grazed the herd a good distance
away. Many days could pass without seeing them. I had been putting
off the task, as if it would somehow get done regardless, but in the
end, I had to go. The slave minding the kine could not booley them on
his own.

I took the blanket from my bed, which, with Ashild's and my father's, were situated at one end of the longhouse. Our home was one
of the few structures still occupied in Linn Duachaill. The Norse had
largely abandoned the settlement half a century before, decamping to
Dyflin, but some families had stayed. My father's had been one of
them. Some might have found it strange to live in what felt at times
like a ghost village, the majority of the longhouses falling into rack and
ruin, but it was all I had ever known.

'How many nights will you be gone?' Ashild was busy at the fire,
stirring something in a pot. Smoke trickled up to the vent hole in the
thatch overhead.

'One, maybe two.' I rolled up the blanket and tied it with leather
thongs. 'Have you food for me?'

'When have I ever let you go unfed, brother?'

'In truth, I cannot remember.' As I had that autumn night, I reminded myself that Ashild was only fifteen. She had the carriage and
assuredness of a woman ten years older. Only a little shorter than I, I
had dark red hair like my own, keeping hers concealed under a linen
cap.

She held out a cloth-wrapped bundle. 'You should have enough
bread and cheese there, if you are not too greedy.'

'I cannot help it if I am always hungry.' I hefted the bundle, pleased by its weight.

'Leave some for the herdsman.' This was our only slave, caring for the cattle far from home.

'Is there enough for me too?' Vekel had entered unseen.

'I do not have to feed you also.' Ashild's sense of humour was acerbic.

'Don't be like that,' he said, slipping an arm around her waist. 'You know how much I love your cooking.'

'Get away.' She escaped his grasp, but there was a smile on her face.

I raised the bundle. 'There is extra in here, for you, I assume.' Vekel's grandmother's cooking and baking was famously bad.

Vekel darted in and began kissing her cheeks. 'You are wondrous, Ashild.'

A snort. 'Should I be scared that a vitki wants to kiss me?'

'Very,' he said, planting one more. 'I will put a spell on Diarmaid and steal you for my own.' Diarmaid, a decent young farmer who lived nearby, was her betrothed.

'You will do no such thing.' Ashild had broken free and her forefinger was wagging in Vekel's face. 'Don't even think about it!'

'Come on,' I said to a grinning Vekel. 'We have a good walk in front of us.'

'You are not to get too drunk at Mainistir Bhuithe.' This was a small monastery on our way. Ashild saw my surprise. 'Do you think I don't know what you have planned after the cattle have been moved?'

Annoyed to be so easily seen through, I muttered something about needing a drink after hard toil, and made for the door.

Vekel blew one last kiss at Ashild and joined me outside. I paused, whistling to Madra and Niall, my two dogs, and checking I had everything ready. Food, blanket, light cloak, bow and quiver, hunting spear. Ironmongery to barter with, safe in a roll of old leather tied at both ends. Also hanging from my belt, crossways, my seax. An all-purpose knife, it had been made by my father. After the sword, it was my most treasured possession.

'I will pray for you. That all the cattle are safe, and the thrall too, and that you both come to no harm on the journey,' called Ashild.

Vekel made a rude noise, muttering something about the White Christ being as useful as Sleipnir, Oðin's eight-legged horse, on a steep icy slope. I also cared little for the Christian god, but there was no need for upset on my part, so I thanked her, and promised that I would say a prayer for our mother at the church of Mainistir Bhuithe.

'I am not setting foot inside the place,' said Vekel.

'There's not much chance of that, looking the way you do.' Although we were only going to booley cattle, Vekel had dressed as if about to perform a sacred ritual. His dress was blue, eyeliner black. A trace of red delineated his thin lips, round his neck hung a woman's glass bead necklace. On his belt was a leather skin-bag, inside which would be talismans needful for the practising of seiðr. Hairy calfskin shoes adorned his feet, the laces of which ended in copper lattens. I thought he entirely looked the part.

He linked his arm with mine, as if we were a courting couple about to take a stroll. 'I shall wait outside and scare off anyone planning to enter the church.'

'No. You can buy honey while I'm praying.' The monastery's bee farm was famous.

Bickering the way old friends can, we went to the forge. My father's dog, a huge wolfhound appropriately named Cú, was sprawled, shaggy grey-haired, at the entrance. He paid my dogs no attention, but his tail thumped the ground at me.

My father looked up from his anvil, where he was beating out a rim for a wagon wheel. 'On your way?'

'Aye.'

'Don't forget a drop of mead.' The monastery's produce was tastier than his own homebrewed ale, and stronger with it.

'I won't.' My attention went past him, seeing the sword on his workbench. It normally lived in the longhouse, under my bed. 'You remembered,' I said, pleased.

A grunt. 'I'll take a look at it when I'm done with this rim.'

Despite the oiled wool inside the sheath, the sword's immersion in the sea had seen some salt damage. I had scrubbed it clean with sand, but tiny pits remained. I had had to oil it well ever since. I checked it regularly for rust spots too, and had mentioned this the previous evening. My father must have fetched it when I went for my daily walk along the strand; that had been a habit come rain or shine since finding the blade.

'Thank you,' I said, wondering if I might finally persuade him to instruct me in its use. If I would ever become a renowned warrior.

The sun shone as we set out. I waved at the few neighbours who were about; they responded, but cast wary looks at Vekel. He saw me scowl.

'They're scared, I know, but they come to me regardless. If they're sick, or going out in a boat to fish, or worried about the harvest.' A knowing chuckle. 'Or like yesterday, when they want to curse someone.'

'Who was that?' I demanded. Linn Duachaill and the land around had a population of a couple of hundred, no more. I knew everyone, to see at least.

A long-nailed finger touched his nose. 'That is between me and the spirits.' When I tutted, he said, 'If I told you, the seiðr would not work.'

I spent the first portion of our journey wondering who in the settlement hated someone enough have a curse laid on them. I asked Vekel twice more, but he ignored me, humming to himself, and calling Madra and Niall to have their ears rubbed.

'I do like that your father's dog is called "Hound", and one of yours is called "Dog",' he said eventually.

I chuckled.

'It's silly to call the other one "Niall", though.'

Inhabitants of Linn Duachaill owed allegiance to a local king, and also to the Uí Néills, supreme rulers of Midhe, the area we lived in. The men of the latter clan were known as 'the sons of Niall', after the dynasty's progenitor, and thanks to their overbearing attitude, universally disliked. I had always thought the name amusing.

'Don't you think?'

I bridled. 'He's four years old and an Uí Néill has never heard me call the dog yet.'

'There's a first time for everything.'

'Pigs might fly,' I said with the confidence of youth.

Having poled across the river Casán in a coracle, we set out westward. Bright sunshine gilded the green, rolling landscape, drying our legs after the fording of a second, shallower waterway. Apart from the tops of the few hills, there was little forest, it having been cut down so the ground could be cultivated. It was pleasant landscape, although mostly flat and unremarkable. Farms were well scattered, but at every last one, dogs barked challenges. Having alerted their owners, they rarely came close. The dwelling houses were small, one-room thatched affairs, surrounded by fields of oats and barley and hurdle-fenced areas for cattle.

There were also raths here and there, built by richer farmers. Circular earthen banks with a single gate, they had animal enclosures within. The name was deceptive, because none of these fortlike structures had enough men for defence. Some raths had dwelling houses inside, but the purpose of most was to keep livestock safe from night-time raids by wolves.

Half the morning's walk from Linn Duachaill, we crested a rise and saw, amid more fields of barley and wheat, the stone tower that marked Mainistir Bhuithe's position. I never tired of seeing it, by far the grandest structure in the area. Built of local stone, and immensely tall – two decent spear casts, by most men's admission – it had been constructed after a particularly brutal Norse raid thirty years before. Able to contain the monks and all their valuables, with a door that was reached by a rope ladder, it had never been needed since.

Nearing the first dwellings, those of the non-religious who had come to live in the shelter of the monastery, I called in Madra and Niall and looped a rope around each of their necks. Otherwise they were wont to chase hens, or scavenge from the tanner's premises, both of which might get us into trouble.

By rights we should have booleyed the cattle first, but I was tired and thirsty. A sup of ale or mead, or both, was too appealing to pass up. Unsurprisingly, Vekel agreed. We beat an eager path to the brewery, which was set close to the monastery's low perimeter wall. No one paid me any heed, a youth in yellow tunic and dun breeks with a couple of dogs. Vekel was a different matter. His outlandish array, not to mention the outrageous swagger of his hips, positively demanded attention.

People crossed themselves as we went by, and at least one housewife retreated into her house and slammed the door. A greybeard dropped his walking stick and almost fell over, so frightened was he. When I stopped at the bakery to buy a loaf – Ashild's supplies would not last us, for we both ate like horses – the serving girl would barely look at me, let alone Vekel. He, loving the effect, kept asking her questions. I told him to let her alone, and he just laughed. 'You will have a babe ere the winter,' he declared, leaving her open-jawed behind us.

'How did you know that?' I hissed. I would not have guessed in a hundred years.

'Seiðr.'

I dunted him with an elbow. 'What else?'

20

He leaned in close. 'Now and again, she rubbed her stomach gently—'

'—in the manner of a woman who's carrying a child,' I said, finishing.

'Just so.'

I shook my head, wondering how much of Vekel's seiðr was related to his acuity of vision.

The monk in charge of the brewery didn't bat an eyelid at either of us. In the main, I suspect it was because he was drunk. This was his usual state; whether he had been like it before, or had acquired a taste for his own produce after taking the job, I had no idea. Red-nosed, whiskerier than monks were supposed to be, his brown robe stain-spattered from neck to ankle, he was an amiable sort.

'There you are,' he announced from behind the taproom's rough wooden counter. It was as if he'd been expecting us, but was also suitable greeting when you didn't know, or couldn't remember, someone's name.

'Greetings, brother,' I said respectfully. Thanks to my mother, I was fluent in Irish.

Vekel inclined his head.

'The blessings of God upon you both.' Vekel arched an eyebrow; unabashed, the monk continued, 'You are both thirsty on a warm day like this.'

'Parched,' I said. 'Beer for both of us.'

The monk dipped a wooden tankard into a barrel, then a second. Liquid spilled as he unceremoniously plonked them down on the counter. 'Come far?'

There weren't many other customers, but I sensed all of their attention.

I had nothing to hide. Downing half the beer, I belched and said, 'Linn Duachaill.'

'Any news?'

'Nothing much.' I drank off the rest of the beer. 'Another, if you will.'

Vekel placed his tankard beside mine. 'And for me. It's good.' Like most of Linn Duachaill's inhabitants, he also spoke Irish.

The monk gave us refills, and without being asked, produced a wooden bowl of water for Madra and Niall.

'My father's fond of your mead,' I said. 'If you could set aside a small barrel, I'll call in for it after booleying the cattle.'

He blinked. 'Ah, yes – the smith from Linn Duachaill! Thorgil, was it?'

'That's right.'

A brown-pegged smile. 'He likes a drop.'

'He does.' Sadness tugged at me. Since my mother's death, my father took himself here on occasion. According to our neighbour Ingolf, also fond of a tipple, my father would drink until he fell down, sleeping on the floor and starting afresh the following day.

'Another?' The monk reached for my tankard.

My appetite soured, I said, 'No. Maybe later, when I come for the mead.'

Vekel was put out not to have a third – he liked his beer – but did not argue when I chided him about our primary task. 'Trying to move kine when pissed is never a good idea. We'll be back before you know it.'

'Very well.' He clicked his tongue. 'Madra, Niall, time to earn your crust.'

The dogs leaped up. I petted them.

'Niall, is that your dog's name?' The question came from a short man further along the counter. Clad in farmers' clothes like everyone else, he had a sharp, stoat-like face.

My heart lurched. I wanted to slap Vekel. Of all the places to say the name out loud, this was the worst. Caught flat-footed, I struggled for an answer.

Vekel jumped in. 'The beer, it's already affecting me. Njal, he is called. Njal. My friend here is half a Norseman, see.'

Stoat Face's expression was disbelieving, but the warning rattle of Vekel's bracelets and the meaningful lift of his staff made sure he didn't say so. With his gaze heavy on our backs, we left the taproom, the red-nosed monk telling us to return soon.

'I'm sorry,' Vekel said the instant we were alone. 'I'm so stupid – and after what I said earlier!'

'It's of no matter,' I said lightly, telling myself nothing would come of it.

The cattle were grazing the slopes of a nearby hill, common land that overlooked the Bóinn River. As always, I searched along the near bank for the sacred and mysterious site of Sí an Bhrú. I knew the spot where it lay, although thanks to the incline, it was not visible until one was much closer. I marked the rath of a large farm – that was where to aim for if I wanted to visit the mysterious, massive circular mound. It had been built untold centuries before, by whom, no one knew. Christians and pagans alike revered it. As Vekel said, a man would have be a corpse not to feel the seiðr there. Seeing my gaze, he said we should visit it at Samhain, the night when the dead walked the land. 'Go on your own. A frost giant could not drag me there then,' I swore, and meant it.

I went back to the task at hand. Our shaggy, brown, black and red beasts were discernible from other stock by the cut in their right ears, and the thrall was with them. We greeted each other warmly. He had belonged to the family since before I was born, and my father treated him well, which was why he could be off minding the cattle on his own. Wolves roamed the area, but there were several stone enclosures where he took the cattle at night.

With his and the dogs' help we cut the twenty-four beasts out, and set off for the fresher pasture, some distance to the east. It was still bright by the time we were done. It was good to stand and watch them graze, all moving in the same direction, the way cattle always do.

'This will suffice until after the harvest, maybe,' I said. The slave grinned and bobbed his head as I shared my food with him.

'I am for the monastery. To be more exact, the taproom.' Vekel set off without a backward glance.

'We need to be careful,' I warned. 'Especially if Stoat Face is about.'

'I'll scare the living daylights out of him.' Vekel waved his staff.

'That might not be the best idea near the monastery.' I did not want to spell it out further. Vitkis and *vitkis*, sorcerers, were feared and respected, but they were also loathed by many. It wasn't unknown for a whipped-up mob to lynch or murder a vitki.

'All right,' Vekel said. 'If he is still there, we shall find a quiet spot outside the settlement to sleep. But if not, I see no reason not to pass an enjoyable evening in each other's company.'

'I'll drink to that!' I raised an imaginary tankard, and laughing, he did the same.

CHAPTER THREE

With no sign of Stoat Face, we did our best to drink the taproom dry. The old monk kept pace. By the time my world began to spin, I was still able to marvel how unaffected he was. Vekel also held his beer better than I, and ribbed me mercilessly about it.

I had no memory of the night's end. There were no dreams either.

I was woken by a pleasant, brushing feeling on my face. Dust filled my nose, and a violent sneeze escaped me, which badly hurt my pounding head. I opened my eyes. I was on the floor, and the whiskery monk was sweeping it. The end of his broom came near again.

'I'm awake.' The words came out as a croak, but he stopped. I rolled my tongue around my dry, foul-tasting mouth. 'What time is it?'

'The terce bell rang a while ago. You needs must get up.' His tone was faintly chiding. ''Tis bad for business if last night's customers are still on the floor.'

'Hungover?'

Grunting, I rolled over and sat up. Vekel was already leaning on the counter, a tankard in hand. He saluted me. 'Join me in hair of the dog?'

'Water is what I need.'

A laugh. 'Have one for the road then!'

I would never hear the end of it if I did not partake; the old monk seemed to realise this, setting aside his broom to fill two more tankards. Wincing at the pain in my head, I stood.

The first mouthful was awful, the second less so. Once half the beer had gone down, I felt more alive. Of course one drink turned into two, then three. Oddly, Vekel had struck up a friendship with the old monk the night before; they roared at each other's jokes, and talked at length about beekeeping and brewing. Feeling a little left out, it was simple enough to announce that it was time to depart. Some of the ironmongery I had brought, nails, buckles, pins and sundry tools, had paid for our beer the night before and the small barrel of mead that sat on the counter. I only had to fulfil Ashild's request, and we could leave.

I went to the church to pray, but Vekel stayed for another. When I emerged, feeling uneasy to have asked something of the White Christ, he was waiting with the dogs. We set off on a track that led northeast, towards home.

'Think it will work?' Vekel asked. 'The prayer for your mother, I mean.'

'Who knows?' I found the Christian religion, its concepts of sin and damnation, and constant striving to find a place in Heaven, tiresome. Norse gods were devious and unreliable, but there were no rules to follow and no obligation to behave in a certain manner or risk eternal suffering.

'It will keep Ashild happy anyway.'

'That is why I did it.'

Still sore-headed, I was in no mood for conversation. Vekel also seemed content not to talk, and a companionable silence fell. Bar a few words when we paused to slake our thirst at streams, it continued until we were nearing Linn Duachaill. More precisely, it lasted until I saw a trail of smoke lifting skyward from the settlement. Far too big to be from a hearth or forge fire, it was too early for midsummer's bonfires.

'See that?'

There was no quick joke from Vekel, as I might have expected. I could have sworn I heard him whisper, 'And so it begins.'

Goosebumps prickled my flesh. I set down the barrel of mead.

We broke into a run, which soon became a sprint. Thinking it was a game, Madra and Niall did the same, nipping at one another as they criss-crossed in front of us.

At the rampart it was clear that the smoke came from our longhouse, or near it. The faces of those we met spoke volumes. As I ran, I shouted: 'My father, Ashild – are they all right?'

'Ashild is a little hurt,' called Old Inga's husband. 'It could have been worse.'

Confusion mixed with my fear, but frantic to get home, I slowed not at all. 'And my father?'

'He lives yet.'

Yet, I thought, nausea washing the back of my throat. *Please, no.* I increased my speed, as if that would change what I would find.

Gunnkel the Bald, whose longhouse was fifty paces from ours, raised a hand in sad greeting. 'Ragnfrid is with him.' That was his wife, who had much herb knowledge, and who had done her best with my mother in her final hours.

'What happened?' I yelled.

'A group of Clann Cholmáin warriors came.'

That was odd, I thought. Clann Cholmáin were overlords to the Uí Chonaing, rulers of the area, and had no particular reason to visit Linn Duachaill. 'And?'

'There was an argument—'

I could find out more afterward. I tore past, running as if my feet had wings.

'Father!'

No answer came.

I skidded to a halt at the open door and entered with Vekel at my back. Ashild knelt by my father's bed, with Cú lying close. Stout Ragnfrid was stool-perched on the other side. I ran over, fear consuming me. Sure enough, it was my father they were tending. His eyes were closed, and his breath had a telltale rattle I did not like. The gloom could not conceal his awful grey pallor either. My gaze went next to Ashild. There was bruising on her left forearm, and a mark on her cheek.

'It's nothing,' she said quietly, although Ragnfrid's lips pursed.

My father was worse off, that was plain. 'How was he hurt?'

Ashild indicated his belly. 'He was stabbed.'

I had to see for myself. Gently lifting my father's hand – he did not wake – I pulled down the blanket. A sigh escaped me. Blood had soaked through the linen encasing his midriff. If I had had to guess, the blade had gone in under the breastbone. I was no warrior, had no medical knowledge, but it did not matter. The wound was mortal.

His eyelids flickered open, his lips crooked. 'Finn.'

'I am here, Father.' I blinked away tears.

'Did you get the mead?'

Despite the grief tearing me apart, I could not but help smile. 'Yes.'

'A drop would be nice.' His eyes closed again.

'I will fetch it,' said Vekel.

I gave him a grateful look.

I had no idea how long the inevitable would take. Nor, when I whispered the question in her ear, did Ashild. Desperate to understand, I held my father's hand and looked at Ashild.

'Clann Cholmáin were here, I know, but what happened?'

'A horse needed shoeing.'

I frowned. The practice was still rare among the Irish, but it was not unknown. A hunting party gone far afield, it could have been, perhaps a diplomatic mission. My father would have been happy to help, I thought. 'Replacing a lost shoe should not end in murder.'

'It was not that, but tribute.' She spat the last word.

I was confused. 'We made our yearly offering to the Uí Chonaing three months ago.' As was customary, it had been in ironmongery.

'I know that.' Her retort was sharp. 'I think it was when one of them saw the sword.'

'My blade?' Oðin was capricious, I thought bitterly, but to do this before I had ever wielded the thing seemed cruel beyond belief.

'There were raised voices, shouts. I came running from the longhouse. One of the group, a noble, wanted the sword. He offered a hundred silver pennies. Father said it was not his to sell.'

Not that that would stop an arrogant young nobleman, I decided. The scene was easy to picture. The young pup in his finery, sneering at my father while his lackeys laughed and fawned. His gaze alighting on the sword. Him picking it up, admiring the ivory hilt and the silverwork on the scabbard, then gasping at the quality of the blade. His surprise that my father would refuse a hundred silver pennies, an enormous sum.

'Why did Father not let him take it?' I hissed. We would have a pile of silver, I could have added. Our father would not be dying, and I might somehow have been able to get the sword back.

'I think he might have offered more, but then he noticed me.' Ashild's colour rose.

My stomach lurched. 'Did he, did he . . .?' I could not say the words.

'No. He manhandled me, but I slapped him across the face, the cur, and he let go. One of his men grabbed me, so I punched him in the guts. I would have stayed, fought, but Father shouted at me to run. I did, all the way to Diarmaid's house.' Her head dropped. 'It is my fault, Finn. I should have stayed.'

I could see it. Enraged because Ashild had fled, affronted because my father would not take his coin, the nobleman had vented his emotions by using the sword to lethal effect. My sister was not to blame, however. I patted her hand, a pathetic attempt to right the terrible wrong that had been done.

'No! If you had, I would have not just a dying father, but—' I battened down my grief savagely, and told myself what was done was done. My purpose now was clear as a swift-running mountain stream. The moment my father was dead, I would seek revenge. Blood for blood, the saying went, a life for a life. And the sword – I had to get it back. 'I need a name.'

'Clann Cholmáin . . .' My father's eyes opened, but they were unfocused. His breathing was weaker too.

'Yes, Father.' To Ashild, I said, 'I need a first name.'

'Cormac. I heard one of them call him Cormac.'

Wild thoughts spun. 'Máel Sechnaill Mór, High King of Ériu and leader of Clann Cholmáin has a son called Cormac.'

'I know,' Ashild whispered.

A noble of his stature would be untouchable. *Let it not be the same man*, I prayed, even as my gut told me different. 'Was it him?'

'I think so.'

I had about as much chance of killing Máel's son, I decided, as beating Oðin in single combat. That did not mean I would not try. My father's murder could not go unanswered. Nor could an assault on my sister, or the theft of a god-given blade.

Vekel came in soon after, chest heaving, carrying the barrel of mead. My father roused enough to drink a little. He smiled, and said we were good lads. 'Look after him and his sister,' he told Vekel. My friend, emotion twisting his handsome face, swore he would. Satisfied, my father closed his eyes.

They did not open again, although he lingered until sunrise. He went peacefully, which was something. I sat, dry-eyed, as his corpse cooled beside me, wondering how my life had turned upside down. I had gone to booley cattle, got drunk at the monastery, and come home to find my father murdered.

Ashild had also stayed through the night. She wept where I had not, but composed herself faster. She lit the fire, warmed a pan of water, and after stripping off our father's clothes, tenderly washed his body. Cú stayed by her side, quieter than normal – he knew.

I watched Ashild, numb, cold, my attention fixed on the wet-lipped, red-oozing wound in my father's belly. Most of me cursed the day I had found the sword, wishing that I had left it to Oðin's raven, but there was a tiny, protesting part that screamed this could not be all that the god intended. I touched the amulet for reassurance.

'We must send for a priest,' Ashild said.

'Why?' My voice was hard.

Calmly, 'So he can receive a Christian burial.'

I came to life. 'Father never set foot in a church in his life!'

'It is what Mother would have wished.'

My fury – not at Ashild, but the mongrel who had slain my father – burst free. 'Mother is dead and gone, sister! It does not matter what she would have done. Father believed in Thor and Oðin, not the White Christ!' I spat the last two words, and then, 'I am the man of the house now. He will have a Norse burial, and that is the end of it.'

We buried my father the same day, beside my mother, a short way outside Linn Duachaill. Cú went to the afterlife with him. I could not do it; instead Vekel drew the blade across the great, shaggy neck. Cú did not resist. It was as if, with his beloved owner gone, he no longer wanted to be alive. In the grave also went the tools of my father's trade: a hammer, pliers, tongs and a variety of ironmongery.

I allowed Ashild to tie a hammer cross amulet around my father's neck. These were worn by people who worshipped both Thor and the White Christ; I hoped his shade would not mind. I shed no tears over his grave, instead swearing a solemn oath that his killer would pay for the death.

I saw Ashild safely to Diarmaid's house, Madra and Niall too. A solid lad, he agreed to look after my sister and the dogs, in particular if I did not return. This last detail was said in his ear. I also made a statement before Vekel, Diarmaid, his father and brother, out of Ashild's hearing. In the event of my death, the longhouse and our land were to pass to her.

My course of action was obvious, if perilous. Questioning Gunnkel and others who had witnessed the party arrive confirmed their identity as members of Clann Cholmáin. What they were doing so far from home, no one knew, but they had come into Linn Duachaill seeking a blacksmith. The group's leader was a young fair-haired man. When they left, he had the sword. Gunnkel said it almost apologetically. I demanded to know if he'd heard anyone address him. 'Cormac. I think it was Cormac,' Gunnkel had whispered. Ashild had not been mistaken, I thought, dread filling me.

There was no point chasing after the party. I had no idea where they were going; I was also on foot. They had horses. The best place for justice was Inis Cró at Loch Ainninn, where the high king lived. Diarmaid and his father and brother did their best to dissuade me. 'The killing was a tragedy, but no good will come of this,' Diarmaid said. 'Who's to say Cormac will even be at Inis Cró? 'Tis two to three days' walk away. Ara, it was probably another man altogether.'

'There is one law for the nobility and another for ordinary folk,' added his father. 'You will not receive a fair hearing. Even if you do, the penalty will not be Cormac's life. Far more likely it is that you will be beaten within a hairsbreadth of your life. Or worse.'

They looked to Vekel for support, but shrugging, he said it was not for him to intervene. It was the Norns, weavers of our life-threads, who would decide when to cut mine.

Diarmaid and his kin stitched their lips at that, but their grim faces made plain their opinion: that grief-stricken, I had lost my wits, and would soon end up dead. I was oblivious to their concern. As long as Cormac of Clann Cholmáin died, it did not matter if I did too. Few people would miss me. My parents were gone, Ashild had Diarmaid, and could look after Madra and Niall. Vekel, self-contained, would survive.

I sought Ashild out to tell her the same, finding her by our father's grave. She rounded on me. 'Typical man! You are throwing your life away, Finn, and for what?'

'For what he did. Father, you . . .'

'I am unhurt!' she spat. 'Yes, he murdered Father, but he is the high king's son. Even if by some miracle you do succeed, you will also die. That is too high a price for honour!'

I heard the wisdom in her words, but my injured pride would not let me climb down. That, and the thought of never seeing my sword again. 'I am going, sister, and that is that.' I made to kiss her farewell, but she pulled away. Defeated, I glanced down at the fresh heaped earth, and hoped that my father would approve. Then I walked away.

'Finn.'

I did not stop. I did not turn.

'I will pray for you, Finn.'

I twisted around, met Ashild's emotion-filled stare. 'Thank you.'

I lingered at Linn Duachaill no longer. A significant journey awaited. Even if Cormac was not at Inis Cró, I wanted to reach it with the crime still recent. I had my bow and arrows, and seax. I also armed myself with a spear, and took my father's old limewood shield down from the wall. For food, I packed some bacon and barley flour.

Vekel insisted on coming. 'I threw the rune bones. It is foretold.' There was something else in his black-rimmed eyes too.

Pleased that the Norns had woven our threads together for a while longer, I gave it no thought. 'There's a good chance we won't come back,' I warned.

One of his sniffs. 'Perhaps. Besides, you won't get far without my help.'

I was heartily relieved. Despite my anger, the idea of going alone to seek justice at the seat of the high king's power was daunting.

On the road west, the same one we had taken to Mainistir Bhuithe, there was time for conversation. Vekel went straight to the heart of the matter.

'How many warriors will be in the royal compound?'

I was ready. 'Answer my question first.'

He looked startled.

It was pleasing to see him nonplussed, so I let him stew.

He broke first. 'Ask!'

It had been niggling at me since burying my father. 'When we saw the smoke over Linn Duachaill, I thought you said, "And so it begins", or something like that.' I stared.

He stared back.

'Was it my imagination?'

A long pause, as if he was considering lying, then, 'No.'

There was a pain in my chest. 'Did you know my father would be murdered?'

'No!'

'Swear it!'

He caught my hand. 'Finn, I swear it on my grandmother's life.'

That was enough. 'What did you mean then? The truth, Vekel!'

'Your life will be full of risk and opportunity, blood and death. There will be love, and loss, and betrayal.'

I blinked; it was a lot to take in. 'Is it because of the sword?'

'Probably. Oðin chose you, not someone else. I did not know when events would take on a life of their own, but seeing the smoke, I knew that was the moment.'

'Could we have prevented Father's death?'

An emphatic headshake. 'No. That was ordained.'

I decided to accept this; madness beckoned on any other path. 'What else?'

'It is unclear.'

I suspected Vekel knew more, but he denied it. It was soon clear that I would get nothing more from him for now. I sighed. 'You asked how many warriors guard the high king.'

'I did.'

I sighed again. My plan, which had seemed bold and obvious when I stood over my father's corpse, now seemed rash, perhaps even ill-conceived. I was loath to admit it. 'Two score?'

'Probably more.'

I walked on, ignoring him.

'When you and I march in, demanding that Cormac pay for his crime, what do you think Máel will do?'

'Listen to my claim,' I said stoutly.

'And then?'

'He will punish his son.' I was less certain of this. The birds in the trees knew that kings and nobles almost never upheld allegations against their own class, let alone their families. Even the chance of Cormac being publicly chastised was small.

'He might do,' said Vekel, echoing my thought. 'Or he might have you drubbed from the hall. Diarmaid was right, you know. To come away from this confrontation with a few broken bones will be fortunate. If the king is in a bad mood, you could end up feeding the ravens, with your father still unavenged.'

I rounded on him. 'So I should do nothing?'

'Of course not. I *am* saying that to charge in like a maddened bull will have one result, and not a pleasant one. If you were to watch and wait, however, Cormac will offer himself to you.'

'How?'

'He's a young man; I wager he often hunts.'

'An ambush?'

'Why not? Or a knife in an alleyway.'

'I want a *holmgang*.' This was Norse tradition, single combat, to the death. It was also, since deepest antiquity, an Irish tradition.

Vekel gave me a look. 'That would just be throwing away your life in a different way.'

'I can fight with spear and seax,' I said hotly.

'And he is the king's son. The filth got given a sword in the cradle, and has been training with it since he could walk. Cormac may not be a seasoned warrior, but he would cut you into little pieces.'

'You're supposed to be on my side!'

'I am,' said Vekel, more gently than usual.

I fell into a sulk, which lasted for some distance. Vekel did not try to lift me out of it. In the end, I came to the realisation that fighting with my one ally was foolish.

'You're right,' I said.

'I know.' His smugness was unmistakable.

Annoyed, I aimed a punch at his arm, but he dodged with ease. 'You'll come to see that I am the wiser eventually.'

I already know it, I thought, but could not bring myself to say the words.

CHAPTER FOUR

We passed by Mainistir Bhuithe. Neither of us was in the mood for beer or mead, and I certainly wasn't going to stop at the church to offer a prayer to the White Christ. Turning the other cheek, as I had often heard Ashild saying, was not an option. Older and truly sacred, set on a panoramic south-facing slope overlooking the River Bóinn, Sí an Bhrú was a different prospect. We broke our journey to make offerings – an iron knife blade and a tiny piece of hacksilver were mine – scooping out handfuls of earth at the front of the great mound and burying the votives as we prayed. There was no way of knowing if the old gods had heard, still less whether they would help. I felt better afterwards, nonetheless, my burden of grief a trace lighter.

Cnogba fort, seat of the Uí Chonaing, was not far from Sí an Bhrú; it seemed foolish not to try and find out what we could there. Vekel did not like parting, nor staying behind, but grumpily conceded that alone, I would draw less attention. Relations between the Uí Chonaing and Clann Cholmáin were frosty at the best of times, but as I explained, that mightn't stop a message being sent to Inis Cró after a colourfully dressed vitki came asking questions at Cnogba. Say more prayers, I told him. Work some magic in our favour. Vekel wagged an admonishing finger, and told me not to make fun of things I did not understand. Feeling reckless, I thumbed my nose and left him to it.

I walked alone to Cnogba, my feet raising dust on the bone-dry track, ignoring the broad fields of wheat, and brooding about my father. Reaching the fort brought me back into the moment. Built on a great earthen mound similar to Sí an Bhrú, Cnogba had a defensive ditch around the base and another at the top, inside which was a stout wooden palisade. Smaller mounds were dotted around it, other remnants of those who had lived and died here in deepest antiquity.

The smith I was after lived and worked in a small house outside the fort, which suited my intention to remain unobtrusive. He was surprised to see me, but gladly paused his toil to offer a beaker of beer. Shocked to hear of my father's death, he crossed himself and enquired how it happened. I flicked my eyes at his apprentice, who was doing a bad job of pretending not to listen in, and lowered my voice to tell the sorry tale. Could it have been anyone other than the Uí Chonaing? I asked. Was it possible that Ashild had got it wrong?

The smith knew nothing of any local nobles or warriors riding towards Linn Duachaill. He had, however, heard the story, fresh in from the countryside, of a party of Clann Cholmáin travelling past Cnogba to the north. He did not know if a young prince called Cormac was among their number, but the information sat in my belly, indigestible, like half-cooked porridge. The smith asked what I would do next. I said the less he knew, the better. He made no protest; I thanked him and went on my way.

Vekel received the news without reaction, and made no attempt to divert me from my course. It made my task feel like that of a man ordered to roll a massive boulder uphill. What could two men do to a high king's son, even if one was a vitki? To return home before having even tried and without the sword, however, was unpalatable. I therefore suggested we continue our journey. Vekel gravely inclined his head. 'It is your path,' he said. So be it, I thought, asking Oðin for his help. He owed me, for it had been his blade that had slain my father.

'You were never destined to be a blacksmith, Finn Thorgilsson.' Vekel's dark eyes fixed mine.

'What makes you say that?'

'The sword was the first real sign, although there were others. The real change came during the time I was away. When I returned, you looked ill at ease, almost as if you had outgrown Linn Duachaill.'

'It is a decent place, but I do not want to spend my life there.'

'Rest assured, you will not.'

Despite the warm sun, I felt cold. I touched the amulet, drawing strength from it. 'And you?'

'Our paths are the same.'

I did not want to ask for how long. Vekel's determination made more sense now. He was a loyal friend, that was true, yet if the gods ordained that he should accompany me, it would add to his purpose.

As was often the case, I wondered if he knew more than he admitted to, but wary of what he might say, did not ask.

Baile Shláine was some distance further on. We passed several patches of woodland, but like the landscape around Linn Duachaill, most of the undulating ground was given over to farming. Earthen raths were more frequent, some with wooden palisade defences. Around them were pastures for cattle, but a lot of arable crops were cultivated too. Rye, barley and oats were commonplace. There was wheat as well, and according to my father, more of it here than in other parts of Ériu. Ulaidh and Connachta, full of bogs and forests, had no land like this.

At the top of the steep hill above the village was a church and friary, at the bottom, running east in a wide silver band, the Bóinn. I had never been further from home. Vekel asked if I wanted to pray at the church, or to seek the blessing of Saint Pádraig, who, centuries before, had lit a Paschal fire there against the wishes of the high king. Once today was enough, I told him, adding that he could shove his suggestion where the sun didn't shine, and he cackled.

The track led to a ford close by. After that, Gunnkel had said, we must follow the far bank of the Bóinn to a southward-aiming bend. It was in a pool here that the legendary warrior Fionn mac Cumhaill had caught the Salmon of Knowledge. Some distance further on, the river snaked southwest, leaving Teamhair na Rí in plain sight.

I drank in the unfamiliar countryside. Well-drained, fertile, it was even more heavily farmed than the ground from Mainistir Bhuithe. The dwelling houses and raths were big, and the herds of cattle large. No wonder the high king claimed the land for his own, I decided.

As we descended the last slope before the bend, Vekel archly observed that only blind men could have missed the great hill. Laughing, I agreed. With the Bóinn guarding its western flank, and flattish ground girdling the rest, Teamhair na Rí stood out in dramatic fashion. The most sacred site on the whole island, it was where the high kings were crowned. A stranger might have presumed that Clann Cholmáin would base themselves there, but the summit had been abandoned for many centuries. The clan's strongholds, a ringfort and nearby crannóg, were at Loch Ainninn, another day and a half's walk to the west.

It was too far to reach before nightfall, young and fit though we were. When we spied a farmhouse with outbuildings and a small rath, I asked permission to sleep in the barn. In return Vekel offered to treat anyone who was sick, and also to bring good luck on the household. Although wary, the farmer agreed; it turned out his son was ill with a fever. Vekel's dried flowers – feverfew – worked a wonder, reducing the boy's temperature. Overjoyed, the farmer's wife fed us on fresh barley bread and roasted pork.

The next day, shown the right road by the grateful farmer, and with his wife's blessings ringing in our ears, we set out for Loch Ainninn.

The landscape changed on the walk west, gradually growing flatter and poorer. Large areas of bog became common. There was no way around, no option but to cross. Knee-high grass gave an impression of solid ground, but our feet soon knew better. The deer sedge and tormentil guided us from dry patch to dry patch, with our shoes sinking into the wet ground between. Despite the discomfort, the bog had a beauty of its own. The bog cotton was just coming into flower, the white, fluffy seed heads moving gently in the breeze. My favourites were the six-pointed flowers on the asphodel, although it would be later in the year before they emerged, and later still when the ling heather purple-flowered. Blue-green lichen covered the jutting rocks, and bright green moss the rotting wood.

There was birdlife also. A golden plover shot up from beneath my feet at one point, its flat *puu* alarm carrying through the still air. There were lapwings, with distinctive wispy crests that came off the backs of their heads, and every now and again, a 'go back, go back, go back' identified a red grouse hiding in the heather. Not that we would go back, I said wryly to Vekel. He snorted, and batted resignedly at his individual cloud of midges. I had one too; they made our lives a misery, following as we walked. Swatting at them brought momentary relief, but they always came back. Our faces and necks were covered in bites, and the itching in my hair was a constant torment.

Late in the morning we came across a group of men standing by a pool of dark brown water. Two bore a long, carved piece of wood. I came first into sight, Vekel being behind me. They were not at all pleased to see me, and things might have gone ill if I had been on my own. One look at Vekel, however, and they lowered their gaze, waiting for us to go past. I glanced at the length of timber the men were holding, suspicion gnawing. Thicker than one of Ragnhild's thighs, it had been carved into the basic resemblance of a man, naked, arms by his sides. The head was the best rendered. Its two deep-set eyes seemed to stare at me, and the expression was glowering, threatening.

We made no greeting; nor did the men.

'An offering,' I muttered to Vekel.

'Indeed. The old ways linger.'

A splash came from behind us; the carving had been thrown into the water.

'Before the Irish worshipped the White Christ, they sometimes used to sacrifice people in the bog,' said Vekel.

I had heard this too. It sounded a dreadful end, held under the surface by wicker hurdles, throat and mouth filling with brown murk. I shuddered, and put the image from my mind.

Loch Ainninn was the biggest body of water I had ever seen inland. Much longer than it was wide, it faced in a northeast-southwest direction. Having asked directions of a farmer, we set off around the northern shoreline. Cranes stalked the water's edge. Bitterns boomed and water rails squealed among the reeds while a marsh harrier quartered the air overhead. Vekel pointed to a pair of white-tailed eagles even higher above, and said that they were a good omen.

I hoped he was right.

In such a natural place to build a stronghold, there were a large number of crannógs on the loch. I assumed the first artificial island to be Máel's, but was soon put right by the warrior guarding its causeway. Vekel's appearance afforded his instant respect. He told us that Inis Cró, the high king's crannóg, and the associated stronghold of Dún na Sciath were further around the lake. Look for the timber stockade on the southwest shore, we were politely informed, and the big crannóg near it. I glanced back to see the warrior making the sign against evil at Vekel. I was content. There was nothing wrong with a bit of fear.

So near to our destination now, my own fears resurfaced. I dawdled first, then stopped to watch a heron in the shallows, motionless as it waited to transfix unsuspecting fish when they came within range of its spear-like bill.

Vekel's intuition was uncanny. 'What are we going to do?' he demanded.

I did not answer.

We had gone back and forth on the best story to present since Linn Duachaill. The most simple, the truth, that my father had been slain out of hand by the high king's son over a sword that was not his, was too dangerous – we both agreed on that. It would be my word against Cormac's, and everyone who had been with him.

Vekel had generously offered to tell Máel that he wished to serve him – I could be his manservant – and by living in the royal household, gain access to Cormac. I refused. If there were oaths to be taken, I told him, it was I who should do so.

His idea had given me one of my own. Even if my idea proved possible *and* successful, every outcome involved Vekel and me suffering unpleasant deaths, either immediately after killing Cormac, or after being pursued and caught as we fled Máel's stronghold. My own death did not matter, but I did not want to be responsible for Vekel's. I would go on alone, I said. He absolutely refused to co-operate. The spirits had told him that he was to accompany me. I was very relieved.

I could come up with no good plan, however. My pace around the lakeshore grew slower.

'There is nothing to stop us seeing the lie of the land, Finn. We are but two travellers, seeking a bed for the night.'

'And you a vitki? You attract attention the way flies are drawn to shite. Everyone, including Máel, if we manage to gain an audience, will want to know why you have come a-visiting.'

'Isn't it obvious? I am wandering the length and breadth of the country, guided by seiðr. There are few who will question that.'

'And if Cormac is not back?'

'He will be. Pups his age never stray too far from the teat. I can weave enough tales to keep us royally fed and watered for a few days.'

I could see Vekel doing this well, but was less sure what approach to take myself. 'What will my purpose be?'

A languorous look. 'You are my companion.'

I had not seen this bolt from the blue. Colouring, I said, 'But we do not . . . we are not—'

'*I* know that. *You* know that, but everyone else will be ignorant.'

Although I did not mind his tendencies, I was uncomfortable with his suggestion. It would have been unacceptable anywhere there were Norsemen, but the Irish were different, and I could come up with no other idea. I scowled and told Vekel to keep his hands to himself. The tart reply, which I expected, was that he would only touch me 'when necessary'.

We did not stop at the second crannóg, which was as small as the first. Inis Cró was the third, a grand structure on the lake's northern aspect, and a good spear-cast in diameter. It was connected to the shore by a bridge, which led directly into a large, bivallate rath – Dún na Sciath. Around that was a settlement; the houses of those not worthy of living within the high king's walls. The place was larger than Mainistir Bhuithe, and to me, mightily impressive. Vekel might have thought so too, but he had always been better at concealing his feelings.

Long heather-thatched wattle and daub houses lined the main thoroughfare. It was thronged; mostly Irish in brown and black clothing, but there were a few Norsemen, and even a dark-skinned trader with a gold earring and outlandish robes. Women stood in shop doorways, bargaining for food, cloth, ironmongery. A balding man squawked at a boy playing too close to his dog. 'You'll get bit,' he cried. 'And then you'll be sorry.' In the lane between two buildings, I spied a carpenter, bent over a sawhorse, shaping a roof timber with a plane. His apprentice, a skinny youth, looked on with a vacant expression.

We slipped in behind an ox-wagon; it was slow moving, but everyone got out of its way. At the stockade's entrance the wagon went in without even stopping. I soon saw why. Three of the four sentries were trying to impress a pretty girl carrying a big bundle of wool, while the other, a good bit older, was leant up against the timber rampart, picking his nails with a dagger.

Vekel drew the interest of this last man, who wore a traditional long tunic, gathered at the waist by a belt. He straightened, shoved his dagger into its sheath and stepped into our path. A whistle left his lips. 'Lads.'

To my consternation, the trio vying for the beauty's attention obeyed the summons.

'Your business, *a chara*?' The question was aimed in my direction; it was clear from the tight grip on his spear that he did not regard me as his friend.

Vekel moved in front of me, staff prominent. 'I was sent by the spirits.' He smiled; his eyelashes fluttered.

Two of the younger warriors took a step back. The other blanched and crossed himself. The oldest was made of sterner stuff, but even he was wary of a spirit-sent vitki. He made a stiff bow. 'And your friend?'

'Company on the road,' replied Vekel sweetly. So sweetly that it was clear we were lovers. It was quick-witted, and the sentries smirked. Their reaction was a stark contrast to what Olvir had called Vekel: ergi and ragr, epithets linked with cowardice, unmanliness and a host of other bad qualities.

Vekel lasciviously rubbed his thumb and forefinger up and down the tip of the staff. 'Was there anything else?'

'There was.' The lead sentry was going nowhere. 'Where are you from?'

'All over,' said Vekel. 'I have never called any place home.'

The sentry let that slide, but his eyes moved to me. 'And you?'

'Breifne,' I lied, using the first name that popped into my head. A small kingdom which lay between Midhe and Northern Uí Néill territory, it was far enough away to make it unlikely he knew anyone there.

He didn't react.

'We seek an audience with the high king,' said Vekel, more politely.

'So do you and half of Ériu,' replied the sentry with a can-you-believe-this look at his comrades. 'What would Máel want with a creature like you? He is a good Christian, like all of us.' His companions bristled, and I thought, do not let this come to violence. We would not come off well.

'The high king loves Christ, but rulers seek wisdom in many places.' Vekel's expression became supercilious. 'And it is for the high king to decide that, not you!'

The sentry considered this, then muttered, 'Maybe so, but you can't prance into the king's presence just because you feel like it.' He continued, explaining that Máel held an audience every three days, and that we could come and wait with those who wished to plead something of the high king.

'When is the next audience?' I asked.

'Three days,' he said smugly, adding, 'There was one this morning.'

Vekel protested, beginning to wax lyrical about his dreams and the messages sent from the spirit world. The lead sentry cut him off, his manner growing less amicable. 'Enough. The high king may listen to your nonsense, but I won't. Away with you.'

We beat as dignified a retreat as possible, the sentries watching in triumphant silence.

41

CHAPTER FIVE

'That didn't go well,' I said sourly.

Vekel scowled. It was clear he hadn't foreseen this.

I took charge. A few questions aimed us at a run-down thatched hut at the settlement's edge. A piece of hacksilver and a blessing from Vekel, and the widow who lived there was happy to rent us a corner of her crop shed. It didn't take long for word to spread of our presence. By the middle of the next day, we'd had a succession of people seeking out the newly-arrived vitki. Christ-worshippers though they were, they wanted herbs or rune-casting, or magic spells. I had never been party to Vekel's dealings before; now I listened in amazement to the requests. To make a sickly child well, to render a woman fertile. To bring disease to a neighbour's crop of wheat, or return a straying husband to the marital bed. To find a missing cow; the list went on.

On a low wooden dais he had had me build, Vekel listened carefully to each respondent. Then he shuffled from foot to booted foot, eyes closed, chanting in Norse, his iron staff moving in and out from between his legs, and weaving intricate patterns in the air. Spell cast, or prophecy foretold, he declared solemnly that their wish would be granted.

Beaming, gabbling their thanks, every supplicant departed confident. Everyone left a gift. Mostly it was something small: bread, a wedge of cheese, a jug of foamy, fresh milk, but one farmer's wife left half a ham, and an arthritic greybeard gave Vekel a wooden bucket of beer. We dined like lords.

Not everything could come true, I said to Vekel when he was done on the second day. It was impossible.

What he had foreseen was true, he told me gravely, but the gods were tricksters. The Norns liked to play with humankind. Evil spirits sent by other vitkis could interfere. It was far beyond his remit to know how many of his predictions would come to pass. 'I am merely the vessel, Finn. The spirits speak through me,' he said. Some men might have laughed in his face, but not I. He had witnessed the raven on the sword, when a god had sent me a gift.

If we had hoped for a warmer reception outside Máel's gate on the appointed day, we had wished in vain. Four different warriors were on duty, and when, with half the morning past, we reached the head of the line of supplicants, they gave us short shrift. The high king, one told us, had no need of pagan filth, particularly arseloving ones. Vekel, composure slipping, threatened to curse the warrior, who sneered and hefted his spear. I took the initiative and dragged my friend away, throwing apologetic looks at the sentries.

'His prick will shrivel and drop off, I swear it,' Vekel muttered.

'Remember why we're here. Angering men like that will guarantee we never meet the king.'

He huffed and sulked for a time, but then admitted I had been right.

Our plan had failed.

We needed a better one.

If we could not go to Máel Sechnaill, Vekel and I decided, he must come to us. It sounded grand, but merely meant that we found a spot with a view of the entrance to the royal enclosure that was far enough from the sentries to avoid attention, yet enabled us to see when the high king emerged.

It did not happen that day; Cormac did not return either. The procession of those seeking out Vekel also slowed to a trickle, before stopping altogether. That was normal, he said; the settlement was not large, and only so many people needed help at any one time. The sour knowledge didn't fill my belly; the remnants of the ham and some fire-baked barley bread purchased from the widow had to suffice.

Vekel cast his rune bones the following morning, and pronounced that our luck was about to change. Irritable, hungry, a scornful reply rose to my lips, but I persuaded myself he was right; if he wasn't, things would improve the day after that.

Fast broken with a mouthful each of ham, we went back to our waiting spot. It was a cloudy morning as usual, and the wind came from the west, as usual. I settled down on my haunches; it was going to be another long day. The original sentry who had denied us entry was at the gate; he gave us a grim look, but our distance did not warrant anything else.

Squatting beside me, Vekel went into a deep reverie, something I had grown used to. I hoped he would come out of it with some kind of spirit-sent guidance. With no one to talk to, I grew bored, but thoughts of my father helped me to find a reserve of patience.

Despite this, the morning dragged by. A messenger arrived and was allowed to enter. The heavens opened, and we took refuge in the settlement's inn until the rain stopped. Returning, I saw that the sentries had changed. The even less friendly warrior, the one who had called us arselovers, was now on duty. I found myself thinking that we were wasting our time; vengeance – and the sword – would never be mine.

A sharp, angry sound dragged me back. 'What's that?'

Vekel stirred, but did not answer.

It was repeated, and I recognised the noise as wild neighing. It came from inside the rath.

Vekel heard it now as well. 'That is one unhappy horse.'

Fearful shouts accompanied the neighing. Hooves thundered around and around. The sentries were staring into the royal enclosure.

'Get some rope, quickly.'

I didn't need to ask why, and aimed for a barn at the back of a nearby house. I found some and luckily, no one noticed me come or go. I ran back to Vekel. The commotion inside the rath continued. 'They haven't caught the horse,' I said, fashioning a running noose at one end of the rope.

'Not from the sound of it,' said Vekel, his face alight.

With that, hooves pounded. The sentries scattered like hens with a fox in the coop. A grey stallion, all flaring nostrils and flowing mane, galloped through the entrance. A merchant who'd clearly been hoping to go in and sell his wares threw himself under his wagon. The stallion hared past, setting the merchant's oxen to lowing.

'Finn,' said Vekel.

I was already moving forward, the rope in my hands. I was used to catching cattle, but not moving at the stallion's speed. There would be one chance only. Closer the stallion came. He was not going to stop for anyone or anything. Closer. My mouth was dry. Fail, and we might as well go back to Linn Duachaill. Succeed, and there was no guarantee Máel would even see us.

44

The stallion charged in, eyes wild.

Whirling the noose, I threw. And prayed.

The rope dropped over his head as neatly as if he'd been standing right by me. A heartbeat's delay, he thundered on, and the knot tightened. Next came the drag, as powerful as if I had caught Sleipnir himself. But for the forge-hardening of my hands, I would have lost the skin on both palms. Death-gripping the rope, I was dragged a dozen paces by the stallion's momentum, and if not for Vekel running in to seize me around the waist, I am not sure he could have been stopped. Halt he did, however, chest heaving, sweat darkening his grey colour.

Vekel let go, went around me. 'Whoa, boy.' One hand was out, fingers together. 'It's all right.'

The stallion reared up, front hooves kicking the air. Fortunately, I'd anticipated this, and there was enough slack in the rope not to rip it from my hands. I knew enough about horses, stayed calm, took up most of the slack when he came down.

Vekel moved forward, murmuring, reassuring all the while.

'The beast won't listen. He's mad!' The voice was that of a groom, come hurrying out of the rath.

'Stay back,' I hissed.

The groom obeyed, but the face on him said he thought the stallion would break free any instant.

He didn't. Vekel took an age to approach, talking, talking. I couldn't hear what he was saying, but that was fine, because the stallion was noticeably calmer. As Vekel came within reach, an apple appeared in his hand. The stallion's velvety lips moved, taking it, and Vekel was beside him, his hand running down the well-muscled neck. His murmuring never stopped.

'I've never seen the like.' The groom had joined me. 'The way that stallion's been acting, I would have sworn it was better off dead. Like something possessed, he is, ever since he come in five days ago.'

'He was frightened, nothing more.' Vekel had uncanny hearing.

'If you say so.' The groom's face spoke differently.

Fresh shouts carried from inside the rath. A man's voice, used to command.

'That'll be the king,' declared the groom, worried.

Vekel pushed the stallion's shoulder, and led him around, calm as calm, to face back the way he had come. 'Quiet!' He pitched his voice low but intended to carry. I heard; so did the people watching.

The sentries who had so curtly refused entry now stood aside as we walked into the unpaved yard that formed the centre of the rath. There were barns, pigpens, enclosures for sheep and cattle, stables, workshops and storerooms. The largest structure was a round, thatch-roofed hall, and it was in front of this that I had my first sight of the high king, Máel Sechnaill mac Domhnaill. A squat, middle-aged figure in a deep red-dyed tunic, he seemed as surprised as any to see the stallion led in like a pet lamb.

Máel barked a command, and the groom scuttled forward, bowing deeply.

'Liath Macha escaped, I take it?'

'Yes, sire. I—' He was cut off by Máel, who directed a shrewd gaze at me and Vekel. 'Who caught him?'

'I did, lord.' I bent my head in respect.

'And you did not let him go. That was well done.' Máel stroked his braided beard, his attention moving to Vekel. 'You, I am thinking, calmed the stallion?'

'Yes, lord.' A trace of deference was evident in Vekel's voice. 'A magnificent beast.'

Máel looked pleased, then rueful. 'Magnificent but unrideable, he is. It's something of a miracle that he is standing there for you.'

'I have a way with horses.' Vekel's black-rimmed eyes slow-lidded.

'So it seems,' said Máel, smiling. He spoke to the groom, who warily took the rope from Vekel. The stallion made no protest, and the king smiled again. 'Let us not stand outside like vagrants. Please, enter my hall.'

This was what I had hoped for, yet it felt like an invitation to enter the wolf's den. We had little option, however, other than to accept.

The circular building was basically a larger, grander version of the Irish houses I was used to. The edges of the chamber, low enough so that only a small child could walk upright, were used as storage space and sleeping areas. There were women here, sitting on benches, working and talking by the light of stone oil lamps, and several children, who stared at us with unabashed fascination.

In the central fireplace, a fire burned. A smoke hole above let in bright sunlight. Behind the hearth was a carved wooden chair, a throne, towards which Máel strode. A thin-lipped priest rose from a stool, as did two noblemen, both eyeing each other and us as we approached. One bore a close resemblance to Máel, but he did not have long fair hair like Cormac. Another son, I decided. All three bowed; Máel paid no heed, sitting, then asking if we were thirsty.

'Some mead would go down well, lord,' I said, scarcely able to believe where I was.

Máel gestured at a servant, who hurried off. 'How came you here?'

Vekel wove a tale of our wandering. He had, he claimed, prophesied for sub-kings and kings, lords and nobles all over the northern half of the island. Guided by seiðr – this word elicited a disapproving tut from the priest – he had come at last to Dún na Sciath. 'I was guided here, lord,' he said, tones as sibilant as water washing over pebbles.

'Doubtless you say the same to every lordling,' said Máel.

The priest snickered; the nobles also seemed amused, especially the high king's son – for son he had to be.

'Mock if you will, lord, but it is true. It was ordained that I come to your hall.'

So that I could kill your son Cormac, I thought.

'Maybe so. But enough of magic and mysticism for now,' said Máel. 'I would know more of your skill with horses. Catching Liath Macha was remarkable enough, but to quieten him in that fashion, well . . . I have never seen the like.'

'There is not much to say, lord. I treat all horses with respect; they recognise that. I am calm and reassuring, but I take no nonsense either.'

'Is he fit to ride now?'

'It might take a little more time, lord. If you wish, I can work with him.'

I had not anticipated it would be Vekel's horse skills, rather than the fact he was a vitki, that gained access to the high king. Nor, I think, had he.

As we said to each other later, it was possibly better that way. Máel appeared to be a devout Christian; certainly, the thin-lipped priest was a constant presence by his side. The high king had seemed interested that I was a smith, although there had been no offer of work. Nonetheless, we had achieved much. It might be a barn, but we were to sleep inside the royal rath.

I would see Cormac when he returned. I just needed an ingenious way to kill him. My own death I did not care about, but with upwards of two dozen warriors also resident in the rath, it seemed impossible for Vekel not to share my fate.

I lay awake every night scheming.

I had known before arriving that Máel Sechnaill mac Domhnaill was fox-wily. How else, as Vekel said, could the ruler of such a small area become one of the most powerful kings in Ériu? His kingdom, Midhe, was tiny in comparison with Laighin, Mumhan, Ulaidh or the territory of the northern Uí Néills. Yet the proof of his ability was everywhere, from his vanquishing of the Norse king of Dyflin fourteen years before, to the defeats of the rulers of Laighin and Connachta since. There had been significant victories in Mumhan also, against Máel's great rival, King Brian Bóramha. Knowing how intelligent he was meant that we had to be very careful in our dealings with him. One wrong step, one inkling of our real purpose, and regardless of the fact that Vekel was a vitki, we would be dragged outside and slain.

A new insight was that Máel's apparent devotion to Christianity did not prevent him listening to Vekel's counsel, out of earshot of the thin-lipped priest, naturally. It helped too that Liath Macha became as docile as a pet lamb under Vekel's hands, allowing the high king to ride him. Soon Máel and Vekel were thick as thieves. The priest didn't like that. Nor did Conchobar, the eldest son and heir apparent, who had been present at our first meeting with the king. His reaction was mirrored by the high king's warriors, although they dared not harm us. It didn't make staying in the royal enclosure comfortable, though, and I slept with my seax in my hand.

The second revelation, the most relevant, was that Máel loved his children dearly. It could even be said that he indulged them. Five sons there were, and two daughters. I never met either of the latter, who were already married off, or Domnall, the son who was abbot of a nearby monastery. The rest lived at Inis Cró with the king and his wife. Conchobar was like his father, cold, calm and calculating. Máel took counsel with him most days. Congalach, next in line, was a withdrawn type who kept himself to himself, but when interacting with Máel, transformed into a happier creature. According to one of the king's warriors, with whom I had become friendly, Cormac was the pick of

48

the lot, handsome, outgoing, and a superb horseman. It was Loki's doing, I would mutter to Vekel, that Cormac was also, apparently, his father's favourite.

Vekel's tart retort was that it did not matter, because Máel would avenge the death of *any* of his children.

I argued and scowled, but my friend was right.

So I did nothing. Sometimes that was the best thing to do, my father had been fond of saying; bide your time, and an answer will present itself.

The next day, with no sign yet of Cormac, I was bored beyond measure. Thinking to work up a sweat with some honest labour, I sought out the royal smith. A friendly type with a hacking cough, he recognised me and hearing that I knew my way around a forge, insisted I enter. Occupying most of the space inside was a light, two-wheeled chariot, wicker-framed and leather-lined. I was familiar with the type, the standard mode of transport for kings and nobles, but had never ridden in one. A couple of Máel's sons, the smith related, liked to chariot race. Bent rims, snapped axles and broken wheels were a common result. So were serious injuries to horses and drivers.

'Not that that dissuades Cormac,' said the smith. 'Far from it. Young men are always the same.'

My interest pricked. 'This is Cormac's?'

'Aye. Wanted it ready the moment he gets back too, but I've not been up to it.' A prolonged bout of coughing. 'There'll be trouble too, if the thing's not fixed.'

My life-thread moved on the loom, as if the three Norns, Urd, Verdandi and Skuld, had heard.

'I could help, if you liked?'

'Are you sure?' Despite the question, it was plain that this what he'd hoped for.

'It would be a pleasure,' I said, excitement filling my veins.

My mind raced. This was how I would meet Cormac. Perhaps I could knife him here too. Dangerous, yes, but far easier than in the hall or the yard. *And the smith*, demanded my conscience, *will you kill him too?* Of course not, I thought indignantly. The answer came straight back: *then you cannot slay Cormac in the forge.* Frustration tore at me, that a golden opportunity might present itself, but be so risk-laden that I dare not seize it.

Under the smith's watchful eye, I fashioned an iron wheel rim and fitted it to the new wheel, which had been made by a local carpenter. The smith wrung my hand afterwards. How much hacksilver for my toil, he asked. No payment was necessary, I said, explaining how busy Vekel was with Liath Macha and the king, and how bored I'd become. If the smith let me work on in his forge, I'd be a happy man. At the very least, I'd decided, I wanted to clap eyes on my father's murderer.

The arrangement suited us both down to the ground – although if the smith had known my real purpose, I doubt he would have been as content.

CHAPTER SIX

Another day went by. The smith was feeling better, but able to do little. Pleased to be busy, I buried myself in work, making new arrowheads and spearheads, as well as several shield bosses. I also had a brief lesson in making horseshoes, which was simple enough work. Morning became afternoon, and I paused in my labour to eat with the smith. The fresh bread and cheese provided by his wife was most welcome. I closed my eyes, remembering with a pang similar meals in my father's forge.

The noise of horsemen reached us; they were riding in through the entrance. My ears pricked.

The smith peered outside. 'Cormac is back.'

My belly knotted, but I kept my face impassive. 'He will greet his father first?'

'He would rather see about his chariot, I'd wager, but yes, I think you're right.'

Mock casual, I looked out of the forge doorway. Most of the group cared for the horses, but two men, one with long, fair hair, went inside the hall. That had to be him, I decided, my heart racing.

I went back to work, imagining my seax in Cormac's flesh as I revealed my identity. I couldn't do it, however. The smith would die, and Vekel was in with Máel. I might get away, but he would not.

Voices carried.

'I had best win the next contest, Father. The pride of Inis Cró is at stake!'

Cormac, I thought.

'Here he comes,' whispered the smith, confirming my guess.

I felt a rush of rage and fear. Rage, at the barbarity of Cormac's actions. Fear, that I could strike him down, but immediately suffer the same fate.

I could almost hear the Norns cackling to one another in anticipation.

Máel walked in, flanked by a young man. No one could have mistaken them for anything other than father and son. The smith and I stood back from our work, and my gaze shot to the sword on Cormac's hip. It was the same one I had found on the beach. The one sent to me by Oðin himself. Emotions in full flood, I prayed that my expression would not give me away.

Máel was in fine humour, delighted to have his son back. 'Can this not wait?'

'No, Father. The race is important!'

An indulgent chuckle. 'Remind me who it is against.'

'I told you before. Niall, the King of Laighin's son. You will have to come and watch.'

'We will see,' said Máel, smiling. He glanced at us.

The smith bowed, as did I. I thought how easy it would be to kill Cormac in that moment. He wouldn't even see it coming. I pictured Vekel then, defenceless against the resulting retribution, and the smith too. I dampened down my hate.

'Lord,' said the smith. Then, 'Your chariot is ready, Prince Cormac.'

'Who's this?' Cormac indicated me.

'A young smith, lord, Finn by name,' the smith answered. 'He's been giving me a hand.'

'He's the vitki's companion,' said Máel, laying emphasis on the last word.

Again Cormac's gaze moved in my direction. He frowned. Nerves taut as a strung bow, I bowed for a second time. There was no reason for him to realise who I was, I told myself. Stay calm.

'His work had best be as good as your own,' said Cormac to the smith.

'It is, lord. Whoever taught him did their job well.'

Cormac spoke again. 'Who was that?'

Fresh panic. 'Th-the local smith, lord,' I said, flailing for a convincing lie.

'Where?'

I was readier this time. 'North, lord, in Breifne.' As with the sentry, I gambled he had never been there.

It paid off. He turned away, inspecting the chariot, and asking questions about the new wheel.

'Breifne?'

Startled, I glanced at Máel. 'Yes, lord.'

'Not too many Norsemen there, far from the sea.' His stare was intense.

I managed a laugh, even as my belly tied itself in knots. 'That is true, lord. I am half-Irish, though. My mother was from Breifne. She met my father at Lughnasadh one year; he was in the area, trading.' The harvest festival was celebrated all over Ériu; vast amounts of beer and mead were consumed, and merchants did a roaring trade.

The plausible explanation saw Máel's interest shift back to Cormac, still busy interrogating the smith. I breathed again, and eager to be distracted from Cormac's presence, I went back to work, hammering the strip of iron that would form a new wheel rim. I took great satisfaction from imagining Cormac's head on the anvil, mine to pound into red, broken-boned ruin.

'That's a new sword.' Máel's voice.

'Yes.' Cormac continued telling the smith that his chariot needed to be taken to the stables at once.

'Where did you get it?' Máel asked. 'The silverwork looks Norse.'

'In that herring-choker settlement called Linn Duachaill,' came the careless answer.

Unseen, I ground my teeth. To be called a herring choker by this cocky lordling was twice as bad as when someone from a village inland did. I imagined whirling, hammer raised, and throwing myself at Cormac, reclaiming what was mine.

'Your hunting took you far from home.'

'A stag led us a merry dance on the first day. Two horses lost shoes. Linn Duachaill was the closest place with a Norse smith, or so we reckoned. I saw the sword there. The smith didn't want to sell, but I insisted.'

'I hope you gave him a fair price. This was made by a real craftsman.'

'He took my offer.' A snort. 'Wisely.'

Blood roared in my ears; my head spun. I had to lock both knees not to fall to the dirt floor. My hammer came down with a weak clunk on the wheel rim.

Máel and Cormac did not notice. Their conversation had moved back to the chariot race, Cormac urging his father to attend, Máel demurring with excuses of 'matters of state' that needed his attention. Without as much as a thank you, they left.

I let out a juddering breath.

'You are pale as three-day-old whey.' The smith looked concerned.

'It's nothing,' I lied. 'I'm just a small bit lightheaded.'

'You've been pounding away fit to burst, that's what's done it. Come, sit down here. 'Twill do us both good to have a sup of beer after the king and his son visiting.'

I accepted, fashioning a smile from somewhere. I felt like the worst type of coward. My father's murderer had been standing before me, admitting he had taken my sword – sure proof that he was the killer – and I had done nothing.

Nothing.

Somehow I got through the rest of the day, burying myself in toil. I had considered damaging the chariot, half-cutting through the axle perhaps, or weakening some of the wheel spokes so that Cormac might be injured or even killed. The chance did not present itself, in the main because the smith fussed over it like a mother hen with newborn chicks. When the work was done, with me helping, he personally delivered the thing into the care of Cormac's groom. A grumpy, tousle-headed youth around my own age, he slept in the stable, which ruled out any opportunity for foul play there.

One of the female slaves liked me – probably because I spoke to her civilly, and didn't molest her at every opportunity – so it was easy to procure a brimming jug of beer. Taking myself far out along the lakeshore, I sat down and began to drink. It was a glorious summer's evening, sunlight glancing off the lake surface, fish jumping at flies, corncrakes calling in the rush beds. Damp-eyed, I toasted my father's shade, and asked for his forgiveness.

'I am a nithing.' The words came out as a whisper. I wanted no one to hear.

'Here I find you, moping!'

Palming away tears, I looked up at Vekel. He was dressed as outlandishly as ever, dark make-up emphasising his eyelids, a glass and bead necklace at his throat, jingling bracelets on both wrists. He saw my state at once, and sat down, uncaring of the damp ground, or the midges that I had been ignoring. He leaned in, putting his head on my shoulder.

'Grieving for your father?'

'That, aye.'

'And wanting to plant a blade in Cormac's chest.'

'Actually, I was going to smash his skull with a hammer.'

'From the forge, of course. How fitting!' Vekel clapped his hands, but he swiftly grew serious. 'You didn't do it, though.'

I made a face. 'I don't have Skíðblaðnir to escape across the lake in.' This was the god Freyr's magic ship. It was kept folded up like a cloth, but when unfolded, could sail immense distances at speed.

'The lake's not that big. You would need Sleipnir on the far side.'

The thought of riding away with Vekel on an eight-legged horse amused me. 'He's not here either,' I said. 'So killing Cormac would cause not just my death, but yours.'

'That's not so bad.'

I glanced at Vekel, but his face was unreadable. 'You may be happy to cross the Bifröst bridge today, but I'm not going to be responsible for it. I'm not ready for it myself either.' Shame scalded me to say the words.

Another elbow, a cackle of laughter. 'You never know when I'm joking!'

'Curse you,' I said, elbowing back, hard.

'It is as well you did not act rashly.' He reached out, and I handed the jug over.

We sat and drank for a while, midges, admiring the reds, purples and golds of the changing sky, and saying nothing.

'If you leave, what about your revenge?'

'It will have to wait,' I muttered, telling myself that my decision was that of a prudent man. I could think of no way to slay Cormac without immediately being implicated.

'Where will you go?'

'Linn Duachaill.'

'And then?'

'I don't know!' Now I was irritated. I had hoped for an easy solution. A quick vengeance on Cormac, returning home, life going back to normal. I had not bothered much to think about what happened afterwards. It was not in Vekel's nature, though, to rest easy. Answer a question, and he would always have another.

'Linn Duachaill is not such a bad place. You'll make your living; there's business enough for a smith. Might even find yourself a wife.

Gunnkel's daughter Grelod, maybe? She has good child-bearing hips.'

'And eyes that look in different directions,' I said, horrified.

'Once your prick's inside her, you'll soon forget that.'

I snorted with amusement, and told Vekel he could marry Grelod's brother Berghard, who was beetle-browed and thicker than a short plank.

'Ha!'

'A double wedding?' I suggested.

We fell about, roaring with laughter. Startled, a coot splashed off across the water.

'Getting away might not be so easy,' I said. 'Máel has taken to you.'

'Leave that to me.'

The graves of Máel's forebears, corpse-pens, as Vekel called them, were located a short distance from the rath. After the evening meal, Vekel made sure everyone knew that he was going to sit out the night there. No one in their right mind, with the obvious exception of a vitki, would choose to do such a thing. 'I will ask about your future, lord. The útiseta magic will be strong,' he said to Máel, who looked startled. The disapproving priest quickly said something in his ear, but was re-buffed. Máel's Christianity was skin-deep, I thought. If there was an advantage to be gained from the old gods, from seiðr, he would take it.

Vekel returned in the morning, gaunt-faced and sombre. He had spoken with several fetches. One in particular, Æesir's Son of Dread, had warned him that Brian Bóramha was machinating against the high king. The priest sniffed and said in a meant-to-be-heard voice that this was no revelation; Mumhan's ruler and Máel had been arch-rivals for years. Unperturbed, Máel demanded more details. Vekel nodded, as if the request had been expected, and closed his eyes.

The clatter of hooves carried inside; a common enough sound, no one paid it any heed.

Vekel's eyelids opened.

Frowning, Máel watched him.

Even the priest looked tense.

I felt nervous myself.

'An army is on the move,' Vekel intoned.

Máel leaned forward in his chair.

Feet pounded. A challenge rang out, and was answered.

The door was flung open.

In came a messenger, dusty from the road. 'Lord, I bring news, urgent news!'

Máel beckoned; Vekel stood aside. The messenger approached, and dropped to one knee. It was not just from respect. The man was exhausted.

The information he carried, from a lord whose westerns lands bordered Mumhan, was grave. Brian Bóramha's army had marched to the frontier with Midhe. It was large, perhaps two thousand strong, and seemed about to invade.

His task complete, the messenger hesitated, and then, puce with embarrassment, begged leave to answer a call of nature. 'My guts, lord,' he explained.

Máel waved permission, and as the man scurried by, I saw Vekel's gaze follow. He quickly revealed to the high king that the fetch had also summoned him away from Dún na Sciath. It was his fate, he said, never to rest long in one place. I would have to go with him. Preoccupied, calling to Conchobar, ordering his advisers to attend him, Máel barely noticed us leave.

'If I were a cynical man,' I whispered as we readied our gear, 'I would have thought it possible to spy a man with diarrhoea stopping to relieve himself before his destination. Noting his shield design, that of a southern Midhe lord, and his urgency to arrive, it is not unreasonable to deduce that he carried serious news.'

A scandalised look. 'Are you questioning what I was told at the corpse-pens?'

Vekel might have seen the messenger, I thought, but couldn't have known the news he carried. Yet what Vekel had told Máel was accurate. I bent my head in respect. 'No.'

Máel was still deep in discussion with Conchobar and his advisers as we exited the roundhouse. People stared at Vekel in the settlement, but that was nothing new. Other than his ability to read the future and cast spells, no one had any real interest. Soon the way home would lie open. My happiness at this was tempered with disappointment. My father was still unavenged, and my sword yet hung from Cormac's belt.

'Where's your dog Niall, herring choker?'

I scowled to see Stoat Face, dusty-footed, on the road from the east. 'Eh?'

A knowing smirk. 'You were drinking at Mainistir Bhuithe not so long since, you and your womanish friend. A couple of mutts, you had, one called Dog, and the other Niall.'

'Njal, his name is,' said Vekel.

'That's not what I heard.'

'Ara, your ears must be full of wax,' I said. 'Njal I called him, after my uncle.'

'If you say so, herring choker.' Stoat Face turned towards the rath.

My stomach flip-flopped. He is here to rat on me, I thought, in the hope of some silver. My eyes went to Vekel, and for once, I could read his expression. He thought the same thing, which was why, unseen by Stoat Face, he was drawing a finger across his throat in a questioning manner.

I actually considered it. We had time – there was no one near – and an alleyway yawned behind Stoat Face. But I had never killed a man, let alone in cold blood. Torn, I hesitated.

If my determination was wavering, Vekel's was not. His face was a cold, rigid mask, and he was wielding his staff like a cudgel. Stoat Face noticed, took to his heels and ran.

'Máel will be too busy. He won't have time to listen to tavern gossip,' I said, as if by saying the words out loud I could convince myself.

'I would not say the same of Cormac. We should have killed him.'

'I will not murder a man in cold blood!'

'And if he succeeds in telling Máel or Cormac?'

'No matter how disrespectful, a dog's name is of no importance when an army from Mumhan is on the doorstep. Besides, it's done now.'

'True.'

Krrruk. Krrruk.

The sound was familiar.

'Look,' said Vekel.

I lifted my gaze. It was not unremarkable to see ravens, but two, overhead, *now*, seemed god-sent.

'How is it with you, ravens? Where have you come from with bloody beak at the dawning of day?' Vekel cried. 'Flesh clings to your claws, your breath stinks of carrion, I think last night you nested where men lay dead.'

I shivered, and rubbed my raven amulet.

'It is Huginn and Muninn, I am sure of it,' Vekel declared. 'Oðin wants you to return to Linn Duachaill.'

I put Stoat Face and Cormac from my mind.

A god had summoned me.

CHAPTER SEVEN

I stared at the bare mast, for that was all the slowly moving vertical length of timber could be. 'There's a ship in the river mouth, or close to it,' I said to Vekel.

He nodded, as if it were an everyday occurrence.

It was not. In Linn Duachaill's heyday, it would have been commonplace. No longer. Although the location, a wide tongue of land bordered on two sides by a river, on a third by the sea, and protected landward by a massive earthen rampart and ditch, was a natural place for a Norse settlement, its heyday was long gone. Not many craft could fit in the river, and the strong currents offshore made anchoring there a risky enterprise. Dyflin, with its sheltered harbour, the Black Pool, was a natural successor.

'A knarr, do you think?'

'Perhaps,' Vekel replied. 'It certainly explains why Huginn and Muninn came.'

I wasn't listening. It was a knarr, I decided, my excitement rising, the same type of fat-bellied trading vessel whose visits had been the highlights of childhood. The merchants' exotic goods and frequent mention of far-off places, Iceland, Serkland, Miklagard, had set alight my youthful imagination. Beside them, Linn Duachaill, Mainistir Bhuithe, even Dún na Sciath seemed positively dull.

Rather than go into the settlement, we turned towards the beach, where I had found the sword. It was empty of people, waves lapping seaweed off the stones. It wasn't far to the mouth of the River Casán, which wound in irregular fashion around Linn Duachaill before entering the sea. The mooring place favoured by merchant craft, it was empty. Around the bend we went, to the mud flats that were exposed at low tide, and there found a longship, hauled up out of the water. She was magnificent, long, lean and narrow, a good hundred paces in length. Painted shields lined the nearest side, but the dragon's head had been taken down. I was pleased; it meant the ship's captain respected the local spirits. I also spied a rock cairn on the mud close to the prow. Decorated with raven feathers, it was surely an offering to Oðin.

'She must have suffered sea damage,' I said to Vekel. There was little other reason for a longship to break its voyage here. Local monasteries such as Mainistir Bhuithe, once a great attraction, were nowadays under the protection of the high king and so longships tended to anchor in the narrow water at Cairlinn when sailing north. Going the opposite way, the port at Dyflin was preferable.

'Unless they have come for Grelod.'

I roared with laughter.

Casting all kinds of aspersions on the poor girl, as is the habit of youths, we made our way closer. As the longship's beauty sank in, I devoured her with my eyes. The tightly wrapped-up sail, yellow and black in colour, was about fifteen paces across. Full-billowing, it must be immense, I thought, and drive the ship through the waves at great speed. I counted the oar holes in the top strake, thirty, along one side.

'Sixty oars, she has,' I said.

'Seventy or eighty men then, or more,' said Vekel. 'A strong raiding party.'

There were not many crew about, but one saw us now. Vekel's appearance could not be mistaken for anything else. The warrior dipped his head, in respect or fear, and said something to a companion close by on the mud flats. He stared; I waved. There was no response.

It wasn't that surprising, I decided, given that I was with a vitki.

'The rest must be in the settlement,' said Vekel.

So it proved. We went straight to the smithy, and there found a crowd around the doorway. Big men, mostly, hard men all. I could tell by the confident way they carried themselves, and by what they wore. Norse tunics and trousers. Silver arm rings. Belts and scabbarded seaxes. And axes. Hand axes, bearded axes, broad axes: each man had one, two or even three. There were spears too, and plenty of swords. These were seasoned warriors.

That wasn't going to stop me entering the forge, I thought stubbornly. This was my home; they were the visitors. I stepped inside, and anger stirred. A warrior was fossicking through the floor-piled ironmongery; another was rummaging about on the workbench. A third was helping himself to the mead I had brought back from Mainistir Bhuithe.

'Hey!' I shouted in Norse. 'That's not yours!'

The three turned; the nearest, the one at the bench, sneered. A little shorter than I, he had high cheekbones and raven-black hair tied back with a thong. 'The smith isn't here.' His tone was light and husky, the accent unfamiliar. 'Not that there's anything worth taking, except the mead.'

A red mist descended. I shoved the warrior in the chest. 'Thief! Get out!'

A seax leaped into his hand; he lunged at me. I scrambled backwards, scornful laughter in my ears, thinking, *I am a dead man.*

'Hold, Thorstein!'

The seax was lowered, reluctantly.

One of the two others in the smithy had spoken. Middle-aged, his entire head was shaved except for a braided strip of grey hair that hung down behind each ear. His tunic was normal enough, but I had never seen such baggy, colourful trousers.

'Finished staring?' he asked. His accent was the same as Thorstein's, and not one I had heard before.

There was more laughter, led by Thorstein, and I flushed.

'Can you blame him, Imr?' shouted a beefy warrior through the doorway. 'You're damned ugly!'

Imr paid no heed. 'This is your smithy, I am thinking?'

'It was my father's. It is mine now, I suppose.'

'He is dead?' No sympathy, but a trace of curiosity.

'Yes.' In my mind, I saw Cormac picking up the sword. How I wished I had been here. But I had not, and he had slain my father and taken my god-given blade. Worry niggled at me, that Stoat Face's intervention might yet make him appear.

'Finn's father was murdered.' Vekel had come into the forge. He got wary looks, and at least one warrior muttered a prayer.

'You saw it happen, vitki?' Imr demanded.

'No. We were away, booleying the cattle.'

'It was one of the high king's sons, Cormac by name,' I said. 'He came looking for a horse to be shod, and saw my sword. When my father would not give it over, Cormac killed him.'

'Your father must have been a mighty smith, to be slain for one of his own blades.' His gaze searched the forge for weapons that were not there.

'It was not his. I found it years ago, on the beach.'

Imr's bushy eyebrows rose. 'Just lying on the sand?'

'A body washed in on the tide. He had a sword.'

'And a raven landed on the corpse first,' said Vekel. Suddenly, he had everyone's attention. 'It was one of Oðin's birds, but he hopped off and let Finn here take the blade. I saw it with my own eyes. Stormcrow, they have called him since.'

'Stormcrow?' cried Thorstein. 'More like Scarecrow.'

More coarse laughter filled the smithy. Freshly enraged, uncaring of how many warriors there were, I threw a punch at Thorstein, who ducked out of the way, chuckling. He was very slim, and, I realised, the only one without any facial hair. At last the husky voice made sense. 'Wait,' I cried. 'You're a woman?'

'I will leave your corpse for the crows!' Thorstein swarmed forward, seax at the ready. 'Huginn and Muninn can feast too!'

'Thorstein!' Imr's voice.

'What?' This from between gritted teeth.

'He was not to know.'

Thorstein glared at me; I was confused. I had never put much store in the fireside tale of a red-haired Norse princess leading a fleet to raid Ériu, yet here, before me, was a female warrior.

'You have the body of a woman. And a very nice one it is too,' said Vekel, caressing the words.

The rest liked that, hooming and cheering.

Thorstein's face was dark with anger. 'I am no woman!'

'We are similar then,' said Vekel, and he wasn't joking.

'Lower your blade, Thorstein,' Imr ordered. 'You cannot slice up everyone who names you as a woman, not least when this one is a smith.'

So they needed someone who can work iron, I thought.

Muttering under his breath, Thorstein obeyed.

A metallic noise. Imr had placed some hacksilver on the worktop.

'What's that?' I asked.

'Payment for the mead,' said Imr, picking up the little barrel. 'I'll take as many nails as you have, and however many you can make in the next couple of days. Arrowheads too.'

The mead was the only drink I had – the rest had been consumed at my father's funeral – but the pieces of hacksilver covered its cost, even if the barrel had been full. I would earn more silver with the ironmongery he wanted, so I muttered agreement and, with Vekel, watched the trio join their comrades outside.

'Is an inn too much to hope for?' someone shouted.

'It is,' I called, 'but if you go to that longhouse yonder, Gunnkel will sell you beer. He has plenty.'

A loud hoom of approval rose into the air.

Cormac did not appear during the two days that followed, and my worries about him diminished. I learned a lot about our visitors. *Brimdýr*, the longship was called, Surf-beast. She was out of the Seal Islands, known to Norsemen as Orkneyjar. Hungry for wealth – the Seal Islands had rocks, wind, sheep and not much else – Imr and his warband had sailed on the spring tides for Ériu. Attacking settlements and monasteries on the coast of Ulaidh, they had been making their way towards Dyflin when a storm hit. Springing a leak, Surf-beast had been lucky not to be taken to the bottom by Rán, the ever-hungry sea goddess. According to Gunnkel, beachcombing as the raiders arrived, the longship had been low in the water, with men bailing for all they were worth.

I understood Imr's need for nails now. He needed cords of wool and cattle hair too, for caulking, and tar to paint on afterwards. Gunnkel and others were able to provide him with the former but not the latter. I told Imr about the nearest tar kiln, on a pine-covered hill some distance to the northwest. I got a grunt of thanks, and he immediately sent off a dozen warriors with barrels.

As I toiled in the forge, aided by one of the Norsemen's thralls – Imr's suggestion, not mine – I went over our time at Inis Cró. Maybe I had been a nithing, but my inaction had saved my skin, and Vekel's. One day, if the Norns wove my fate that way, a chance to kill Cormac and retrieve the sword would come. As for our encounter with Stoat Face, it troubled me less and less. Compared to Brian Bóramha's threat to Midhe, not to mention the host of daily problems Máel must deal with, a dog called Niall was of no importance. Vekel agreed.

Of more concern was whether I could join Imr's crew. The moment he had asked for nails and arrowheads, this had been my hope. Until now, there hadn't been even a hint of interest. Proud, wary of refusal, I had not asked either. Time was running out, however. The repairs to *Brimdýr* were almost complete. She would sail on the morning tide of the third day.

On the last afternoon, I was still making nails. Heating one of the square iron rods I had previously fashioned, I would cut off individual lengths, and beat each nail to a point at the free end. While I repeated the process, the thrall would pick up the still hot nail and beat it through a hole in the anvil, flattening the head nicely.

There was a lot of noise, two of us constantly wielding hammers. When I heard shouts through the clamour, therefore, I paused in my labour. Wiping my face with a rag, I walked to the forge door.

Gunnkel was outside his longhouse, peering towards the rampart.

I cupped a hand to my mouth. 'What's going on?'

'The sentries are yelling and pointing.' Gunnkel looked worried.

I had thought Imr overcautious to place guards at the rampart, could not understand why his men went everywhere armed. 'No one knows you're here,' I'd said. 'You don't have anything to worry about.'

He had given me a pitying look and spoken the verse:
'Out in the field no man should move
A foot beyond his weapons.
For a man never knows, out on the trackways,
When he may need his spear.'

What a fool I had been, to try and teach a warrior like Imr his trade, I thought, going inside for my own spear and shield.

The thrall gaped. 'Keep working!' I ordered. 'This does not concern you.'

It was Cormac, I decided, my guts churning.

Of course it was Cormac. In he charged at the head of a group of twenty riders, girded for battle to a man. Helms, shields, mail shirts on almost half. Spears, swords, daggers. A strong enough force to crush Linn Duachaill's few inhabitants, should it be necessary. More than enough to do whatever it was he had planned. Stoat Face had been believed. I could imagine no other reason that Cormac should have come with such haste. I should have cut Stoat Face's throat, I decided, but it was too late. Now I was about to die, and with nothing achieved.

Cormac dragged his horse to a halt so close to the forge I had to retreat inside not to be barged over. I came out again as, high-spirited, nostrils flaring, it skittered back a little. I lifted my shield up, so it protected my body, and gripped my spear overhand, ready to thrust. If I was to leave this world, I thought, I would take Cormac with me.

'Finn Thorgilsson,' he cried, face alight with anticipation.

'You know that is my name, lord,' I said, eyeing my sword, still hanging from his belt. I had a bad, bad feeling in my belly, but had to keep up the pretence. 'What business brings you here?'

'I was told a tale about a smith's son from Linn Duachaill who had the impudence to call his dog Niall. Are you that man?'

'No, lord.' Cormac hadn't yet realised that I was my father's son, I decided. He merely thought I had insulted his family by naming my pet after them. I considered denying I was from Linn Duachaill, that I had any dogs, but all Cormac had to do was ask questions of Gunnkel, say, to find out I had been born and bred here, and owned two. 'He is called Njal, lord, after my uncle.'

A knowing sneer. 'Really?'

'Yes, lord.' I kept my face blank. Let that be the only reason he's here, I prayed. I will get away with a beating, maybe a broken bone or two. Cormac's gaze never shifted, though, and my unease grew.

A frown. 'Remember that day in the forge, when you were helping the smith with my chariot?'

I felt sick. 'Yes, lord. I hope you won the race?'

No reply. His brow lowered further. Then, 'You said you were from Breifne!'

He had me. I did not answer. I thought about thrusting forward my spear – he was just within reach – but the riders flanking him were watching like hawks. A move out of place, and they would gut me like a fish.

'So you're from Linn Duachaill, not Breifne . . .'

Time stopped.

My heart banged off my ribs. Again I wondered about trying to kill him, but one of the riders eased his horse forward a little, and I knew the moment, if it had been there, was gone.

Shocked realisation on Cormac's face. 'You're *that* smith's son!'

'You murdered my father for a sword. *My* sword,' I cried, throwing caution to the wind.

'A herring choker has no right to such a weapon! You must have stolen it.'

The insult stung as much as at Dún na Sciath. 'I found the sword on the beach. The god Oðin sent it to me.'

His warriors, Christians all, didn't like that. Several crossed themselves. It didn't stop Cormac sliding from his horse's back. He tossed the reins to a nearby warrior. Out came the sword; he levelled it at me. 'You pagan savage. Where is your god when you need him?'

Rage took over, and if there had been any bridge left to me, I set fire to it now. 'You are no prince,' I said.

Cormac's lips pinched white.

'You are a murdering piece of arse-moss,' I shouted. 'Come here and I will end you!'

'Lord,' said a warrior in a mail shirt. 'Let me.'

'Stay where you are!' Cormac stalked closer.

I retreated inside, blocking the doorway with my shield.

'Master?' The thrall sounded frightened.

'Keep making nails,' I snarled.

Only Cormac could come at me. I had a chance, I told myself.

'I came seeking an impudent herring choker, and found not just him, but the pup of the man who tried to stop me taking what is rightfully mine.'

'Oðin gave the sword to *me!*'

'Ever wielded a spear before, herring choker?' Cormac asked. 'Doesn't look like it.'

I did not answer.

He shifted from foot to foot, appraising me.

I waited, nerves taut, unsure what to do.

His blade flickered forward. First at my shield, then a feint at my foot.

I slammed down my shield, knocking the sword tip to the dirt, and stepped back, panting.

Worse perhaps than another assault, he laughed. 'You cannot win. You must know that.'

'It'll be hard for you too.'

His scowl revealed that he wasn't completely confident.

It was obvious why. My spear was longer than his sword, and I was standing in a narrow doorway. He couldn't swing his blade overhead or from the sides, but only come at me with thrusts.

A saying of my father's came to mind. An angry enemy was one with a chink in his armour. Keep digging away at him, I thought.

'Scared?' I asked.

He cursed, and told me that my father had begged for his life.

Completely forgetting my father's saying, furious, I lunged. My spear thwacked into his shield once, twice. He took the blows and stabbed back with his sword. By some miracle, I dropped my shield enough to prevent him burying the blade in one of my ankles, but the action unbalanced me. I staggered backwards, and sensed him follow. If he forced me into the forge, I was done. Desperate, I poked my spear out in front of me. It was clumsy, childlike, but the tip connected with his shield and he checked. Somehow I regained my footing and drove forward, filling the doorway once more.

Cormac smiled. 'Let's see if you can do that again.'

This was life and death for me, I thought, but a game to him. If he grew bored, he could force me out by setting a fire in the roof. It was a sour realisation. I could think of no tactic other than rushing him. I might get in one meaningful thrust before he ended the fight. Before the Norns' shears cut my life-thread.

I tensed.

His expression tightened.

Shouts. Cries. 'Lord!' yelled a voice. 'The Norsemen are coming!'

Cormac's heard turned, just a little.

I charged. He heard, but couldn't stop me hitting him with my shield. The boss met his midriff with a solid thump, and I came after, eager as a rampaging bullock. Down he went, onto the flat of his back. I stamped on his right hand, and he let go the sword. My spear point resting right below his eye, I said, 'Lie still.' Paling, he obeyed. It was so tempting, but I cooled my bloodlust. My life hung in the balance.

I waited.

Our clash had been so brief that the warrior in the mail shirt hadn't seen. He was twisted around on his horse. So were nearly all the other warriors. 'What in God's name is going on?' Mail Shirt roared.

A warrior came running in. 'We killed a Norseman.'

'What? Why?'

'It was Cerball. He lost the head, and rode after one of the sentries, cut him down from behind.'

'Fool! And the other one fetched his comrades.'

'Aye. They are coming from the longship.'

CHAPTER EIGHT

Give him his credit, Mail Shirt did not panic. In two shakes of a lamb's tail, he had the warriors in a double line, with their backs to the forge. Then a man who'd noticed what had happened to Cormac spoke to him. He wheeled his horse.

'Lord!'

'How many Norsemen are there?' asked Cormac from the ground.

'Sixty, lord?' said Mail Shirt. 'Seventy, maybe?'

I looked down. Cormac's face had gone fish-belly pale.

I wondered if Loki, fickle as ever, had thrown the dice in my favour.

The stamp of feet, the shink of mail, carried. Came closer. Halted.

Some of the horses shifted to and fro, but the line of warriors held firm. They muttered to one another.

'Name yourselves! I would know whose man murdered one of mine.'

I recognised Imr's voice. His Irish was shocking, *gioc-goc* as it was known, all mispronunciations and incorrect emphases, but it was understandable.

'We are of Clann Cholmáin and the Uí Néills,' said Mail Shirt.

'You're a long way from home.'

'The king's son led us to this dungheap.'

'King's son?' Imr sounded disbelieving. 'Where is he?'

'Here!' I roared.

'Show yourself.'

I stepped back, keeping my spear point close to Cormac's face. 'Up. Face the wall, close.' As he obeyed, I discarded spear and shield and whipped out my seax. Wrapping an arm around his neck, I laid it along his collarbone, point resting against the side of his throat.

'I have nothing to lose, understand?' I whispered in his ear. 'Make a wrong move, and I *will* end you.'

A stiff nod.

We walked forward, giving Mail Shirt and the riders a wide berth.

I could sense Cormac drinking in the Norsemen, staring at Imr, out in front of his men. They filled the space between the forge and the nearest longhouse. An impressive sight they were, a line of mail shirts, helmets and overlapping painted shields. I counted more than fifty. They were eager-faced too, ready for a fight. Ready to avenge their fallen comrade.

Best of all, I noted half a dozen Norsemen on the nearest longhouse roofs, each with a nocked arrow at the ready. Half of Cormac's warriors did not have armour. If the archers loosed, the toll on men and horses would be heavy.

'You,' said Imr to me. 'This I had not expected.'

'It's Scarecrow,' said Thorstein.

Snickers.

'Tell him who you are,' I ordered Cormac.

'Cormac Sechnaill mac Domhnaill I am, of Clann Cholmáin and the Uí Néills.'

'More,' I said, pushing just a little with the seax. Cormac hissed with pain. A drop of blood ran down his neck.

'My father is Máel, High King of Ériu,' he said.

Imr glowered. 'I don't give a rat's arse who your daddy is. One of my lads lies dead over there, the back of his neck opened. Which of your nithings did it?'

None of the riders moved.

Imr's baleful gaze returned to me. 'What in Hel is going on?'

'The king's son came for Finn's dog.' Vekel emerged from Gunnkel's longhouse. 'It got a little complicated after that.'

'The ragr vitki,' said Cormac, mockingly using the Norse words. 'I should have known you'd be here too.'

'This makes no sense,' said Imr to me and Vekel, 'and my temper is growing short. Explain!'

Vekel laid it out. How he and I had got blind drunk at Mainistir Bhuithe. How Stoat Face had heard him call Niall by his name. The return to Linn Duachaill, finding my father dying, the sword gone. Our journey to Dún na Sciath and Inis Cró, and how we had left, guided by Oðin's ravens. Stoat Face must have gone to the high king's residence, Vekel went on, and at the very least, spoken with Cormac.

Imr looked less than happy. 'So one of my men died because of a bastard dog, that's what you are telling me?'

Vekel's lips pursed. 'In a word, yes.'

71

Imr came stumping over. Several of Cormac's warriors put hands to their weapons. 'If a single Irisher moves,' Imr cried to the bowmen, 'Start loosing, and do not stop!'

In an instant, they all resembled statues.

Imr stopped in front of me, shoved his face into Cormac's. 'I've half a mind to cut your throat and be done,' he said conversationally, and as if I had no say in the matter.

'I wouldn't do that.' Cormac's voice was husky with fear.

'Why not? Blood for blood. And Kalman was twice the man you will ever be. A wife he has in Orkneyjar, and two weans who will grow up never knowing their father.'

'Kill me, and Dyflin will feel Máel Sechnaill's wrath afresh. Blood will run in the streets.'

'I am from Orkneyjar,' Imr scoffed. 'Not Dyflin.'

'That's as maybe. Ten horses to one says that you are Sitric Silkbeard's man.' This was Sigtrygg, king of Dyflin, but also a man under the power of the High King. Cormac continued, 'If my father demands it, Sitric will hand you over.'

That silenced Imr.

It was hard to admit, I decided, but Cormac was brave.

'Cut off his balls instead,' suggested a warrior, and axe heads banged off shields in agreement.

Imr leered.

The Norns' rune-marked fingernails were moving my life-thread, and I didn't like its direction one bit. It was time to seize control of my own fate, if I could. 'He's not your prisoner,' I said loudly. 'He is mine.'

Imr's jaw dropped, just a little. 'Hear this cub!'

'What are you going to do, Scarecrow, leave with him?' called Thorstein. 'Can you outrun arrows?'

Imr's eyes were on me, intent as a those of a mouse-watching cat.

'You can have him, on one condition,' I said.

Cormac said nothing. He knew as well as I that all the best pieces left on the tafl board belonged to Imr. The risk to me was as great. I was gambling not just his life, but my own.

'And that condition is?'

It was clear as running water that whether Cormac lived or died, I could not remain at Linn Duachaill. When word reached his father of my involvement, as surely it would, vengeance would be swift.

Whatever about naming your dog Niall, it was not for commoners to effect violence on members of the royal family. Various fates awaited. Drowned in a bog under wicker hurdles, or a blade death, if I was lucky. Being flayed alive if I was not.

Silently, I asked Oðin to have a word in Loki's ear. Then, with all the confidence I could muster, I said, 'Vekel and I will join your crew.' This of course was no guarantee of safety, particularly if Máel decided he wanted to revenge himself upon Imr for the mistreatment of his son, but I didn't have too many other options.

Imr didn't laugh at my suggestion, which was something. Thorstein did, but that, I decided, was to be expected.

'I have watched you work. You are a decent smith,' said Imr. 'Are you able to fight, though?'

'I can handle myself.' My words were mostly bravado. I had just been in an I-kill-him-or-he-kills-me situation with Cormac, but I had never fought in a battle, still less slain a man.

He *hmph*ed, but did not scorn me yet. 'And you, vitki – can you wield axe or spear?'

'No,' sniffed Vekel, and my heart sank. But he wasn't done. 'I can weave powerful spells, however, and read the future. I am thinking those qualities would be of use to a man like you. To a warband like yours.'

Imr grinned, reminding me of a cornered wolf baring its teeth. 'Frigg's tits, you're a cocky pair.'

I looked at him, and thought, he knew full well that I was in no position to bargain. I could kill Cormac and thereby avenge my father, but the high king's men would soon be on my trail. To let him go, shove him towards his warriors, scarcely guaranteed mercy either. Sailing away in *Brimdýr* was by far my best option, but Imr had to think it was worthwhile.

He let me swing in the breeze for what seemed an age. Then, a simple, 'Very well.'

I stared at him open-mouthed, like Gunnkel's son, never the same since a bull kicked him in the head.

'Give the princeling here, before I change my mind,' ordered Imr.

I released Cormac, and shoved him in the back. 'I will come for you one day,' I said.

Convinced, I think, that Imr was bent on murder, he did not reply, but his look back at me was of pure vitriol.

Imr didn't even draw a weapon, so confident was he. 'I have a simple offer for you, lord. There will be no retribution against me or any of my crew for what happened here. Do I have your word?'

'Aye.'

'Swear it on the White Christ.'

Cormac obeyed.

Imr's grunt was satisfied. 'Another thing.'

Cormac seemed as enthusiastic as a man presented with a bowl of fresh sick. 'What is that?'

'I want the man who slew Kalman.'

Cormac did not answer at once. Mail Shirt's face darkened. I caught Scar Face glancing at a ruddy-cheeked warrior who had taken a sudden, intense interest in his horse's mane.

'Now,' said Imr, and there was iron in his voice.

Cormac hesitated, then pointed at the ruddy-cheeked man, who looked up, terrified.

'Kill him,' Imr shouted, and six bows twanged.

Feathered chest and back, Kalman's murderer fell from his horse. He made a few gurgling sounds and was still.

'And all your men's mail shirts,' said Imr.

Soon nine lay at Imr's feet. He'd taken four swords as well, and seemed content.

A little of Cormac's courage returned. 'My father will be angry,' he told Imr.

'You have not been ill-treated by me. As for the armour and weapons, they count as the blood price for Kalman. Your father will see that.'

Cormac glowered, but kept his trap closed.

This was my chance, I decided. I almost said the words, 'My sword – I want it back,' but instinct sealed my lips.

It was as if Cormac knew my mind. He half turned, trying to look unobtrusive.

Imr's attention was on him in a flash. 'That's a fine blade you're wearing.'

'A gift from my father.' Cormac's eyes met mine. Butter wouldn't have melted in his mouth. I wanted to punch his face in, because he knew the same thing as I. If Imr took the sword, he would keep it for himself.

'Your father, eh?'

'The High King of Ériu, yes.' The words were emphasised. 'He would be mightily put out to know it had been taken from me by force.'

Imr weighed up his avarice against how far he could push Máel, then he made a dismissive gesture. 'I have no need for such a trinket.'

Cormac's chin dipped, hiding his smirk.

I battened down my anger. The wretch could keep it for now. Taking it back as he died would complete my revenge.

Given permission by Imr to leave, the Irishmen rode off, Cormac throwing evil looks over his shoulder at me.

Heedless, I prayed to Oðin, who had approved my finding of the sword, and asked him for the chance to avenge my father. With the blade returned, I would pay honour to the god with every man it slew.

Imr decided not to wait for the morning tide. Better to leave now, he said, and have to row for a time, than to find Cormac returning with warriors from Cnogba, say. Just because he had sworn on his god didn't mean his father would leave things be. It wasn't beyond the realm of possibility. I hurried with Vekel to Diarmaid's, there to bid farewell to Ashild.

Horrified by my tale, she asked if Cormac would raid, take slaves. I told her that was highly unlikely. Vekel jumped in too. The people of Linn Duachaill had done nothing, he said, still less Ashild or Diarmaid and his family. Thor and Oðin's protection would also help. Her angry response was that she needed no divine help but that of Christ, and that in fact we had no idea if Cormac would come. If I had not taken Niall to Mainistir Bhuithe, she wailed, and if Vekel and I had not gone to Inis Cró, 'none of this would have happened'.

When Vekel said that the Norns weaved as they pleased, she told him to shut his mouth. Shocked, he obeyed. It was rare to see him silenced, but when angry, my sister had a tongue on her.

Ashild rounded on me next, demanding to know if I had anything useful to say.

I observed sourly that Cormac would still have murdered our father, and that I had not been trying to cause trouble, but to avenge him. 'Look where it got you,' she snapped, furiously wiping away tears.

'Nowhere! Thanks to your pride, you are a fugitive, brother. Not only that; everyone dwelling in and around Linn Duachaill has to live in fear. If only you could have slain Cormac when he was far from home!'

Defeated, ashamed, with no grain of comfort to offer, because she was right, I muttered something about *Brimdýr* needing to sail on the tide.

'Go on,' she said. 'Go.'

I made to embrace her, but she pushed me away.

'Look after the dogs,' I said. There was no possibility of taking them on the longship.

A sniff. 'Of course. They will not suffer because of your stupidity.'

Heavy-hearted, I apologised to Diarmaid, who told me what was done was done, and that I should not worry about my sister. 'She is blood-kin to me,' he said, 'or will be soon.' I thanked him, feeling even worse inside. I would miss their wedding, and had nothing to give as a gift now. Promising that I would send something fitting, I shook his hand and after giving Madra and Niall a hug, took my leave.

Before we went to sea, Imr had us swear our allegiance. I was not over-comfortable binding myself to a sea-wolf I barely knew. Watched by the entire crew, solemn-faced, it was clear that the oath was non-negotiable, and I was unprepared to stay in Linn Duachaill, so I said the words and kissed Imr's sword hilt. Vekel did the same, but whispered afterwards that his vows to the spirits took precedence. What he meant was not explained, and I did not ask.

I did my best from the start to memorise men's names, and to see how they fitted into the crew. The first I learned was that of Ulf, my oarmate, an amiable type who almost seemed out of place in a band of warriors. His friend Havard was a tall, sarcastic man whose gangling limbs were clearly the reason he was known as 'Heron'. Bowlegged Kleggi's name meant 'horsefly' – I did not know why – and he loved to sing. Stocky and muscled, Odd Coal-biter had fearsome filed teeth, which made me wonder why he had the nickname of someone who liked to sit by the fire. I didn't ask. The largest warrior in the crew, Thorir, Crimp-beard's real name, stood three hands taller than I. Inordinately fond of his appearance, he was forever combing his hair and beard. Wisely, I didn't comment. I also knew Hrafn Harbour-key, who had, unasked, told me of his ability to creep into a port without being seen and steal a ship. He had a fine opinion of himself, it was clear, but this too, I kept to myself.

The voyage south to Dyflin began well enough. With no sea experience other than fishing close to shore in a sealskin and withy coracle, I expected the fine weather and calm waters to mean a smooth passage. Vekel and I had each been tasked with helping to man an oar each. It wasn't so bad rowing, I decided; I was used to hard labour. The technique of rowing was not that simple, but with Ulf's help I managed it. Vekel, sitting on a chest beside Thorstein, looked as if he'd drunk curdled milk, but he was rowing too.

We did not go far. Perhaps five spear casts from the shore, the oars were shipped, and the mighty yellow-and-black sail unfurled. What had seemed a light breeze at Linn Duachaill was stronger on the open sea, and soon *Brimdýr* was scything through the waves. The timbers thrummed, ropes snapped taut, and the whole ship moved. Moved constantly. Up, down, up, down, canted now to the left a fraction, and now the right.

Clutching the base of the dragon head at the prow, gazing ahead, Vekel cried out with delight, like a small child given his heart's desire. I wanted to join him, but the motion had set my head to spinning. With the stink of tar and sheep's wool adding to my queasiness, I cast about aimlessly, wishing I could magic myself back to solid land.

'Feeling sick?' Ulf asked.

I nodded. The small motion made the nausea even worse.

'Get it up, that's my advice.' He mimed putting two fingers to the back of his throat. 'An empty stomach is better, see?'

His gesture was too much. I rushed to the side and leaned over. Up came the bread Ashild had given me, and more besides. Miserable, I hung there, staring at the blue-green water until the involuntary heaves died away. I wiped the drool away with the arm of my tunic, and turned around. I got a few knowing looks, and a smirk from Thorstein, but to my relief, no one else was paying any attention.

'Does it get better?' I asked Ulf.

He looked up from the tafl game he was playing with Havard. 'Eh?'

'The sickness – does it improve?'

'After a time.'

'Not always,' said Havard. 'Remember Giard? He puked whatever the weather. Shouldn't have gone to sea, really.'

'He did it to get away from his wife,' said Ulf. 'She was a right shrew, always nagging him. "Are the sheep fed?"'

Havard chuckled. '"Have you put a new hinge on that door?"'

'"Why is that roof still leaking?"'

'"We need more firewood."'

It was clearly a well-worn thread that Giard had endured from his oarmates.

'Where is he now?' I enquired.

The banter stopped. 'Valhöll,' said Ulf. This was Oðin's feasting hall, where half the warrior dead gathered.

Despite the nausea, I was able to drolly think that Thorstein might ask how they could be certain he had not gone to the goddess Freyja's massive seat-room, Sessrúmnir. That was where the other warriors who had died went. Where I suspected Thorstein might go.

'I am sorry—' I began.

'Don't be. He's happy there, I am sure,' said Havard, glancing at Ulf.

'Because he's not having his ear bent by his wife!'

They both laughed, in the way men who have spent years in each other's company do. I did too, but awkwardly.

Leaving them to their game, I picked my way towards Vekel, still at the prow. I leaned against the timbers beside him and focused on the horizon. He didn't speak, and I, roiling-stomached still, didn't want to. I longed to see Dyflin, to know that my misery would soon end. Our destination was about a day's sail away, however, so Imr had said. I closed my eyes, as if that would make time pass quicker. Startled to feel a sharp increase in my nausea, I opened them again, and fixed my gaze on the far-off junction of sky and sea. To my wonder, it wasn't long before my stomach settled. I sighed with relief.

'Feeling better?' asked Vekel.

'Aye. Staring at the horizon helps.'

'Better keep doing that then.'

'Finn! Vitki! Get your arses over here. This isn't a pleasure cruise.' It was Imr, and he sounded impatient.

Vekel also seemed aware that our situation aboard *Brimdýr* was by no means certain, because he made no protest either at answering the summons, or gutting the fresh fish that would serve as the evening meal. I was of little help, the strong smell causing uncontrollable retching that left me weak-kneed and bathed in sweat. Vekel told me to go to the side and stare into the distance again. I gladly obeyed.

'Not much use, are you, Scarecrow?' It was the familiar husky voice.

I did not move my head. 'Thorstein, I meant no offence.'

No answer, but no sharp retort either.

'I won't call you a . . .' I groped for the right word, and failed, lamely adding, 'that is to say, I will treat you the same as Vekel, or any of the others.'

No reply, just the soft shush of leather as he walked away.

I took heart. Compared to our previous interactions, this had gone well. I hoped it would continue. I had enemies enough – and would, no doubt, make more – without adding crew members to the list.

CHAPTER NINE

Dyflin, east coast of Ériu

I stared at the wooden palisade running down the southern shore of the river mouth, and behind it, the houses. I had never seen so many. Scores of them, there were, and if the streets leading away from the gates went far, they ran into the hundreds. That meant thousands of people, I decided. Those numbers far outstripped the largest crowds I was used to, at Bealtaine, the festival marking the start of summer. It was a little unnerving.

'First time to Dyflin?' asked Havard.

'Of course,' said Ulf. 'His eyes are as big as plates.'

'It is big,' I said, annoyed that I was so easy to read.

'Dyflin is nothing special,' said Imr with a snort. 'If you want to see an impressive place, go to Miklagard.'

'You have been to the Great City?' I had only ever heard about it third- or fourth-hand. Miklagard had mythlike status. With a hard-to-believe half million population, it sprawled over a massive area. Many buildings were built on a scale that was similarly hard to credit. Its markets were full of exotic spices, silk, and satins. A man could buy a Damascus-made blade, the steel even better quality than Frankish. The finest horses in the world could be bought there, and the most beautiful female slaves. It was also the gateway to the holy city of Jórsalir, where Jew-men and Arabs lived side by side. Men travelled even further afield from Miklagard too, to eastern Serkland and beyond, to the fabled regions were silk was made.

Ulf gave me a dig. 'Can't you tell by his trousers?'

'They're not from Miklagard, fool,' said Imr.

'Serkland, Miklagard, Jórsalaland, they're all the same,' Ulf declared. 'Burning hot in the summer, balls-freezing-cold in the winter—'

'They're not the same, you great ox. You travel through part of Serkland to get to the Great City, which has lands of its own. I've not

80

been to Jórsalaland, but it's even further, on the shores of the Middle Sea.'

Ulf continued without drawing breath: '—full of savages that want to steal everything you've got or kill you, or both.'

'The Khazars aren't as bad as the Pechenegs,' said Imr. 'And know that the Greeks in Miklagard call *us* savages. You get to know the looks, even while they're haggling with you.'

Ulf *hmph*ed. 'I'd knock sense into them.'

'Not with no weapon, you wouldn't,' said Imr. 'Take them off you at the gate, they do, and no more than fifty Norsemen allowed in at a time.'

'I'll wager you and your oarmates all had seaxes tucked away,' said Havard with a wink. 'The small of your back, eh, or high up your thigh, close to your balls?'

'We did, but I tell you, it didn't pay to fight in the Great City. Get caught by the city guard, and they crucify you.'

'Like the Jew-men did to the White Christ?'

'Just the same, if that story's true. It's a stinking death. Three days, it can take a strong man to cross the Bifröst bridge, if he's given food and water.'

'I would sit below that cross,' said Vekel, materialising by my side. 'The seiðr would be strong.'

Havard rubbed his horse-tooth amulet; Ulf looked away. Even Imr seemed to find it distasteful.

I shoved away my own dread. 'A jug of beer says you couldn't stomach the smell.'

'Done,' said Vekel, seizing my hand, 'although I'm not sure when we will next see a crucifixion.'

'No time soon,' said Havard with feeling. Everyone laughed.

'Would you travel to Miklagard again?' I asked Imr.

'Again?' cried Havard. 'I'd rather be tied to a cow's tail and scuttered to death than go there once!'

I ignored him.

'Maybe one day,' said Imr. 'You'd come?'

'In a heartbeat.'

'Better learn to fight then, smith. It's a hard road, that one.'

I nodded. 'Ulf says he will teach me.'

'I'll test you soon, see how you're coming on.'

Pleased but nervous with it – I had not seen Imr fight, but to be leader of these sea-wolves, he was probably skilled indeed – I muttered my thanks.

'Reef the sail! As soon as that's done, I want oars out,' Karli ordered. Karli Konalsson was his full name, which told me he had an Irish father, Conal. It suggested that not all of Imr's crew were from the Seal Islands or Lochlann, the land of fjords and mountains, where my grandfather had been raised.

So eager I wasn't paying enough attention, I nearly slid our oar into the wrong oarhole. In doing so, I blocked Thorstein and Vekel from sliding out theirs. With Thorstein's curses filling my ears, I self-consciously pushed the end through the next hole along.

'Look for the rune the next time,' said Ulf.

I stared. Above the attachment for the sliding oarhole cover, a rune had been carved, an upwards-pointing arrow. I could not read much, but I knew my runes. 'Týr,' I said. 'For the one-handed god. I hadn't seen it before.'

A moment later, Karli's shout had us all run out our oars. Keen not to make another mistake, I followed Ulf's lead. Pull the oar towards my midriff, forcing the other end deep through the water. Push down and back across my thighs, lifting it, dripping, high in the air. Raise my arms and pull again.

'Sing us into port, Kleggi,' said Thorstein

'Aye, do!' 'Make it a good one, Kleggi.' Other men hoomed in agreement.

Kleggi grinned and began to chant.

'Don't say "It's been a good day"—' This as we pulled.

'"Till sundown!"' The response, as the oars rose from the water again, was deafening.

'Don't say "She's a good wife"—'

'"Till she's buried!"' roared the rest of the crew. Even Imr joined in.

Don't say "It's a good sword"—'

'"Till you've tested it!"'

'Don't say "She's a good girl"—'

'"Till she's married off!"'

'Don't say "The ice is safe"—'

'"Till you've crossed it!"'

'Don't say "The beer is good"—'
'"Till you've drunk the last of it!"'

Oars shipped at Karli's command, *Brimdýr* nosed towards the bank. He had guided us past the mouth of the small waterway that joined the larger River Ruirthech close to the sea. A short distance on from that was the famous black pool, *dubh linn* in Irish, which had given the town its name. It was a perfect mooring place for ships, but according to the shouts of a couple of men in a small fishing coracle, it was full.

Karli had had us row against the Ruirthech's current instead, directing us along the southern bank until a space presented itself between a knarr on our larboard side and a trim, smaller longship on the starboard. We got looks from left and right as we glided in: they were noticeably different. Neutral, sidelong or avoidant from the knarr's crew; hard, closed, even hostile from the longship. With no wish for trouble, I kept my eyes averted from both.

Twenty of the crew leaped into the thigh-deep shallows; catching the ropes thrown by Karli and his right-hand man, Olaf Twin-brows, they heaved the ship close in and tied the ropes fast around boulders placed there for that purpose. Eager to get ashore, I clambered past the dragon's head, taken down as we neared land, towards the prow.

'Where d'you think you're going, boy?' Twin-brows' voice was booming.

I turned. 'What?'

'This is Dyflin. It will rain, if not now, then overnight.' He gestured gruffly at the sail. 'That's our roof.'

Apologising, for I did not want to get on Twin-brows', or anyone's wrong side, I came back to help. So did Vekel, meekly enough. Damp from the sea air, made of wool, the massive rectangular sail must have weighed the same as six men.

Or three, Ulf opined, if you were Crimp-beard's size.

The mast down, we stayed out of the way as the mast lock was removed, but stepped in to help with a score of others as the massive piece of timber was lifted free of the keelson and mast fish, then laid flat on the decking, between the warriors' sea chests.

We went back to the sail. Again I got it wrong, fumbling as the others manhandled it across the ship, then unrolling the thing along the top strake. Vekel, more deft than I, showed me how it was to be held in place, passing a strip of leather through the regular seamed holes in the sail's edge and on, through every fourth oarhole. Each strip was fastened with a loop and antler toggle.

'Who taught you how to do that?' I whispered.

'Thorstein.'

I cast a look at him, setting in place vertically, one after another, the lengths of timber that raised the centre of the sail so it became a tent. 'Is he being friendly?'

'I'm not sure Thorstein does "friendly",' said Vekel. 'He's talking to me, though.'

'Put in a good word, eh?'

'Fancying your chances?'

'Ara, you and your filthy mind! No, I just got off on the wrong foot with him. There's no point making an enemy close to home.'

'Don't worry overmuch. Thorstein's bark is worse than his bite.'

'Are you mad? I saw him with Crimp-beard.'

The pair had had a practice bout as we sailed, axe and shield against axe and shield. Blades wrapped in leather covers, mail shirts also on, they had ducked and weaved, each using their weapons' beards to try and rip the other's shield from his grasp, or shoving suddenly, to off-balance and send their opponent arse-first to the deck. Neither had been going at it with full force, it had more been a limbering-up exercise, but watching had rammed home how skilled the pair were, not to mention the depth of my inexperience.

'Done,' Karli said, his stern visage relaxing. 'I'm for a tavern, and as much beer as my belly can take.'

Loud approval met this comment. Imr spoke up at once. Ten men had to remain behind, to stop would-be thieves from climbing on board. Men grumbled, and argued, but not very much, and as a leather drawstring bag was handed around, each pulled out a stone. There were ten white inside, Karli declared; the rest were black.

Imr did not stay to watch. Sliding on thick silver arm rings and a magnificent cloak brooch, he went to seek an audience with King Sigtrygg. Four warriors, Thorstein, Crimp-beard, Hrafn Harbour-key and Odd Coal-biter went with him. These, I whispered to Vekel, had to be his best men.

The ability of Thorstein and Crimp-beard had been evident earlier.

The other two were clearly cut from the same cloth. I decided to walk carefully around all four.

Happily brandishing a black stone, Havard offered the bag. 'Your turn.'

I took it, thinking it would be typical, my first time in Dyflin, to get a white one. To my delight, the stone I chose was a glossy black. It reminded me of the spherical piece of glass used by my mother to smooth fabric.

It was Vekel's turn next. 'Black!' He held up his stone in triumph.

To his disgust, Ulf's was white. His head turned, and my gut screamed, *he's going to demand we trade places.*

'Come on,' I said to Vekel, indicating Ulf with a tiny inclination of my head. He caught my meaning. Ignoring Ulf's calls, I hurried to the prow and threw a leg over the side.

'Finn!'

'I'll bring back some beer, Ulf, never fear!' With a jaunty wave, I dropped onto the mud.

Vekel was right behind me. 'I thought you wanted to stay on the right side of everyone.'

'I'm not staying on board,' I said, ignoring the fact that I was going against my own advice.

'Ulf will make you pay at weapons practice. The others will have noticed too.'

'I'll worry about that tomorrow.' Full of youthful exuberance, I wanted to sample the delights of Dyflin now. True, the mud, discarded rope, a rotting woollen sail and the carcase of a sheep in front of me weren't inspiring. Nor was the huddle of miserable-looking slaves, wrists tied with rope, who were waiting to be loaded onto a nearby vessel. Ignoring the stench of human and animal waste, I decided that the town itself would be a wonder.

Vekel linked his arm with mine. 'We are not getting drunk.'

'Of course not.' I was happy enough to avoid the tavern closest to the river, which by the loud, enthusiastic conversations I had heard, was where the crew were headed.

'Mind your purse,' Thorstein said.'

My hand went to the leather bag attached to my belt. I had no hack-silver, still less any coins, but iron pins, needles, and fish-hooks also served as currency. I felt for the handle of my seax, and was reassured. I had it, and Vekel. No one would try to rob us.

Through the gate we went, past a pair of spear-wielding guards who were busy arguing about who was the prettier, the one's wife or the other's new thrall.

The winding street was paved with timber, something I had never seen before. Rutted over with mud, it was perhaps a dozen paces in width and had houses on either side. Built end-on to the thoroughfare, and set a little way back, they were rectangular houses different to those at Linn Duachaill. Smaller versions stood behind, the sleeping areas for slaves and animals. Low wicker fences separated one property from the next. Many also had pig pens out front. Hens pecked in the dirt; I saw geese too.

An irritated warrior – not one of our crew – shoved past, mouthing something uncomplimentary in Norse.

'Walk,' said Vekel. 'It's best not to look completely like the herring chokers we are.'

We moved on. Despite himself, Vekel stared almost as much as I did.

There was no particular order to the layout, the streets gently twisting this way and that, like multiple branches of a river. There were densities in certain areas of smiths, coopers, and craftsmen working amber, metals, antler, but businesses were also found on their own: millers, clothmakers and tavernkeepers.

We continued our exploration, and in the south-eastern corner of the town, reached the royal great hall. Surrounded by a ditch and palisade, backing onto the Black Pool, Dubhlinn, there was a great open space before it. Warriors in mail shirts lounged about on benches near the entrance, drinking beer and boasting to one another. I was keen to set eyes on Sigtrygg, but after Inis Cró and Dún na Sciath, suspected that his guards would be as stern as Máel's. I led Vekel away, taking a different street to the one we had arrived on.

'Thirsty?'

'As Oðin was after nine days and nights hanging on Yggdrasil,' Vekel replied.

Asking directions to the nearest tavern, we were sent along the street and down a smaller way that led back towards the river.

The alehouse was rundown, its heather thatch mouldy, the door broken-hinged, but the hum of conversation from within was encouraging. I stooped to enter, Vekel one step behind, my eyes adjusting to the dim interior. The building's front half was given over to business, a counter separating the owner's living space from the customers. Rushes covered the floor; benches ran around the sides, under the low angle of the thatch. Most were taken, and quite a few of the occupants were staring at us.

While Vekel went to buy beer – in a town, it had to be good, I told him – I found a space to sit. There was room between a man who appeared to be asleep and a couple of Irishmen in long, belted tunics.

Their gaze was fixed in horrified fascination on Vekel. I was pleased; this increased the chance of not having to talk to them. My father had always warned me to take care who I spoke to at Mainistir Bhuithe. Christ-lovers were just as likely to thieve as anyone else, he would say. Dyflin, I decided, with its visitors from every corner of the world, was far more dangerous. Minding our own business would keep trouble at arm's length.

Vekel came back with two brimming tankards. He was beaming. 'On the house!'

'Why?'

'The place is plagued with mice. I put a curse on the little creatures. '"There shouldn't be a single one left by tomorrow," I told him.'

This was going too far, I thought. 'We'll just be drinking here the once then.'

'Maybe.' Vekel's face was serene, innocent.

The beer was as good as I'd hoped, and the free refills provided by the grateful landlord soon put paid to our intention of staying sober.

We talked in low voices, about Cormac and what he might do. It was comforting to conclude that because Imr and his crew were not from Linn Duachaill, he would leave the place alone. This did not stop me from wondering whether Ashild and Diarmaid were in danger. They were not, Vekel declared. He had dreamed my sister's future, had seen her with a babe in arms, Diarmaid by her side.

A surge of relief. 'And Madra and Niall – did you see them?'

A flutter of long eyelashes. 'They are also well.'

Reassured – vitkis were renowned for their ability to read the future – I settled back on the bench. Noticing a young, black-skinned man emerging from behind the counter, broom in hand, I nudged Vekel. 'A *blámaðr.*' It was truly a day of firsts, I thought.

'*Fear gorm,*' Vekel said in Irish.

The term meant 'blue man'. It made no sense, I decided, given that he was blacker than pitch.

Vekel beckoned.

Surprised, the youth pointed a finger at his chest as if to say, 'Me?'

Vekel nodded.

The youth approached, looking nervous.

I smiled, to show we meant no harm. 'Speak gioc-goc?' I asked in Irish.

'A little.'

'Norse?'

'Yes.' Hesitant, accented.

'You are a thrall?'

'Yes.'

'How long have you been here?'

'Long time.' His face was a mask, protection against the world, I judged.

'What do they call you?' Vekel asked.

'Slave. *Blámaðr.* Fear gorm.'

'No, your real name.' Vekel paused. 'What your mother and father called you.'

Hesitation, then, 'Lalo.'

It sounded strange to my ear; I had never heard the like.

'La-lo,' said Vekel. 'That is god-given. Powerful.' He grinned at the youth, who returned it with a tentative one of his own.

'Get back to work, boy!' It was the proprietor. To Vekel, he said, 'My apologies, vitki. He knows not to annoy the customers.'

'Peace. I wanted to speak to him.'

The proprietor gave Vekel an obsequious head bob, and the youth resumed sweeping up the hazelnut shells and cheese rinds dropped by customers.

'I would not be surprised if we see more of him,' said Vekel.

Assuming that meant Vekel wanted to drink here regularly while we were in Dyflin, I said that the mice plague had better end soon.

Vekel gave me a look.

'Where do blámenn come from?'

'Bláland, a burning region far to the south of the Middle Sea. They say the sun is so hot it burns their skin black. Curls their hair too.'

I shuddered. A hot summer's day in Ériu was more than I could bear. 'I would not like a place like that.'

'I imagine he feels the same about here.' Vekel continued, 'Clouds almost all the year round. Rain just as often, and fog as well. Damp. Cold. Hardly any sun. He must hate it!'

'I suppose.' I glanced at the youth, who studiously kept his gaze on the floor, and wondered if he thought much about his home.

We fell to talking about Imr, and where he might next take *Brimdýr*. We had not been on board long enough to be told, although as Vekel said, he might be discussing that very thing with Sigtrygg. Mumhan was a good possibility, we decided. Sigtrygg was no friend of Brian Bóramha; he would surely not care if the king of Mumhan's territories were raided. Another place to raid, if we were daring, was Vedrarfjord in the southeast. Its ruler Ívarr had deposed Sigtrygg only a year before. It was well known that since his retaking of Dyflin, Sigtrygg was out for revenge. A third possibility, and a rich source of slaves for more than a century, was the coast of Britain.

I mentioned Serkland and Miklagard.

'Listen to the fledgling, and it barely out of the nest,' said Vekel.

A little fuzzy-headed from the beer, I glowered. 'I am no fledgling.'

'Nor are you a seasoned warrior like Imr. There are dangers enough in Dyflin and Ériu without going halfway across the world to find them.'

I didn't like him telling me what to do. 'Scared?' I jibed.

'When have you ever known me back down?'

Vekel wasn't a fighter, but nor was he one to retreat if there was an argument to be had. I glared at him anyway. He returned it with feeling.

I was more likely to fly back to Linn Duachaill than I was ever to travel to Miklagard, I decided with a sigh. 'Let's not fall out.'

Beer slopped as Vekel bumped his tankard off mine. 'To friendship. Our friendship.'

I nodded.

Amity restored, we downed the lot. It was my round next, but as Vekel said, the landlord still thought the sun shone out of his arse.

'Better drink as much as we can, while we can,' he said. I wasn't about to disagree. Off he went.

Nature called. I went outside. Spying a dungheap to the side of the next house along, I emptied my bladder into that. Adjusting my breeks, I wandered back, whistling. All was well with the world.

My happiness was brief.

CHAPTER TEN

'What kind of man dresses like that?' A male voice, speaking in Norse, inside the tavern.

A reply came, too low for me to discern the words, or who had spoken, but my pace quickened anyway.

'A *bod salach*, that's what,' said a second voice, in Irish. 'A dirty prick.'

I ducked inside. Vekel had his back to the bar, with three men around him in a little semicircle.

'I want no trouble,' said Vekel, who hadn't seen me.

'Then you shouldn't have come in here, arse-plunderer,' said the first man, Irish by the cut of him. He poked Vekel in the chest.

'Do that again, and I'll put a spell on you. Your cock will wither and drop off.'

The man checked, but his friend, who was dressed in Norse fashion, laughed. 'We're God-fearing Christians. We have nothing to fear from pagan filth!' He cocked a fist.

I rushed forward. Seizing his shoulder, I whirled him around and drove a mighty punch into his belly, just the way my father had taught. His mouth gaped, eyes widened, and he dropped.

I spun, ready to take on the others. The Irishman was sinking to his knees, both hands clutching his groin; Vekel had kneed him in the balls. But the third, also Irish, was grabbing for a knife.

Dragging Vekel with me, I made for the door.

The knife-wielder charged after, and things might have gone badly – stabbing a man in the back is easy – but the young black slave was just outside. He gave me a firm nod as we emerged. I sensed rather than saw his broom slide across the doorway at ankle height. An instant later, there was a meaty thump as the Irishman landed face first in the mud.

'Move,' I told Vekel, pushing him in what I thought was the direction of the river.

I chose badly. Two hundred paces later, around a bend, the street was blocked by a wagon. Packed high with straw, standing beside a longhouse with a half-finished, half-underlaying-sods-exposed roof, and men moving to and fro between, it was going nowhere anytime soon. The blockage meant there were no passers-by, just the workmen, and a snot-nosed child sitting in a doorway. As we screeched to a halt, he stared at Vekel with unabashed fascination.

Shouts. Cries. The sounds of pursuit.

'*Skítkarls*,' I said, eyeing two men running in our direction. I say run – the one Vekel had kneed was thirty paces behind his friend, and he was struggling. In front was the Irishman who'd gone for his knife. It was out too, gripped in a way that suggested he was no stranger to a fight.

'The third one is still winded,' I said confidently. 'At least we won't be outnumbered.'

'Is that so?'

My attention followed Vekel's, past the limper, and I groaned. Walking slowly around the bend was the Irishman I had punched.

'We should run,' I said, searching for an alleyway, even a gap between houses. Where they would lead, I had no idea, but anywhere was better than a fight with blades, two against three.

'Go if you want.'

I couldn't believe it. Vekel was pacing towards our pursuers, his iron staff gripped in both fists, like a fighting cudgel. 'What are you doing?' I cried.

'Choosing my own thread.'

'Vekel!'

'I am tired of being called a ragr-man, or an ergi. Tired.' There was real venom in Vekel's voice. 'Those men need a lesson in manners, and I am going to teach it to them.'

Not for the first time, I decided that part of the reason my friend had become a vitki was because such men – feared, respected and despised – were generally left alone. Womanish men who were not vitkis had a much harder time of it.

Vekel kept walking.

Two stark choices faced me. Flee, and leave my oldest friend to be butchered, or stay and end up with my guts decorating the street. The former was too awful to consider, the latter easy to imagine.

Swearing under my breath, I hurried to catch up. 'This is a bad idea.'

'Not if we get to the first one before his comrades do.'

He was right. Pulling out my seax, I broke into a lope.

Vekel kept pace.

The first man saw us coming for him like two dogs chasing down a hare, and he twisted around, looking for his friend. He was still thirty paces off. Courage failing, the man shuffled backward, keeping his seax ready.

This was not good. Two against two could go either way, and the winded one would soon join the fray. He and Knee-in-the-balls might be a little incapacitated, but outnumbered, Vekel and I risked injury or death.

I broke into a sprint.

The Irishman, whose face was dominated by an oft-broken, flattened nose, increased the speed of his backward shuffle.

I yelled in triumph and kept after him. We would catch up before his comrades got there.

Something moved under my left foot, shifted, and the next thing, I was falling. I went down hard, left side towards the ground, but somehow kept hold of my seax. Struggling to get up, I heard the Irishman laugh. I heard him coming too, telling me he would open my throat. And then Vekel was there, screaming like a *bean sidhe*, and swinging his staff like a battle-frenzied berserkr.

I rolled over and got up. The Irishman had decided not to fight Vekel, instead retreating to join Knee-in-the-balls. The winded one had found a reserve of energy; he was almost there too.

'Ideas?' I asked.

'You go for Broken-nose. I'll take the one I kneed in the balls.'

'And the third one?'

'Whoever's finished first can have him.'

A cackle escaped me. This was mad, Loki mad, and it was happening. We closed.

'I'm going to cut off your bod salach and feed it to you,' wheezed the Irishman.

Broken-nose said nothing to me, just came in with his knife, a ripping movement that would have unseamed my belly had I not skipped away. I cut wildly at his face, but I wasn't nearly close enough, and he sneered. Somewhere close by, I was aware of Vekel chanting.

Again Broken-nose attacked, slashing, then converting the swing to a quick stab. Somehow I avoided it, already wishing I had the experience of men like Imr, Thorstein or Crimp-beard. I was barely able to keep him at arm's length. The one-sided fight would soon be over. I took a step back, as if that would help.

An anticipatory smile played over Broken-nose's lips. 'Ready to die, herring choker?' he asked.

I readied my blade for another futile attempt. My mind was full of dark images. Loki splitting his sides with laughter. Oðin uncaring, probably not even watching this pathetic contest. The Norns arguing over which one would cut my thread. I hoped my end would be quick at least, no lingering for days while my wound putrefied.

Swipe. Broken-nose advanced. I retreated, thrusting and missing. Slash.

Behind my opponent, the most welcome of apparitions, Vekel, staff raised high. Down it came, full force, taking Broken-nose across the back of the head. The iron staff wasn't heavy enough to break his brainpan, but his eyes rolled upwards, and he fell.

I looked for Knee-in-the-balls. He was lying in the dried mud, moaning softly and clutching his groin again. Respect for Vekel surging, I searched for the Norseman whom I had punched. To my amazement, he was also down, the shards of a broken jug scattered around him. I had an impression of a lithe, black-skinned shape vanishing into a side alley.

Amazed, I glanced at Vekel. 'Was that the *blámaðr*?'

'Unless he has a twin brother in Dyflin, yes.'

'Why would he help us?'

'Because we didn't treat him like an animal?'

I had no chance to ponder the matter. Somehow Knee-in-the-balls had got up, and knife at the ready, was throwing himself at an unsuspecting Vekel. I violently shoved my friend sideways, and without thinking, stabbed Knee-in-the-balls as he came hammering forward. My seax went into him as easily as a hen for the pot. He folded up, *oof*ing, and collided with me. I braced, holding onto my seax, then shoved it in even further. He screamed, all his strength gone, and collapsed. My seax came free with a distinctive, soughing sound. I stared at it, dazed; the entire blade was reddened. A similar colour was rapidly spreading around Knee-in-the-balls' hands, clutching his middle. His eyes were closed, and he was moaning.

The world rushed in. Broken-nose was unconscious, and from the look of him, the winded Irishman wasn't getting up any time soon. Our fight had not gone unnoticed, however. The thatchers were watching, horrified. The little child who had been amazed by Vekel was now in its mother's arms, bawling. The shock in her face said it all.

'The best thing to do is leave,' I said, calmly. 'Now.'

Plenty of daylight remained as we reached *Brimdýr*. To my relief, there had been no pursuit. The spectre of what I had done hung over me, though, like a fetch tracking my steps through the winter darkness. The man I had stabbed was for the next world, that was certain. What would come of his death was much less clear.

'Should we say anything?' I whispered to Vekel.

'Of course. If we don't, and a dozen men come looking for vengeance tomorrow, what do you think Imr will do? He'll feed us to the wolves, and he'd be right to.'

'They might not realise we're on *Brimdýr*.'

Archly, 'Have you seen any other vitkis?'

I sighed. He was right. Even if Vekel hid aboard, enough people on the shore had seen him to be able to answer questions.

'Finn, you skítkarl! Come here!' It was Ulf, and he wasn't happy. A skítkarl was literally a shit-man.

I groaned, but quietly. Louder, I said, 'I am sorry.'

'You will be!' Ulf came storming down the deck, the other sentries watching in amusement.

He had been regaling them with all the ways he would punish me, I decided. It was understandable, though, and my own fault. He didn't care that I was neck deep in a dungheap, needing his, Imr's and everyone else's help. And so I did nothing to avoid his swinging, open-handed slap. My vision blurred; I staggered sideways, preparing myself for the next blow.

It did not fall.

Confused, assuming he was waiting for me to look at him before he attacked again, I straightened, blinking away tears of pain.

Ulf was staring at my knife-wielding hand, which was covered in blood. 'You've been fighting.'

'I killed a man.'

Ulf's face was a picture. 'You?'

'He's not dead yet, but will be soon enough. Stabbed him in the guts.' I thought this might impress.

Slap. I reeled. Another blow followed, a punch to the stomach this time. I bent double, spattering sour beer over my shoes, and Ulf's. He hit me again, on the back of the head, and I went down on one knee, into the vomit.

'That for being a stupid-arse nithing! Stand up!'

Through the pain, I wondered why Vekel wasn't helping me. How I had assumed Ulf's amiable manner to mean he wasn't capable of brutal behaviour.

'Up!'

Struggling, I obeyed, and found myself face-to-face with an irate Ulf.

'First you sneak off when I want you to do my sentry duty. Second, you return pissed, with a tale of bloodshed and murder, all over nothing, no doubt. Give me one reason why I shouldn't turf you overboard, or better still, decorate the deck with your brains!'

My gaze went from his to the faces of the nine others. I discerned not a trace of sympathy. 'They started it,' I mumbled.

A cynical laugh. 'Didn't mean you had to finish it! I've had half a hundred brawls. Most end with cuts and bruises, maybe a broken nose, or a couple of ribs. They don't have to finish with men dying, especially when your ship is in a foreign port.'

'We tried to get away,' I protested. 'We ran, but there was a wagon blocking the street—'

'Save your lies,' said Ulf, drawing back his fist.

'It's the truth. Finn wanted to get away even when the street was blocked,' Vekel broke in. 'It was I who turned to fight.'

'You?' Ulf didn't look happy, but he didn't try and punch Vekel.

'Yes.'

'How many were there?'

'Three.'

'The two of you against three?' He could not contain his disbelief.

'I am not the one to question the spirits. "Fight," they said. "Do not run."'

Ulf had no answer to that. He gave me another punch, which sent me to the deck again, then hoiked a gob of phlegm onto the planking beside my head. 'Skítkarl,' he said, and walked away.

When I judged it safe to move, I rolled onto my front, and wincing, got onto all fours. A moment later, I managed to stand, but not straight.

'That went well,' said Vekel.

Wiping drool from my lips, I gave him a sour look. 'How, exactly?'

'You're not dead. He didn't heave you over the side. And he didn't lay a finger on me.'

I sucked on the marrow of his words, and decided the taste wasn't as bad as my aches and pains said it was. Even as I took a crumb of comfort from that, a niggling doubt tickled the back of my mind.

Ulf's restraint didn't mean Imr would take my side.

Imr didn't come back that evening. As Havard said — *he* was still talking to me — Imr was probably drinking Sigtrygg under the table. Or trying to, Twin-brows added, to much amusement. I wondered if that meant Imr couldn't hold his beer, or that Sigtrygg was a champion drinker, but didn't dare ask. For the foreseeable future, my voice was best left unheard. Sore all over, head aching, I hunched up in the prow, cloak protecting me from the worst of the drizzle, and kept watch. This had been Ulf's command, which I had obeyed with alacrity. Vekel hadn't been told to join me, but did so anyway. I asked if he knew what Imr would do; he said not, and his tone suggested it would be wise to drop the subject.

I wanted to tell him that we should have run, not fought, but there was no point doing that either. His glib answer would have been that seiðr was behind it. Cursed seiðr, I thought, and was consumed with instant panic in case the very idea brought harm upon me. One breath followed another, however, and a soul-possessing fetch did not appear. The men walking the shore paid *Brimdýr* no attention either.

I tried not to brood further, but failed. Vekel stood out from a crowd. Upon his return to Linn Duachaill as a vitki, Gunnkel had humorously observed that a blind man would have seen him, even at night-time. He wasn't far wrong, I thought, looking at my friend. A few questions on the riverbank would reveal Vekel was aboard the

Brimdýr, and where he was, I was. Unless the companions of the man I had stabbed made no effort at all, it was hard to see how they would not find us, and soon.

I thought next about running. Leave the ship, leave Dyflin, and I would be safe. Safe from revenge, it was true, but where would I go? Linn Duachaill was the obvious choice, even though I had only just left it, but there I risked being caught by Cormac, and possibly placing Ashild at risk also. A third choice, joining the crew of another ship, stood little chance of success because of my lack of seafaring skills and battle experience.

Time passed, and I could think of nothing other than staying put and hoping for the best. It was tiring, chewing over my problems, and darkness had long since fallen. The riverbank was quiet, the town too. The drizzle had stopped, and I was warm in my cloak. There was an inevitability to my eyelids drooping. I pinched myself repeatedly, and when that didn't work, stood up. The day had gone badly enough. To fall asleep would put me beyond redemption, not just with Ulf, but with the other sentries as well. Eager not to burn every bridge, I paced to and fro, watching the shore, and thinking of happy times in my childhood.

As the sun peeked over the eastern horizon, Ulf came creeping along the deck. I was still awake, greeting him with a nod. He couldn't quite hide his disappointment; clearly, he had expected to find me snoring. When he next told me to get some rest, I decided he didn't think I was a complete nithing. I grinned and went to take his place, halfway along the deck, beside Havard. His snores were not enough to stop me from slipping away into welcome unconsciousness.

Pain in my ribs. I cried out. Another kick, and I was rudely awake. I stirred, finding Imr standing over me, his right leg already drawn back.

I raised a hand in protest. 'Stop!'

'Why?' He kicked me again. 'You're a horse turd, with the wits of a hen.'

I struggled into a sitting position. 'Ulf told you about my fight.'

'He merely confirmed it was you.'

'I don't understand.' I got to my feet, grateful not to be kicked again, grateful that Vekel was by Imr's side.

98

A clatter to the side of the face. 'I heard the sorry tale just now, in Sigtrygg's hall. Not what I wanted or needed when I've a bad head on me.'

'Sigtrygg's hall?' I hated how stupid I sounded.

'The Norseman you fought, Biarn, is known to Sigtrygg. The man you killed was his friend.'

The death was sooner than I had expected. 'Killed?'

'He died overnight. That's why Biarn came raging to Sigtrygg. His story is that you and the vitki picked a fight with him and his friends in some dingy tavern, and when they chased you out, there was a set-to in the street. You stabbed his friend, then ran off.'

'Lies,' I snarled.

'So you didn't knife his friend?' Imr's fists closed.

'I did, but he's lying about how it happened.'

'Spit it out then.'

Hard faces ringed me. I could put names to many now. Thorstein. Crimp-beard. Hrafn. Odd Coal-biter. Twin-brows. Karli. Havard. Ulf's, as angry as he had been the previous evening. None were remotely friendly.

Struggling to maintain my composure, I said, 'I went for a piss outside the tavern. When I came back, three of them were picking on Vekel.'

'Three?' demanded Imr.

'The Norseman and two Irishmen. There was a bit of a scuffle, just fists, and we ran.' I continued, laying it out exactly as I remembered, until the point where our three opponents were down.

'You say the *blámaðr* helped you?' I had mentioned speaking to him in the tavern. Imr cocked his head. 'Strange, no?'

'We treated him decently,' said Vekel.

'Why? He's a thrall, like any other thrall.'

'He's a person too,' said Vekel. 'Not that you'd ever think such a thing.'

Imr stared, not quite believing his ears, then he snorted in amusement. 'It explains how two wet-behind-the-ears herring chokers like you beat three men. The *blámaðr* struck one from behind, and somehow the vitki managed two on his own.'

I coloured, but there was no denying it. 'Aye.'

'So how did one end up with a blade in the belly?'

99

'It was over, or so we thought. Then one of the Irishmen picked himself up and ran at Vekel. He was going to stab him in the back.'

Growls. Angry hooms. Glances at Vekel, who nodded to confirm my words.

'What did you do?' demanded Imr.

'I pushed Vekel out of the way, and stuck the Irishman. It was self-defence. He was coming in hard with a dagger. I did not mean to kill him, though.' I made no mention of ramming home the seax, to make sure.

Imr's slate-grey eyes held mine, vicelike. At last, he spoke. 'I believe you.'

I blew out my cheeks, letting out a long breath, but my nerves were yet stretched like a thread tested by the loom weight. One test had been passed, but another had replaced it. I knew this as if Huginn and Muninn were perched on Imr's shoulder, delivering a message from Oðin.

'What did Sigtrygg say about it?' Vekel asked.

'He wasn't best pleased,' Imr replied, 'but said that these things happen, and that finding the man responsible would be like trying to pick out a single sheep from a flock.'

Everyone stared at Vekel, with his jewellery and eye make-up, and woman's dress.

'Biarn laughed,' Imr continued, 'and said that one had been a vitki, and he had already tracked him down, to a ship called *Brimdýr.*'

I sighed. 'And Sigtrygg looked at you.'

'He did. Wasn't too happy either.'

I was on the wrong side of two kings now, Máel and Sigtrygg, I thought blackly. 'What is he going to do?'

A chuckle. 'Sigtrygg? Nothing.'

This was too easy. My gaze went from Imr to Vekel, who shrugged, to Thorstein, who leered, and back to Imr. 'I don't understand.'

'Biarn demanded a holmgang, and the king agreed.'

'Until first blood?' I asked, in hope rather than expectation.

'To the death. Biarn wants vengeance for his friend.'

I knew well why Imr was pleased. I stood no chance whatsoever in the single combat. My death would satisfy Biarn, who afterwards would not seek retribution from Vekel, a vitki. It would also smooth out the friction between Imr and Sigtrygg, bring things back to what

100

they had been. I cast a sideways look at Vekel, whose bland expression seemed to say that he had known this would happen.

'Where? When?' I enquired.

'Outside Sigtrygg's great hall, at midday.'

'It's normally three days or more after the challenge,' I protested, as if delaying would make any difference.

'Sigtrygg wants it done and dusted.'

A king's word was law in his own town, I thought.

Far above, I could have sworn I heard the Norns cackling with glee.

CHAPTER ELEVEN

'Stand up straight. Hold your shield so,' Ulf ordered.
I copied him, aware that I had too much to learn, and too little time.

We were standing on the shore, not far from *Brimdýr*. I had on Havard's simple leather helmet, and was armed with my limewood shield and one of Ulf's axes. There was no question of borrowing a mail shirt – armour was not allowed in a holmgang.

Ulf had set aside his anger over the way I had run off into Dyflin, and volunteered to teach me what he could before the contest. 'It won't be enough of course,' he'd said to Imr, 'but maybe I can teach the skítkarl a few tricks.'

Imr, irritable and hungover, waved a hand in acknowledgement and went to lie down under the sail. 'Do not wake me until it is time,' he'd growled.

He wasn't watching, therefore, but Vekel, Thorstein, Havard and a few others were. Mostly, I suspected, they had come to laugh at me, and to discuss how bad my odds would be with the bet-takers.

'Pay attention, boy! Unless you want to die quickly, without a fight.'
I fixed my attention on Ulf again. 'Sorry.'
'Did he look like a swordsman or an axeman?'
'I don't know.'
'He was in a hole of a tavern, so I'm going to say he prefers an axe.'
'I should use a sword first then.' We were allowed more than one weapon each, as well as three shields, and as the challenged, the choice was mine. It felt like clutching at straws. I had no idea if Biarn was also a swordsman.
'We'll see. Axes for now.'
I sucked in a ragged breath, and advanced to meet Ulf.

*

Imr waited until it was almost midday before leaving *Brimdýr*. 'Nothing worse than waiting for a fight to start,' he muttered, and I believed him. Bar the unfortunates who had been selected to guard the ship, the entire crew came too. Most obviously expected me to die, and from their conversations would gamble on that eventuality, if the odds were good enough. I found it oddly comforting that a few were prepared to risk silver on me. I did not know if I could win, but I was certain of one thing.

I would not die without a fight.

A big body of men we were; the streets cleared as if by seiðr. Imr led the way, the same four warriors around him as the day before. I was next, with Vekel, who had painted his face an unsettling, deathly white. Ulf walked on one side of us, Havard on the other. I chose to think of them as an honour guard, rather than an accompaniment to the grave, although the loud conversation behind me between Kleggi and Coal-biter about how quickly I would die gave the lie to that.

Vekel had wanted me to eat something, strength for the fight. Unwilling to trust my stomach or my guts, I refused. Ulf tried to press some mead on me, saying it settled the nerves, but I said no to that as well. Better to be bowel-loosened with a clear head, I decided, than to be mead-brave and over confident.

The open ground in front of Sigtrygg's great hall was jammed. As Imr's guards pushed their way through, allowing the rest of us to follow, he laughed at my circle-mouth. 'It's not every day there's a holmgang, boy.'

Ulf saw my confusion. 'Sigtrygg doesn't often allow them, else they'd be happening after every drunken brawl.'

'Why did he agree to this one?'

Imr wolf-smiled. 'Biarn is a crewman on another longship. His captain and I got to talking yesterday, before news came of your squabble. We hatched a plan to do something together. Sigtrygg liked it.'

Suddenly, I saw it all. The bad blood between me and Biarn was a potential bone of contention between Imr's crew and that of the other longship, and that could jeopardise whatever scheme Imr and his new ally had contrived. My death in the holmgang would see Biarn's honour restored; with the matter settled, Imr's business could continue, which would also please Sigtrygg.

It was a sour realisation, because Imr had had a hand in it too. 'You think I'm going to lose.'

Imr shrugged in a 'yes, I do' way.

I stuck out my chin. 'And if I win, what will the other captain do?'

He looked a little disconcerted, then declared bluffly, 'If he knows what's good for him, he will grin and bear it.'

I imagined wiping the smirk off Biarn's leader's face, and shocking Imr into the bargain. My spirits rallied, but then we reached the clear area right in front of the great hall, and the immensity of my task sank home.

Hundreds of townsfolk were there, waiting. Imr worked his way free of the press, beckoning. I obeyed, noting the lines in the dirt. They marked out a square patch, ten paces to a side: the space for the holmgang. Three larger squares surrounded it, each also demarcated by bootheel-dragged lines. Hazel staves marked the four corners of the outer square.

'You know the rules?' Vekel asked. 'You can cross the first two lines without penalty. Put a foot beyond the outermost line, however, and you lose.'

I nodded. Given that our fight was to the death, the price of stepping outside the boundary would be execution by the other party.

Imr steered us to the nearest corner. He had spied Biarn in the one diagonally opposite. Ulf came after, setting down the two shields he was loaning me, along with his sword, a pair of his axes, one bearded, the other broad. I picked up the sword, wondering what it would feel like to slide it into a man. According to Ulf, Biarn was probably an axeman first and foremost, so I was going to take the risk, and choose swords.

Vekel and the rest had now spilled out, filling the space all around my corner. His dark eyes were on me. 'Fight well. Fight bravely. The gods are watching.'

Empty words, I thought, wondering if he'd seen the future, if there was any way I could win. My new comrades clearly didn't think so; Kleggi had given me a pitying look, and I'd heard Crimp-beard saying he hoped it was over quickly, so they could go and find drink. It wasn't just their dismissive attitudes that made the resignation swell in my chest. Sparring against my father, training for a short while with Ulf were worlds apart from a holmgang against an experienced warrior. In all likelihood, I was going to lose. I was going to die. I reached under my tunic, and caressing the raven amulet, found some determination. I would not go into the endless night easily, I decided. Biarn would know he'd been in a fight.

A fat-bellied, middle-aged Norseman swaggered into the square's centre as if he ruled Dyflin, not Sigtrygg. His tunic and breeks were of good quality, but scars marked his face and hands. I decided that this once-was-a-warrior was the king's steward or some such. In pompous tones, he announced that the holmgang between Biarn Skafhogg and Finn Thorgilsson would take place at once. It was a contest to the death, he said, with the loser's property going to the victor. Loud cheers erupted.

Good luck to Biarn, I thought with black humour. All I had were a spear, a shield, my seax, some clothes and a bit of ironmongery.

Once-was-a-warrior asked what weapon I would use. I told him sword first, loud as I could, and Biarn sneered. I hoped that meant he wasn't pleased.

'Step forward,' boomed Once-was-a-warrior.

Vekel squeezed my shoulder. 'May the Norns be with you,' said Ulf. 'Loki guide your blade,' said Thorstein, which was a surprise. That was it. I walked away, noticing Crimp-beard haggling odds with someone. Evens was not fair, he grumbled. Biarn wasn't that good. 'Give me two to one at least!'

The odds being mentioned for me were far worse. I heard twenty-five to one, thirty to one, even forty to one. A devil took hold.

'Vekel!' I shouted.

'Yes?'

'Put a piece of hacksilver on me, best odds you can get.'

'I will!'

Biarn heard; he positively strutted from his corner. 'Wasting your friend's money, eh?'

'A vitki knows which bets are good, and which are not.' He sneered, and I decided words might be a powerful tool.

'Following tradition, each man only has a sword and shield,' Once-was-a-warrior declared.

We both raised our shields high, and then after a nod from Once-was-a-warrior, drew our blades. How I wished mine was the sword I'd found on the beach.

'Remember the rules. If either of you steps over the threshold marked by the hazel staves, your life will be forfeit.' Done, Once-was-a-warrior moved out of the way.

Biarn and I stared at each other.

'Biarn-i!' bellowed a voice. 'Biarn-i!'

The majority of the crowd instantly took up the chant. No one called my name.

Biarn smiled.

'Was your friend moaning as he died?' I asked, shouting to make sure he heard. 'A barrel of beer says he was.'

Raising his sword, Biarn charged.

I retreated, shield held in front of my body, sliding my feet back, one-two, one-two. Time to find the chink again, I thought. 'Did you love him?'

'Like a brother!' Biarn was spitting with rage.

'You're lying. It was rich to call the vitki a bod salach, when in fact your friend was.'

'Coward!' He swung his sword down hard, aiming for my shield, but I danced out of the way.

'You're no bod salach.'

He checked, looking confused.

'No, it's a pillow-biter you are,' I yelled.

He charged again, and cut sideways, catching the iron rim of my shield with his blade. My arm jarred, but the shield did not break.

'Pillow-biter,' I taunted.

'Nothing wrong with that,' cried Vekel.

A few spectators laughed; Thorstein was one.

'Biarn-i!' went the shouts. 'Biarn-i!'

'Your bed will be cold from now on, with your friend gone,' I said.

Biarn's eyes bulged. He came at me like a madman, hacking and thrusting with wild abandon. I retreated, desperately blocking his blows and managing an occasional, weak counterthrust.

'You've crossed one line!' Ulf's deep voice carried through the wall of noise.

Another two steps, and I would be outside the final square. I threw myself sideways, back into the central space. Biarn's sword licked out, and the tip connected with my left calf. It was a glancing blow, or at least that was what I hoped. I ignored the throbbing pain and the warm sensation running down my leg, and shuffled back as fast as I could.

'Maybe it's time to find yourself a bald girl,' I said. This was a derogatory term for a monk, tonsured and robe-wearing.

'Think you're clever, eh?' Biarn stabbed at the bottom of my shield, Ulf's move.

Luckily, I anticipated it. I could not stop my shield-top being driven forward. Instead I ducked down low, almost onto my haunches. Rather than skewer me through the upper chest, his sword whistled over my head, so close I fancy it parted the hair. I drove my blade at him, blind. It didn't hit home, but I sensed him back away. I came up fast, driving forward with my shield. The boss smacked off his one, and as he was forced back, I headbutted him. The edge of my boiled leather helmet split his nose like an overripe plum.

'How do you like that, pillow-biter?' I asked in jubilation.

Blood was pouring from Biarn's nostrils, running down into his beard. If he had been half-crazed with anger, he was totally consumed by it now. He attacked like a boar cornered by the hounds, wild, savage, uncaring of injury. He wasn't aiming straight, but that didn't matter because the first blow cracked my shield. The second split it clean in two. Only the boss, curved around my left hand, prevented me from losing several fingers to his blade.

My roar for a replacement could have been heard on the far side of Bifröst bridge. Once-was-a-warrior came skipping between us with his staff raised, and ordered us to halt.

I hurled the broken shield away and went slowly back to my corner. The breath sawed in my throat, and the pain in my calf was bad. I glanced down. The lower left leg of my breeks was red-soaked. It didn't matter, I thought. Biarn would kill me before the blood loss did.

Ulf proffered a new shield, this one with a black raven painted on a white background. 'Should have given you this first, what with Storm-crow being your name.' He sounded apologetic.

I looked for Vekel, who gave me a wink.

It was infuriating. I was about to die.

'Ready?' called Once-was-a-warrior.

'I am.' I turned, horribly aware that I had succeeded in angering Biarn, but not enough to make him lose reason altogether. I flailed for an idea, anything that could help me not just to win, but to survive more than the next few moments.

I came up with nothing.

'Begin!' Once-was-a-warrior removed himself to the edge of the square.

Biarn ran forward, eager to renew his attack.

I felt black despair.

Eight paces separated us.

Six.

I decided to try Ulf's strike the bottom of the shield move.

Then, to my amazement, Biarn skidded – one of his boots must have caught on something in the dirt – and like that, his legs flew up in the air and he landed on the flat of his back.

I seized my chance, stamping on his outstretched arms. His sword and shield fell to the dirt. Ignoring the pain from my injured calf, I kicked away the blade and as the cheering from my corner – Vekel's louder than anyone else – rose to the grey skies, I lobbed my own out of the square.

The cheers stopped.

'What are you doing, skítkarl?' It was Ulf's voice, incredulous.

I dropped onto Biarn's chest, straddling him, and my fists already swinging. I wasn't his equal with a weapon, but by the All-Father I was as strong, probably stronger. I hit his broken nose once, twice, and blood sprayed. I felt his cheekbone crack with the third punch; it made him scream. His hands flailed at me, but I leaned back out of the way and punched him in the jaw, and again in the nose. He roared.

It was so satisfying, I hit him a few times more, reducing his nose to mushy pulp. Frantic, he caught the skin below one of my eyes with his nails and ripped. Sweet agony blossomed down my face; I cursed him for a nithing, and reaching back and around, found his groin and grabbed. As luck would have it, my hand closed around his ball-sack. I squeezed as if my life depended on it, squeezed and twisted and wrenched.

He wailed like a baby then. Roared. Screamed. Cried. His heels drummed the dirt, his hands waved in the air. He begged me to stop. Instead my grip tightened. Harder and harder I squeezed, imagining I was getting every last drop of juice from a ripe plum.

Dimly, through the noise of blood pounding in my ears, I became aware of a harsh, repetitive sound. I stared down at Biarn. His head was turned sideways, and he was vomiting.

I did not release my hold on his ballsack even a little.

A moment later, he lapsed into unconsciousness.

I waited, to make sure it wasn't a trick.

Silence had fallen, but I could have been alone again, on the beach at Linn Duachaill, with a skull-cloven corpse, a sword and a raven. I relaxed my grip, brought a hand around to the handle of my seax, and drew it. Calm as a mother rocking her babe, I cut his throat from one side to the other. I took the blade deep, sawing down through flesh, tendon and windpipe until I hit bone. Blood poured, flooded out of him; the Dyflin dirt sucked down every drop. Biarn's arms moved a little; his lips twitched, but no sound came, just more blood.

I got up, becoming aware of the spectators again. My gaze moved, taking in the stunned expressions, the open mouths, the shock. The fear, in some men.

'Storm-crow!' It was Vekel. 'Storm-crow!'

The *Brimdýr*'s crew took the cry up with gusto.

Crowds are fickle. 'Storm-crow!' came a shout from near Biarn's corner.

In the blink of an eye, most people were chanting my name.

Crimson-edged seax raised high, I let the acclaim wash over me. There could be no clearer sign of an intervention by Oðin. I was sure of it. And in return, I offered him Biarn's life. Take him to Valhöll, great Oðin, I said in my mind, if you deem him worthy. I will sit beside him when my time comes.

CHAPTER TWELVE

K ing Sigtrygg soon heard about my victory, and the manner of it. I was summoned to his presence. 'He wants to see you *now.*' Once-was-a-warrior's tone suggested immediate obedience would be wise.

'He can wait,' said Vekel waspishly. 'My friend is busy bleeding to death, in case you hadn't noticed.'

Once-was-a-warrior huffed and puffed, but when Vekel pointed his iron staff at him, he quietened.

I was content to lie down and let Vekel examine my left calf. I heard the shears cut away my breeks. Fresh agony burst upwards from the wound as he began to probe. I winced and bit the inside of my cheek, but I let out not a sound. There were people watching.

Vekel had come prepared. Out of his bag came a small roll of linen. Expertly wrapping it tight – 'but not too tight', he explained – around my leg from knee to ankle, he tied it off. 'That will do for now.' He sniffed and gave Once-was-a-warrior one of his looks. 'We don't want the king to get impatient.'

I let Vekel help me up, and found myself face-to-face with Imr. To my delight, there was respect in his eyes.

'That was well done, Stormcrow,' he said.

I gave him a half-smile.

'The boy deserves more credit,' interjected Ulf. 'He has no skill with weapons, but no one can deny he's a fighter.'

'Grabbing a man's ballsack – I didn't see that coming,' said Crimp-beard, shaking his head. 'I lost a lot of silver.'

I laughed. 'You should trust a crewmate better!'

'No arguing with that,' he admitted. 'I'll know in future – especially if you've worked on your weapon skills, and I will help you with that.'

'My thanks.' That was a big step forward, I thought. Remembering, I caught Vekel's arm. 'Did you place the wager?'

'Ara, course I did. But until you mentioned it, I had forgotten!' His head twisted, searching the crowd. 'We'd best be quick. The bet-taker will be making himself scarce.'

Ignoring Once-was-a-warrior's complaints, and Imr's advice that it was not good policy to make a king wait, Vekel and I began looking. The man was not where he had been, and I wasn't much good thanks to my limp, and the fact that I only had Vekel's description to go on. Short, bearded, brown tunic, breeks, a belt with a purse and a seax described one man in every two.

It was Ulf who spied the bet-taker making for a street that led away from the great hall. Not only that, he and Havard scruffed the blackguard and brought him back to us.

'Do you have winnings to collect as well?' I asked Ulf.

A sheepish look. 'If I'd bet, I would have put my silver on Biarn.'

My gaze switched to Havard.

'So would I.'

'More fools the pair of you.'

They had the grace to laugh, and I decided they might accept me after all.

I rounded on the bet-taker, who fawned and smiled an oily smile, and said he had been going to fetch the vitki's silver.

'So you haven't got it here?' Ignoring the man's protests, Vekel emptied his purse into my hands. Perhaps a dozen pieces of hacksilver fell out. His iron staff whipped up, coming to rest under the bet-taker's chin. 'Well?'

'I have it! I have it, in my house! Do not put a spell on me!' The words poured out in a terrified babble.

'I'll go with him, fetch the silver,' Ulf offered. 'You had best present yourself to King Sigtrygg, oarmate.'

I grinned. The last word meant more than my winnings.

His back stiff with annoyance, Once-was-a-warrior led me, Vekel and Imr towards Sigtrygg's great hall. It was a far grander building than Dún na Sciath, which was ironic, considering Máel considered himself lord over whoever ruled Dyflin. Long and almost rectangular, its sides swelled out to the middle and back in again to the far end, like a ship. The roof was straw thatch, and atop each gable end perched a magnificent carved dragon's head.

'Be careful what you say to Sigtrygg,' Imr said in my ear.

'Why?'

'He's prickly, and not to be trusted.'

And you *are*? I thought. My fate was bound to Imr's now, however, and those of his crew, so I told him I would be careful.

The door, guarded by mailed warriors, was pulled open, leading into an anteroom. Guiding us through another door, to the left, Once-was-a-warrior turned immediately right, and we entered the great hall proper.

My mouth fell open.

Once-was-a-warrior snickered. 'Impressive, eh?'

Awestruck, I nodded.

The hall was like a longhouse, but grander and far more majestic. Down either side of the central aisle, holding the roof up high overhead, were lines of posts. I say posts, but they were trunks, as thick around as Crimp-beard's middle. Oil lamps mounted head high illuminated intricate painted patterns and shapes. Each post, I saw, bore a tale or myth told in timber.

Dominating the aisle was a long rectangular firepit, as wide across as I was tall. It was summer, so only a small section had a fire, enough to cook on, but it was easy to imagine a vast roaring blaze therein during winter, when the winds howled and rain battered the hall.

Living space ran the building's length to left and right. The left had benches, and the best, for the king and his closest allies, were midway along, near the fire. The right had benches, as well as storage chests, weapon racks, and rolled up blankets and furs.

Dozens of people were within. Household thralls, whose incurious stares did not last long. Warriors, lounging about on the right-hand side benches, honing blades and combing beards, whose bold eyes warned, do not get above yourself here. Womenfolk, slaves or servants, who kept their gaze averted from men they did not know. Children, of whom there were a number. Their fine garments probably meant they were Sigtrygg's offspring.

A woman with similar features, also well-dressed, sat by a loom. Sigtrygg's mother Gormlaith, I decided. Daughter of the last king of Laighin, sister of the current one, and widow of Sigtrygg's father, ruler of Dyflin and Jorvik in England, she was still a fine-looking woman, and had no fear of staring at us. I gave her a bold smile, which she acknowledged with a slight nod.

One of the youngsters, a mop-haired boy of about twelve or thirteen, noticed the red seeping through Vekel's bandage. He was knife sharp. 'Were you in the holmgang?' He paused, then realising, asked, 'You won!'

'I did,' I told him.

'I wasn't allowed to watch, but they say you grabbed his balls!' A face.

'That is true.'

Another face. 'What kind of warrior does that?'

'One with Loki's cunning.' And I would have lost otherwise, I thought.

The royal scion had no reply to that, but he tagged along as Once-was-a-warrior led us towards the king's seat. I felt Gormlaith's eyes on us; it was no surprise that her seat was within earshot of the king.

Sigtrygg was a slight figure with fox-red hair and beard, and eyes that could have come from the same creature. Bright, rapid-moving, they fixed on me when we were still ten paces off. His famous beard was sleekit with oil, but he could equally have been called Refr, Fox, as Silkenbeard, I decided. Clad in an embroidered tunic, he was dripping in jewellery. Arm rings, finger rings, and a huge silver thistle brooch at one shoulder, Irish chieftain style. There were men sitting close, but not too close, advisers or allies, I presumed. I noticed two more than the rest.

The first was a monk, a fleshy-faced individual who deliberately made the sign of the cross as I glanced at him. I remembered my father's scorn of the White Christ, and his dislike of the control priests exerted over their flocks. This power, he told me, was the same reason many kings liked Christianity.

The second figure close to Sigtrygg was a Norseman with a beard woven into two braids, each end enclosed by a little silver ring. He too had his gaze intent on me.

I was the centre of attention, and I did not like it.

'Your pardon, lord, for taking so long.' Once-was-a-warrior spoke a great deal more obsequiously than his outside performance.

'W-w-what is the r-reason for the delay?' demanded Sigtrygg.

Once-was-a-warrior cleared his throat. 'The winner of the holm-gang, lord, he was wounded. His injury had to be treated, lest it grew worse.'

The whole truth – how we had had to chase down the bet-taker – would make him look bad, and his lie suited me and Imr as well. I decided that Once-was-a-warrior was not all hot air and bluster. It remained to be seen if the king would be satisfied with his explanation.

'He's bleeding still, Father!' The boy danced in to Sigtrygg's side. He pointed. 'Look.'

'I s-see.' Sigtrygg ruffled the boy's hair, then gave him a gentle shove. 'Run along, Artalach. There is m-men's t-talk to be had.'

The boy pouted, but obeyed, giving me a broad grin as he passed.

'S-so y-you are Biarn's killer.'

It was strange, I thought, for a king to have a stutter. Normally, infirmities prevented men from ruling. Not so in Sigtrygg's case. Along with wresting back the throne from Ívarr, this proved his capability. I bowed my head. 'Yes, lord.'

'Ball-s-squeezer is your n-name, I am told.'

Snorts of laughter from all sides. Imr was struck by a coughing fit. Vekel cackled like an old crone. 'Ball-squeezer,' he repeated. Scandalised, the priest looked at the rush-covered floor. Sigtrygg's eyes remained on mine. He wasn't smiling. Nor was Twin-braids; his stare was stone-hard.

My cheeks were warm – I didn't like the name, nor the laughter – but I could not make a scene, lest I offended a king. 'I prefer Stormcrow, lord.'

'B-but you did s-squeeze Biarn's balls until he passed out, before you s-slew him?'

'I did, lord.'

'Then Ball-squeezer you shall be called!' The entire sentence came out word perfect.

Amid the hilarity, the feet pounding the floor and the cries of 'Ball-squeezer!', I doubt anyone noticed Twin-braids' scowl but me. He was Biarn's chieftain, I guessed.

'Ball-squeezer is far better than Stormcrow. I wish I'd thought of it,' whispered Vekel, who had crept in behind me.

Had I not been in the presence of a king, and lame with it, I would have boxed his ears. Sigtrygg's sharp-as-a-fox eyes were also still on me;

he was waiting for a response. I bowed, deeper this time. 'Who am I to protest a king-given name, lord? I thank you.'

He liked that. His attention went briefly to Twin-braids and then past me, to the bench-sitting warriors. 'S-see that B-Biarn's possessions are delivered to *Brimdýr*.'

Two men got up at once and made for the door.

'A f-fine mail shirt will soon be y-yours, I s-suspect, and some good weapons too.'

I didn't say what I wanted, that I had won Biarn's things, not him. I would have swapped the lot for the sword Cormac had stolen, but that offer wasn't on the table, so I smiled, and thanked the king again.

'I am t-told' – Sigtrygg glanced past me, to Imr – 'that y-you are half-Norse, a smith from Linn Duachaill, and along with the v-vitki, newly part of *Brimdýr*'s c-crew.'

'Yes, lord.'

'S-so you are Imr's man.'

Sure that this was a test, but not why, I nodded. 'I am, lord, oath-sworn.'

Sigtrygg's fox-eyes went past me, to Imr. 'See that you keep this one on a tighter leash. Holmgangs are best avoided.'

'I understand, lord.'

Sigtrygg twisted to look at Twin-braids. 'The result is not what we expected, but honour has been served. There shall be peace between your crews. I will not have it any other way.'

Twin-braids had a sour face on him, but muttered his agreement.

'The task takes precedence over quarrels,' Sigtrygg said to Imr.

'There will be no trouble from my men,' Imr replied.

Sigtrygg seemed content. His hand moved – he was about to send me away – when a voice cried, 'Ball-squeezer deserves a prize, Father!'

From deep in the shadows on the hall's far side came the mop-haired boy.

Sigtrygg tutted. 'I told you this was m-men's talk, Artalach.'

'You are a mighty ring-giver, Father.' As Sigtrygg smiled, Artalach continued, 'Surely the holmgang's winner shall not leave your hall empty-handed?'

From anyone else, this would have been a grave affront, impugning the king's honour. The priest scowled, but Sigtrygg gave his son an indulgent look. His attention returned to me. 'I-I am a ring-giver, it is true. Y-you shall have a g-gift.'

'Thank you, lord.' From the corner of my eye, I sensed Artalach's delight. He was a good lad, I thought, even if his father was as crooked as a dog's hindleg.

Sigtrygg worked a ring off a forefinger and threw. Winking in the lamplight, it spun through the air.

I caught it. An incomplete circle made from twisted rods of silver, it was simple but beautiful. 'I am grateful, lord,' I said, and bowed again.

Sigtrygg waved a hand. I was dismissed. 'I-Imr,' he said. 'Asgeir t-too.'

Asgeir was Twin-braid's name, I decided, as he walked with Sig-trygg and Imr towards the back of the hall. The priest looked none too pleased to be left behind, but said nothing. Gormlaith did not speak either, but she was watching.

Vekel dug me in the back. 'Let's not outstay our welcome.'

Asgeir *was* Twin-braid's name, as it turned out. He was also known as 'Norseman-shaker'. If the legend was to be believed, Thorstein told us in the tavern afterwards, he had once killed an entire ship's crew, Norsemen from Kaupang. As I said to Vekel behind my hand, he had either had help, or he'd somehow scuttled the vessel.

'Careful where you say that,' Thorstein advised, indicating the rest of the room with an inclination of his head.

Startled twice over, for I thought I had spoken quietly, and this was the second time Thorstein had been friendly, I nodded my thanks. *Brimdýr*'s crew took up a lot of the benches, but there were other customers too.

Afternoon had passed into evening and we were steadily and determinedly drinking our way through my substantial winnings. True to his word, Ulf had returned from the bet-taker's with a bulging-at-the-seams purse. Having escaped certain death, I was in an expansive mood; it seemed right that I should lead the way into the nearest hostelry, and there pay for everyone to get rat-arsed drunk. Most of the crew seemed pleased that I had won, even if they had not expected it, but when the free ale began to flow, any reserve melted away. I was slapped on the back, hugged, toasted, soaked in beer, and told I was one of them. It felt good, I have to say.

Ulf, slurring his words after downing no less than four tankards in succession, said I was a fast learner. I would be ready for a shield-wall in no time. Havard proclaimed he'd known from the start that I was a good one. Crimp-beard insisted on an arm-wrestle, and after slamming my hand to the tabletop with disgusting ease, announced to general hilarity that if I was Ball-squeezer, he was Sack-crusher.

The easing of Thorstein's aggression was another pleasant development. I wondered if he had noticed how close I was to Vekel, and deduced that if I was friends with a vitki, I would hold no animosity towards a woman who dressed as a male warrior.

'How long have you been on the *Brimdýr*?' I ventured.

Thorstein looked at me over the rim of his tankard. 'Two years.'

'And before that?'

'A farm, if you can call it that. Rocks and stones, they were the only crops that grew.'

'On Orkneyjar?'

A nod.

I suspected there might be more to joining Imr's crew than poor land, yet I judged it prudent not to ask further.

Instead I accepted Coal-biter's challenge to see who could finish a tankard quicker. He had been drinking for a decade longer than I – he must have been just shy of thirty – but I was the best competitive drinker in Linn Duachaill, and although he did not know it, able to open the back of my gullet and empty a tankard in two great swallows. So it proved. Mine banged on the table a good three heartbeats before his. Mightily annoyed, he threw down some hacksilver and demanded a rematch. I met his wager, and beat him again.

He glared at me, clearly unable to understand how I had bettered him. 'Again!' he roared. 'Third time lucky!'

The significant amount of beer I had consumed had not drowned all my common sense. 'Another night,' I told him. Catching a serving lad's eye – I had greased his palm on the first round so he paid attention – I ordered not two, but four tankards. They arrived fast, and I slapped Coal-biter's back. 'Those will keep you going.'

'Not for long,' he retorted, but I was already gone, slipping between Ulf and Havard so that he could no longer see me.

I could get no sense from them either – they were arguing over the physical attributes of two wenches behind the bar – so I found Vekel.

He was sober, possibly the only one in the room, apart from the proprietor and his thralls.

'Did you foresee my victory?' There hadn't been time to ask until now.

'I did.'

He could have been lying – I could never tell with Vekel – but that didn't stop my skin from crawling. 'Why didn't you say?'

'Would you have believed me?'

I pictured Biarn, heard the roars of support, remembered my certainty that I would lose. 'Maybe not.'

'You see?' An arch of plucked eyebrows.

I growled in annoyance, and finished my beer. 'I wonder what Imr and Asgeir are scheming about with Sigtrygg. D'you know?'

A headshake.

'I don't trust Asgeir.'

'And you would be right not to.'

'You saw him also?'

'When Sigtrygg was telling him and Imr what's what, Asgeir looked as if he was licking piss off a nettle.'

I chuckled. The expression was old, but still funny. 'Mumhan has to be one of the most likely places we'll head for.'

'My thought also. Maybe Sigtrygg wants us to sting Brian Bóramha in the arse.'

I laughed, giving no consideration about how wise it was to antagonise another of the most powerful rulers in Ériu. Names went through my head, Irish ones, and places settled by Norsemen, places I had heard talked about but never seen: Waesfjord, Vedrarfjord, Luimnech, Dún Corcaighe.

A dig in the ribs. 'It doesn't matter where we go. What's important is for you to learn how to use axe and shield.'

Beer-cocky, I said, 'I know how to do that.'

'If Biarn hadn't slipped,' said Vekel, 'you would have been food for Freki and Geri.' These were Oðin's wolves, corpse-eating roamers of battlefields.

Even though I was drunk, the point was indisputable. 'I will learn.'

Vekel kissed me on the cheek. There were a few looks from our oarmates, but I didn't care. Nor did Vekel, who had done it for effect as much as anything else. I caught Thorstein glaring, and thought, no, please, not again. I had no time to brood. The next instant Vekel was telling me not to look, but he'd seen Lalo in the doorway.

'Who?' Soused, the name meant nothing.

'The *blámaðr*.'

I peered across the room. 'He's not there now.'

'He seemed scared. Come on.'

I nabbed one of Coal-biter's beers without him noticing and drank the lot.

Then I went after Vekel.

CHAPTER THIRTEEN

It wasn't the best idea to go wandering Dyflin's streets at dusk, but Vekel's mind was made up, and trying to change that was like trying to stop rain from falling. I would not let him go alone either. I slipped my much-lightened purse inside my tunic, where it was held in place by my belt. It was the safest place I could think of. I kept a hand on my seax too, and moved with such caution that eventually Vekel told me if I didn't keep up, he'd leave me behind. Muttering that we could have just stayed with our oarmates, I picked up my pace and followed.

We found the tavern after a little wandering. Vekel went straight to the innkeeper, as if he hadn't a care in the world. Wary in case some of Biarn's friends might be inside, I lingered by the door, ready to extricate Vekel or fight, or both.

'He's not here.'

'Lalo?'

A withering look. 'Who else are we searching for?'

I noted the innkeeper's sour expression. 'His owner doesn't know where he's gone.'

'He ran off this afternoon, apparently.'

I shrugged. 'It's nothing to do with us. Let's go back – the night is young.'

'We're going to *Brimdýr* first.'

'He won't have gone there.'

'How do you know?'

Defeated before I even started, I tried a different tack. '*Brimdýr* is in the opposite direction to the tavern we were drinking in.'

'Do what you want. I am walking back to the ship.'

Grumbling under my breath, I followed him out the door.

Towards the river.

It soon became clear that Vekel was more interested in searching the shoreline than returning to *Brimdýr*. Why were we looking for Lalo, I demanded, but got no answer. I wove after him. There was so much beer in me at this point, I couldn't have found my arse if someone shone a light on it. But Vekel's nose was sharp; he soon stopped by a pile of rotting wooden barrels, which were half-covered by an old, sodden mass of stinking wool. Once a sail, it had been discarded thanks to the great rip down the middle, storm damage.

'Lalo?' Vekel pitched his voice low.

No response. Loud, drink-fuelled conversation carried from a group of men sitting round a nearby fire. From the river's opposite bank, a reed warbler called.

'Lalo, it is the vitki and his friend. We spoke to you yesterday. Come out. You have nothing to fear.'

Still nothing.

'Lalo.' Vekel could really sound persuasive when he wanted.

A face appeared from under the sail. It was Lalo, and he looked absolutely terrified. It was no wonder. Escaped thralls could expect to receive a good hiding, maybe worse.

'You ran away?' asked Vekel.

'Yes.'

'Where are you going to go? Your home is very far.'

'I go . . . you.' Lalo's expression was pleading, like a small child looking for a hug.

Even as my mouth opened with a vehement 'no', Vekel said, 'That is a good idea.'

My indignant protest was stopped by Vekel's hand on my mouth. 'Quiet,' he hissed, 'or those drunken fools over there will hear.'

'I stay . . . you?' Lalo's eyes, full of hope and fear, were not on Vekel, but me.

I shook my head violently. 'Vekel, I—'

'*Marabout?*'

I stared at Lalo, uncomprehending. He was pointing at Vekel.

'Marabout?' he repeated.

'He's asking if I am a sorcerer.' Vekel tapped his chest, and said, 'Marabout, yes. Vitki.'

121

Lalo made obeisance, like a peasant to a king, and muttered something in his own tongue.

'How much hacksilver is left?'

I sensed Vekel's purpose, and liked it as much as coming face to face with Niðhöggr, the dragon that gnawed the roots of Yggdrasil, the World Tree.

'Well?'

'Not that much.'

'Give it here.'

I had a better chance of pissing into the wind and not getting showered by it than preventing Vekel from getting his way. Jaw clenched, I handed over the bag.

He jiggled it up and down, estimating. 'With what I have, it'll be enough.'

'I tell you, Lalo's owner is not going to sell him!'

Vekel ignored me. 'Hide in there until I come back,' he ordered.

'We go . . . ship?' Lalo asked.

'Tomorrow, yes.' Vekel waved a hand until Lalo retreated under the sail.

'This is not wise' I said, hating how the beer-fuzziness impaired my thinking.

'Move,' said Vekel, as if I hadn't even spoken. 'Someone might see you, and Lalo must stay hidden. Either come with me, or climb aboard *Brimdýr*.'

'I could go back to the tavern.'

A sniff. 'I have the hacksilver, remember.'

'Which is mine!'

'And I placed the wager, remember, with *my* silver. What's left is my portion.'

Unable to answer, because he *was* entitled to a decent portion of my winnings, and seething with frustration, I walked after him into the gloom.

Inspired, I said, 'Imr will never allow a *blámaðr* onto the ship.'

'Let us see about that.'

I groaned.

Vekel's plan to sneak Lalo on board while the sentries dozed worked like a dream. Lifting two of the removable planks in front of the mast, he ordered Lalo down into the tight space below the deck. It was used to store weapons wrapped in oiled fleeces, shields, foodstuffs, spare equipment and the like. He did not get discovered until the next day, some time after we had set sail.

Havard, fossicking about for a length of rope, got the fright of his life, and threw himself back so hard he landed on his rear end. 'A fetch! There's a fetch in the hold!' he roared.

Men stood up from their sea chests. Shouted in alarm and drew their weapons. Imr, who was sleeping off his beer, stirred in his blankets.

Vekel shot to Havard's side, waving his arms. 'It is no fetch, but a *blámaðr*. He is my thrall.'

The news spread through the ship quicker than a spark lighting bone-dry tinder. A circle formed around the hole in the deck, and it wasn't a friendly one. I shoved my way through to find Lalo cowering down amid the wool bales.

'I recognise this *blámaðr*. He's not yours, vitki,' said Crimp-beard, bristling. 'He's slave to a tavern owner in Dyflin.'

'Not anymore.' Vekel could sound self-satisfied whatever the situation.

'And how is that, vitki?' Imr had arrived. Sunken-eyed, wild-haired, he did not look well, or happy.

'I bought him.' It hadn't been that simple, Vekel had told me, chortling. The tavern proprietor wanted more silver than Vekel had. It had taken the threat of a plague of mice and rats, and barrels of beer gone bad – as well as the silver – to change his mind. Vekel eyed Imr boldly. 'He belongs to me.'

'Even if that's true,' Imr snarled, ''Tis bad luck, having a blámaðr on board.'

I had never heard of that superstition, but there were nods aplenty, and muttered ayes.

'Into the sea with him!' This was Glum Geirason, a sour-faced warrior with a limp, and one of the crew I had thus far had little to do with. 'He'll make a fine offering to Rán.'

'No!' Vekel shouted. 'I say he will bring us good fortune!'

Glum's hand was on his seax. He and Vekel stared at each other.

Threat hung heavy in the air, like an autumn murk. Time slowed, as it must have for Oðin during his nine days on the World Tree. Lalo, who didn't need Norse to understand, let out a soft moan.

'Imr?' demanded Glum.

'The blámaðr is my thrall,' Vekel intoned. 'Any man who lays a hand on him will be forever cursed. I am a visendamaðr, remember, a man who knows.'

'Vitki,' said Glum, and spat. It hit a wool-wrapped bundle beside Lalo, who shrank back.

'I am also a sorcerer, yes,' said Vekel.

Imr rubbed his face, in the manner of a man whose head aches so badly that any decision is confounding.

Vekel's hard eyes roved around in challenge. Ulf couldn't meet his gaze, nor Havard. Thorstein gave him a tight smile, which was encouraging. So too was Kleggi's nod. Plenty of other faces, however, were grim and implacable.

Glum's friend, Ketil Gramr – the Fierce – was beside me. From the corner of my eye, I noticed him tense, like a farmyard cat about to pounce. I slipped behind him in the blink of an eye, and twisted his right arm up and towards his shoulder blade, until he squawked. 'Move,' I hissed in his ear, 'and I'll break your arm.'

Ketil muttered something foul, but he didn't struggle, and despite the press, no one grabbed me from behind, or slipped a blade between my ribs. I hoped that meant that the cliff edge my life and Vekel's – not to mention the blámaðr's – rested on, was enough to keep our footing.

'Lalo,' said Vekel. 'Out of there. Onto the deck with you.'

The blámaðr scuttled up and on his knees, clung to Vekel's legs like a shy child with newly arrived visitors in the house. 'Marabout,' he said.

'Stand,' said Vekel gently. 'On your feet.'

Lalo obeyed, gripping Vekel's hand tight.

'The blámaðr's name is Lalo, and he is not to be harmed.' Vekel was staring at Imr. 'Not now. Not when he is cooking food, manning an oar, or helping to sail *Brimdýr*, nor even when he is asleep.'

In the momentary lull, gulls screeched overhead. A gust of wind billowed the sail. *Brimdýr* cut through the waves, timbers thrumming. It was a fine day to be at sea, I thought, randomly.

'You heard the vitki.' There was weariness and perhaps a tone of resignation in Imr's voice. 'The blámaðr is not to be harmed.'

Vekel's right arm shot out. 'Handsala.'

Imr stared. He knew, as everyone did, the weight of a handshake.

'Your word, jarl.' Never before had Vekel called Imr his lord.

Imr made a face like a cat's arse. 'He had better pull his weight, vitki,' he snarled, 'else you and the blámaðr will both have to swim to shore one day. Ball-squeezer too.'

'You will see his worth soon enough.' Confidence oozed from every word.

They shook hands, and despite the rancour between them, there was a noticeable change in the crew's demeanour.

Imr's tongue worked; he scowled. 'My mouth tastes as if someone took a shit in it. Someone fetch me beer!'

'I have two barrels,' said Vekel, pitching his words to carry. 'Enough for everyone to have a few scoops.'

Imr's sour expression cracked into a semblance of a smile, and the mood changed further, like a cloud slipping away from the sun. I say that, but as I released Ketil, he gave me a poisonous look. His friend Glum was equally disgruntled, but had the wisdom not to speak against Imr. He and Ketil did not join in the beer-drinking, but hunched up together, muttering and glaring at Lalo.

I moved to Vekel's side, ignoring Lalo's grateful look. 'We can't keep watch night and day,' I said quietly, in Irish. 'Someone will knife him.' And one or both of us, I almost added.

'We'll see about that,' Vekel replied.

I grinned. I wasn't entirely comfortable with Lalo's presence, but Vekel had taken him under his wing. That meant he was one of us. I would die before letting Glum or Ketil lay a hand on him.

While the crew, Imr foremost among them, set about finishing his barrels of beer, Vekel took Lalo to the small brick-built fireplace close by the base of the mast. He rummaged in his bag and dropped something onto the flames. Curls of smoke rose, to be whipped away by the wind, and a pungent smell spread outwards, before it too was carried off. Vekel danced, now hopping from foot to booted foot, now rubbing his iron staff off his groin, and chanting, half-singing in a low, monotonous tone. Lalo watched, mesmerised, lips moving in some prayer of his own.

Still chanting, Vekel moved to the ship's side.

All eyes followed.

A jawbone came out of Vekel's bag; that of a young pig, he had had it the day before from a townsman butchering outside his house. Incanting, mumbling, he hurled it in the air. Falling end over end, the jawbone hit the water with a splash that I saw but did not hear. Next was a goose's wing – I had no idea where Vekel had got that – and more chanting. Held aloft for longer, perhaps because of its lightness or the feathers, it spun and whirled gracefully, before landing on the sea. It was still floating when a wave hit sideways and carried it off, down into a trough. I strained my eyes trying to find it again, but could not. Like the jawbone, it had gone to Rán's realm.

I hoped she accepted the offerings.

A clatter on the deck nearby brought me back to *Brimdýr*.

Vekel was crouched on his hunkers looking at his ox-bone runes, which lay scattered across the timbers. Lalo wouldn't look, his eyes were closed, but everyone else was staring with a mixture of fascination and dread.

'Well?' Imr's lips were beer-frothy; he looked more human with a few bevvies inside him. 'What do you see, vitki?'

I stared at the ash-marked lines and shapes on the bones, and was grateful for my tunic, which concealed the sudden gooseskin on my arms. I wasn't always sure about Vekel's predictions, but when he cast the runes, I felt the gods watching.

'Our raid will go well.' Vekel was rocking back and forth on his haunches, like an old crone watching a soup pot on the fire.

Imr liked that. Together with Asgeir's crew, we were more than a hundred warriors, a strong force, enough to best those of Ívarr's men who were at Vedrarfjord. We were relying, however, on the reports that had several of his ships either at sea, or trading down the coast to Dún Corcaighe and Luimnech.

It was clear that Imr burned to ask questions, but only a nithing interrupted a vitki who was rune-casting.

'I see cattle, many cattle,' said Vekel.

Imr grinned his wolf-grin, teeth showing. Crimp-beard and Ulf were hooming, Thorstein too.

'Good numbers of thralls as well.'

Oðin was in a good mood, I decided, and the Norns were busy unpicking other men's lives, leaving us to our own devices.

'There will be blood,' said Vekel.

No one blinked. We were raiding after all; bloodshed was inevitable.

'Men will die.'

'Aye, Ívarr's men!' cried Hrafn, to much approval.

'I see oars without rowers, on *Brimdýr*.'

Silence fell with the speed of a snuffed-out candle.

'At least two oars.' Vekel's head lifted, and his eyes went first to Glum, then Ketil. 'It could be more.'

They both went as pale as the winding sheet used by Christ-worshippers to shroud corpses. Kleggi, more superstitious than most, shifted a couple of steps from the pair.

Everyone was staring at them, but for some reason, my attention returned to Vekel, which was why only I saw the look he gave Lalo. Deciding that Glum and Ketil would be no loss, imagining myself the proud owner of cattle and thralls, I made nothing of it.

There was more to a raid than my imagination had suggested. My mind had been full of images of jumping off a ship before dawn and running amok with my oarmates as our enemies panicked. That might work if all we wanted was to burn houses and seize thralls, but we were after cattle. Even if the kine stayed calm, a hard-to-predict outcome, not too many would fit on *Brimdýr*'s deck, or that of *Sea-stallion*, Asgeir's ship.

No, Imr had eagerly explained, his eyes clear of ale-haze, we would creep unseen into the settlement in the depths of night. Once everyone was in position, the houses' thatch roofs would be set alight. At the first sign of flame, with chaos ruling, the cattle were to be driven out into the countryside. Ívarr's men would be so distracted by their burning homes, they wouldn't even notice their livestock vanish. So the plan – concocted by Imr and Asgeir on a ship-friendly beach west of Vedrarfjord – went.

It was more complicated than that, naturally. Vedrarfjord was on the southern bank of the River Siúr, while Dyflin, where we intended to drive the cattle, was far to the north. Imr was somewhat at a disadvantage here, because neither he nor any of *Brimdýr*'s crew knew the area well. Asgeir did, and according to him, the Siúr was not especially deep. There were narrow points too. Once the livestock were a safe distance from the settlement, they could be swum to the other side, reaching the relative safety of Osraighe. A slender kingdom squeezed between Laighin to the east and Mumhan to the west, Osraighe was nonetheless a military power in its own right, and Gilla, its king, was no friend to Norsemen.

Asgeir had suggested that his warriors herd the cattle from there to Dyflin, where they could be divided. That, or if the opportunity arose, the beasts could be sold on the way. In Imr's words to us afterwards, the chance of a fair split if Asgeir got his way was as likely as a man with a soup wound surviving more than a few days. He had insisted that the two raiding parties be formed of his warriors and Asgeir's.

No one on *Brimdýr* liked that. Driving cattle to Dyflin with men we didn't trust seemed a sure path to trouble. When Imr asked for volunteers for the attack on the settlement, the air filled with raised hands. No one responded when it came to the men needed to steal the kine. Cursing us for nithings, telling us that this was how it had to be, he directed Karli to hand round his bag of black and white stones.

I was to be a cattle-thief; so too were Thorstein, Ulf and Havard, and Crimp-beard. They grumbled, but Imr, the bit between his teeth, brooked no refusals. You can slaughter one or two on the way, he declared. Roasted meat all the way to Dyflin, imagine that.

Thorstein and the others settled down. They didn't mind what troubled me: Glum and Ketil the Fierce were also to be in the party. Normally, Vekel's announcement that he was to come too would have raised my spirits, but as we huddled around our shoreline fire the night before the raid, blanket-wrapped against the unseasonal cold, I told him it wasn't a good idea.

His rejoinder was instant. 'Why not?'

'What about Lalo?' I countered.

'He's going too.'

'That's even more unwise!' It was easy to imagine Glum or Ketil creeping towards us at night.

'I can't send the poor boy with the settlement party.' It sounded as if Lalo were Vekel's son. 'Staying with *Brimdýr* wouldn't work either. Karli doesn't like him.'

'You bide by the ship as well then.' Imagining myself in Biarn's mail shirt, the equal of Ulf or even Crimp-beard, ignoring the fact that my suggestion meant we would be separated for the best part of a month, I added brashly, 'A vitki has no place on a raid.'

'You have a short memory.' His lips quirked at my irritable, questioning look. 'Have you forgotten the street fight in Dyflin?'

The gloom hid my reddening cheeks. 'I've killed two men,' I growled.

'One day you will be a mighty warrior, Stormcrow, but not yet. I am coming. So is Lalo.'

That was the end of it.

CHAPTER FOURTEEN

Vedrarfjord, southern Ériu

I peered into the darkness. Dawn could not be far off, although I could discern no lightening of the eastern sky. More than fifty of us lay in dew-soaked grass, about five spear-casts from the southern aspect of Ívarr's settlement, which ran for twice that distance along the riverbank. According to Eyjolf, the warrior charged by Asgeir to lead his men in the cattle-raiding party, this was the closest point to the pens used by Ívarr. There were livestock at almost every house, but rounding them up now posed too much risk. The change in plan had come about at the last moment; our scouts had brought word of three longships moored along the shoreline. It meant that Ívarr had close on two hundred warriors. Taking away the handful of men left to guard the ships, the crews of *Brimdýr* and *Sea-stallion* numbered a touch under six score.

Disappointed, sure that the raid would be called off, I had been surprised by Imr and Asgeir's decision to proceed. The firing of houses would still go ahead, but the only kine to be stolen would be Ívarr's. Young and headstrong as I was, the thought of pissing off a third king appealed mightily. So did the thought of stealing a herd of cattle from under the noses of so many warriors.

Eyjolf came belly-crawling in from the right; another warrior was with him. Like all of us, both had smeared mud on their faces and hands, the better not to be seen. 'Ready?' he mouthed to Crimp-beard.

'Been wondering what's kept you.'

Eyjolf sneered. 'We go when the owl calls, no sooner.'

'It best be soon, eh, or next thing dawn will arrive, and we'll be lying out here in plain view.' The only cover was the shrouding dark.

Eyjolf's mouth worked, but he held back a retort. 'Follow me,' he whispered and began worming his way towards the ditch. Crimp-beard and Thorstein exchanged a look, and went after.

'They seem as likely to kill each other as the sentries,' I whispered.

Vekel's lips touched my ear. 'Neither Crimp-beard nor Thorstein are that stupid, and Asgeir will have picked Eyjolf because he's reliable. The other warrior will be like that too.'

Vekel didn't see everything, I thought. Sigtrygg's wish for peace after my holmgang had had little effect. The passionate hatred with which both crews regarded each other was currently matched by the mutual desire to get rich, but how long that would last was unclear.

'That's not to say there won't be trouble ahead.'

'What have you seen?' I asked, wondering how he always read my mind.

'You will find out in good time.'

Lalo repeated the words.

Aware that he was only trying to learn Irish, I shoved away my irritation at Vekel's reticence and pricked my ears. An owl call was to be the signal that Imr and Asgeir, together sharing the task of attacking the settlement, were about to scale the palisade with their warriors.

It wasn't long before a prolonged, unearthly screech carried to us. It stopped, then repeated itself, a harsh, echoing shriek that set my teeth on edge. My mother had hated the noise, identifying it as the cry of a bean sidhe, signifying a death. The noise had consequently terrified me as a small boy. I knew it was Coal-biter now, however; he had mimicked the owl call multiple times, until we all recognised it.

Imr and Asgeir had heard too. Soon red-orange light appeared in the sky above the settlement, and I fancied I heard the crackle of burning thatch. I searched for Eyjolf and Crimp-beard, but the ramparts were pitch-black beneath the illumination cast by the just-set fires.

'Ready?' This was Ulf, next in command after Crimp-beard, or so he liked to think. 'Wait for Sack-crusher's whistle, Ball-squeezer.'

Vekel let out a strangled, just-stifled snort.

I glared at Ulf, which amused him all the more. He eyed Vekel. 'Vitki, keep the blámaðr out of the way.' Without waiting for a response, he crawled on to the next men.

I wondered what Ulf would make of Lalo's seax, slyly given by Vekel as we waited. It would be murder to lead him into Ívarr's settlement without the means to defend himself, Vekel had explained. I had not argued; my friend always did as he pleased. It was also, I decided, perhaps a way for Lalo to gain some acceptance from the crew.

Crimp-beard's whistle came, and we were all on our feet. Despite the weight of Biarn's mail shirt, I was younger and, it seemed, fitter than the rest. I was soon out in front. Vekel had always been fleet of foot; he kept pace. Lalo, limpet-like to his new master, did too.

Crimp-beard met us at the open gate. There was blood on his axe blade, but he was grinning. 'Well met, Ball-squeezer.' Since the holmgang, he'd been a great deal friendlier, but he loved to poke fun.

I came back with my usual, 'Sack-crusher.'

Crimp-beard laughed.

'The sentries?' Vekel asked.

'Dead. On this wall anyway.'

Thorstein loomed up out of the darkness. 'Four – one for each of us.'

'The pens are this way,' said Eyjolf, who was shadowed by his comrade.

Weapons at the ready, half the group loped after him. The rest stayed outside to prevent the cattle from escaping when they exited the palisade.

Ívarr was a wealthy man. Perhaps eighty cattle, cows, calves and young stock, were penned up close to what I assumed was his longhouse. Several were white with dark-red ears, a rare, valuable type from Britain; the rest were a mixture of local breeds.

No one was anywhere near. Shouts and cries carried from the rest of the settlement; as we wanted, the inhabitants' attention was on the burning houses. I copied Eyjolf and threaded the handle of my axe into my belt, then slung my shield across my back. Men formed a line, which would guide the cattle towards the gate, and Eyjolf lifted aside the gate timbers.

The beasts, unsettled by the noise, milled about, none moving towards us. As much stockman as smith or warrior, I was about to climb into the pen but Vekel, followed by Lalo, beat me to it. Working their way through to the far side of the pen, they began waving their arms.

'Sook, sook, sook, go on!' Vekel shouted.

Lalo might not have understood the Irish, but he valiantly repeated it.

Led by a horned dun-coloured cow, her head going up and down with unease, the cattle began to emerge. Soon all the kine were pushing to get out, with Vekel and Lalo urging them on from behind.

'Cattle-herders, we should call you both, not vitki and blámaðr,' I declared.

'If you want me to call you "Ball-squeezer" from now until Ragnarök, keep saying that,' came his tart response.

Eyjolf and his companion had gone off to take the lead; so had Crimp-beard and Thorstein. Staying with Vekel, I ended up at the back, which was why I saw the youth hurtle out of Ívarr's longhouse. Perhaps he was a herdsman, or maybe he'd heard us. Either way, he had a spear, and he was stupid with rage.

Ulf lobbed a hand axe, easy as if he were in a throwing contest. It hit the youth squarely between the eyes, killing him deader than dead. 'Nithing,' said Ulf, retrieving the axe. 'Could he not see how many of us there are?'

'I understand. He loved his cattle,' said Havard.

Ulf harrumphed. 'Arse-wipe.'

'Me or him?' Havard demanded.

'Both of you.'

Even Havard chuckled at that.

As we walked behind the last of the cattle, I cast a look back at the settlement. 'Someone has set a torch in the roof of Ívarr's longhouse,' I said.

Ulf twisted. 'It's burning nicely. As if losing his cattle wasn't bad enough. I'd give a handful of hacksilver to see his face.'

I laughed.

Relaxed, for there was no pursuit, we neared the gate. Ulf and Havard were already arguing over who would eat the most meat that night. I asked Vekel how many thralls the other party might have taken. We would see when we saw, he replied, and it was best not to count eggs before they were hatched. I gave him a dunt for that, and called him 'Cattle-herder' again. Delighted to find a rare chink in his armour, I decided it was worth the name 'Ball-squeezer', from him at least.

'Man!' Lalo was pointing, his face twisted with alarm.

Too late my head turned. Too late Ulf and Havard stopped talking. It was too late even for Vekel, with his vitki wits. A sentry on the palisade's walkway, bleeding from a head wound, but not dead as he was supposed to be, hurled a spear.

Havard went down, skewered through the neck. He looked faintly surprised.

'No!' Ulf's roar might have been heard in Dyflin. Up the ladder he went, faster than a rat into a hole. The sentry didn't have a chance. Head cloven by the same hand axe that had slain the herd-boy, he died. Ulf wasn't finished. Once, twice, thrice, and another two times he hewed, reducing the sentry to a headless, limbless torso. 'That for you, you whore's get!' he roared, kicking each body part off the walkway.

Bile filled my mouth, went up the back of my nose. Helpless, I spewed a mixture of bread and beer – what I'd had before leaving *Brimdýr* – all over the ground, right beside poor Havard.

Ulf clambered down the ladder, and pulled the spear from his friend's neck. Without a word, he slung Havard's corpse over his shoulder as if it were a butcher-split half pig. Only then did he take in the three of us: me, Vekel and Lalo, rooted to the spot.

Curiosity creased his face. 'What?'

'Nothing,' I said, coughing and snorting drool, remembering how amiable he'd seemed the first time we had met.

Lalo didn't utter a word.

'We had best get after the cattle,' said Vekel.

'Go on then,' Ulf ordered.

Ulf laid a last rock onto the pile, and stood back to appraise his work. 'It's not a fire, old friend, but it will have to do.' He muttered a prayer.

The grave was not deep. With no spades, we had had only axes and our bare hands to fashion Havard's final resting place. Hindered by the heavy clay and the pressing knowledge that pursuit might be close on our heels, Ulf had given up digging. Laying the corpse in the shallow pit we had thus far managed, and with it, Havard's weapons and shield, he built over it a stone cairn. I and a dozen of the *Brimdýr's* crew helped, which meant it was swiftly finished. Eyjolf and his cronies, who had refused to halt, were gone on with the cattle; so too were the rest of our oarmates.

Dawn had come not long since. In the middle distance, smoke rose to join the clouds: Vedrarfjord was still burning. The rolling countryside and the bends in the Siúr made it impossible to see if Ívarr had sent any warriors after us, but as Vekel observed, it was safe to assume that he would. The sooner we crossed into Osraighe and entered the mountains on the northern horizon, the better.

'Done?' I asked Ulf.

He bristled, but knew as well as I the need for swiftness. 'Aye.'

'Time to run,' said Vekel.

Lalo echoed him.

'Good,' said Ulf, and was rewarded with a smile.

The language lessons were beginning to irritate. 'If you're finished . . .' and I broke into a ground-eating lope.

Cattle move slowly; we soon caught up. For the first time, I was able to appreciate properly the stock taken from Ívarr. They were fine, well-fed beasts, black, crimson-red, flame-red, and brown. As well as the horned dun cow, there were five white-backed, with black bodies, and three of the rare, white, red-eared type. There was one bull also, black, thick-necked, a placid enough creature. Now that we had the kine in a compact group, surrounded on all sides, they moved along without giving any trouble.

We passed farmhouses, raths and fields of barley and wheat, but it was too early for people to be stirring. Dogs barked. If anyone responded, and realised there were strangers close by, they had the sense not to challenge us.

'Where's the ford?' Ulf eventually demanded of Eyjolf.

'Close.'

He wasn't lying. Not long after, we reached the Siúr, which was a lot broader than the Casán at Linn Duachaill. Thirsty, the kine moved between the alder trees to the river's edge without being urged. A pair of moorhens swam away from the invaders to their territory, and a flash of bright colour darting off low over the water marked a kingfisher.

I had never herded cattle across a river, but Eyjolf had. A dozen men who could swim went over first; once they were on the far bank, we closed in on the herd, shouting and sooking, forcing them forward. Most beasts can swim, even if they don't choose to, and soon enough the kine were entering the water, and with strong kicks of their legs, crossing without mishap. A few of the younger calves had to be bodily heaved in after their mothers, but even they managed the passage.

The same was not true of all the warriors. Perhaps half could not swim; they had to lie on their backs and be hauled over by those who could. There was much cursing and protesting, not to mention splashing and swallowing of water, but no one drowned. Asgeir's advice, to leave mail shirts on the ships, was proven wise. I was one of the few who had ignored it; I now counted myself fortunate to be a strong swimmer, and able to cross with my precious armour.

Relieved to have entered Osraighe, amused by the complaints of the men who'd been helped across, the dozen who had swum over first weren't paying attention to our surroundings. I wasn't either. Truth be told, I was admiring the cattle again, half listening to Vekel grousing as he wrung out his hairy calfskin shoes.

'Men. Men!' Lalo's voice.

He's right, I thought, as hooves drummed the earth.

'Shieldwall!' Crimp-beard yelled. 'Some of you, keep the cattle from straying!'

The dozen who had been first across formed up at once. Men who had been squeezing water from their clothes, or complaining about the rust that would soon be evident on their weapons, scrambled and cursed and tried to do the same, but the response was low. Perhaps twenty shields formed up, with Crimp-beard raging in the middle and swearing he'd rip off heads and shit down necks if more didn't join him.

A score of men, Lalo and Vekel among them, made a loose circle around the herd. To my intense relief, the kine, alarmed by the thundering arrival, settled.

The noise had been a group of horsemen, eighty at least, warriors all. They fanned out in a great semi-circle, easily overlapping our pitiful shieldwall, their spears at the ready.

I joined the formation, guts churning. I was no veteran, but it was plain that a quick charge would take the riders around us and into the midst of the rest, and the cattle. One barked order, and bloody mayhem would break out.

'Declare yourselves!' This was a thin-faced rider, not much older than I. On his left shoulder was a beautiful, long-pinned cloak brooch similar to Sigtrygg's. 'You are in Osraighe, where Gilla is king. None travel here without his leave.'

'We are sworn men to Sigtrygg, Dyflin's ruler, who is on good terms with Gilla,' replied Eyjolf.

'We are no friends to Ívarr of Vedrarfjord either,' Crimp-beard added.

'As if you would be, leaving his territory with a herd of kine,' said the brooch-wearer.

His men's laughter was loud, and had a tone that filled me with unease.

'Where are you going with these fine beasts?'

'Dubhlinn, lord.' Eyjolf used the Irish name, and his tone held just enough obsequiousness not to sound grovelling.

'That's a long way.'

'If we encountered any of Gilla's warriors, lord, men such as yourselves, Sigtrygg bade us pay our deepest respects, and to seek safe passage through Osraighe,' said Crimp-beard.

This was almost true. Gilla hated Ívarr with a passion, Sigtrygg had told us, which meant he'd be well disposed towards us, but he was also stingier than a moneylender from Mumhan. In Sigtrygg's exact words, 'Eat his food out of a storage chest, Gilla would, so he can shut the lid if anyone comes knocking on the door. If you meet his men, a hefty toll will be exacted.' Asgeir had reckoned we had a decent chance of making it through Osraighe unhindered; Imr had been less sure, but as he said, there was little to be done other than offer a prayer to Loki, and roll the dice.

Currently, we had a three and a two, I decided, and Gilla's men were looking at fives.

Eyjolf, who had been quick to shove his way into the centre of the shieldwall beside Crimp-beard, seemed about to speak. Crimp-beard gave him a none-too-gentle nudge, though, and he said nothing.

'Ara, of course you can herd your cattle across Osraighe,' said Brooch-wearer.

This was far too easy, I thought. Crimp-beard, frowning, was of the same mind. So too was Eyjolf.

'Can we offer you a few head in thanks, lord?' asked Eyjolf.

'Ten, maybe,' said Crimp-beard, ignoring Eyjolf's scowl.

Brooch-wearer rubbed his chin, the way a man does when he's pondering. 'That's a little miserly, don't you think?'

Eyjolf looked as happy as a constipated man squatting over a reeking dung-pit, but he managed not to protest. Perhaps realising that his temper would get the better of him, he appeared content to let Crimp-beard do the bargaining too. The latter did his best to appear content. It wasn't convincing. 'How many were you thinking, lord?'

'Two dozen.'

This was almost a third of the kine, I calculated, an extortionate price. I wondered if Crimp-beard, clearly unhappy, and Eyjolf, outraged, would decide to fight. Ulf, still grieving Havard, muttered that we should just get on with it. He wasn't entirely out of his mind. Everyone who wasn't watching the cattle was in the shieldwall now; we numbered almost fifty. The Osraighe-men might win the clash, but stood to suffer plenty of casualties. Even if we accounted well for ourselves, however, the fighting would cause the cattle to stampede, many probably never to be seen again. We would be left with nothing to show for the raid but dead and injured men.

'Twenty?' Crimp-beard didn't sound convincing.

'You're quite the joker!' Brooch-wearer's smile was toothy. 'Two dozen, it is.'

'Men! Men!' cried Lalo.

In all the excitement, we had forgotten Ívarr, and the warriors he might have sent after us. Even the Osraighe-men hadn't been watching. Running down to the far bank between the alders came a large group of Norse, a hundred at least. They came to a halt at the water's edge; shouted insults and threats carried across almost at once, but they made no move to swim over. Only those seeking death would try to secure the crossing coming out of the river against an enemy, ready and waiting, and greater in number.

Their predicament didn't stop ours from having worsened, greatly. If we'd had a two and three on our dice, I thought bitterly, we had ones now. Brooch-wearer's fives had become sixes. Everyone knew it. Eyjolf looked as if he'd swallowed a wasp. Crimp-beard was cursing under his breath. Over by the cattle, Vekel looked unsurprised, which was predictable but infuriating.

Somewhere, I decided, Loki was chortling, the tricksy bastard.

'You could always go back over the Siúr,' Brooch-wearer offered. 'Maybe you could strike a deal with Ívarr's men.'

There was, I decided, more chance of an appearance by Ymir, the frost giant slain and later dismembered by Oðin and his brothers, than of us driving the kine over the river into a welcome of axes and swords. As my father would have said, a man held by the short and curlies does what he's told.

'Well?' asked Brooch-wearer.

'We'll stay here, lord,' said Crimp-beard, grimacing. 'Two dozen cattle are yours, and welcome.'

'Choose as you please!' Eyjolf's gesture was expansive, but his eyes went to the three white, red-eared cows, showing he hoped they would not be part of the price.

'Did I say two dozen beasts?' Brooch-wearer's giggle was unexpectedly high-pitched, like a girl's. 'I meant three.'

Eyjolf couldn't help it. *'Thirty-six?'*

'That's what three dozen is, yes.' Brooch-wearer spoke as if to an addlepate. 'Including the white, red-eared cows, obviously. The king is very fond of those.'

'You drive a hard bargain, lord.' Crimp-beard's jaw was gritted.

'I think it's fair, considering. If you'd rather' – Brooch-wearer indicated the far bank, and Ívarr's irate warriors – 'you know, deal with the other party, be my guest.'

'We can fight,' hissed Ulf. 'Those pretty boys' horses won't charge our shieldwall. The cattle will be lost, sure, but the Osraighe sheep-humpers will leave half their number in the dirt by the time we're done with them.'

Crimp-beard wavered. He was a proud man, and the humiliation was not sitting well with him.

My first experience of a shieldwall might well be my last, I thought, but if it comes to it, I will play my part.

'We'll take your offer, and thank you for it.' Vekel had come around the side of the shieldwall, unnoticed.

'Finally, someone with sense,' said Brooch-wearer.

'It is not your decision, vitki!' shouted Crimp-beard.

Moving light-footed as a cat, Vekel was suddenly right in front of Crimp-beard, his iron staff pointed, a clear threat. 'Fight then,' he said, voice casual. 'You will not see tomorrow.'

'Ha! Do you think I care about that?'

'A gladdener of the raven you would be. I see clouds of them here, feasting.'

I had goose skin again. I hated how Vekel could do that to me. He was talking sense, though.

Bull-stubborn, Crimp-beard could not see it. 'Eh? Why?'

'Almost every man from the *Brimdýr* will join you. Truly, the wolves will howl in the hills tonight.' As Crimp-beard's face fell, Vekel turned on Eyjolf. 'The *Sea-stallion*'s crew will fare no better.'

Eyjolf, whey-faced, glanced at Crimp-beard. 'Sigtrygg doesn't have to know how many kine we stole from Ívarr.'

'I suppose.' Crimp-beard looked at Vekel again. 'Are you sure?'

'I have never been surer.'

'Take your three dozen beasts, lord, but not a single one more!'

'I am a man of my word,' Brooch-wearer said, feigning hurt.

'You had best be, or there will be blood.'

Brooch-wearer chose to ignore the comment, which as I said placatingly to Crimp-beard, meant he knew the threat was genuine. We watched and glowered as the Osraighe-men cut out the cattle they wanted. When Ívarr's warriors realised what was happening, their threats redoubled. A prolonged slanging match ensued, threats of sexual assault, torture, killing and dismemberment being hurled from three directions. It was all hot air, I commented sourly to Vekel. Ívarr's party had seen sense: the Osraighe-men had their minds fixed on the prize, their kine; and our warriors, well, they had given up.

'Posturing is important,' Vekel said. 'You should know that by now.'

'Posturing?' Lalo's face was quizzical.

'Acting,' I said. 'Putting on a show. Pretending.'

Lalo repeated my words, but still didn't understand.

Vekel began to explain in more simple terms, and I left him to it.

Of more concern was the journey to Dyflin.

He was all smiles and friendship now, but I had my suspicions about Brooch-wearer's guarantee of safe passage. It wouldn't be a surprise, I thought, if it lasted no longer than it took him to disappear from sight. There was some advantage to staying in Osraighe, I decided. It avoided southern Laighin, whose king was no friend to Sigtrygg.

Noticing Glum and Ketil Gramr, who continued to throw evil looks in Lalo's direction, I decided that there were also dangers closer to home.

CHAPTER FIFTEEN

Four days passed. We took a meandering path north through the heather- and gorse-covered mountains. Few people lived there; it was home to deer, foxes and wolves. There were hawks aplenty too, hanging above like airborne sentinels. I saw no ravens, though, which was unsettling. A halt twice daily allowed the cattle to feed on the scrubby grass. We could have driven them harder and reached Dyflin sooner, but as I told Eyjolf, they would have lost a lot of condition and not regained it before winter. There was no point pissing off Imr, Asgeir and Sigtrygg any more than they would already be when they heard about Brooch-wearer's extortionate toll.

We spent more time in Osraighe as a result, but fickle Loki favoured us now, and there were no encounters with any of Gilla's warriors. Vekel and I kept Lalo away from Glum and Ketil, which prevented that pot from boiling over. Eyjolf and his lot sneered and swaggered around us, but there was no bloodshed. A wolf pack came one night, prowling to and fro in the nearby trees. Their howls greatly unsettled the cattle, and so I led out a dozen men with flaming torches. The wolves fled into the darkness, and had the wisdom not to return.

The grazing break in the middle of each day meant there was time for weapons training, and Ulf was my main teacher. It was fortunate that Vekel insisted on leather covers on our weapon blades, because, still grieving for Havard, Ulf did not hold back. Having demonstrated various moves, he would then insist on practice bouts. They all ended the same, humiliating way. Me in the dirt with Ulf standing over, often having to be prevented by Vekel or one of the others from finishing the job. Bruised all over, in severe pain, my head ringing, I would get up and ask to start again. Practice and repetition were the only way to learn.

Thorstein offered to teach me on the fifth day, and to my surprise, Ulf agreed. We used swords rather than axes, which took me straight back to being a complete novice. Unlike Ulf, though, Thorstein did not beat me black and blue. The leather-covered blade at my throat or thigh, or tip pressed against my belly, was enough reminder of the damage it caused in skilled hands. Thorstein was surprisingly patient, showing me how to hold the sword and shield, the best posture to take, and so on. A lot of his exercises were repetition. Ready myself, shield high, sword held at right angles to the body. Thrust. Follow through with a punch of the shield – strike with the iron boss, Thorstein advised, and you could break an enemy's nose – and then deliver a final, life-ending sword thrust. Do it again. And again. And again, until my arm muscles burned.

Swinging from on high was to be avoided, because it invited a skilful opponent to bury his blade in my armpit. Stabbing was safer, and just as effective. 'Sink this much into a man's belly,' Thorstein said, marking a hand's length on the steel, 'and he'll go down, screaming. There's no need to push it in further. That enemy is done, finished. Move on to the next one.'

'Stamp hard on him as you walk over, though. Make sure, eh, Glum?' Crimp-beard advised to much laughter. He saw my incomprehension. 'Most often, what Thorstein said is right, but every now and then, a gut-wound doesn't immediately end a warrior. That's why Glum walks with a limp.'

Hooms, roars of amusement. 'You should have told him always to look down, Thorstein!' shouted Goat-Banki, so known because of his skill at breeding goats. 'Stuck Glum good, that Saxon did!'

Rather than turn on Goat-Banki, not the brightest spark in the hearth, Glum glared at me. 'What's so funny, eh?'

Wary, I hadn't joined in the merriment; to my knowledge, I hadn't even shown any amusement. 'Nothing,' I said quickly.

'Doesn't look like that from here.' He stumped over.

'There's no need for this,' said Thorstein.

'Keep your nose out of my business!' Glum shoved in front of Thorstein. 'You were laughing at me.'

'I was not.'

'I saw you, Ball-squeezer.' He shoved me in the chest.

The slightest reaction would escalate the situation beyond

redemption, so I didn't retaliate, even though the young, prideful part of me wanted to. 'I didn't say it, Crimp-beard and Goat-Banki did. Pick an argument with either of them, why don't you?'

'He's right,' said Thorstein, although he didn't intervene.

'Crimp-beard is an oarmate.' Then, with a little reluctance, 'Goat-Banki too.'

'So is Ball-squeezer,' Thorstein declared.

'Not to me.' Another shove. A leer. His hand went to his seax.

My mouth was dry. I wouldn't get the leather cover off my sword blade before Glum stuck me. I'd have to try a head butt, or a gut-punch, and hope that that granted me time enough.

'Stop!' Crimp-beard's yell caught everyone's attention, as it was intended to. 'All we have lost this far on the raid is some kine.'

'Three dozen kine,' said Eyjolf, but it was only said for the benefit of his cronies.

'None of us are raven's meat yet, like the vitki foretold, and I would like to keep it that way,' said Crimp-beard. 'Leave it, unless you would like to fight me.'

Glum's expression could have curdled fresh milk, but he wasn't about to take on Crimp-beard. With careful precision, he spat, the gobbet landing on the toe of my left shoe. 'I'm watching you and your arse-loving friend. Not to mention the cursed blámaðr. So is Ketil.' He walked away.

I imagined what it would feel like to ram my blade into Glum's mouth and out the back of his neck. My fingers toyed with the leather covering.

'Your balls aren't that big,' Thorstein said in my ear. 'Even if you killed him, Ketil would do you in revenge. You're not fit to take the two of them, one after the other.'

'Yet,' I said.

An appraising look, the faint suggestion of a smile. 'We'll see.'

'Let's keep practising.'

'No. That's it for now.'

'Why?'

'It's time to get the cattle moving.' Men were getting up from where they had sat, stretching, and farting.

'Glum bad man,' said Lalo as I joined him and Vekel.

'He is,' I replied. 'Him and Ketil both.'

'Ketil. Glum.' There was a venom I had never heard in Lalo's voice. He was a thrall. I thought nothing of it.

Afternoon moved towards evening, and finding an abandoned rath atop a small hill, we drove the cattle inside, finding it sufficient for stock and men both. Interwoven branches lopped from trees in a patch of nearby oaks were used to close off the entrance. This done, our minds turned to food. We were hungry, and running low on provisions. Goat-Banki said he'd try his luck afield. He didn't have much between his ears, Vekel whispered, but he was a fine archer. Sure enough, Goat-Banki was back before sunset with a gralloched red deer hind slung over his shoulders. The warriors from the *Brimdýr* cheered him to the darkening skies; even Glum seemed pleased.

A couple of Eyjolf's men had also gone out with bows, but returned empty-handed. He and his companions looked on sourly as we built a roaring fire and fashioned two wooden tripods between which, at chest height, ran a stout branch. Then, lashing the carcase to the 'spit' with leather thongs, we suspended it over the flames. It was lacking a handle, but there were plenty of willing hands to see that it got turned when the part closest to the heat began to scorch.

Crimp-beard, never one to hold back, was first to cut a hunk off with his seax. The venison was warmed at most, in all likelihood still raw, but that didn't stop him eating it in two great swallows. He smacked his lips. 'Oðin's balls, that's delicious!'

Like that, we were all leaning in, jostling and slicing off meat.

Raw or not, it did taste good. I cut myself another chunk, and gave some to Lalo, who smiled red-lipped thanks.

'All we're lacking is beer,' said Ulf. 'Or mead.'

'It'll be Dyflin before we see either of those,' said Thorstein. 'Worse luck.'

'We should have a story,' I suggested.

Everyone seemed to like that idea.

'Vekel?'

'If I talk, you savages will eat all the venison, and leave none for me.'

Thorstein spiked a great lump of meat onto a length of branch. 'I'll cook this for you, vitki. It will be ready when you're done.'

Vekel's eyes roved, assessing the audience. 'A tale, eh?'

Ayes from round the fire. Even Eyjolf's lot seemed keen.

'Seeing as we're thirsty, a story about mead seems fitting,' said Vekel. Plenty of hooms.

I knew what was coming. 'Listen closely,' I said to Lalo, who was perched by Vekel's side. 'This is a good one.'

'Some of you have heard of the giant Suttung, who took possession of the mead that gives men poetic power,' said Vekel. 'How he got it is another tale. Just know that Suttung intended to keep the mead for himself. He put it into three cauldrons named Odrerir, Bodn and Son, and hid them within a mighty boulder, where they were guarded by his daughter Gunnlod.'

Lewd comments rained in.

Vekel continued, 'Oðin knew of Suttung's mead, and its wondrous power, which had originally belonged to a man named Kvasir.'

'And we all know where he came from,' said Ulf, hawking phlegm into the fire.

Everyone laughed, including Vekel. As I had about the cauldrons, I clarified for Lalo. Kvasir, the wisest man in the world, had been formed from globules of godly spit. Murdered by the dwarves Fjalar the Deceiver and Galar the Screamer, Kvasir's blood was used to make mead; the resulting brew contained his ability to dispense wisdom.

'If dwarves make, how did Suttung get . . . mead?' asked Lalo.

'As I said, that is another tale, for another night,' replied Vekel. 'But in short, he took it from Fjalar and Galar.'

Lalo nodded.

'Oðin knew of Suttung's mead and its magical properties, and he wanted it for himself. He left home in search of it, and after a time, came upon nine thralls mowing hay. He asked if they wanted their scythes sharpened. They agreed, so he took a whetstone from his belt and set to work. Soon their scythes were much sharper. Impressed, the thralls asked Oðin for his whetstone. Anyone could have it, the god said, if they gave him an appropriate price. All nine wanted it, and suggested that he sell it to them alone. Instead he tossed the stone into the air, and as the thralls, pushing and shoving, tried to grab it, they each managed to cut their own throats with their scythes.'

'That would have been a sight,' said Thorstein, to ayes and hooms.

'Oðin found lodging for the night nearby with Suttung's brother, a giant by the name of Baugi,' Vekel went on. 'Baugi was in a difficult position. His nine thralls had killed one another, he complained, leaving him insufficient labourers for his fields. Oðin, who had given his name as Bolverk—'

'Stupid bloody giant obviously didn't speak Norse!' interrupted Ulf.

I joined in the laughter, but Lalo's face was blank.

'Bolverk means "Worker of Misfortune",' I explained.

Lalo grinned.

'—so Bolverk offered to do the nine thralls' work. His pay was to be one drink of Suttung's mead. Baugi said that he had no control over his brother, but agreed to go with Bolverk and see if they could persuade Suttung to grant the request.'

'Some chance of that!' roared Goat-Banki.

'Over the summer, Bolverk did nine men's toil. When winter arrived, it was time to be paid. They went together to Suttung, and Baugi told his brother of the bargain he had made with Bolverk. Suttung flatly refused a single drop of mead.'

'Typical giant,' muttered Thorstein.

'Bolverk persuaded Baugi that they should get the mead through cunning. He pulled out a gimblet' – here Vekel glanced at Lalo – 'a special tool for boring into rock. They went to the boulder in which Gunnlod and the mead were hidden, and he asked Baugi to bore into the stone. After a little while, Baugi said he had gone right through. Bolverk blew into the hole, but rock dust came back; this showed that Baugi was trying to trick him. Keep boring, he ordered, and Baugi did. This time, the gimblet entered the boulder's centre. Quick as a flash, Bolverk turned himself into a snake and wriggled through, avoiding Baugi's attempts to stab him with the gimblet.'

As Vekel spoke, I studied the faces around the fire. Rapt, they were, entranced, just as I and everyone in Linn Duachaill had been when my friend wove his magic. Vekel was not just a vitki, I thought, but a skald.

The story went on. Disguised as a handsome young man, having slept with Gunnlod for three nights, and drained Odrerir, Bodn and Son in the same number of gulps, Oðin put on his eagle's skin and flew off at top speed. Chased by Suttung, also in eagle form, all the way to Asgard, he regurgitated the mead into buckets left out by the gods. A few drops went astray, falling from his beak down to Midgard, where humankind live.

''Tis clear that you have drunk none of that, vitki,' said Ulf to loud approval.

Vekel's chin dipped in pleased acknowledgement. The tiny amount of mead let fall by Oðin gave the poorest and mediocre poets their ability, while fine skalds and taletellers received theirs straight from the gods.

'An excellent rendition, vitki,' said Thorstein, with more warmth than I had ever heard in his voice. 'You must be thirsty.'

'I would not refuse a drink.'

Thorstein proffered a waterbag.

Vekel took a swallow, and his expression went from surprise to delight. 'This is beer!'

Thorstein shrugged.

The astonished accusations that Thorstein was a conniver of the first degree, to have had beer when no one knew, were matched only by demands for a taste. He let it go around the fire willingly, saying Goat-Banki was to have it after Vekel, and that there was enough for each man to have a mouthful and no more.

'How about another tale, vitki?' asked Ulf.

'I'm done for the night.'

'You tell one, Ulf, about Havard,' I said.

'The filthier the better,' suggested Crimp-beard. 'He was a randy bastard.'

'I saw him hump an old blanket once,' said Kleggi. 'Honest to Thor, I did.'

Chuckles, hooms and obscene gestures. More mention of Havard's sexual exploits.

Cheered by the colourful memories of his friend, Ulf settled down and began.

I was woken by shouts. Voices, calling the alarm. Blanket thrown off, rubbing sleep away with one hand, seax ready in the other – since the confrontation with Glum, I had lain down with it unsheathed – I got up.

Vekel was awake too, but there was no sign of Lalo. I had no time to wonder why.

'Guard the entrance, some of you! Banki! Banki, I need you and the others here with your bows!' Crimp-beard was a dark outline atop the rampart. 'Eyjolf, send up your archers! Quickly!'

I seized my shield and axe, and hurried to where we had stacked cut branches to prevent the cattle escaping. A great hole gaped in it – someone had been tampering. Ulf was there, and Ketil Gramr, and several of Eyjolf's comrades, all peering into the night. Movement was audible beyond the rath, but I could see no one.

'Are any of the kine gone?' I asked.

'I don't think so,' replied Ulf, turning to regard the milling beasts. 'If some did get out, it wasn't many.'

'Who was it?'

'Locals. Has to be,' snarled Ketil. 'Thieving Osraighe filth.'

Considering how we had come by the kine, that was a little rich, but I said nothing. I wondered about going outside, but took my lead from the others, who were staying put. It would be impossible to tell friend from foe, I decided, not to mention the risk of being skewered by Goat-Banki. Even now, he and the other bowmen were loosing shafts, loudly encouraged by Crimp-beard.

We stayed on guard. The noises outside the rath died away. Banki and his fellows, who had apparently not hit any of the would-be cattle thieves, ceased shooting. Vekel came, Lalo now with him. I wondered where the blámaðr had been.

'We have counted the kine,' said Vekel. 'None are missing.'

'Loki be thanked,' said Ulf with feeling.

'The sentries be thanked, more like.' Ketil cupped a hand to his mouth. 'Glum, was it you who raised the alarm?'

There was no immediate answer. Ketil clambered up the hacked earth steps to the top of the rampart, still calling for his friend.

'That was a lucky escape,' said Vekel. 'It would have been a shame to lose any more cattle.'

'No lose cattle,' said Lalo with a shy smile.

I clouted his shoulder. 'In part, no doubt, thanks to you and your stockmanship.'

He looked puzzled. 'Stock-man-ship?'

'You are good with livestock,' I said, waving my arms as we did when encouraging them to move. 'Sook, sook.'

His face lit up. 'Sook, sook!'

'Glum! Glum!' Ketil sounded angry and concerned. 'Someone help me find him!'

'He couldn't find his own prick if it wasn't attached,' said Ulf, putting a foot on the bottom stop.

147

I couldn't have cared less about Glum, so I busied myself with staying alert, in case the thieves returned. Ulf and the rest made desultory conversation. Vekel and Lalo vanished, presumably to get what rest they could before the dawn came. That wouldn't be long; there was a paling in the eastern sky.

'Glum!' Now Ketil's voice thrummed with alarm.

I heard him jump down from the rampart. More shouts of dismay and anger. Ulf and a few others ventured outside, weapons at the ready. Soon it was evident that Glum's corpse was lying outside the rath; his throat had been opened ear to ear. He must have heard the cattle thieves, Ketil raged, and been killed before he could call for help.

Everyone thought the same.

So did I.

Until I went back to my sleeping place by the fire, and mentioned something along those lines. Lalo and Vekel glanced at one another, which triggered a memory of the look between them when Vekel had predicted an oar on *Brimdýr* without oarsmen.

Lalo had gone off when the alarm was raised, I decided. Black as the night, no one had seen him, or how, in the confusion, he had slain Glum. I wondered about saying it to Vekel, but as he loudly lamented Glum's death, and how sorry he was that his vision had been correct, I thought it prudent to keep quiet. It seemed that Lalo was not just a herdsman, and his hitherto unseen skill might prove useful again.

Ketil would be lucky to reach Dyflin in one piece.

CHAPTER SIXTEEN

Dyflin

Glad to leave the hills of northern Laighin behind, we pastured the cattle in a paddock close to the western edge of the town. Everyone wanted to head in and start drinking – Thorstein's water-skin was but a distant memory, and Eyjolf's band had had none of that – yet the herd could not be left unguarded. Crimp-beard and Eyjolf didn't agree on much, but they were of one mind when it came to the number of sentries. Twenty at least, and lucky it wasn't more, they told us, ignoring the grumbling and sour looks. Karli and his bag of black and white stones were on the *Brimdýr*, so we made do with varying lengths of grass, ten at a time, held in Crimp-beard's giant paws.

To my delight, I chose a long one. Kleggi had to stay behind; so too, to his immense displeasure, did Ulf. That was, until Thorstein offered to change places. 'Drown your sorrows,' he told Ulf, handing over a silver coin. 'Have a drink for Havard from me while you're at it.' Emotional, Ulf replied with a gruff nod. Crimp-beard didn't make Vekel choose; he wanted the vitki by his side when they met with Sigtrygg. We had been with the *Brimdýr* for less than a month, and already Vekel was indispensable.

It was uncomfortable to think that I wasn't in quite so secure a position. I had been accepted, it was true, but I hadn't yet proved myself. Until there was a fight or a battle – in which I wasn't maimed or slain – I was still a young pup to many of the crew, a smith and not much more. As we walked towards Dyflin, I moaned about it to Vekel, who said that patience was a virtue. My retort, acid-sharp, was to ask if, with monkish words like that, he was becoming a White Christ worshipper. This slipped inside his guard; he shut up. Relishing this rare victory, I did my best to reassure Lalo, who was visibly out of sorts. It wasn't surprising; Dyflin was where he'd been kept as a slave, and his former owner would not have got over his grievance at being blackmailed by Vekel.

'You don't have to worry,' I said. 'You're with us.'

This made no difference. Lalo hunched his shoulders, and withdrew further into himself.

I tried another tack. 'You are Vekel's thrall now, not the tavern keeper's.'

'He belongs to no one.'

I looked at Vekel, startled. 'What do you mean?'

'I freed him.'

'When?'

'After the cattle-raid. The attempted cattle-raid.'

I gave Vekel a sharp look. This gave weight to my suspicion. 'Why then?'

'He proved his worth yet again, preventing the cattle from stampeding.'

'That's not enough to warrant being freed.' Quietly, I said, 'It was killing Glum, wasn't it?'

Feigned shock. 'I have no idea what you're talking about.'

'Pull the other leg, it has a bell on,' I said.

Vekel made no acknowledgment. Then, 'He was my thrall. It was my decision.'

'Except you used my hacksilver to buy him!'

'No. *Your* portion paid for our comrades to get pissed, remember? *Mine* went towards Lalo's purchase.'

I gave up on that line of attack. 'When were you going to tell me?'

An elegant up-down of his shoulders. 'You found out now.'

'Vekel!' I was being unreasonable, and I knew it, but he was so hard to read, to understand.

He smirked.

And smug, I thought. I was about to shove him arse first into the ditch, when—

'No horseplay. We are not boys in Linn Duachaill any longer.'

'I know.'

'Act like it then. The others must see me *only* as a vitki, someone to be feared.'

It was preferable, I decided, that the others respected Vekel and his power. 'Very well. But know that I know you're not above trickery when it suits.'

He threw me a look.

'You predicted Glum's death, then brought it about yourself, or should I say, got Lalo to do it. Ketil is next, I assume.'

His eyes were slits. 'Perhaps. Only the Norns can tell.'

'Which one are you then – Urd, Verdandi or Skuld?' I shot back.

'Are you going to tell anyone?'

'Of course not!'

'That is good.'

I wanted to ask more questions, but Vekel went into one of his silences.

We did not talk for the rest of the journey.

Crimp-beard and Eyjolf found something else to agree on: going to the Black Pool first, not to Sigtrygg's great hall. There was a pleased, not to say a little relieved, reunion with Imr on *Brimdýr*. Asgeir's *Sea-stallion* was moored alongside our longship; he had also safely returned. They had been in port for four days, Imr told us, and beginning to wonder if our group had come to harm.

'We knew you had taken the cattle – the pens were empty – but after that . . .'

'Just as we had no idea about you,' said Crimp-beard. 'Did you capture many thralls?'

A wolf-grin. 'Close to two hundred, all told. We were low in the water coming back. Sold already, they are. Sigtrygg was pleased with his cut. You will be with yours too.'

'Did many fall?'

'A handful.' He mentioned a few names, but none were men I called friends.

Crimp-beard grimaced. 'It could have been worse.'

'And you? Ívarr's pens were a decent size – you must have had the whole herd.'

'Not quite.'

'How many head then?'

'About forty-five.'

Imr's lip curled. 'Is that all?'

'It is a long road from Vedrarfjord to Dyflin.'

Even trying his best, Crimp-beard was shit at lying. Imr had the truth out of him in no time, heard the sorry story of how we had been caught between Brooch-wearer and his Osraighe-men, and on the other side of the Siúr, Ívarr's warband. How we had been forced to hand over the best beasts.

'He took three dozen?' Imr swore. 'Why didn't you fight?'

'We might have beaten them off,' said Crimp-beard, 'but a lot of the crew would have died, and the cattle would have scattered to the four winds. This way, there were no casualties, and we saved forty-five kine.'

'No men lost at all?' Imr was surprised.

'There was one – Glum – he was killed a few nights later by cattle-raiders. They didn't take any of the herd,' Crimp-beard quickly added.

'Glum was a miserable shit,' said Imr. 'Amazing that his mother knew what to name him when he was a babe.'

Crimp-beard snorted, and I decided, neither of them liked him. Thinking of Ketil, I glanced at Vekel, whose expression was smooth as fresh-fallen snow. He was expert at hiding his emotions and real motives. Even if there was an element of trickery to his art, he had real power too. I was glad to be his friend, not his enemy.

'Well, vitki,' Imr said to Vekel. 'You were right about the raid. Lots of thralls, bloodshed, but not too many dead. You were wrong about the cattle, but I suppose you cannot see every movement of the Norns' fingers on the threads.'

'Even so.'

Imr grunted. 'And the blámaðr didn't bring any ill fortune upon you?'

'He was useful,' said Crimp-beard. 'Right good with livestock, he is. Worth keeping around, I'd say.'

'Good enough.' Imr didn't seem to care one way or another, which suggested that his desire to throw Lalo overboard had not come from true fear, more dislike of the unknown.

'He is no longer a thrall,' said Vekel.

'Eh?' A swarm of flies could have flown into Imr's open mouth.

Vekel explained, calm and confident, what he had done. 'Lalo will stay with me, as is the custom, but he is not a slave. He is to be treated accordingly.'

It was common knowledge that the status of freedmen was only one ladder rung above that of thralls, but Imr wasn't about to antagonise his vitki, so he nodded in agreement. His attention soon moved on: 'I see Asgeir and Eyjolf disembarking. They'll be going to Sigtrygg. Come on! Otherwise the mangy dogs will take all the credit.'

Once-was-a-warrior brought us into Sigtrygg's presence, his swagger no different to the first time.

Artalach spotted us first, and came running. 'Ball-squeezer, you're back!'

'Lord.' I bowed.

'Were you at Vedrarfjord with Asgeir and Imr?'

'I was, lord.'

'You were part of the group who seized the kine?'

'Indeed, lord,' I said, thinking, he's a sharp one. He listens in on Sigtrygg's conversations.

'Your pardon, lord,' said Once-was-a-warrior politely, 'but your father is waiting.'

Artalach made a face, but let us continue towards Sigtrygg's dais.

The king spoke to me first. 'S-squeeze any m-more b-balls in V-V-Vedrarfjord?' His voice was pitched to carry. Asgeir and Eyjolf glowered at me – they had not forgotten Biarn – but genuine amusement rippled through the rest of the hall. Artalach was particularly entertained.

It was tempting to mock Sigtrygg's stutter, as I might have done in childhood. Instead I muttered that I hadn't had the chance.

He wasn't even listening. 'How many cattle have you for me?' he demanded of Imr and Asgeir.

Sigtrygg's face soon grew sour. His cut was one third. 'F-fifteen beasts,' he grumbled. 'I could get m-more by s-sending Artalach and his friends into Midhe one night.'

Artalach puffed himself up like a fighting cock. I could almost see him trying to do just that. Stranger things had happened.

'What happened to the rest of Ívarr's herd?' asked the king.

Again the sorry tale had to be told. Crimp-beard pitched it as well as he could, making much of the fact that we had only lost Glum. Eyjolf emphasised the Osraighe-men's numbers. Sigtrygg was having none of it, and said as much. 'You should have f-fought. F-from the s-sound of it, you would only have had G-Gilla's m-men to deal with. Í-Ívarr's lot didn't have the b-balls to cross the river.' His stutter, I noticed, got worse when he was angry.

'Casualties would have been heavy, lord,' said Imr.

A contemptuous *phhhh*.

In the minds of kings, ordinary mortals' lives were of no conse-quence compared to wealth and riches, I decided. Imr and Asgeir took the disrespect without reaction. Eyjolf also managed to keep an impas-sive face, but Crimp-beard, proud, bristled. Vekel laid a hand on his arm, unseen, and he quietened.

'If there had been a battle, lord,' Vekel said, smooth as butter, 'the kine would have stampeded in every direction. We would have been lucky to get a quarter of them back.'

'If that,' I added.

Imr rowed in, mentioning the almost-seventy thralls given to the king as his cut. Fine slaves they were too, Asgeir went on, young and hale, desirable to anyone.

'There's no point c-crying over spilt m-milk,' said Sigtrygg, and I thought with relief he was going to leave it at that. If he demanded more than his share, Vekel whispered in my ear, no longship captain would want to serve under his banner.

Sigtrygg addressed Imr and Asgeir. 'Y-you are to divide the c-cattle equally?'

'Yes, lord.'

'As I th-thought. Imr, I shall have your b-beasts – that will give me thirty.'

'My lord? I don't understand.'

'That is none of my concern.'

'Why am I to be punished and not Asgeir?' Angry, Imr forgot to – or deliberately didn't – add the word 'lord'.

'No messenger has come from Máel Sechnaill demanding Asgeir's head, as well as those of two of his men.'

I could not help looking at Vekel. I had worried about Ashild since leaving, but away from Linn Duachaill, Cormac's threats to *me* had soon faded away. That, I realised, had been foolish.

Imr kept a straight face. 'Why would Máel do that, lord?'

'O-One of his s-sons was badly handled at L-Linn Duachaill. He was bandied about, like a f-for-sale thrall, and his life threatened by a local s-smith, a man with a d-dog by the name of N-Niall.' Sigtrygg's gaze fell on me. 'What h-have you to say, B-Ball-squeezer?'

My throat closed. If I lied, and Imr did not, I was in deep trouble with Sigtrygg, but telling the truth would result in the same thing.

'Well?'

There was no difference between the frying pan and the fire, I decided, and began to tell my tale. A little to my surprise, Sigtrygg listened without interrupting. Artalach paid close attention too.

I held back nothing. Booleying cattle, the encounter with Stoat Face at Mainistir Bhuithe. Returning home to find my sword gone, and my father dying of a murder-wound inflicted by Cormac. Vekel and I travelling to Inis Cró, and leaving again without exacting vengeance. Seeing Stoat Face for a second time. *Brimdýr*'s presence at Linn Duachaill; dealings with Imr. Cormac's arrival, the killing of Kalman, and the confrontation that had come after. The bargain made with Imr as I stood with my blade at Cormac's throat.

The last detail elicited a gasp from Artalach.

Sigtrygg liked it too. 'A h-hard neck, you have, B-Ball-squeezer.'

'I had nothing to lose, lord,' I said.

He turned on Imr. 'I c-can understand why B-Ball-squeezer and the v-vitki earned Máel's enmity, but y-you did not have to. Why did you not just g-give them up?'

'Cormac's men killed one of mine, lord. It did not matter who the little shit was – vengeance had to be taken. Handing Ball-squeezer and the vitki over to him afterwards would have felt too much like arse-licking.'

'And you did not think to tell me of this?'

Imr shifted from one foot to the other, a rare display of uncertainty.

'I should deliver the three of you to Máel.' Sigtrygg's fox-eyes were flat and cold.

There it was. The threads of three lives: mine, Vekel's and Imr's, with the Norns' shears poised to shift them forever, and not in a good way.

'Let us continue to serve you, lord,' said Imr, 'and I will deliver to you riches untold. *Brimdýr* will be the scourge of Ériu's coastline, I swear.'

Sigtrygg sucked on the marrow of that, and it seemed he liked the taste. 'Riches untold, eh?'

'You will see, lord.'

A sniff. 'Very well. I will tell Máel that I know nothing of the men he seeks. He is busy enough not to pursue such a trivial matter, I wager.'

Artalach's face gladdened.

'Thank you, lord.' Imr even sounded genuine, though the words must have galled worse than a burr under a saddle blanket.

Sigtrygg wasn't finished.

He beckoned, and we came closer. When Artalach did the same, Sigtrygg did not send him away, but warned him to keep silent about what he heard, on pain of a severe beating. The boy promised earnestly that his lips were sealed.

Sigtrygg muttered, 'I w-want you to raid C-Cluain Mhic Nóis next.'

He mangled the Irish words, but I knew where he meant. A monastery built on the great river Sionainn, it had been sacked countless times by Irish and Norse alike. It was also allied to the high king, which showed his intentions towards Máel remained malicious. There had never been any intention of surrendering the three of us, I thought, seeing the same bitter realisation in Imr's face. We had been used.

Asgeir was more focused on the task, and the potential risks. 'I thought you worshipped the White Christ, lord.'

Sigtrygg made the sign of the cross, as if that would excuse him from ordering the plundering of a sacred place. 'The church will receive its share of what's taken.'

Maybe this was why the fleshy-faced monk wasn't present, I thought. The king's donation would be a token, and stick in the gullet of any cleric, even a brown-nose like the monk. He might even feel moved to tell Máel what Sigtrygg was up to.

'And what share will I get, lord?' asked Imr, recovering some confidence. 'We will not raid for nothing.'

'You will not go empty-handed. One fourth.'

Imr bridled to learn that Asgeir would get one third, as before, but he had the wits not to protest any further.

Sigtrygg was fox-shrewd, I decided. A single leech did not hurt that much, and a quarter of the plunder was better than none. Give Imr and the *Brimdýr*'s crew any less, however, and he risked them sailing away, choosing to be their own masters.

I caught the king looking at me sidelong, and wondered if Vekel and I were to be an offering to Máel. It might be you alone, a voice said in my head. Sigtrygg isn't going to get rid of a vitki, but you're not worth anything.

'Have you heard the tale of how Stormcrow – Ball-squeezer to you, lord – came by the sword that was stolen by Máel's son Cormac?'

Vekel's mind-reading was eerie. There was goose skin on my arms again.

'Do I care?' Sigtrygg had what he wanted; there was no more need to humour.

'You might, lord.' Vekel put a light emphasis on the word 'might'.

The king's expression became sly again. 'Very well. Tell me.'

Artalach came closer to hear.

Half-embarrassed, half-proud, I listened as Vekel related my discovery of the head-cloven corpse on the beach, and how I had taken the sword with the approval of one of Oðin's ravens.

'You saw this yourself?' asked Sigtrygg. 'This is not some story, expanded on with each telling, that you heard third- or fourth-hand?'

'I saw it all, lord,' said Vekel, his tone reverential. 'I saw the raven land on the body. Rather than attack the eyes, as you would expect, it pecked at the sword hilt. I saw Stormcrow approach slowly, with deference, heard him speak to the raven. It did not fly away, no, it hopped onto the sand, and watched, as close as we are to you, while he took the sword. It croaked at him too.'

Artalach's expression was stunned.

Sigtrygg was holding his Thor's hammer amulet. 'Anything else?'

'Other than Oðin's sacred bird offering a sword to Stormcrow?' Vekel chided.

Sigtrygg laughed. 'It was a remarkable thing to have witnessed.' To me, he said, 'Speak.'

'I saw the blade first, lord. I was about to take it when the raven landed on the corpse.' I heard muttering, could guess what the king's warriors were saying, that they would have left well alone. 'I said that I would offer myself to Oðin if I could have the sword.'

'Out loud?'

'Yes, lord. I spoke to the raven. I swore an oath to Oðin.'

Another gasp from Artalach.

A slow shake of the king's head. 'B-Ball-squeezer I named you, but S-Stormcrow is your rightful name.'

Like that, I knew Sigtrygg would not sell me out to Máel. I also knew, from the questions he asked, that if I ever came into possession of the sword and the king found out, he would take it from me.

When I thanked Vekel later for weaving in the story, I mentioned this.

He enquired if I would rather have been dunted in the back of the head on a dark night and carried off to Dún na Sciath, there to be delivered into Cormac's hands.

There was only one answer to that.

And, as Vekel warned, Sigtrygg's forbearance would only last as long as it suited him. If word came that Máel would pay good silver for our hides, the king would easily enough forget he was a vitki, and that I was Oðin-favoured.

It was a sobering thought.

CHAPTER SEVENTEEN

Cluain Mhic Nóis, on the Sionainn river

Dawn would not be long coming. Off to my right, where sky met land, I detected a tinge of rosy pink. *Brimdýr* nosed upstream, faint plashes coming from the oars as they rose and fell. We had practised this the day before, Karli and Imr stalking up and down, watching intently until everyone got it right, quiet enough. The crew of Asgeir's *Sea-stallion* had done it too, the two longships beating up and down a stretch of water a good distance downriver from the monastery. Bogland, empty of people, it had been sufficiently far to prevent a turf-cutting peasant from running to Cluain Mhic Nois with a warning.

We had set out in the middle of the night, and rowed until buildings could be discerned on the marshy shore. They were impossible to miss, even in the half gloom. It was flat terrain, the monastery and surrounding settlement sprawled across a large area.

Peace still reigned, if you discounted the two crowing cocks vying with each other for supremacy. By Imr and Asgeir's calculation, we would land just as the monks were about to get up for the second service of the day. It didn't much matter if they were wrong, Ulf had joked earlier, because bald girls didn't know how to fight. Attacking a monastery, Thorstein explained, was a bit like taking sweets from a child. All they did was cry.

Even though the monks were defenceless, I had elected to wear my mail shirt. I had ignored the jibes thrown by Ketil, jerking my head at Crimp-beard, Thorstein, Hrafn and Coal-biter, who had done the same. That had quieted Ketil. Glancing across the narrow gap between *Brimdýr* and *Sea-stallion*, I noted that Asgeir's warriors were also clad in just tunics and breeks. Some hadn't even bothered to don their helmets.

'Don't say "It's been a good day",' Kleggi whispered behind me.

'"Till sundown!"' I replied, amused, as my oar came out of the water.

'Don't say "She's a good wife",' Kleggi softly continued.

'"Till she's buried!" More men had heard, and responded.

'Shut your traps!' hissed Imr.

I choked back a laugh, and received a clout across the head. Kleggi got kicked in the back.

'Quiet, all of you!' Imr ordered.

'What does it matter?' Ketil lifted an arse cheek off his chest and let out a thunderous fart. 'That for the Christ-loving monks!'

Imr glowered, but Karli's low-delivered announcement to dig in the starboard oars and lift to the larboard stopped him from saying more. Men obeyed, *Brimdýr* turned towards the bank, and a moment later, she came to a gentle halt in the reedbeds, disturbing an indignant water rail. *Sea-stallion*, manoeuvring in with Asgeir standing tall at the prow, also stopped.

Ulf was first over the side, lowering himself into the waist-high water. I handed down his shield and broad axe; he gave me a predatory smile and began wading shoreward. The monks weren't to blame for Havard's death, I thought, but they were going to pay, nonetheless. Crimp-beard and Thorstein were close on Ulf's heels; so too were Hrafn, Coal-biter and Karli.

'Just going to stand there and watch?' Vekel's tone was waspish.

Without a word, I gripped the side planking, and swung over and down. The water was colder than I liked, the bottom sucking and muddy. I took my shield from a grinning Lalo; two axes and my seax were in my belt.

'Stay in the ship,' I told Lalo.

Vekel chuckled as he joined me. 'There's no chance of that.'

Sure enough, Lalo clambered down, and shorter than either of us, ended up chest-deep in the river. 'Very c-cold,' he said, teeth chattering.

We pushed into the shallows, surrounded by our comrades. On the bank, I saw that Lalo also had a seax on his belt. Vekel was fearsome-looking: daubed-white face, and heavy black colouring around his eyes. Despite his lack of weapons, I thought, monks would run from him, screaming.

To my amusement, the water was deeper where *Sea-stallion* had come in. The first warrior to disembark vanished beneath the surface and came up, spluttering. He had to swim ashore. I could hear Asgeir swearing, and ordering anyone wearing a mail shirt to take it off, unless they wanted to drown.

A loose circle gathered around Imr, who was also in armour. He had donned it just before leaving *Brimdýr*. In the lightening air, he was quite a sight, spectacled helmet, fine sword, painted limewood shield, colourful trousers.

'Spread out. Move fast, head for the big buildings – that's where the riches will be. Keep any mead or beer until later. You can get pissed on *Brimdýr*.'

The tense faces relaxed; many laughed quietly.

Imr glanced at Vekel, and received a grave nod. The omens were good, Vekel had told him the night before. Our raid would be successful.

'Go on!' Imr ordered. '*Sea-stallion*'s crew are still arsing about. This is a real chance for us. Regroup here by the time it's full day. We'll get on the river again fast.'

Men loped off in twos and threes towards the settlement. Beyond it was the monastery, set back some distance from the river. I heard Ketil complaining that there was no need to hurry. 'Oðin's sake, they're only monks!'

Vekel and Lalo came with me. Thorstein joined us, which was surprising. Then a memory tickled. I had noticed them together on *Brimdýr*, more than once, but assuming that Thorstein wanted a reading of the future or some such, had paid no attention. There had been looks, though, and men talking behind their hands. Now, for the first time in my life, I wondered if Vekel had feelings for someone. Feelings of the heart, that is. I cast a look. He and Thorstein were walking side by side, and talking to each other in low voices. Lalo dogged their heels, seax in hand.

A shout in Irish carried from the houses ahead. Cut short, it turned into a gurgling shriek. Another cry, another abrupt end, and it really began. A woman screamed. A dog barked, the short, frantic barks that signal utter fear. Shouts rang out, men, calling to each other.

I pulled out an axe and broke into a run. I wasn't really looking for a fight, and I had no great desire to kill anyone – I just wanted silver, and gold, if I could get it. It was hard to see how bloodshed could be avoided, however. During our voyage around the southern coast of Mumhan and into the mouth of the Sionainn's estuary, most conversations had revolved around previous attacks the crew had made with Imr. All had been violent.

From the narrow gap between two straw-thatched houses, a man came charging at full pelt. His spear was aimed at my chest. There was time only to duck behind my shield. A massive impact; the iron point rammed through the limewood, and punched into my chest. I staggered, and instinctively swung my axe. The man, struggling to drag free his spear, didn't even see. The axe blade took him where neck meets shoulder. He was clad in only a tunic. Flesh split open. Bone smashed. Warm red blood misted over my shield and face. The man went down, a rag doll, a half-cut-asunder corpse.

I looked at what I had done, and my stomach roiled.

'You would never make a butcher,' said Thorstein drolly, stepping over the dead man as if he were nothing but a rock.

Lalo didn't look; Vekel said, 'Fool. What was he thinking?'

'He wasn't,' I replied, pulling the spear from my shield, glad that my belly was empty. 'He was probably just defending his home, or his family.'

'Better to run,' said Vekel.

'Run,' said Lalo, but he sounded unhappy.

This is a warrior's life, I told myself. A raider's life. It's what you always wanted.

The horrors continued. In the settlement, houses were burning and people dying. A dog lay in a pathetic jumble of limbs, head severed from its body. There was a child about the same age as Artalach sprawled on top of its dead mother; their faces bore expressions of terror. A pig ran past, squealing blue murder. A naked crone haunch-rocked back and forth, cradling the bleeding stump of one arm with the other.

Another man appeared in a house doorway. He ran at me with a pitchfork. Face twisted with rage or grief, I could not be sure, he lunged the tool at my face. More prepared now, I leaned to the side, the pitchfork skidding off my mailed shoulder. Propelled forward by his own momentum, the man came within reach. An instinctive axe swipe took off the top of his head. A neat disc of hair and bone flopped onto the ground beside him.

I was angry now, aggravated by the stupidity of those who attacked armoured warriors with pitchforks and old hunting spears. Was there no one in the settlement, I asked Vekel, who could fight?

Probably not, came the answer.

I decided there was no point entering any of the one-roomed houses, which were miserable and poor-looking. Anything valuable would be in the monastery, and plenty of the crew were ahead of us. Asgeir's party could not be far behind either. Breaking into a ground-eating lope, with Vekel and Lalo following, I found the gate in the low earthen rampart. It was open. A short distance inside lay the door-man, a monk, dead. He had been going to raise the alarm. What difference it would have made, I had no idea, because the *Brimdýr*'s crew were running amok. Monks charged hither and thither, wailing and calling on the White Christ for help, and if they came near, dying.

Crimp-beard, a barrel balanced on one shoulder, was arguing with Hrafn about which church would have the most treasure. Hrafn's acid reply was that gold and silver bought more mead than one pissing little barrel contained, and they had better move fast, else there'd be none left.

I didn't go for the largest building, cathedral in size, which would already be mobbed. Instead I headed towards a small, almost square church behind it. I twisted the latch, and pushed. To my amusement, the door, strengthened with iron knobs, wasn't even locked. It swung open, revealing a bare, stone-flagged room with an altar at the far end, and behind that, a large cross on the wall. Below that was an inset box. I knew what it was; my mother had dragged me to enough masses when I was small. It had an odd name, the tabernacle, and inside, if I was lucky, would be at least one silver chalice.

'Who is that?' Lalo was pointing at the figure nailed to the cross.

'The White Christ,' said Vekel, making the sign against bad luck. 'Have you never been in a church?'

An indignant shake of his head. 'My owner in Dyflin tried. Dragged me to one. I bit his hand, and ran back to the tavern. I have my own gods.' A perplexed expression. 'He is nailed to it. Why is he suffering?'

'Odd, I know,' said Vekel. 'He did it for those who worship him.'

'A god, suffer for us?' Lalo muttered something annoyed-sounding in his own tongue.

'So they say. Three days he was on the cross, wearing a crown of thorns, and only being given sour wine to drink.'

'Oðin did it for nine days and nights on Yggdrasil,' I said.

'That was for his own benefit, to gain understanding of the runes.'

'He's still a better god.'

'Obviously,' said Vekel.

I offered up a silent prayer, and ignored the White Christ, who seemed to be staring at me. I wasn't about to ask his permission. A few raps from my axe head shattered the lock on the tabernacle. Inside, to my delight, were two chalices, one larger and more ornate.

'What are they?' asked Lalo.

'This' – I lifted the smaller – 'is used to hold wine that the priest drinks during mass.'

'Wine? Mass?'

'Not now.' Annoyed that I had not thought something to carry valuables in, I went to shove the chalice into my belt.

'Here.' Vekel had his leather bag wide open. 'We don't want the others to see.'

I handed it over, and took out the bigger chalice, marvelling. A beaten silver plate served as a cover. Around the vessel's rim ran a band of gold, decorated at intervals with dark red stones. Gold also encompassed the outside of the bowl's bottom, another fat band shaped the circle of the flat base.

'That is worth a fortune.' Vekel, not easily impressed, was.

Mesmerised, I did not answer. The chalices I had seen used were simple things, dross compared to this.

'Quickly, before someone comes,' said Vekel.

I lifted the cover and tipped. Little white discs spilled onto the floor. Lalo was entranced. 'What are those?'

'Communion bread.' A blank look, so I explained, 'Sacred bread for the White Christ followers to eat.'

'Food? Is not much.'

'It's not meant to be,' said Vekel. 'They think it is the White Christ's flesh.'

Lalo recoiled, and kicked a few away with his foot.

'It is strange,' I said, stashing the large chalice alongside the smaller. The only other thing in the tabernacle was a long-handled silver strainer; I took that too.

'The same might be said about hanging an ox carcass from a tree, or a man,' said Vekel.

'Those are offerings to the gods,' I said, offended.

'You and I know that, but a White Christ worshipper who chances upon a sacred grove thinks it is barbaric savagery.'

'What are you doing?' The fearful but determined voice belonged to a tonsured monk in the doorway. He came into the room, protuberant eyes fixed on the open, empty tabernacle. 'Those vessels belong to God and this monastery.'

'They're ours now,' I said, striding forward.

He had courage, that bald girl, and he came to meet me.

Thoughts swirled around my head. The monk didn't have a weapon, but he would try to impede me. I could easily split his head open, as I had with the second man in the settlement, but the thought of killing someone unarmed, a monk sworn to peace, did not appeal. I decided to chest-smack him with my shield. He might suffer broken ribs, but that was better than dying.

'What have we here?' In strolled Eyjolf, and an ill-featured warrior I recognised from *Sea-stallion*. Both their axes were bloody, and Eyjolf's face was crimson-splashed.

The monk, caught between us, quailed. Eyjolf smiled, and crossed himself. The monk, pleased, did the same.

'Well?' demanded Eyjolf.

'We found nothing,' I said, and beckoning to Vekel and Lalo, walked past the monk.

'The box in the wall was empty?'

'It was,' I said sourly. 'Someone got here before us.'

Eyjolf scowled, and that might have been that, but for the fool of a monk.

'He's lying! The sorcerer has the holy treasures in his bag!'

Eyjolf's expression darkened. 'I should have known you for a liar, Ball-squeezer. Empty it, vitki!'

Vekel stared at Eyjolf. He said nothing.

'Don't make me hurt you, vitki!' Eyjolf took a step forward; so did his leering crony, Ugly Bastard.

'You'll have to come through me first.' It was strange, but I felt no fear. Instead I hefted my axe, and thought, Eyjolf's brains on the blade will be a good thing.

Eyjolf stalked closer.

'God will reward you!' The monk actually clapped his hands with excitement. Afterwards, I concluded that he had mistaken Eyjolf's mockery in crossing himself for reverence. That in turn made the monk think Eyjolf would help him against me and Vekel. The halfwit was still smiling when Ugly Bastard unseamed him with his seax. A horrific cry of pain, and the monk collapsed amid his own entrails.

'Give me what's in the bag, ragr-man, and you can all walk out of here alive,' said Eyjolf. 'Even the blámaðr.'

'Not blámaðr,' said Lalo, and there was a fury I had never heard in his voice. 'Mandinka.'

'Nithing is a better name for you, blámaðr.' Eyjolf spat on the floor.

Vekel also looked angry now. He and I fronted up to Eyjolf and Ugly Bastard; Lalo went skirting around the side of the room, his intent clearly to get behind them.

I could taste my fear. Eyjolf and Ugly Bastard weren't wearing mail shirts, but they were experienced warriors. I was not, and Vekel had only his staff. As for Lalo, well, he was a slip of a thing.

'I'll kill Eyjolf, then help you,' I said quietly.

'Stay alive long enough for Lalo to reach you,' came Vekel's answer.

There was no time for a response. Eyjolf was coming at me, his accompaniment the eviscerated monk's awful moaning.

Bang. Eyjolf's bearded axe bit into my shield. He wrenched, pulling me forward even as it came free. I hewed at him, my axe blade cutting a deep notch in his shield rim. I punched forward with my own shield, fast, trying to unbalance him, and then Thor's hammer Mjölnir hit my head. Knees buckling, I cut sideways at one of Eyjolf's legs as I fell. I saw blood spray, and thought he cried out before darkness took me.

Water. Cold water, on my face. Helpless, I inhaled some. After a bout of paroxysmic coughing, which made the pounding in my skull twice as bad, I came to. Cold stone pressed against my back; I was lying on the church floor. Vekel was kneeling over me, my upturned helmet in his hands. Lalo was perched on my other side, looking concerned.

'What happened?' I mumbled.

'Eyjolf knocked you senseless. Can you sit up?'

I tried, and could. Eyes slowly focusing, I saw Eyjolf and Ugly Bastard lying close by. Neither was moving. They weren't asleep either; the guddling pools of scarlet were evidence of that. The monk was almost dead. 'What happened?'

Lalo answered. 'Vekel threw his bag at the ugly one. He tried to catch it, and Vekel hit him with the iron staff. He stumbled, and I cut his throat from behind.'

I stared. This former slave could have been talking about slicing a joint of meat. I found my voice. 'And Eyjolf?'

'You cut his leg badly. He was lamed, couldn't move fast. Lalo and I finished him off. Not bad for a ragr-man and a blámaðr.' Vekel stood, and offered a hand. 'On your feet.'

I stood, and the world spun. If Lalo hadn't grabbed an arm, I might have fallen. 'I feel as if I drank an entire barrel of beer last night,' I said, my tongue fat and hard to use.

'You'll be all right.' Vekel picked up my helmet. 'Put this on – it's already proved its worth once today.'

I eyed the helmet with respect. An axeblade length dent ran along its top helmet from front to back. It had saved my life, no question. I put it on gingerly, noticing that the felt and wool liner was soaked through. 'You scooped water from the font,' I said, realising.

'And poured it on your head,' said Lalo with evident enjoyment.

Oddly, I thought of my mother, and how horrified she would have been at the profaning of holy water so. I didn't let myself consider what she would have made of me helping to sack Cluain Mhic Nóis, nor of my stealing sacred vessels.

We hurried outside.

Smoke rose to the skies; several monastery buildings were aflame. A group of the *Brimdýr*'s crew was watching the cathedral burn; the barrels of mead stacked nearby another source of their enjoyment.

I rolled my eyes. It was as if Imr had said nothing. To many, getting pissed was just as important as finding treasure.

Booo. Booo. Dazed or not, I recognised Olaf Twin-brows's vallhorn. He wasn't making music now either. *Booo. Booo.* The sound went on and on, a clear alarm.

Vekel had heard it too, and Lalo.

So, to my intense relief, had those watching the conflagration.

'Trouble,' said Ulf, draining a cup and wiping his mouth.

'It's coming from over there,' I said, pointing east.

'We had best get back to the ship,' said Vekel.

'No,' said Ulf, annoyed. 'We go to find Twin-brows.'

Vekel didn't argue for once.

Forming up with the swiftness of a wolf pack, Thorstein and

Crimp-beard led the way. A dozen more joined as we ran; a rough headcount came to about thirty-five. Hearing the racket, seeing us, a score of warriors from *Sea-stallion* came too.

'Did you foresee this?' I demanded of Vekel.

No answer.

He hadn't, I realised, which was why he looked as if he'd drunk a bowl of sour milk.

Twin-brows met us before we were halfway to the furthest limit of the monastery wall. He came at the run, slowing now and again to sound the alarm.

'What is it?' Crimp-beard called out.

'Warriors, horsemen and foot.'

'How many?'

'Two hundred at least.'

'Someone saw us yesterday, and went for help,' said Thorstein, swearing.

No one was up for that fight, drunk or not.

A few resentful glances were thrown at Vekel, who pretended not to notice, and then we ran for *Brimdýr*. Weighed down by my mail, head still pounding, I could not keep up. There was nothing wrong with my ears, however, so I heard the shouts from the ship at the same time as everyone else. It was Imr, and he was roaring as if his life depended upon it.

Which, as the large group of warriors approaching from the west came into sight, it did.

CHAPTER EIGHTEEN

The second group of newcomers, men from Midhe by their shield designs, were too close to allow us to embark safely on *Brimdýr*. *Sea-stallion* was behind us, which meant that Asgeir and his warriors were protected to some extent. They made no attempt to join us, which ought not to have been a surprise yet still was. The whole stinking lot of them clambered into their ship as fast as they could.

We had to stand and fight, though, else a wholescale slaughter of the *Brimdýr's* crew would have resulted. Imr ordered a shieldwall. Under normal circumstances, I would have been in the second, or more likely, the third rank, but being one of the only warriors wearing a mail shirt, I was ordered into the front rank. Ignoring the pain in my head as best I could, I took my place beside Crimp-beard and Thorstein. Imr was on my other side; Kleggi, who had seen the enemy coming and thrown on his mail shirt, was beyond him. A few others came off *Brimdýr* as well, but I wasn't trying to recognise faces, I was staring at the Irish, who were preparing to attack. A hundred at least, there must have been, about half mounted, half on foot.

'The horses will charge first, eh?' I asked.

A snort from Thorstein. 'They will all come together.'

'Try and break us the first time,' added Crimp-beard.

'Banki!' roared Imr.

'Aye?' He was on *Brimdýr*.

'Are you ready?'

'Aye, me and the other lads with bows.'

'When they come, shoot over our heads—'

'Aim for the horses, I know!'

Imr grunted, satisfied or irritated, it was hard to tell. 'If Banki and the rest do their job, we'll charge ourselves, d'you hear?'

It seemed insane – however many of us there were against a far larger force – but Crimp-beard hoomed, and Thorstein banged his axe off his iron shield boss. Others copied him, and as the loud metallic noise filled my ears, my fear receded. 'Oðin!' I shouted. 'O-ðin!'

Men snarled in agreement. Next thing, everyone in the shieldwall was roaring the god's name, and rhythmically battering his shield boss. 'O-ÐIN!' we shouted. Clatter. Clatter. 'O-ÐIN!'

I almost forgot that if we broke, there was little chance of boarding *Brimdýr*. A watery death in the Sionainn beckoned instead.

As if spurred by our challenge, the Irish riders clapped heels to their mounts' flanks and drove forward. The warriors came after, in an uneven, screaming tide of shields and spears.

The distance between us halved in the blink of an eye. I could see the Irishmen's expressions, could pick out individual horses' markings.

Shoot, Banki, I thought.

An arrow hurtled over my head, then another. Four more followed, one for every bowman on *Brimdýr*. Down the arrows came, into the mass of animals and men. They could not miss. Struck in the neck, one of the lead horses staggered, barging into another. It stumbled, and an arrow hit its rider, who lost control. Each shaft had a similar effect. A heartbeat later, another half dozen arrived.

'Boar snout!' Imr yelled.

Instructed by Thorstein, I formed up behind him and Imr. Crimp-beard, the biggest, stood beyond them, at the point. The others in mail shirts completed the left and right sides of the rough triangle; the warriors without armour were in the middle and back. Shields, and axes ready, we advanced towards the milling, disorganised Irish.

'Hold your position,' Thorstein told me. 'Remember what Ulf taught you.'

'Aye,' I said, determined not to let my comrades down, felling what I recognised afterwards as the hot surge of battle rage. For the same reason perhaps, my memories of the fight were splintered.

Crimp-beard's axe splitting the head of the first Irish warrior to come within reach, and his bellowing, triumphant laugh. A horse's thrashing leg knocking down its dismounted rider, and Thorstein burying his axe in the man's belly. Arrows from Banki and his comrades flighting in, landing among the Irish who had yet to close with us. A constant sweat-sting in my blinking eyes, a numbness in my fingers from tight-grasping my axe and shield grip. The snarling mouth of a warrior who charged me, and his shocked expression when my blade carved open his upper arm. The incessant screaming of an unarmoured man struck by a spear.

Our charge broke the Irish. They retreated in poor order. Battle-mad, I would have gone after; so would others, but Imr, wolf-wise, roared at us to hold. Back to the ship we went, moving as fast as men can when walking backwards, facing the enemy. This was Banki's saga moment, his and the other archers. They laid down such a volley of shafts that the Irish, rallied by their leaders, thought twice about attacking again.

Men pulled themselves on board, laughing like madmen, laughing like men who have braved the storm of steel and come out the other side. I stayed onshore with Crimp-beard, Thorstein and Hrafn, and several others. Together, straining, we heaved Brimdýr backwards, into deeper water. Karli bellowed that she was afloat, and men waiting on either side of the prow sent knotted ropes snaking down, and dragged us up one at a time. Sensing that we were going to escape, bravado swelling, I stayed behind until only Crimp-beard was left. We were chest-deep in the river now, and my feet were mud-sticking. Another few steps, I realised, and my heavy mail would drag me under. I no longer had the strength to swim with it.

'Come on, fool!' Thorstein was staring down from above.

Heaved upward, hands working the rope, feet walking the timbers, I obeyed. Standing square on the deck, seeing the Irish helpless on the bank, feeling Brimdýr turn – Karli was directing those at the oars – I realised I was going to live.

All at once, I had an overwhelming need to piss.

I wasn't the only one.

A row of men lined up, joking, throwing insults and arcing yellow streams of urine over the side in the direction of the Irish. Furious, still wanting to fight, they shouted threats of their own. Spears were hurled but fell short, vanishing into the Sionainn. Brimdýr was in midstream now, beyond reach, and as more warriors joined the rowers, she moved downstream, away from Cluain Mhic Nóis. In the distance, all oars out, prow aimed towards the sea, was Sea-stallion. I hoped it sprang a leak and took every warrior to the bottom.

Turning away, responding to Karli's demands for oarsmen, I noticed Hrafn sitting with his back to the mast, legs out in front. His face was grey, and worse, there was blood all over the planking. Vekel and Lalo were kneeling, their hands pressing in vain against Hrafn's thigh.

Worse was to come.

'Hey!' The shout came from the bank, and the voice was familiar.

No, I thought.

It was Ulf. Ulf, somehow left behind. Shouting as if we could turn *Brimdýr* around and go back.

The Irish weren't deaf. Men pointed, began to run towards him.

'Swim,' I roared. 'Swim!'

Ulf needed no encouragement. Tossing aside his shield, he plunged into the river.

I rushed to Karli. 'Stop rowing! It's Ulf!'

Karli went to the side, and swore. He rounded on the oarsmen. 'Stop! Back water!'

The risk of turning was too great. Some of the Irish had found coracles on the bank, and were coming downriver. All we could do was resist the current as much as possible, not move away at speed. It was not enough. Ulf, as I later learned, had taken a wound. Weakened, not a strong swimmer, he floundered perhaps half the distance to *Brimdýr* before his head went under.

Tears running down my cheeks, I made myself watch. His death, pointless, had to be honoured in some way.

A hand on my shoulder.

Half thinking myself still in battle, I whirled, reaching for my axe.

It was Karli, his face understanding. 'Can you row your oar alone, Stormcrow?'

'I can.' Palming my cheeks, I went to take my place.

By general consensus, we passed by Luimnech and Inis Cathaig without stopping, just as we had on the voyage in. Somewhere between Vedrarfjord and Dyflin in size, the twin settlement was also ruled by the Norse, but situated within Mumhan, its residents lived in fear of Brian Bóramha. They were likely to do us harm, Imr declared, or to send word of our presence.

Vekel was quick to join in. We had done well to escape once, he said. Testing the Norns again so soon would be downright foolish.

Mourning Ulf and Hrafn – who had died before the sun went down – and the others who had fallen, no one protested. There was grumbling, however, that Vekel should have known that the Irish were coming, that he should have warned us. It was no surprise that Ketil was chief among the grousers. Hearing him that night, anchored in the wide mouth of the Sionainn's estuary, Vekel took the bull by the horns and challenged Ketil. At once the men whom he'd been talking to slid their arses further away, which was encouraging.

It was impossible, Vekel shouted, pointing his iron staff at Ketil, to know every movement of the Norns' fingers on the thread of more than fifty men's lives. 'I am not a god, but a vitki,' he said. 'Do you know the difference?'

Men laughed, and Ketil flushed. 'Of course.'

'Best remember it then, lest you be cursed.' Vekel thrust the iron staff back and forth, and said lasciviously, 'Or take it like a ragr man.'

Ketil was furious to be insulted so, but no one was supporting him. He stitched his lip.

Better it would be, Vekel went on, to look for vengeance on Asgeir and his treacherous crew. If they had also stood their ground, the outcome of the battle would have been different. Rather than flee to the ship, we could have plundered the fallen Irish, and taken our time leaving. Ulf would not have been left behind, he said to loud approval. Perhaps others who had fallen might have reached *Brimdýr* also.

This was pure speculation, and disregarded the numbers of Irish, but it fell like spring rain on seedling crops. Names went around the ship, crew members who were gone. Svein Estridsson, the best singer on the ship. Hallfred, a likeable drunkard, who, I heard men saying, was probably still in one of the monastery's barns, sleeping off the barrel of beer he'd snaffled for himself. Steinunn, grumpy and bald, who had, despite his age, wielded a spear with a youth's dexterity.

Asgeir was to blame, Vekel said, Asgeir and the arse-wipe nithings who followed him. He looked at Imr, who growled approval. Vekel drew a deep breath, as if making up his mind about something, and then he said, 'There will be a reckoning. In blood.'

A sharp look from Imr. 'Retribution in Dyflin would be ill-advised. Sigtrygg would come down heavily on everyone.'

Vekel's smile was sly, conspiratorial. 'The king need know nothing of what happened. We can tell Asgeir not to feel bad too, that we would have done the same thing. Water under the bridge, we shall tell him. No hard feelings.'

'He won't believe that.'

'Throw a feast for him and his crew to celebrate the raid, and his misgivings will ease. Arrange another voyage for Sigtrygg with Asgeir, and an opportunity to strike will come.'

'Lull him into thinking we have forgotten,' said Imr, smiling.

'Precisely. The sweetest revenge is served cold.'

Only I noticed Vekel's eyes brush against Lalo's. Here it was, I thought, his trickery again.

It was no surprise to me when, off the Laighin coast several nights later, Ketil vanished while on watch. Goat-Banki, who had also been on duty, swore blind that he had seen nothing. There was immediate mention of his habit of falling asleep on sentry duty. Banki, thin-skinned at the best of times, threatened a holmgang with any accusers. If it had been Crimp-beard or Karli, or Thorstein, or anyone else popular who had disappeared, he might have had a taker, but Ketil, like Glum, had not been liked.

No one took up Banki's challenge.

No one mentioned the pair from that day forward either.

Another good thing that came of the raid on Cluain Mhic Nóis was a general acceptance of me by the crew. I wasn't just Ball-squeezer or Stormcrow any longer, or the man who had paid for a night's drinking in Dyflin. I had been in the boar's snout which had broken the Irish, who would have slain us all. My daily practice bouts – Thorstein had offered to take Ulf's place – were watched with interest now, and encouraging comments replaced the jibes of before. Crimp-beard gave me tips; so did Odd Coal-biter.

Imr was pleased with me as well because of the larger chalice and the strainer, handed over by Vekel. As Imr loudly announced, it was the match of anything else plundered from the monastery. Wily, he had asked if that was all we had found, but appeared to believe Vekel's vigorous assertion that it was. The smaller chalice, naturally, had been held back for us both to share. Cut up into hacksilver, it would more than make up for our cut of the fifteen cattle taken by Sigtrygg after Vedrarfjord.

Lalo was also making good strides forward. I initially assumed that

Vekel's describing our fight with Eyjolf had been to increase the crew's antagonism towards Asgeir and his warriors. Watching men's faces as the tale was told, though, I realised that it had other purposes. To prove that Lalo was not just a good stockman: he could also fight. When he offered to join me on my oar, where Ulf had sat, there were a few looks, but no protests or name-calling. Lean and strong, he learned fast, even joining in the choruses to Kleggi's stroke-keeping songs. It went on. A few nights later, Thorstein told Lalo to help himself from the cooking pot – as everyone else did – and there were no objections.

I wondered about declaring that he was part of the crew now, but decided laying it out as bald as that could wait. Gradual acceptance was better than ramming something down men's throats. I told Lalo quietly that he was one of us, however, and he beamed from ear to ear.

'You used a word at the monastery,' I said, curiosity returning with the memory. 'Man— . . .'

'Mandinka.' He tapped his chest. 'My people.'

'Mandinka.' I rolled the strange word around my mouth. Then, intrigued, I asked, 'What is Bláland like?'

'Where?'

How stupid, I thought, to call his land by its Norse name. 'The place you come from.'

A broad smile, a wistful look. 'Mandé.'

'Mandé?'

A nod.

'They say the sun is hot there, burning hot.'

'Oh yes, it is wonderful. You would not like it, Stormcrow!'

'You know me well.' When we stopped laughing, I asked what had been in my head since the first time I saw him. 'How is it that you ended up here, half a world away?'

His face grew serious.

'I am sorry. You don't have to say.'

'No – I tell you, Stormcrow. The Mandinka often fight with other tribes, like other peoples. Here it is Laighin and Mumhan, Osraighe, Connachta, Dyflin and Ulaidh. Where I come from, it is Mandinka, Soninke, Ligbi, Vai, Bissa. We steal cattle, sheep and goats from each other; slaves are taken too.' He saw my surprise, and said, resigned, 'It is the same everywhere. Usually, the slaves are sold to other tribes, but sometimes they are taken to the coast and bought by foreigners – Araboo, for the most part. That was my fate.'

'And the Araboo' – I stumbled over the word, which was unfamiliar – 'took you where?'

'Valland, you would call it.'

'From there to here is not so far.' I knew of the land of the Franks, and of the fine swords made there. It lay some days' sail from Ériu's southeastern coast.

'You would not think that during a storm on the open ocean.'

I gave him a rueful nod. Seasickness no longer troubled me much, but when it did, I was prone to decorating the deck with vomit. Lalo, on the other hand, could eat a full meal even as the wind threatened to rip the billowing sail free. He was also better travelled than I was, and in all likelihood, most of *Brimdýr*'s crew. Even Imr, who had visited Miklagard, might not have been as far. I noticed Lalo's expression, and trying to reassure, imagining what I wanted for myself, I said, 'One day you will return home.'

'Do not lie to me, even if you mean well.'

Wrongfooted, I said, 'It is *possible*. You made the voyage from your land, after all.'

'As a slave. What do you think would happen to me if I tried to take passage to Mandé? It is the Araboo who sail those waters, remember.'

I am a fool, I thought. 'They would enslave you again.'

'You see?' Lalo's voice was full of bitterness. 'I am free now, and yet I am not.'

He faced the same danger everywhere, I decided. It wasn't just from the Araboo and Franks. The Norse, Irish and Saxons would also see him as a blámaðr, an escaped slave. I tried to imagine how it felt to live with that truth, and didn't like it at all.

'You are a sea-wolf now,' I said.

He smiled, and it was as if he realised my own predicament.

Linn Duachaill was less than a day's voyage from Dyflin, yet I dared not go back there, not while Cormac, Máel's son, lived. And that could be decades.

I would never forget my father's murder, though.

Or the sword.

PART TWO
AD 999

CHAPTER NINETEEN

Near Gleann Máma, southwest of Dyflin

The wind howled down off the mountaintops, wild as any I had experienced at sea. I was grateful not to be on *Brimdýr*, because this gale would have had me emptying my guts. Snow skirled down, light enough for the moment, but the heaped grey-yellow clouds filling the sky threatened more. It was a cursedly stupid time of year to make war, I decided, pulling my gaze away and fixing it on the back of the next man along, Crimp-beard. Vekel was beside me, and Thorstein on his other side. No one was talking. We were part of the army's long column, somewhere between the front and the middle, and Dyflin lay a day and a half's march behind us. Warmth, shelter and a full belly were but distant memories. So was being in bed with my Irish thrall Dearbháil. And being able to feel my toes.

My face was all right, covered by a woollen arming cap and my helmet, with a long scarf wound round and round the lot, leaving only a narrow slit to see. I had on two thick wool tunics and a padded felt jacket, but the fourth layer was my mail. Parts – the arms, and the lower border, protruded beyond the limits of my cloak, the fifth layer – and soaking in the cold, transferred it through my garments. My legs had only a pair of woollen breeks for protection. Other than my head, I felt half-, or completely frozen.

There was no point grumbling. We were all in the same boat, and Brian's army was on the march towards us. Not only that, so was Máel Sechnaill's. Unforeseen, unpleasant and unwelcome, war had come in midwinter, and on two fronts.

Its beginnings, as was often the case, had been innocuous.

Two clans ruled northern Laighin, one led by Donnchadha Uí Dunchadha, the other by Máel-mórda Uí Faeláin. The latter was Sigtrygg's ally, but the former had orchestrated his ousting and replacement by Ívarr of Vedrarfjord five years before. Unsurprisingly, Sigtrygg had often punished Donnchadha since. Rather than quench the flames of discontent, it had driven Donnchadha into Brian Bóramha's arms. He in turn had sent a host from Mumhan to ravage Máel-mórda's lands the previous autumn. Sigtrygg's response to that was swift: Donnchadha had been languishing in Dyflin's gaol for three months now.

Now the whole world knew what Brian's answer – and Máel's – would be.

Dyflin's walls were not fit to withstand a siege, so staying put had not been an option. We were marching towards Gleann Máma, which lay south-southwest of Dyflin. According to Máel-mórda, this was the best place for battle. It was as well to have his support. With two of the most powerful kings in Ériu allied against us, and Sigtrygg able to rally perhaps twelve hundred warriors, Máel-mórda's men were sorely needed. The tally conducted in Dyflin had come to somewhere short of two thousand eight hundred.

We would be outnumbered at least two to one, perhaps more.

Failure to reach Gleann Máma, therefore, risked being outflanked, slaughtered, or both. The sour as gone-off milk idea came that we could be outflanked and slaughtered anyway. There was nothing to be done about that either, so I thought of happier times, Linn Duachaill when I was a boy, and my mother still alive. It worked for a short while, and then my glance fell on Lalo.

If I was in poor shape, he was twice as bad. He had on far more clothing than I – four tunics and three pairs of breeks, two cloaks, and a pair of scarves – but the cold still affected him worse than anyone. It was no surprise, him being from Bláland, but he was a piteous sight. The little of his face that I could see was pinched and greyish, and he could not stop shivering. To try and keep warm, he had volunteered to be our eyes and ears, regularly running to the front of the army and back. It helped a little, but the abuse he received from Máel-mórda's warriors – we heard some of it the most recent time he had returned – meant that Vekel had forbidden him to leave again.

'They're savages,' Vekel said as Lalo protested. 'One might put a spear in you as you went past, and no one would say a thing.'

'We accept you, Mandinka,' said Thorstein, 'but men from Laighin don't.'

Others had heard me talking to Lalo that day, and the name

Mandinka had stuck. To be honest, I think men just preferred it, and Lalo didn't seem to mind.

He uttered something in his own tongue, definitely uncomplimentary, and started half-running on the spot as he walked. He looked ridiculous, but I copied him anyway. Two fools we could be together, I thought. At least we'd be a bit warmer.

'A jug of ale, or a joint of roast lamb, Stormcrow?'

I gave Kleggi a sour look. 'Eh?'

'Which would you prefer now? Choose one.'

'Easy. Roast lamb.' The mere thought set my mouth to watering.

He came back at once. 'The lamb, or a decent spell in front of a fire?'

'Warming my bones,' I said, trying to ignore my snarling belly.

'That, or a hut to spend the night?'

The chances of this were slim indeed. We had passed a few miserable cottages, but the last one had been some time since. Even if we saw one when the time came, I thought, there would be twenty men to each of us also looking for shelter.

'Shut up, Kleggi. I don't want to play.'

Undeterred, he tried Thorstein, who gave him short shrift. A look from Vekel saw Kleggi move on to someone else. Crimp-beard liked the game, though, and so did Coal-biter. When Kleggi had done with them, he began to sing. Everyone joined in, even Lalo. Kleggi could be a pain in the arse, I thought, but he was good at keeping men's spirits from falling. Whether he could do so until we made camp was another story.

In fairness, he did, but by the time darkness fell, Kleggi had lost his voice. Accustomed to raiding inland, we hacked branches off the nearby rowan and hazel trees and built shelters. There was little natural protection, and without moss to fill the holes, the wind whistled through the crude shelters, but the edge had been taken off the cold air, or so we told ourselves, huddling together inside.

There were smiles all round when Thorstein produced *hnjóskr*, touchwood, from a leather pouch. This was a fungus collected from trees in autumn, and soaked in urine among other things, before being dried and beaten and worked into a felt-like material that was easily set ablaze. Lalo and I reduced a heap of twigs and smaller branches to kindling with our seaxes, and heaped them before Thorstein. He arranged hnjóskr fragments on top, and taking a curved steel from his belt, he knocked off sparks with a flint, letting them fall onto the precious touchwood. Cupping his hands, he blew until tendrils of flame danced upward.

The small fire that resulted was a distant relation of the massive one in Sigtrygg's hall, but to us, shivering, hungry and footsore, it felt Oðin-sent. Food left from the previous night – stale bread and hunks of hard cheese, mostly – was shared around. Men chewed in silence, unable to keep their eyes from coveting others' portions. When the meal, such as it was, ended, not a morsel remained.

It was lucky that Gleann Máma wasn't far, I remarked dourly to Vekel, and that the scouts reckoned Brian's and Máel's armies would reach it the following afternoon. Deep in thought, he did not reply. His continuing reticence did not help my mood. Belly unsatisfied, chilled to the bone, set for a poor night's rest, and imminently facing an enemy whose numbers dwarfed our own, it was hard to imagine victory.

I threw the grim thought into the recesses of my mind and locked the door. Whatever the outcome, I would fight.

'I'm too cold to sleep,' Thorstein announced.

Crimp-beard chuckled, and Kleggi, who had somehow squirmed his way into our shelter. Lalo, shrouded in his wrappings, just chattered his teeth.

'Tell us a story,' I said to Vekel.

He ignored me.

'Come on, vitki,' said Thorstein. 'It's a long time until sunrise.'

'You know you want to.' I nudged him.

Vekel huffed and puffed, but our eagerness was so obvious that only a stone-heart could have refused.

'I will tell you of Asgard,' he said. 'The reward for those slain in battle.'

No one protested. It was an apt choice. Many men would die on the morrow, and likely some of us. Asgard was where we all wanted to go, except maybe Lalo. I didn't know where he thought he might end up after death. For me, I wanted Valhöll, Oðin's enormous hall with its 540 doors. Grim reality returned. Despite my oath, and the beach encounter with the raven, I had no guarantee the god would accept me. If he did not, Freyja's hall Sessrúmnir would do. I deserved that, I told myself.

As Vekel laid out, Freyja chose first. I had not given much thought to this before. In my youthful arrogance, I had assumed I would live to be a greybeard. No longer. It was ridiculous, however, to worry about whether I was picked by Freyja or Oðin to be one of the *einherjar*, the immortal warrior dead. Neither might. If my time came the following day, the only thing within my control was to die in the best manner possible. Between them, the Norns and the gods would decide my fate.

This might be my last night in this world, I thought. The last time I would spend with my oarmates. With Vekel. Lalo. Dearbháil, who despite being a thrall, was dear to me. I fought back sadness.

Then, mercifully, the tale drew me in. I imagined standing in Val-höll, holding in one hand a tankard of the exquisite mead produced by the goat Heidrún, and in the other a choice cut of pork from Saehrímnir, the boar who was roasted and eaten every day and whole again the next.

I was carried away by Vekel's skill, forgetting the cold, the hunger, the fateful morn to come.

It was milder by dawn. A lot of the snow had melted, exposing the ridges in a piece of ploughed ground nearby. The previous day's cutting wind had been replaced by a gentle breeze from the south. The cloud cover complete, it was a grey day, like so many at this time of year. Yawning and farting, we emerged from our shelters and began to prepare for battle. There was no food, just water from our leather bags to drink. I didn't care; I wasn't thirsty or hungry. I wanted to find the Mumhan- and Midhe-men, and destroy them.

I caught sight nearby of Sigtrygg's hot-headed brother Harald, a man with the same fox-look as Sigtrygg. Fond of his own voice, he liked to drink, fight and hump, and not much else. He was in charge of Dyflin's warriors, although it would fall to each longship's captain to lead their warriors into battle. Two of Sigtrygg's sons were also with us. The older, slender-framed Oleif, was a skilled rider, but he had none of his father's refr-cunning. Artalach, eager as a hunting hound, was too young to lead men into war, and so it had fallen to Máel-mórda to command the entire army.

The scouts he had sent out returned with news of the enemy host, camped half a morning's marching distance from Gleann Máma. Brian's scouts, identifiable by their blue and gold patterned shields, were a lot closer; there had been a short clash, resulting in the withdrawal of the Mumhan-men. If we moved fast, the lead scout told Máel-mórda, the high ground on either side of the gleann could be ours.

Máel-mórda and Harald took him at his word. With no tents to pack away, and having slept in our gear, it didn't take long to get ready. An air of nervous excitement was palpable, but I could also hear joking and laughing, the usual banter. It helped *Brimdýr*'s crew that Vekel cast his rune bones before we left, and pronounced the omens good. Victory would be ours, Imr told us, walking up and down the line. We would wreak such a slaughter as had not been seen in Ériu this hundred years, and by the day's end, each of us would be laden down with booty: swords, armour, silver. Hooms and even a cheer met the last announcement.

I waited before asking the question that was preying on my mind. Carved from sheep's tail vertebrae, Vekel's rune bones were covered in odd dashes and lines that held no meaning to ordinary men. I had never tried to understand them either – the seiðr in the yellowed bones was for vitkis and *völvas,* not me.

I pitched my voice so that even Lalo, close to Vekel on the other side, could not hear. 'Is it true that the omens were good?'

No answer.

'Vekel.'

His eyes, rimmed with fresh black, turned on me. 'What?'

'Were the omens favourable, or did you lie so that men would not feel afraid?'

His gaze held mine – I could not look away – and he said, 'Do you really want to know the answer?'

When put like that, it was easy to choose.

'No,' I replied, determined not to let fear take root in my heart.

'I didn't think so.'

We marched.

Gleann Máma wasn't much of a gleann, not compared to the ones in the mountains further south. Nor was it a great place for an ambush. The grassy slopes leading up to the woodland on the left and right were gentle, scarcely steep enough to put a man out of breath. That was good, Máel-mórda told us. There was little risk of falling as we charged down on the unsuspecting enemy. A steep incline would not have worked. I wasn't convinced, and by the faces around me, nor were many others, but no one disputed the point. There was nowhere else to fight the enemy other than the flat terrain to the west, and that would end in disaster.

The army split into two halves, Norsemen and Laighin-men moving into place between the trees on either side of the gleann. It was imperative, Máel-mórda's orders had come, not to walk on the flat ground at the bottom. It made sense. Brian's and Máel's warriors might well see us hiding as it was; to announce our presence with thousands of boot prints would have been catastrophically stupid.

As I observed to Vekel under my breath, it felt catastrophically stupid anyway. Hazel, ash and rowan trees made up the majority of the trees; all were autumn-shedders, and completely leafless. If we tried to hide behind them, a cloudy-eyed dotard would see us before he entered the gleann proper. The only real concealment was the holly bushes, green-leaved and red-berried. There were plenty, but they were scattered about with no rhyme or reason. We had no other choice, however, and so took up the best positions possible. It meant that there were large gaps in our line; and in Máel-mórda's on the other side.

'This is no ambush. It is pure horseshit,' said Crimp-beard, breath clouding before his face.

'A big, steaming pile of it,' said Kleggi.

I was not happy either. This would be my first full-scale battle, and against superior numbers. Things looked ominous, whatever Vekel's runes might have indicated or not indicated.

The warriors to our left were under the command of Styrlaug, captain of the longship *Giálfrdýr*, which meant 'beast of the crashing sea'. A stolid, quiet type, he was brave and reliable. So were his men. I wish I could have said the same of those on our right, who were led by none other than Asgeir.

He had come skulking back to Dyflin two autumns after his disappearance at Cluain Mhic Nóis. There had been no reckoning about what had happened, but Sigtrygg made him work hard to regain favour. He never sent us raiding together again either. The years since had seen a steady increase in tension between the crews. Brawls were the norm when we encountered Asgeir's lot, bloodshed too. It was something of a Christ-miracle that no one had died, and I decided that we needed to watch our right flank as well as the Mumhan- and Midhe-men in front of us.

I studied my close companions. Coal-biter didn't care about survival. His self-confessed purpose for being in the world was to kill his enemies. Thorstein was calm too, but then he always was. I had seen him stand and fight four men once rather than run, and come out on top. Another occasion also stood out, a storm years before. *Brimdýr* had been climbing waves taller than barns and then, barely under the control of those at the steering oar, shooting down the other side. Each time – and there had been a score at least – we had been within a hairsbreadth of flipping over. I had seen fear in everyone's eyes then, even Vekel's – but not in Thorstein's.

I would fight like him, I decided. Play my part. Fight until victory was ours, or defeat overcame us. If I died in the process, I died.

Harald and Oleif worked their way up and down our positions, declaring that if we hit the enemy hard enough with the first charge, they would break. Break an enemy, Harald declared, and he will run. Running men are easy to kill. 'Follow me,' he said, 'and one day we'll be telling our sons and grandsons about today's victory.'

They were fine words, fighting words, and they lifted spirits for as long as it took Harald to disappear from sight. Then men stared at the gaps in our line, and those in Máel-mórda's opposite, and their courage leached away again. Realising that the fainthearted might begin to slope off, abandoning the rest to an inevitable fate, Imr and the other captains strutted the lines. They slapped backs and filled ears with encouraging words, and did it until the tramp of feet, thousands of feet, became audible.

An army makes a lot of noise, there's no two ways about it. There were horsemen too, curse them, Mumhan scouts, out ahead of the main body of Brian's and Máel's host.

They were alert too, doing their job. The nearest riders were perhaps two hundred paces from the trees when a great cry went up. The same man who'd given voice pointed straight at us, and shouted again. He and his comrades reined in, secure in the knowledge that they were at the extreme limit of arrow range, and took a good look. They also stared at the trees where Máel-mórda's warriors were hidden, and more cries of alarm went up.

'That's it,' said Crimp-beard. 'There'll be no cursed "ambush" today.'

'Just a toe-to-toe contest.' Coal-biter's voice was anticipatory.

It would be brutal, I thought, and with little chance of victory. Part of me exulted, though. I had always dreamed of standing with comrades in a shieldwall, fighting overwhelming odds.

I tested my axeblade for the umpteenth time. Finding it pleasingly sharp, I told myself that my oarmates and I were better than any warriors from Mumhan or Midhe, that we would cut down anyone who came within reach. If Cormac was here, I might even get a crack at him. And if the battle went against us, we would retreat in good order, and return to Dyflin.

It was also possible that I would go to Valhöll today. If I did, I decided, I would take plenty of the enemy with me.

'Out of the way. Move!' It was Goat-Banki and his friends, the archers among us. They walked to the treeline, arrows already nocked, and we cheered.

'Quiet, you fools!' said Banki.

His warning came too late. The Mumhan scouts saw him and his friends, but clearly thought the chances of being hit were remote, because they didn't budge, just sat on their horses and continued assessing our numbers.

Their nonchalance allowed Banki and the rest to get a feel for the wind, and the distance. Almost in unison, they bent their bows to full draw, aimed high and loosed. All eyes followed the six arrows. Up they went, virtually disappearing into the clouds. Down they came. A pair of horses dropped, kicking, and a rider took a shaft in the shoulder.

We cheered like men watching a race when the outsider they have wagered a fortune on comes in first.

A single arrow in the second volley hit a target, another rider, but it killed him stone dead. The Mumhan scouts beat an undignified retreat, leaving two wounded horses and a corpse, and their ears ringing with our insults and jeers.

Brian's and Máel's response didn't take long.

Their combined army continued to advance, spreading out as it came. By the time it entered the gleann, it would fill the flat ground, a great rectangular bloc of warriors that far outnumbered us and the Laighin-men. We would break off it, I heard a man say, like waves against a harbour wall. Even if our charge or that of Máel-mórda's warriors was successful, he continued, the formation would not split apart. It was too bloody big.

I turned. 'We do what Harald and Imr said.' My voice was loud. Hard. Determined. 'We are braver than those Irish whoresons. Better hewers of flesh. We feed the wolves and ravens better too.'

Those who could hear liked that, but then Imr appeared, face black as thunder.

'What?' I asked, my belly tightening.

'They are too many,' he said quietly.

Coal-biter bared his filed teeth. It was a terrifying look, one I had never been tempted to copy. 'Run if you want, Imr. I am staying.'

A few voices joined Coal-biter's, but most men's eyes were on Imr. He was our leader, the one we trusted. The one who would decide for us all.

'I gave Sigtrygg my word, shook his hand. We stay. We fight.' Imr's cold stare travelled from warrior to warrior, even to Lalo. 'Victory *is* possible! Hit those sheep-humping Mumhan- and Midhe-men at full tilt, and they *will* break!'

Men clattered blades off their shield bosses, rumbled their readiness to fight.

Krrruk. From above, the croaking call I knew so well. I glanced upwards, through the leafless branches. It was a solitary raven, floating over the gleann.

It might well have been looking for food, a deer carcass, or a sheep that had strayed from the fold, but naturally, I took its presence to mean that it was Oðin-sent. The god was watching, I thought, touching my amulet. He had not abandoned me. He was with us. 'LOOK!' I pointed. 'A raven comes!'

'A sign from Oðin!' Vekel declared.

Imr seized the chance. 'Oðin!' he shouted, and also pointed. 'Oðin!'

Other men saw. Joined in. Beat weapons off shields. Hearing the din, Máel-mórda's warriors began yelling their own battle cries. It was an almighty clamour, and it gave me strength. Purpose. Conviction.

Today was similar to when I had won the holmgang, I decided. I had beaten Biarn. Our army would defeat Brian's and Máel's. I gave no consideration to the blood-price.

As the cheering faded, Vekel continued what he had been doing all morning, standing on the low platform he'd had us make. He cast spells to fill the minds of the Mumhan- and Midhe-men with fear and confusion, and to weaken their limbs and weapons. He wove them to make us invulnerable, able to kill our enemies with ease. The spells had many verses, but one stuck in my mind.

'This third I know,' Vekel chanted. 'If I have real need to hold my foes in check, I blunt the blades of my adversaries, their weapons and staffs cannot bite.'

Men liked that. So did I.

The gods were on our side, Vekel told us, and we believed him.

The Mumhan-men and Midhe-men did not hurry to the fight. There was no need. The scouts came again to look at us. Wary of arrows, they stayed much further away. Small groups broke away and rode off to left and right, their purpose to go around the woodland, to the far end of the gleann. There they would ascertain we had no reinforcements, no surprise other than the one that had already failed. And frustrating though it was, we had to stay put. Charge out from the trees, and the scouts would simply ride away, leaving us on flat ground, exposed to the entire enemy army.

Midday was drawing close when the same riders came galloping back to join the scouts at the gleann's entrance. After a brief conferral, the whole lot withdrew towards the main body of the Mumhan- and Midhe-men.

A warrior loped out of the trees opposite, a messenger sent by Máel-mórda to Harald. The order soon passed down the line. We were to let our foes come as close as possible before attacking. No one was to move until a horn sounded three times. We would meet the Laighin-men in the middle of the enemy.

CHAPTER TWENTY

The horn blew once.

My knuckles bulged on the haft of my bearded axe. Over my shield rim, beyond the trees, all I could see was Mumhan-men and warriors of Midhe. Thousands of them. They were walking slowly, facing three ways, towards us, forward and towards the Laighin-men. Prepared for our charge. My gaze rose. I could almost see the valkyrjur in the air above. I certainly sensed them.

Another horn blast.

'Lord of the Dead, I will give your ravens food enough,' Crimp-beard shouted. 'Raw meat!'

I will also, Oðin, I promised calmly, wondering if my own flesh was part of the offering.

The third horn blast came, and the time for thought ended.

We surged forward, roaring like madmen.

Crimp-beard was on one side of me, Thorstein on the other. Coal-biter was there, and Imr, to left and right, and beyond them the rest of *Brimdýr's* crew, and all the Norsemen. From the trees opposite, Máel-mórda's warriors were running towards the enemy too.

My mind was focused. I would kill as many foes as possible. Victory would be ours. If I was to die, I intended to die well. A worthy einher-jar then, Oðin or Freyja would take me for their own.

The Mumhan-men were ready. So were Máel's warriors. They halted and formed a shield wall, a good approximation of a Norse one. A line of overlapping shields, many painted in Brian Bóramha's colours of blue and gold, awaited us. The same, but patterned with Máel's design, faced the Laighin-men.

We closed to twenty paces. Cold air rushed past my face. My breath sawed in my throat. Coal-biter was yelling. Crimp-beard had edged in front – he would hit the enemy first. The Mumhan-man I would meet had a simple leather helmet. I readied my axe.

Ten paces.

Five.

The din – shouts, the crashing of shields, screams – was so loud I discerned nothing else. Time lost meaning. My vision narrowed. Killing distance.

I saw my opponent's expression change, and intuited his move.

I dodged behind my shield, and a mighty spear thrust went over my shield and head.

I sprang up off my haunches, and with an overhand swing, split helmet and skull in twain with my axe. One, I counted.

The warrior behind made no immediate response as his comrade died, his muscles perhaps frozen by the valkyrja Herfjötur. He screamed when I hewed off his right arm at the shoulder, though. He twisted, still mewling, and spray from the stump crimson-misted my vision. I battered him away with my shield boss, and shoved onward to the next man.

He had seen me coming. Down came his sword, its hammering power smith-worthy. If the strike had connected, my collarbone would have snapped like a twig, mail or no, but the valkyrja Mist was with me. I twisted, causing his swing to go a fraction awry. The blade spanged off my helmet, clacking my teeth together, and most of its force spent, bounced off my mail. Double-visioned, I was still close enough not to miss. A short, vicious side-chop with my axe almost cut his head from the neck. The face registering complete surprise, it fell sideways, prevented from separating entirely by a few tendrils of sinew. Three, I counted as blood jetted.

I screamed, a wordless cry from the pit of my stomach, and when I went at the next Mumhan-man, he quailed and tried to back away. There was nowhere to go. The press was too great. I snagged my axe-beard onto his shield-top, ripped down and as his arm, engaged in the straps, pulled him forward, I went in with a headbutt. Nose reduced to mush by helmet steel, eyes pain-closed, he did not see my axe. Another chop at the junction of neck and shoulder. Another head all but severed. Another corpse falling to the trampled, frozen grass. Four.

A small space yawned in front of me. On the other side was another Mumhan-man, a youth who looked to have pissed his breeks. He made no move at me; I risked a look to left and right. Thorstein was there, mail spattered red, helmet dented, but chopping his opponent into fleshy ruin. The next warrior to face him looked ready to soil himself also. On my other side, Crimp-beard was still in front, and there was an empty semicircle – axe-swing in size – before him. I laughed. We *would* drive Brian's host from the field. The Laighin-men would see our success and win their own.

It wasn't just Oðin who was with us, I decided, my spirits soaring. The valkyrjur were here in force, exulting in the chaos, seeding fear in our enemies' hearts, ensuring that their blows were poorly aimed. Vekel had invoked them before the battle, asking for their aid. And it had come, from Herfjötur and Mist. Hlökk and Sveið were here also, Skalmöld and Randgníðr, Sigrdrífa and the others. Not all their actions would be helpful. They were, after all, the choosers of the slain.

'Coal-biter's down!' Thorstein's voice.

Not for the first time, I wondered if a divine being had read my mind.

I couldn't look, because Piss-breeks had actually found enough courage to charge. I let him drive his spear into my shield, and as he tried to dislodge it, cut off his right arm at the elbow. Five, I thought. His shriek was ear-piercing, and I used the moment to belt my axe and wrench the spear from my shield. I succeeded, but did not have enough time to arm myself again before another Mumhan-man was on me. This one was a veteran, and clad in mail, armed with axe, Norse style.

He did what I had done to the fourth man, and hooked his axe-beard to the top of my shield. He pulled, and instead of trying to stop the shield being dragged down, I shoved forward, like a man heaving at the mud-bound wheel of a wagon. Unbalanced, he staggered back. Rather than carve me open at the neck, his axe swing went harmlessly over my left shoulder.

It allowed me to bury my seax in his upper thigh, just where his mail ended. It went in nice and deep. He staggered as it came out. Blood gushed, but he was still able to fight. Too close to swing properly, he battered the back of my head with his axe, once, twice, thrice. Again I saw stars. Another few blows, and I would fall. The will to live took over. I probed forward with my seax again, and stabbed and stabbed. The blade grated off bone, and his throat opened in a visceral scream. His right arm flopped over my shoulder, as if he were a drunk needing help to walk, and I stuck him another time for good measure, driving the seax right up into his groin. Warm liquid covered my hand, proof that I had cut the great vessel there.

Six went my count.

The veteran's eyes had glazed over; I don't think he knew where he was, dying. I wondered if he had prayed to the White Christ beforehand, asking for his intercession as we had with our gods and the valkyrjur. If so, it had done him scant good.

'Stormcrow!' Thorstein, sounding more urgent than I had ever heard.

My head twisted. Crimp-beard was staring in astonishment at the spear jutting from his right armpit. Horrified, my eyes followed its shaft. The Mumhan-man wielding it was as big, maybe even bigger, than Crimp-beard. Grimacing, he ran it in deeper, and Crimp-beard emitted a horrible groan. He tried to raise his axe, but failed. The spear slid another handsbreadth into his chest, and his strength vanished. Nerveless fingers let go of his axe, and his great shape almost folded in on itself as he went down.

An animal roar rose from the Mumhan-men. I barely heard. Anger, white-hot battle rage, had erupted inside me. Seax sheathed, I dragged free my axe. As the enemy swarmed forward like a pack of hungry wolves, I charged back. Alone. I knocked the first warrior down with my shield, and smashed another's chest. Seven. A spear rammed into my right shoulder, but the mail didn't give, and heaving myself sideways and off its point, I somehow back-chopped up into its wielder's face. The axe sheared his nose in half and ruptured an eye, juddering to a halt in his brow-bone. Howling, he fell away, and I leaped into the gap, thinking, *eight*.

Nothing would stop me. No one would stop me.

I was going to kill them all, for Crimp-beard.

I must have slain three more Mumhan-men, before, chest heaving, no foeman immediately in front, I felt a hand seize my left shoulder. I spun, axe coming up, and found myself eyeball to eyeball with Thorstein. He rapped his axe haft, hard, off my helmet. 'FINN!'

Sense returned. I focused. 'What?'

He jumped past, met a jabbed spear with his shield and killed its wielder with a casual axe cut. The Mumhan-men hesitated, and Thorstein cried, 'Our attack has failed. We need to retreat!'

'Crimp-beard—'

'—would not want you to die in vain!' Again his haft clattered me. 'Come on!'

I wanted to keep fighting, but the battle-rage was slipping away, like frost in the morning sun. Suddenly aware that nothing separated Thorstein and me from half a hundred Mumhan-men but a few corpses and the momentary fear my battle insanity had birthed in their hearts, I let him lead me backwards. We moved slowly, without turning our backs, and still numbed by the violence we had inflicted, they merely watched. We soon rejoined the rest of the Norsemen, who were making a fighting retreat. I glanced about, trying to recognise shields, or faces. I saw Hrafn, Banki, and a few others, but there were many missing.

'Coal-biter?' I asked.

'Dead.'

'Imr?'

'Haven't seen him.' Thorstein raised his shield, and an arrow tonked off it, spinning away to the right. 'What happened to you?'

'Eh?'

'If I had to wager, I'd say you turned berserkr like Coal-biter.'

An arrow hissed in, and I lifted my shield. It punched through the limewood, and I had to snap the shaft to get it out. 'Maybe,' I said. I hadn't had time to think, and whatever it was had gone.

'You were like a man possessed.'

'It was because of Crimp-beard.' My voice was thick.

'Aye,' said Thorstein sadly.

We kept moving. The situation was the same or worse all along what had been our line. There were Asgeir and his warriors, also pulling back. I spied Styrlaug's shield, white with a black raven, so he was still alive. Harald was dead, but Oleif and Artalach were unhurt. Out on the battleground, the Laighin-men had also retreated. There were far more Norse and Laighin dead than Mumhan- or Midhe-men. That didn't mean Brian's and Máel's casualties were light. Far from it. Their warriors had been given a real bloody nose. Rather than give pursuit, they just dragged away their wounded, and regrouped.

In the shelter of the trees, we found Imr. He was bleeding badly from a leg wound, but his fire wasn't gone. Even as Vekel, who had stayed behind with Lalo, dressed his injury, Imr was declaring that we had to charge again.

'Why?' I demanded. Battle rage gone, I could see were between a rock and a hard place.

'They didn't break the first time,' Thorstein added.

'Look at them!' Imr spat. 'Do they look like an army that wants to win?'

'They look like an army that has held its ground, and seen off an attack,' I said.

'Are you afraid, Stormcrow?' he taunted.

I squared up to him. 'Ask that of the Mumhan-men who died after Crimp-beard fell!'

Vekel shoved in, and with a hand on each of our chests, pushed us back. 'Brian and Máel have surely won if you start fighting each other! And Crimp-beard will have died for nothing.'

Imr's face changed. 'Crimp-beard . . .'

'He's gone, and Coal-biter,' I said.

'And the guts of a score more,' added Thorstein harshly.

Imr shook his head, clearing his mind. 'That many?'

'It's the same everywhere,' said Vekel. 'See for yourself.'

In the end, we did make a second charge, in the main because the Laighin-men made to do so first. Norsemen are proud, and it seemed cowardly to let them fight alone. I wanted to avenge Crimp-beard, and others did too. Giant not just in frame, he had been one of the most popular crew members.

The attack also went badly, and sooner than the first. The battle rage didn't appear again. Banki fell, and another half-dozen from *Brimdýr*. I was injured in my left, my shield arm. It was a flesh wound only, but I could no longer defend myself, or at least do so well. When Imr, now nursing a cut to his face, said that we were done, no one argued. The Mumhan-men had had their noses bloodied enough not to come after us into the trees, but they had given no ground either. One way or another – either through and over us, Vekel said, or with us watching – they were going to march on Dyflin and Máel-mórda's stronghold.

Asgeir had already gone, of course, sloping away instead of joining the second attack. We heard this from Oleif, who didn't argue with Imr's statement that it was time to retreat. The battle had gone badly with him also; perhaps half of Sigtrygg's household warriors remained.

195

Artalach protested; he wanted to try and ambush the enemy in a different place, closer to Dyflin.

'No. It's over,' Oleif said.

'Father will be furious!'

Oleif scowled. 'Aye, well, he wasn't here, was he?'

'So Brian Bóramha and Máel Sechnaill are just going to walk into our town and do what they want?'

'That's right. And anyone with a titter of wit won't try to stop them.'

Artalach genuinely looked as if he might attack Oleif, but he never got the chance, because Lalo said, 'The Mumhan-men are charging again.'

They were too, the bastards, a great section of their line, loping towards us with horrible intentness. Someone had lit a fire in their bellies. Even if we stood and fought, they easily outnumbered us four to one. There were also archers, at the back, and they were loosing already, high over their comrades' heads.

'We go. Now,' said Imr.

I could hear Artalach still protesting to Oleif as we began to run. 'No! I'm staying!'

I glanced back. Most of Sigtrygg's warriors were retreating. Only Artalach, Oleif and a handful of others, the most loyal, remained. One went down, an arrow in his leg, and the Mumhan-men whooped.

'Let's help,' said Vekel, but I was already turning.

Shoving away the pain of my arm wound, telling myself that I could still fight, I joined the brothers. Vekel came too, which surprised me. So did Lalo, which didn't.

'Lord,' I said to Artalach. 'This is not wise. We should retreat.'

'No. At least one of Sigtrygg's sons has courage.'

A savage oath from Oleif. 'You're a fool, Artalach! The battle has been lost!'

'Run then.'

'Your brother is right, lord,' I said.

'I am staying.' He went to put on his helmet, which he had taken off to wipe his brow.

'Forgive me,' I said, and smacked him on the back of the head with my axe. His eyes rolled up to the whites, and I caught him as he fell. Oleif gaped, and I said, 'Are you going to help me, or just stand there?'

'Take him, lord,' said one of the household warriors. 'We'll hold the Mumhan-men.'

Oleif gave him a tight, grateful nod.

We each hooked an arm under one of Artalach's, and with his legs dragging, half walked, half ran east, towards Dyflin. Arrows smacked into the earth around us, but they were speculative shots. As long as Sigtrygg's household warriors stood firm for a time, I decided, we would get away.

'You better not have cracked his skull, Stormcrow,' said Oleif.

If it wasn't for me, he'd be dead already, I wanted to say, but instead I muttered something trite about Artalach being a tough lad.

More shafts came down. I could see Imr and the rest up ahead, though, and my heart lifted. Brian Bóramha's army might be coming to Dyflin, but we could get away in *Brimdýr*. I didn't know where we would go. It didn't really matter.

'Finn.' It was Vekel.

'What?'

'The boy has been hit.'

Oleif heard too. We gently lowered Artalach, and stared in dismay at the arrow jutting from his thigh. It had been a freakish shot, I thought, and hit him completely by chance. It was bad, too. His breeks were already soaked with blood.

'Can you remove it, vitki?' demanded Oleif. 'Or work some seiðr to save him?'

'Maybe, but I need time.'

'We don't have any of that,' I snapped. 'Most of the warriors who stayed have fallen.'

'Lord?' Vekel asked.

Oleif hesitated, then looked again whence we had come. 'Do it later. Otherwise we're all dead men.' He stooped towards Artalach again.

I did the same, telling myself the boy would be all right.

Relieved that the enemy had given up their pursuit, we decided to spend the night in a barn. The short day meant there was no possibility of reaching Dyflin in one march. Twenty-nine of *Brimdýr*'s crew remained, many wounded. With no food, we huddled together in the straw, glad just to be out of the freezing night. We weren't alone.

Styrlaug and the remnants of his crew were in possession of the other half of the barn.

Artalach was still alive; as soon as we'd arrived, Vekel set to work. First, he had chanted, and danced, and waved his staff over the boy. No one dared ask what he was doing, what spirits he called on. This done, he had set to work on the barbed arrowhead, removing it with a great deal of difficulty and even more blood. The flow had been staunched with cautery, an iron heated in a smouldering fire. I had not been alone in gagging at the burning smell as Vekel worked the long metal probe deep into the meat of Artalach's thigh. Finishing, strapping up the wound with lengths of fabric from a ripped up tunic, he told Oleif that the boy had a slim chance of survival. Even if he did, infection could set in. Amputation would then be necessary, which came with its own risks.

Oleif's expression, switching between rage and grief, suggested he would have struck anyone bearing such news, but even a king's son thought twice before attacking a vitki.

Artalach was stiff and cold the following morning. No one was surprised; seiðr was unpredictable, and the blood loss had been significant. Oleif was composed, but it was clear it had hit him hard. I was sad – the boy had been likeable – but I was also glad it wasn't me. My oarmates' expressions suggested they felt the same way.

'Father will take this hard,' said Oleif. 'Harald and Artalach both dead.'

'We had best move,' said Imr. 'Else he will only find out that we lost when that whoreson Brian marches into Dyflin.'

Oleif nodded. 'We carry him home. He should have a proper funeral.'

A pang of grief hit me. Crimp-beard, Coal-biter, Banki and the rest of the slain were lying in the open, left on the battlefield. There would be no earthly interment with their weapons; instead the flesh would be picked from their bones by the wolves, ravens and other carrion birds. It was a harsh fate, but one I could do nothing about.

I sought out Imr on the march. 'What's your plan?'

'Getting back to Dyflin alive.'

'Assuming we do that . . .'

'The gods know what Brian and Máel will do, but it won't be pleasant. Brian might not know that we raided Cluain Mhic Nóis a few years ago, for example, but he'll suspect everyone from the longships.'

'He will. Britain then?'

'Perhaps, aye.'

'We might come away with a lot of silver.' Everyone knew that the English king Æthelred paid tribute to Danish raiders, chief among them Svein Forkbeard, and Olaf Tryggvason of Nordvegr. This was Norse for Lochlann. Even though Olaf had recently made peace with Æthelred, and Svein had his own troubles at home, some raiding continued.

'That is my hope.'

'We are short of crew.' It hurt to think about it. So many would never pull an oar on *Brimdýr* again.

Imr was all business. 'There'll be a few at Linn Duachaill, maybe, and if not, on Man. There are always men there with too much time on their hands.'

I spent the long, cold walk back to Dyflin imagining raiding settlements in Bretland and England.

CHAPTER TWENTY-ONE

We fled Dyflin before the victorious Mumhan- and Midhe-men arrived, on the first day of the year that the Christ-worshippers called 1000. With Styrlaug's *Giálfrdýr* alongside, Imr aimed *Brimdýr*'s prow north. *Sea-stallion* and the other longships had scattered to the four winds.

Sigtrygg was on board our vessel. He was prickly and difficult to deal with, true, but he was openhanded with silver, especially when his life was in danger. As Imr said, and everyone agreed, only a fool looked a gift horse in the mouth. The riches offered by Sigtrygg – silver, hack-silver, Christ-chalices, gold – were worth half a hundred horses, and fine ones at that. It made sense to take him and his family as paying guests on *Brimdýr*. The remnants of his household filled the shortage in the crew nicely.

I avoided them and Sigtrygg both, as much as was possible on a long, narrow ship. It was plain that the king had not forgiven my out-spokenness before Gleann Máma, and even though Oleif had told him I had tried to save Artalach, Sigtrygg blamed me for his death. By his looks, he felt the same way about Vekel, who had removed the arrow, but didn't dare say it.

The king's warriors picked up on his anger towards me. Cowed like beaten dogs by the defeat, however, and the fact that I was friends with a vitki, they did not offer any violence. Gormlaith alone seemed to believe my story; she smiled if I ever caught her eye.

We stopped at Linn Duachaill, but could not linger. It was too close to Dyflin, and that was without considering Máel Sechnaill, Brian's ally. There was a brief reunion with Ashild, still with Diarmaid, and now the mother of a sturdy little boy. I gifted enough silver to widen her eyes, kissed her, and ignored her warnings about the life I led, and the sure path to damnation I was taking. 'The White Christ has no power over me. I am one of Oðin's chosen warriors,' I declared, and believed it. Gleann Máma had seen to that.

She sighed, and crossed herself, and said she would pray for my soul. When Vekel asked if she would do the same for his, and pinched her arse as he did so, she slapped him. Laughing, he blew her a kiss and said he had laid protective spells on the house, the farm and all of her family. Ashild's protests at this were at best half-hearted. Despite her outward piety, she had not given up on all the old ways, which pleased me.

On up the coast we took the longships, braving gales, heavy seas and relentless rain. It seemed even the elements were against us. Men would usually have asked Vekel to read the future, or cast spells, but not now. I wondered if it was because he had been wrong about winning the battle at Gleann Mama, and whether they still believed in him. I did, because I knew that he had lied to keep up morale.

Sigtrygg hoped to find refuge with the Dál Fiatach clan, rulers of the Ulaidh, the largest population in the kingdom of the same name. He was sorely disappointed. King Eochaidh mac Ardgail allowed us just two days to procure supplies and water. A strong force of warriors guarded the harbour, to ensure a prompt departure.

We found no safe haven either at Ulfreksfjord, a small Norse settlement perched on the northeast coast of Eochaidh's kingdom. Its ruler Snorri was full of what seemed genuine apologies. Eochaidh had eyes and ears everywhere, he said, and if word carried that he had welcomed Sigtrygg, there would be serious consequences.

More winter storms awaited as *Brimdýr* and *Giálfrdýr* battled around Ériu's northern shores. Styrlaug lost three men overboard, but not a single warrior of our crew drowned. Rán did not take us to the bottom either, or Thor. Whether it was thanks to the many offerings we threw overboard for both deities, Karli's incredible skill, or both, I was not sure, and did not care to try and decide. Pulling into the bay close to the main settlement of the Cenél nEóghain, rulers of a small kingdom west of Ulaidh, I had never been gladder to be in calm water. For once, I wasn't alone. Even Karli, stoic to the last, declared his relief.

King Aédh of the Cenél nEóghain wasn't on particularly good terms with Eochaidh, which had given us hope that he might prove more friendly, but it was not to be. Once again, Imr and Styrlaug were allowed to replenish food, water, rope, sailcloth and suchlike, and then we had to leave.

If Sigtrygg's mood had been black when forced out of Dyflin, it plumbed new depths on that second voyage. I felt some sympathy. Between his fury at being deposed by Brian, his grief at losing a brother and son, his failure to find refuge in Ériu and his seasickness – he had no sea legs – the man was entitled to feel out of sorts.

His mood improved at Man. A large island close to the English coast, it belonged to the king of Dyflin. Man's Norse inhabitants had no intention of swearing allegiance to Brian Bóramha, but they wouldn't kiss Sigtrygg's arse either. Secure in their own fastness, they only paid lip service to him, but they offered a friendlier reception than anywhere thus far on our voyage. Sigtrygg decamped to a hall kept for his visits. Imr and Styrlaug bargained with a local jarl, who offered us a ramshackle longhouse on the settlement's outskirts. It meant I did not have to be around the king, which was good. Things between us had not improved.

Man provided a welcome base for several months; it was also the first time anyone had had to grieve the comrades who had fallen against the Mumhan-men. We did that in style over many nights, toasting Crimp-beard, Coal-biter and Banki – also remembering Ulf – even as we drank ourselves under the table.

Imr was busy from the outset, recruiting warriors. It ought to have been hard. News had come of the slaughter at Gleann Máma, and Sigtrygg's expulsion from Dyflin. Fortunately, *Brimdýr* had a reputation. Imr had plenty of silver too, not just his own, saved over years, but recent payment from Sigtrygg. The promise of raiding in a renowned longship is attractive, but few things persuade a man to take service like hacksilver in his palm.

Vali the Strong was the first. A smith like myself, barrel-chested and with tree trunk-thick arms, he wore no fewer than three hand axes in his belt. When Imr asked why, he whipped out one and flung it through the air. The axe was still quivering in the mast when a second joined it, followed by the third. All were stuck deep in the wood in an area not much bigger than a shield boss.

Imr didn't often look impressed, but he was by Vali, who had also been on plenty of raids. 'If you ever have the need,' he announced, 'I can geld a man, and 'e won't bleed to death neither.'

'An odd skill to possess,' Vekel commented. 'Is it something you practice on your enemies?'

Chuckling, Vali wagged a finger at Vekel, whom he didn't seem the slightest bit afraid of. 'A funny man and a vitki?'

Vekel ignored him, which I knew meant that he had been discomfited.

'No, that's not why I do it,' Vali went on. 'It's on account of my wife, see. Hlif Horse-gelder, she's called. Learned it from 'er.'

'A woman who cuts horses' balls off,' said Thorstein, grinning. 'She sounds formidable.'

A vigorous nod from Vali. 'She is that, and beautiful with it.'

'You wouldn't want to tumble a shapely thrall with such a wife. Is that why you want to join *Brimdýr*? Out of sight, out of mind, eh?' Vekel poked his forefinger in and out of a ring made by the thumb and forefinger of the other hand.

We laughed.

Vali took it in good spirit. 'A man likes to get away, is all. I miss the sea.' He stamped the deck. 'I miss this.'

I understood that. So did Imr, and they shook hands.

After Vali came two brothers, Thormod the Tough and Hrolf Red-beard. Confusingly, both had red beards, as well as hair, and Hrolf was quick to assert that despite their names, he was the tougher of the pair. What was clearly an oft-repeated argument began, but they shut their mouths when Imr told them to. They were also experienced raiders.

Another was a cocky, beardless youth by the name of Kar, who swaggered up to Imr by the prow, the spot he liked to interrogate potential crewmen. Kar proudly announced that he was Mursi's son. Imr gave him a blank look – we all did. Nonplussed, Kar explained that Mursi's skill with an axe had been famed throughout Man for years.

'That is all fine and good,' Imr replied, 'but can *you* wield one?'

Kar bridled that his youth counted against him, but did not protest when Imr suggested he and I have a bout. With leather covers on the axeblades and the entire crew watching, we went at each other on the deck. To my surprise, Kar was indeed proficient, and it took considerable effort not to be hurt. Imr saw too, and swiftly ordered a halt. 'You'll do,' he said to Kar. 'What about your father? We would have space for him too.'

A sad smile. 'A fever took him during the winter.'

'Family?'

'Mother is dead, and my sisters are married off.'

Imr nodded. 'Understandable why you're looking to leave.'

I understood too; Kar's story felt similar to my own.

With time on my hands, I often thought of Dearbháil, who had been an exciting bed companion, but also sharp-witted. There had been no space on *Brimdýr*, so I had left her in Dyflin. Imr's shock that I had freed her at the same time was memorable. 'She was pretty! Young too, with most of her teeth. No children either. You'd have made your money back on her at least.'

I hadn't bothered to explain. Until Vekel had liberated Lalo, I felt similarly about thralls. They were possessions, like cattle and sheep. But years spent in Lalo's company, eating, sleeping and fighting beside him, had changed my opinion. True, his skin was black where mine was white, and his hair curled tight against his head while mine fell to my shoulders, but there the major differences ended. His blood was red in colour. His piss and mine were yellow, and his shit stank too. He was a man like me, who had been born free, and only enslaved through ill fortune. Dearbháil's story was little different. She had been captured in a Norse raid as a small girl.

Imr would have said I was going soft, but he was wrong. Lalo and Dearbháil were special cases. I would still take thralls on raids, because they were currency. And sometimes, when silver and other treasures were in short supply, thralls were the *only* currency.

Thoughts of Dearbháil made my groin tighten, and more than once I considered buying a female thrall. I had seen several still-attractive ones in the marketplace. With regret, I decided it would be a waste of hard-earned silver. We might not be here much longer.

Word had come fresh from Dyflin. If it was to be believed, Brian Bóramha wanted to sit down and talk with Sigtrygg, man to man. It sounded too good to be true. Sigtrygg was no slack-jawed nithing, to believe the story at first hearing. That very morning, Styrlaug had gone off to find out what was what.

One thing was certain in my mind. If the story proved accurate, Sigtrygg would jump back to Dyflin quicker than a flea onto a dog. His return made a bizarre kind of sense. Brian had no interest in ruling the town. He wanted hostages and silver, and an oath not to cause trouble again, and he'd be happy enough for Sigtrygg to reinstall himself in his great hall.

The fifth month of the year arrived, and *Brimdýr* was back in the Black Pool. After the manner of our last departure, it was strange to be here. Just one other longship was at anchor, Styrlaug's *Giálfrdýr*, evidence that Sigtrygg's position was still weak. I did not like that, or being in Dyflin. Things had changed. Sigtrygg was king again, in name anyway, but Brian Bóramha was the master now, and Sigtrygg danced to his tune. Whether he would mastermind raids all over Ériu and get fat on profits from the town's bustling slave market remained to be seen. Imr was content to wait and see. He spoke to no one of his intentions, always his tendency. Restless, I hoped that the time spent on Man had awakened in him a desire to take *Brimdýr* elsewhere.

We had returned fresh after the withdrawal of Brian Bóramha and his army. The King of Mumhan had gone after accepting Sigtrygg's word, sent by messenger, that he would faithfully serve Brian from this moment forward. This, Vekel and I agreed, had been done to allow Sigtrygg and his household to re-enter the town with some pride and thus avoid further humiliation.

I had looked for Dearbháil, but she was nowhere to be found. It gladdened my heart. According to the innkeeper where we had stayed, she had set out for Ulaidh. I hoped she had found her family.

Brian had not gone far from the town because the treaty went further than hostages from Dyflin and oaths of loyalty. Sigtrygg was to marry one of Brian's daughters, and Brian would take Sigtrygg's mother Gormlaith as his wife. The joint ceremony was to take place the very next day, strengthening the peace.

I was in an odd mood, resenting being here, while looking forward to the morrow's festivities. I didn't want to leave the company of my shipmates, yet I had little desire to drink myself senseless, the intention of most. Vekel and Thorstein had vanished together, as they sometimes did. Their disappearances, indeed their entire relationship, was ignored by Imr and the rest of our shipmates. Their reasoning was simple, I had decided. What wasn't spoken of wasn't happening.

I *had* given it some thought. Since forming a relationship with Thorstein, Vekel was the happiest I had ever seen him. That made it straightforward enough to accept them as a couple. Presumably, the two lay together, yet Thorstein's belly had never swelled. Vekel had to be the reason why. Thanks to the herbs I'd bought on his advice, Dearbháil had never got with child either.

Good luck to him and Thorstein both, I thought.

A purpose for the afternoon appeared. I would buy Vekel a gift, simply because he was my dearest friend. What it would be I had no idea – yet. Deciding that there was enough in my purse, and no need to visit my personal hoard, buried in a field a short distance north of Dyflin, I got ready. Clean tunic donned, hair combed and seax in my belt, I clambered off *Brimdýr*. It wasn't far to the gate in the wall, where the sentries' greetings were friendly. Our role in Sigtrygg's escape had not been forgotten.

The open space before the king's great hall bustled; preparations for the royal weddings were in full swing. Once-was-a-warrior was in his element, pointing and gesturing, shouting at a slow-moving thrall, ordering benches carried inside before a party of musicians were allowed to enter. Ribby mongrels hung around a butcher's cart laden down with sides of beef, pork, and lamb. Chickens had escaped from a broken wicker cage and were running about, getting under people's feet. A couple of young lads were in pursuit, but they were laughing so hard I doubted the hapless birds would ever be caught.

I picked a way through, remembering the holmgang I had fought here years before. Many would have said Biarn's slip and fall was ill fortune; I had always put it down to an intervention by Oðin himself. Inexperienced and callow, there was no other way I could have won that fight. I thought of the beach at Linn Duachaill then, and the beady-eyed raven, and the skull-cloven corpse, and the god-given sword.

News came of the last now and again, stories of Máel Uí Sechnaill's son wielding it in battle, and of men swearing allegiance to Midhe on its silver hilt. The knowledge pricked, galled, like an ill-fitting saddle girth, a bitter reminder of my still unavenged father. Nor was there ever any mention of the blade's rightful owner – me. It would be mine again one day, I swore to myself. There would be a reckoning with Cormac, in blood. I would offer his life to Oðin, as I had Biarn's, and every life I took with it thereafter.

'Need a guide?' The question came in gioc-goc, its utterer a filthy-garmented, bare-footed boy of about ten years. He was blocking my path, the gouger.

'I know Dyflin well enough.'

'Do you?' He had the cockiness of the young and the stupid. 'Where's the best ale sold?'

'The Thatch.' This was our favourite haunt.

His turn to snort. 'Every eejit knows it's The Brazen Head.'

'Watch who you call an idiot,' I warned. The truth was, I'd heard the same, but that inn was on the western edge of the town, a long walk when sober, worse when ale-soused. This was the principal reason I'd never crossed its threshold.

'It's not drink you want anyway,' he declared.

This was perceptive. 'How can you be sure?'

'On your own, aren't you?' A lascivious wink, bizarre from such a youngster. 'Want a tumble? There's a place full of pretty young wans close to here.'

'I do not.' Nonetheless, I felt a pang of nostalgia for Dearbháil.

'Is it a man you fancy? A boy?'

'No!' I'd never had those kind of feelings for Vekel, or any man.

'You're looking to buy something then.'

I strode off in the direction of the closest shops. He kept pace, delivering an amusing, running commentary on what I might want. Shoes, boots, a belt. A tunic. Breeks, for mine were in poor repair, he opined. A knife. An axe or spear. A sword.

I made no answer, but my silence added fuel to his fire.

'A shield?'

'A helmet?'

'Armour?'

Despite myself, I was amused. His suggestions were shortening the list of possible gifts for Vekel. Inspiration hit, yet I could not remember ever seeing a silverworker's shop in Dyflin. Searching, I continued down the street and into another, and another. I had no luck. Locals would have known, but I was not going to ask for directions, because that would give the boy the upper hand.

I was acting like my ten-year-old self, I realised, arguing and tussling with Vekel. I gave in. 'I'm looking for a silversmith's.'

Hands on hips, as Ashild did when she was proven right, the boy said, 'I was starting to think you'd never ask.'

'You hadn't guessed right either,' I countered, smiling.

'True.' One word, so solemn. His hand came out. 'There's nothing free in this life, as my uncle says.'

'You'll get paid if the shop has something I like.' I stared him down. At length, with an exaggerated sigh, he led me down the next alley to the left, coming to a triumphant halt outside a nondescript house. 'Here.'

'It was this close?'

A sly look. 'Not my fault if you don't know Dyflin as well as you claim.'

I chuckled, and knocking on the open door, entered. Cloth-covered tables spanned the width of the building, separating it into unequal parts. A small quantity of silverwork was on display: brooches, rings, simple necklaces with glass pendants, and one engraved arm ring. It was prudent; a nimble-footed thief could be in and out in the blink of an eye.

Other things were for sale: a polished oak tafl board with antler and stone pieces, a lovely wooden panpipe, goose-bone flutes, drilled pig bones on twisted cords. If the premises' owner made these as well, he was talented indeed, I decided. The chances of finding a gift for Vekel seemed good.

'Well met, sir.' A portly, red-cheeked man in a leather apron stood, laying a slender hammer on his workbench. I spied a small anvil, clippers, pincers, punches and sheets and lengths of silver. 'Are you after anything in particular?' he asked in Norse.

'Just looking,' I said, studying the arm ring. A solid tube, it bore a striking design of hundreds of little triangles, each studded with one or more pellets. The style was familiar; Imr had one, and Thorstein.

'That'll cost plenty.' My guide had come in, uninvited.

I didn't want him hovering, so pouch-fumbled and produced a piece of hacksilver worth a day's labour. His eyes widened, and I said, wagging a finger, 'This, but you will take me wherever I ask for the rest of the afternoon.'

A quick nod.

I dropped the silver back into my purse and drew tight the string. 'Later.'

He managed to strangle most of the protest that came bubbling up his throat.

'Wait outside.'

An indignant whisper, 'Without me, you might get cheated!'

'I'll manage.'

With many a backward glance, he slunk out the door.

'Appointed himself your guide, eh?'

'Something like that.'

'He's all right.'

'You know him?'

'Aye. Orm, his name is, an orphan. Lives with his uncle, a smith, who works him like a dog.'

It explained the boy's keenness to earn his own money, I thought.

The silversmith's fingertips caressed the arm ring. 'You like it?'

'I do,' I replied, quickly adding, 'but I'm not here for myself.'

'A gift for a lady?'

'Not that either. Show me your other merchandise.'

He moved to a strongbox at the back of the room. Pulling a thong-hung key from under his tunic, he opened an impressive barrel padlock, the like of which I had rarely seen, and lifted the lid. He returned with a thick bundle of wool. A swift, practised motion saw it unrolled, revealing a wealth of finger rings, arm rings, six stunning but unfamiliar little seashells, and a beautifully carved pair of dice.

'These are not silver,' I said of the last.

'They have been shaped from the tusk of a hrossvalr.'

My memory tickled. A lifetime before, in Linn Duachaill, Egil the Fat had had a whole tusk.

'A what?' A feminine voice speaking Norse, but with an Irish accent.

CHAPTER TWENTY-TWO

The silversmith bowed in welcome. 'Hrossvalr, lady.'
'That is a strange-sounding name,' she said in Irish. She was shorter than I, young, red-haired and disconcertingly, seemed very aware of how attractive I found her. She was confident too, and uncaring of the disapproving face on the middle-aged woman behind her – a servant, I decided.

'It means "horse-whale",' I said. 'They are like seals, but much larger, and dangerous with it.'

'Where are they found?'

'Groenland.'

Interest in her green, green eyes. 'Have you been there?'

To lie would have impressed, but I had always been bad at it. 'No, sadly.'

'They say it is even colder and more inhospitable than Iceland.'

'I have heard that,' I replied, amazed by her knowledge.

A *tsk*. She had seen my surprise. 'It is not just you Norsemen who voyage far across the seas! Saint Breandán sailed to Iceland hundreds of years before any of your race. That is common knowledge.'

It had escaped me. I coloured, and noticing the smith's amusement at my embarrassment, felt irritated as well.

She was sharp as a pin. 'I meant no insult.'

'None taken,' I said, forgiveness coming easily.

Smelling business, the silversmith interjected in serviceable Irish. 'How may I be of assistance, lady?'

'Do you fashion brooches?'

'But of course.' From under the table came another woollen bundle. Its contents, numerous pairs of intricately engraved brooches, soon had the young woman and her servant oohing and aahing.

My attention now strayed more towards the lady than the items I'd been looking at before.

'You like those dice, young sir.' The silversmith, an old hand, brought me back to the matter at hand. 'I will give you a good price.'

'Another time.' I replied in Irish, so the young woman could understand. I picked up one of the little shells, mesmerised by its smoothness and the dappling of spots on the top. The only shells I was used to were razorshells, whelks and mussels. 'Where is this from?'

'Have you heard of Jórsalaland?' The place name sounded bizarre in Irish.

'Naturally,' I said, grateful I had listened to Imr's tales. The young woman's head turned; she was listening, which pleased me. 'Its capital is Jórsalir, the Christ-worshippers' holy city. Both lie a long way south of Miklagard.'

A grave inclination of his head. 'And further south still is a narrow sea controlled by the Araboo. I am told the shells come from there. The local people use them as currency, as we do with silver.'

'How much for the six?'

His price was eye-watering. I laughed, and made to leave.

His next breath halved it. I offered him a seventh of his original demand, and we settled on a fifth.

'I would have paid more,' said the young lady.

The silversmith was scandalised. 'Why did you not speak, lady?'

'I did not want to seem rude.' A glance at me. 'Are the shells for your wife?'

'I am not married.'

'Your woman then. A fine warrior like you must have one.'

I liked this even more. 'No. The shells are for my friend, Vekel. He is a vitki, a druid.'

A little fear came into her eyes. 'It is as well I stayed silent. It would be ill-advised to get on the wrong side of a druid.'

'The shells are yours if you wish,' I said, thinking, I can get Vekel something else.

'No.' She folded my fingers around them, and gave a light squeeze.

'Very well.' I bent my head in respect, and to calm myself, for her touch made my head spin a little. To my relief, she went back to examining the brooches.

I accepted a wrap of cloth so the shells did not get chipped in my purse. Secreting them away, I thanked the silversmith. Calmer, my pulse returned to normal; this was the moment to speak again with the young woman, but my mind was empty as an upturned bucket. I knew well why. Dearbháil aside, and she had been a thrall, I was unused to speaking with attractive women.

She gave me a half-glance, and I seized the opportunity.

'Found any brooches you like?' It was a weak first attempt.

'I am not sure.'

'Any of them would look good on you.' All I could think of, this sounded even worse.

The servant's scowl would have curdled milk, but her cheeks dimpled.

I wanted to continue the conversation, awkward as I found it, but hearing loud voices outside, among them Vali, Hrolf and Thormod, I decided to go while the going was good. We would probably never meet again, she being a visitor to the town, and I did not want the young lady's last impression of me to come courtesy of lewd suggestions by my crewmates.

With a polite nod at her, ignoring her servant, I exited the premises without Vali and the others noticing. I let them go on down the street. Although I had not bought the arm ring, I was in a mood to buy something for myself, and that would not happen in their company.

'Friends of yours?' The boy was lolling against the shopfront.

'Yes.'

'See? I knew you weren't in any shape for drink.'

I grunted.

'You liked that girl. I could tell the tone of your voice.'

'Is that right?' I retorted, again surprised by his perception.

'She wasn't from round here.'

'Where is her accent from?' I couldn't tell.

'Osraighe, maybe, or Mumhan.'

It was ridiculous to feel disappointed, I told myself. A chance meeting like that would never amount to anything. Even so, the memory of our encounter stayed with me.

'Well, it is time.' It was the following day, when two kings were to wed, and Imr had dressed to impress. Beard oiled, in his finest tunic, he was wearing every last one of his arm rings. He had even had his thrall wash his baggy, colourful trousers. 'We best not be late, else all the beer will have been drunk.'

The crew, gathered in the inn where Imr stayed, laughed. No one cared about attending the marriage itself, held in the largest of Dyflin's Christ-churches, but every man on *Brimdýr* intended to take up the invitation to the feast afterwards.

It was typical that Vekel wanted to see the brides, especially Brian's daughter Sláine. Old to be wed, she was sixteen, and if the stories were true, a beauty. I had no interest in the girl. The daughter of a king, she was from a different world to mine, and would be all airs and graces. If I ever found someone, I decided, she would be like the spirited young woman in the silversmith's.

I did not glimpse Sigtrygg, Brian, Gormlaith or Sláine when we reached the great hall. The place was packed to bursting point; with tables and benches set up outside and the day warm and bright, we did not even try to enter. The throng was in part household warriors and thralls, but there were hundreds of guests and well-wishers too. They had arrived from Dyflin and Mumhan, Laighin, Osraighe and Midhe. Thankfully, Máel Sechnaill had not come, nor his son Cormac. The king of Connachta had sent one of his sons, however, and the Ulaidh, wary of Brian and Sigtrygg's new alliance, had sent a party of high-ranking nobles.

There were jarls from Man too, full of smiles and health-toasts, practised at keeping their feet close to the fire. Ívarr of Vedrarfjord was present, barely able to conceal his resentment, but he had always been stiff-backed. Emissaries from Luimnech and Dún Corcaighe were here, a show of respect to Brian, the largest fish in their pond. Last but not least, I spied Snorri of Ulfreksfjord, forgiven by Sigtrygg, or so he said.

Once-was-a-warrior, who had also escaped on *Brimdýr*, greeted us like old friends. Apologising for the lack of room inside the hall, he had tables brought out, and importantly, two large barrels of beer. We set to with a will, toasting Sigtrygg and Sláine, Brian and Gormlaith and Once-was-a-warrior too. Pleased, he sat himself down and had a tankard with us. The wedding had gone reasonably well, he said, celebrated by two bishops and the thin-lipped priest.

'Only reasonably?' I enquired.

'A jarl from Ulaidh puked on the floor. Too much ale. It was during the sermon, luckily, and he was near the back. I don't think Sigtrygg or Brian saw.'

'Someone will tell them,' said Thorstein.

'No doubt,' I said. 'Another reason for Sigtrygg to hold his grudge against the Ulaidh.'

'Here's to the king's health anyway,' said Once-was-a-warrior. 'May he get Sláine with child soon.'

We raised our beers and drank. Duties calling, Once-was-a-warrior then took his leave.

'Better get used to such toasts. For the king will be our master, should we stay. Him and Brian.' Imr's eyes roved, gauging reactions.

'I am for greener pastures,' said Thorstein, never afraid to speak his mind.

Lalo nodded; his feet were always itchy. Vekel cupped his chin in one hand. He was watching too.

'It will be politics and nothing else from now on, that is certain,' I said. 'Brian is the most powerful man in Ériu, and no one can deny it. I for one have no wish to be his man, any more than I have been Sigtrygg's.'

'There will be raiding, but only to Ulaidh, that is my prediction,' said Vekel. 'Its kings have still not bent the knee to Brian, and Sigtrygg will want revenge after the way they treated him.'

Grunts. Mutters. The coast of Ulaidh was prone to storms, and its people did not roll over the way soft-handed monks from Cluain Mhic Nóis did, say.

Imr sucked foam from his moustache, and continued to hold his own counsel. It was impossible to tell which way he would lean.

If he stayed, I was not sure I could. Relations with Sigtrygg had been strained before Gleann Máma, and had worsened after Artalach's un-fortunate death. Our spell on Man had seen no improvement; sitting on his hands, Sigtrygg had had time to brood, and not just on how he had been deposed. Despite my trying to avoid him on the voyage back to Dyflin, his stares had been murderous. To remain, I decided, would eventually see me bleeding out in an alley some dark night, or floating face down in the Black Pool.

When I left, I would not be alone. Thorstein had already spoken his mind, and Vekel would not linger if both I and his lover were leaving. That meant Lalo would also come. I studied my comrades.

The majority of the newcomers would probably stay, among them Vali, Thormod, Hrolf and Kar, but some of the original crew might be persuaded. If so, well and good, I decided. If not, we would go anyway. Knarrs carrying merchant goods often crossed the sea to Britain and Man during the spring and summer, and we had the silver to find passage.

I thought of my father, and decided that staying or leaving made no real difference to the chances of retribution for his murder, or regaining possession of the Oðin-sent sword. My one chance at Dún na Sciath had been squandered. To go there again on my own, or even with my friends, would see me dead rather than Cormac. My father would not have wanted me to die avenging him, I told myself. It was some solace. So was the heartfelt hope that when I returned to Ériu, Oðin might grant another opportunity, not just to kill Cormac, but to claim the sword again. I would not waste it.

Mood brighter at the thought of seeing new lands, determined that Sigtrygg would cause me no problems before my departure, I decided to join in properly with the festivities.

Some time later, much the worse for wear, I wandered away from my friends. Not wishing to piss in the open like everyone else – I was drunk, but not a complete savage – I wandered down the side of the great hall, leaning against the wall every so often until my head cleared. When I was far enough from the crowds, I undid my breeks and let my relieved bladder empty itself. I had just finished when my attention was caught by voices to my left, towards the back of the building. My head turned. A figure stood perhaps thirty paces away, tall and broad-shouldered, with his back to me.

'You're pretty. Give us a kiss.' He spoke Norse.

'Have you any idea who I am?' A woman, her Norse accented.

She was in front of him, and smaller, so I could not see her, but my memory stirred.

'Don't know, don't care. Go on, kiss me.' He took a step forward.

'Leave me alone, you brute!'

The sound of a slap.

'Bitch!' The man lunged forward, and there was a cry of pain.

I began to run. I had seen violence against women before, but not in a peaceful town, and most certainly not at a wedding. Busy grappling, the woman's assailant did not hear me. I hooked a foot around one of his ankles and heaved. He did the splits, and tumbled backwards against me. I punched him in the face as he gawped upwards, and when he fell onto his back, kicked him wherever I could. Ribs, head, belly, head again.

His arms flailed, trying to grab me. I stamped, and had the satisfying feeling of his nose breaking beneath my boot. 'That for being a skítkarl,' I said, and stamped again. He roared, and curled into a ball, which allowed me to look at his victim. A feather could have knocked me over. It was the young Irishwoman from the silversmith's, the one who had captivated me. But today she was in a magnificent blue dress, with a floral wreath in her red hair. She was stunning.

'It is you.' The comment was so pathetic, I cringed inwardly.

An eyebrow arched. 'This is a surprise.'

'Are you hurt?'

Her hand rose to her neck, and the red weal around part of it. 'Only a little.'

I kicked the man again, and he groaned. 'Ill-mannered brute.'

'If Sigtrygg finds out, he's dead.'

I was dumbstruck. The shock was as great as the occasion one winter, when, to the amusement of my oarmates, I had fallen headfirst into the Black Pool.

'Leave your mouth open that wide, and a fly will go in, my mother would say.'

'You are Sláine, Brian Bóramha's daughter.'

'Unless Sigtrygg married someone else today.'

It was incredible how easily she discomfited me. I kicked out again, eliciting a satisfying groan. My mind spun. 'What . . . why were you outside, my lady?'

Her turn to colour. 'I needed some fresh air.'

This was familiar ground, or so I thought. 'Had too much ale?'

'No! Because I am just wed to a man with sons my age!'

'Forgive me. I didn't think.' She made no answer, and I said, 'You did not agree to the marriage.'

'I had no choice!'

'I suppose not.' Sympathy filled me that the daughter of a king, now wife and queen to another, should have as much control over her life as a thrall.

'Sigtrygg wedding me and my father marrying Gormlaith helped

216

to solidify the peace. It is for the good of the people. My wishes count for naught.'

'I am sorry,' I said, not knowing what else to say.

A dismissive gesture. 'Yours is not a Dubhlinn accent. Where are you from?'

'Linn Duachaill, a small settlement a day's sail to the north.'

'I know the name. It was Norse originally?'

'Indeed. My father was Norse, my mother Irish.'

'Both are gone?'

'Aye.' I could see them both, the one pale and cold in the birthing-bed, the babe laid alongside, and the other, victim of Cormac's greed. 'My mother died years ago. My father's death was more recent.'

She touched my arm, making the skin tingle. 'His was not an easy passing?'

'He was murdered by one of Máel Sechnaill's sons. Cormac.'

Her mouth made an 'O'. 'Why?'

'He came into my father's forge and saw a sword – my sword. I was away at the time. Cormac wanted it, and my father said the blade was not his to give. Cormac slew him and took it for his own.'

'How terrible! Did you seek justice?'

'Faugh! I did not even try.' I was not going to mention Dún na Sciath and how I had not slain Cormac.

'Why?'

'Only one thing happens when people of my station seek redress from the nobility.'

A shocked look, then, 'I have never really thought about that.'

I forbore from the sharp retort that rose to my lips. 'I hope to meet Cormac again one day. Nothing will stop me from taking my revenge. Oðin strike me down if I lie.'

Silence.

I saw her face. 'You worship the White Christ.'

'And you are a pagan.' She looked slightly scandalised, but there was a flush to her cheeks.

'Proud of it.' I reached into my tunic and brought out my raven.

She recoiled, as one might from a snarling dog.

I laughed. 'You are scared of the old gods.'

'I am not!' To my surprise, she reached out and grasped the amulet. Our fingers touched. Self-conscious, I let go, although the contact exhilarated. She held on. We were close now; she was studying the ravenhammer, which allowed me to breathe in her perfume, to admire the light pattern of freckles on her fair skin, to note the curl of red hair around the base of one ear.

'You are beautiful.' The most beautiful woman I have ever seen, I thought, feeling a light-headedness that had nothing to do with beer.

Her head rose. Her eyes met mine. Less than a handsbreadth separated our faces. 'Thank you,' she said, smiling.

It took all of my self-control not to lean towards her, and . . .

'It's a raven?' she asked.

'Yes. Muninn, one of Oðin's birds.' The words came out whispered. I did not know why.

'My lady?' A woman's voice, insistent, even strident.

Sláine stepped back, her chest rising and falling rather faster than before. 'What do they call you?'

'Finn, my lady. Finn Thorgilsson.'

'I am grateful to you.'

'My lady, where are you? Your husband is calling!' The voice was nearing the doorway through which she must have emerged.

Sláine stepped within, preventing her maidservant from coming outside and seeing me.

'Shall I kill him?' I kicked her assailant in the groin, who let out a deep, pit-of-the-belly groan.

'You would do that?'

'For what he did to you, aye.' I meant it too. 'Dead men tell no tales.'

I had shocked her, that was evident. She vacillated, with the maid's cries growing louder, then said, 'No. Just make sure he talks of it to no one.'

I gave her a firm nod, waited until the door closed, then leaned down and grabbed the front of the man's tunic. Dragging him up off the ground, I slid the tip of my seax into his left nostril. His eyes, petrified, went down to it, and back up to me.

'What's your name?'

'Rognald.'

'You crew on a longship?'

'Aye. *Sea-stallion*.'

'It makes sense that you're one of Asgeir's men,' I snarled. 'I know you, Rognald, and I know your longship. Breathe a word of this to anyone, ever, and I will hunt you to the ends of the earth. Your death will be incredibly unpleasant. Fingers and toes cut off, balls sliced away, eyes gouged out – you'll be begging for release long before I'm done. Understand?'

Tears were running down his unshaven cheeks. 'I swear it,' he sobbed, 'on the All-Father, and the White Christ too.'

I stared into his face for a long moment, until the smell of piss – he had soiled himself – told me he was probably telling the truth. And then, flick, I sliced his nostril right open, and let him drop, screaming, to the ground. 'Do not forget,' I told him.

That done, I was thirsty for more ale.

CHAPTER TWENTY-THREE

Amid the singing, arm-wrestling, dice-rolling and grabbing of any female thralls foolish enough to come close, no one noticed my return. That is, save Vekel. He never drank much these days, even at times like this, declaring that if he was to lose his head, it would be with herbs that brought dreams or second sight.

I poured myself a fresh cup of beer from the barrel and went to join him.

'That was the longest piss a man ever took,' he said.

I elbowed Kar to one side, sitting beside Vekel.

'Well?'

I feigned ignorance. 'Eh?'

'You were gone a long time.' He stared. 'A woman?'

'No.' But I could not meet his gaze.

'I knew it! Get a quick hump in?' This wasn't unusual behaviour from our oarmates.

'Ara, get over yourself!' I was indignant.

'It wasn't a thrall then.'

I buried my nose in my tankard, and hoped he would give up.

'A freeborn servant caught your eye.'

I did my best to ignore him, but Vekel was like a child worrying at a scab. He would not give up until it lifted off, ready or no.

'Did you kiss her?'

'No.' I could imagine it, clearly.

'Are you going to see her again?'

'I hope so,' I said, thinking, beyond the most banal of greetings, it will be easier to put a pack-saddle on a colt than to speak to her. That was before even considering the danger of doing so.

'You look miserable, suddenly.'

'It's nothing.'

'Doesn't seem like that.'

I drank deep of my beer, and reflected sourly that it would have been a better idea to have taken my leave the instant it became clear who Sláine was.

'What is it?'

I scowled, and thought, it will never come to anything. I might as well tell him. I placed my lips against his ear.

A leer. 'Ooh, that's nice.'

I punched him. 'All right, I won't tell you.'

'I'm sorry, Finn.'

This was rare from Vekel. I looked to see if he was being genuine. He appeared to be, so I relented, and leaned in again. Quietly, I said, 'I met Sláine.'

Vekel blinked. 'And?'

'She might like me.' I explained what had happened.

'The girl is grateful you stopped her being raped. That's not the same as thinking the sun rises in your eyes.'

I told him next about our meeting in the silversmith's, and her comments about my having a wife.

'That is more interesting. You might be right. Is the feeling mutual?'

I nodded. I expected him to leap in with warnings not to get involved with Sigtrygg's wife, that I would get myself gelded, or killed, or both, but instead Vekel smiled.

'Quite the moonstruck calf, you are.'

I did not know how to reply, so I said nothing.

'I'm unsurprised she's not happy. Sigtrygg is no looker, and old enough to be her father besides.'

I ground my teeth, trying to put the image of him climbing on top of Sláine from my mind. 'It would be madness to pursue this – you must see that.'

He was rummaging in his bag. His fist came out, gripping something.

'No,' I said. 'Not the runes.'

Vekel cast them anyway. He leaned over the beer-soaked table, mouth pursed in concentration, poking at one bone, then another with a long fingernail.

My guts were in knots, but I could not take my eyes off him.

He muttered something inaudible.

'Well?' I demanded.

'Ooh, the vitki is reading the future.' This was Kar, slurring, but face alive with interest. 'Where are we raiding next?'

My heart lurched. The last thing I needed was for another person, especially someone I did not know well, to find out.

Vekel brought his black-lined eyes up to Kar's. 'That's not what I am looking for.'

'What are you doing then?'

'Determining when you will die.' Cold words, delivered in a flat monotone.

Kar's face paled, and a hand went to his mouth. Lurching to his feet, he hurried off.

'He's going to be sick,' Vekel observed.

'That was uncalled for.'

'Would you rather I told him the truth?' He had me, and knew it.

I wasn't up for any more game-playing, however. 'Tell me what you see. I need to know, Vekel.'

'The Norns have woven your threads together.' There was an unusual reverence in his voice.

My heart sang.

'I see them part. It will not last for long.'

Disappointment met realism. Sláine was married, Sigtrygg was in good health. 'She loves me?'

'She will. And you will love her.' A chuckle. 'You are halfway there already.'

I thought beyond the attraction and the passion to the consequences if Sigtrygg found out, and felt a tickle of fear. Quickly, I rolled the bones this way and that, upsetting the pattern. Vekel made no move to stop me.

'A lot of men don't want to know it all,' he said, shrugging. 'Look at Kar's reaction.'

I kept silent, partly wishing I had destroyed his reading even sooner. I might have held back, not gone to Sláine's aid. Now, though, it was clear fate had brought us together. Who was I to try and stop that?

He raised his cup. 'To you and your lady love.'

Lifting my own, setting aside thoughts of death, I grinned. My earlier decision to quit Dyflin quite forgotten, I began to imagine ways to meet Sláine, and how Imr might be influenced to tarry a while.

*

In the event, I did not have to try the latter. Late on in the night, Imr, who as he said afterwards, should have known better, agreed to a wrestling bout with Vali. The smith's mighty strength soon told, and Imr was grappled to the dirt once and then twice, thumping his arm on the ground to concede. Even though he could no longer win – the contest was the best of three – he insisted on going ahead with the last. Going low, he wrapped his arms around Vali's knees and took him crashing down, somehow managing to leap astride the smith's chest, knee-pinning his arms and forcing Vali to admit defeat. Jubilant, Imr only noticed afterwards that he had badly wrenched a hamstring.

In considerable pain, unable to stand for long, he was ordered by Vekel to rest. When Imr asked how long, Vekel replied, 'as long as a piece of rope'. Be more precise, Imr demanded, to be told that a rope could be any length at all.

I had no wish for Imr to be bed ridden, but I was mightily pleased that he was unfit to take us to sea. Hamstrings were unpredictable injuries. As Vekel told me, winking, sometimes the recovery took months.

I was in no state to seek out Sláine the next day, which was as well, for the newly wedded couple emerged from their bedchamber only to see the bloodstained sheet from the bed, proof that she had been a virgin, was brandished outside the great hall. Then, thralls having changed the bedlinen, they vanished again, as Sigtrygg loudly observed to the crowd, 'to ensure more seeds were sown'. This was related by Lalo, who had gone to watch.

It sent me into a bad temper. Although I had only spoken briefly with Sláine, I hated the idea of her underneath a heaving Sigtrygg. I wondered tetchily if he stuttered at the climax. Not wishing to brood, I dug out my weapons and put an edge on them such as I never had.

Karli, who never liked to be away from the ship for long and had slept on board overnight, commented. 'Know something I don't, Stormcrow?'

I gave him a quizzical look. 'Eh?'

'You're preparing for battle. I wondered if Sigtrygg told Imr this morning to go raiding.'

'No.' I ran the whetstone along my axeblade, up, down, up, down, then the same on the other side. I tested the edge with my thumb. It was deadly sharp, and would part Sigtrygg's head from his shoulders with ease. 'Clearing the beer fog, that's all.'

Karli *hmph*ed in disbelief, but he knew when a man didn't want to talk, and left me to it.

The repetitive task had tired me out, drink-weary as I was, so I curled up in my blanket between the sea chests, and closed my eyes. Awakened by the screeching of gulls, I judged afternoon to be almost gone. There was no sign of Karli; my only companions were the disgruntled-looking sentries, men chosen by lot. The reward for missing the wedding feast was to be given two days off duty, starting at midday just gone. I decided that their disgruntlement had been significantly added to by the complete absence of the crewmates who should have been replacing them. This was confirmed when I asked. Hiding my amusement – I did feel for the sentries – I offered to go back to the great hall and wake the latecomers.

This suggestion was met with hearty agreement.

I packed away my weapons in an oiled cloth, pulled the worst tangles from my hair, and clambered over the side. The walk from the Black Pool wasn't long, but a brisk sea breeze blew away the worst head-cobwebs. Revisiting the previous day's events, I admitted inwardly that there was more to my offer than rousing the layabouts. Sláine was in the great hall too. I told myself at once not to be a fool. Even if I somehow gained entry to the royal quarters, and by some lucky chance Sigtrygg happened not to be with her, I would not go undiscovered for long. There could be few surer ways of losing my head than being suspected of carrying on with the king's new bride. Not that I would ever get that far. There would be sentries outside his door, and sober ones at that. I buried the fantasy, and concentrated on searching out my oarmates.

They were easily found, lying under the very benches provided by Once-was-a-warrior. I picked out the nearest four. Nudging didn't work, nor did a few gentle kicks. A bucket of water taken from a kitchen thrall did the trick. Retreating from their curses only when I had an agreement that they would relieve the sentries on *Brimdýr*, and soon, I aimed for the sidewall of the great hall, and the door where Asgeir's warrior had attacked Sláine. She would not be there, I knew that, but standing on the spot would sharpen my memory of her.

It did, and also increased my frustration severalfold. The headstrong part of me wanted to hammer on the door and demand entry. The wiser part made me walk away, wondering if Vekel's reading of the runes had been incorrect. It wasn't unknown, he admitted it himself. Maybe he'd just been trying to make me feel good, I thought, or maybe the Norns were behind it, cackling as they moved my thread away from Sláine's. The beer-headache threatening to return, a cold sweat on my temple, I decided to forget about the Queen of Dyflin and head for The Thatch. At least one of my oarmates would be up for a drink.

A little whiskery dog, brown with a white flash on his chest, was nosing about the open space before the great hall. There was plenty to attract his attention, from gobbets of table-fallen meat to half-gnawed bones that had dropped from drunken hands. He was young, too young to be out on his own. I cast about, looking for the person who should be looking for him. I saw no one. The majority of those who were actually upright were thralls, beginning the massive process of cleaning up. Once-was-a-warrior was supervising, bleary-eyed and still loud of voice, but as far as I knew, he didn't have a pup.

I walked towards the dog, still searching for an owner. At ten paces, I stooped, and said softly, 'Hello, pup! Handsome boy, aren't you?'

He wagged his tail, but didn't stop chewing on his latest find. He did not run, though, as I came closer, and let me pick him up willingly enough. Stroking him, my fingers stopped on a fine leather collar with an intricately designed, silvered buckle. 'You do have an owner,' I said, 'and a rich one too.'

'Cú! Where are you, Cú?' A woman was calling from inside the great hall. She sounded worried.

He wriggled in my arms. 'Is that your name?' I felt a pang of sadness; at my father's funeral, Vekel had sent his dog Cú to the afterlife. Spying a thick-waisted, middle-aged woman in typical Irish dress exiting the main doors, I headed towards her. 'Is this the fellow you're after, mother?' I asked.

Her glare would have stopped a charging berserkr. 'I am not your mother, Christ be thanked,' she snapped. Her face softened to see the pup. 'And yes, that is him.'

It came to me. 'You are Sláine's servant!'

'The queen's maid, yes,' she said, stiff and formal, as if we'd never met, 'and that is her dog. Her pride and joy, he is.'

'I'm sure – he's a lovely little thing.' I made no move to hand him over. 'We met yesterday.'

A blank look.

'In the silversmith's.'

A long, appraising glance, a sniff. 'Ah yes, I remember.'

Nice to see you too, I thought. 'My father had a dog of the same name. 'Tis some coincidence that Sláine does also.'

'Indeed. Give him here.' She reached out.

'I would like to return the pup to Sláine myself. I found him.'

'Absolutely not!' Again I was subjected to the berserkr-stopping stare. Her fingers beckoned.

I let out an exaggerated sigh, and just as she was about to take him, stepped back. 'Be sure to tell Sláine who found Cú, won't you?'

Her third hard stare was met with one of my own.

'Christ and all his saints.'

I petted Cú, and pretended not to have heard.

A murderous scowl. 'Very well, I'll do it.'

'Thank you, mother.' I passed over the pup with a sweet smile. 'Good boy,' I said to him, and he wagged his tail.

'He likes me,' I called after her.

No answer, and I wondered if Sláine would hear how her maid had caught the dog, with no mention of my part. I hoped not.

Seven days went by without my seeing or hearing from the new queen. When entering the town, I made sure my feet carried me past the great hall on the off-chance that Cú might have escaped for a second time, or that Sláine herself might be coming or going. I had no luck in either regard. From the casual conversation I had one afternoon with Once-was-a-warrior, she was keeping to her quarters or the great hall. 'It must be hard on the creature, not just married but taken from her family, and living the Norse way rather than the Irish. It is fortunate she has her maid,' he said. His perception surprised me; evidently, there was more between Once-was-a-warrior's ears than I had assumed.

There was no Sigtrygg-believable reason for me to send a message to Sláine, or to seek out her company, so I did my best not to think about her by keeping busy. I trained with Kar; went fishing for mackerel with Vekel, something we had done as boys; I even had time for a swift rustling expedition into Midhe with half a dozen oarmates. We weren't greedy, taking only three sheep, enough to feast *Brimdýr*'s entire crew for one night.

Belly full of mutton and ale, I slept deep and dreamless, wakening to a warm, sunny morning. Sláine came to mind, and I did not try to bury the thought this time. I hadn't been given any duties for the day by Imr, so I decided to try my luck again outside the great hall. I donned the cleanest of my tunics, combed my hair, and was ready. Vekel asked where I was going; I told him, and he winked. 'Loki be with you,' he said.

I nodded, thinking, the scheming trickster won't be bothered with me, with something so small. I was completely wrong, because a few moments later, just inside the town gate by the Black Pool, who should I see coming towards me but Sláine's maid. This could not be coincidence, I decided.

'Are you lost, mother?' I asked in Irish.

'*Amadán*,' she replied. 'Do not play games.'

I nodded, deciding it wise not to anger my only contact with Sláine. 'Are you looking for me?'

'Why else would I come anywhere near the Black Pool, a place overrun with savages?'

I smoothed my features. 'Here I am, mother.'

'The queen wishes to meet.'

My heart leaped. Vekel had not been wrong. 'When?'

'Tomorrow.'

My heart leaped again. 'Where?'

'Do you know The Brazen Head?'

'Aye.' I hadn't been there yet, but remembered Orm declaring it had the best ale in Dyflin.

'Be there tomorrow at midday. Tell the innkeeper that you have come to see an old friend.' Her mouth was a thin line. 'When asked, say that you are from Mumhan.'

'I will. Tell the queen nothing could keep me from meeting her.'

A fearsome scowl, a shake of the head. Clearly, she did not like Sláine's orders.

'Thank you,' I called softly.

She walked away without responding.

*

It was cloudy the following morning, which made the time hard to judge, so I erred on the side of caution, leaving *Brimdýr* early, and following the Ruirthech to the west of the town. The Brazen Head was easy to find. White-washed, the street outside swept clear of the usual detritus, it was a two-storey structure, larger than most houses. Knowing I had a little time to kill, I was drawn to the smithy on its right. Smoke eddied from a hole in the roof; the smith was busy within. By the door was a wooden table upon which ironmongery had been neatly laid out. To my surprise, on a stool behind it perched no one else but Orm.

He returned my grin. 'Shopping?'

'Something like that.' Under his beady eye I picked over buckles, pins, hooks, clasps, belt ends. There were stirrups too, which I was unused to.

'These are well made,' I said.

'Of course,' he said huffily, as if I had intimated that this was surprising.

'Your uncle's work?' I peered inside. The bare-to-the-waist man inside did not look up, focused on the piece of metalwork on his anvil.

'Yes.' There was more behind his one-word answer, and I remembered what the silversmith had said.

I held up a ring-headed dress pin, as nice a piece as I might have made. It would go well with my cloak. 'How much?'

'A silver penny.' His eyes were bold.

'Do you think I came down with the last shower?' I winked to take the sting from my words.

'Orm!'

'Yes, Uncle?'

'Are you being fair?'

A scowl, quickly hidden. 'Yes, Uncle.' To me, he said, 'Half a silver penny.'

'That is twice the price I would charge for a dress pin.'

Trickster or not, he was still only a boy. His mouth fell open. 'You're a smith?'

'I am.'

'What have I told you, Orm, about robbing customers?' His uncle, who *had* been listening, came barrelling outside, a too-slow hen squawking and fluttering out of his way. His meaty arm went back, and the lad cowered.

'Hold,' I said.

Surprise on the sweaty, soot-marked face. 'Why?'

'Your nephew was only trying to make money. He's inexperienced, that's all.' I turned to Orm. 'Next time, study your customer's hands.' I held out my own, calloused, marked with old burns.

Orm was careful not to look at his uncle, who muttered something under his breath.

'Next time, be less greedy,' I advised. 'Start with the price at half a silver penny, and be prepared to drop it a little. You will still make a profitable sale.'

'I cannot argue with that.' The smith gruffly held out the pin.

In return I offered a piece of hacksilver almost half the weight of a penny. 'This is yours. You sweated over the pin, and the boy's food and clothing do not grow on trees.'

He took the silver with a nod. With a warning look at Orm, he went back inside.

I waited until the ting of his hammer carried outside before, using Orm's shape to block what I was doing, laying down another piece of hacksilver. His astonished gaze went to it, then to me. A question began to form on his lips, but I shook my head, no.

'This is for you,' I said quietly, 'not your uncle. You might see me more often, entering The Brazen Head. Keep an eye on the customers, eh? Anyone unusual, or odd-looking, around the times I am here, I want to know. There's plenty more where that came from.' I tapped my pouch so it clinked.

'You in trouble?'

'Not at all.' I shoved away the thought of Sigtrygg's reaction if he found out I was meeting his new wife in secret.

'Why d'you want to know who's coming and going then?'

'That's my business, not yours,' I said. Noticing the smith staring, I picked up a stirrup, and called out, 'Very nice. I might come back for a pair of these.'

'The boy will give you a good price.' Satisfied, he returned to his work.

Advising Orm to keep a good lookout, I ventured inside The Brazen Head and found a table at the back, from where I could see who entered and left. It was not yet midday, so I did not approach the landlord, a potbellied Norseman with a long beard. Nursing a tankard of good beer – it *was* far better than the stuff served in The Thatch – I kept my head down and spoke to no one.

My mind was busy. Even if Vekel approved, getting involved with Sláine was reckless. There was still time to leave, but that was a nithing's way out, I decided. If I was going to rebuff Sláine, I would do so politely, and in person. My inclination after making this decision was to drink more – my nerves were jangling – so it was a relief to see two women enter a while later. The first was the fearsome maid, and the second had her hood up, shielding her face. I watched, my heart thumping as the maid spoke briefly to the innkeeper, who led them up the wooden staircase. A door opened and closed, and he returned alone.

I went to the bar. Waving away a grey-haired serving thrall, I beckoned the innkeeper.

'Aye?' He wasn't the most communicative.

'I am here to see an old friend.'

His rheumy eyes narrowed. 'Where are you from?'

'Mumhan.' I indicated the staircase with a jerk of my chin.

His gaze went over my shoulder, studying his other customers, and I thought, his palm has been well greased to make sure no one has followed Sláine. She is young, but no fool.

'Last on the right.' He was already moving along the counter, greeting another customer.

I risked a casual look around the room myself. Satisfied that no one was paying any heed, I trod lightly up the stairs. There were four doors, a pair on each side. I stopped outside the second on the right and raised my hand. It was still not too late, a voice said inside my head. I remembered Sláine's beauty, and rapped softly, twice.

The door opened a fraction, revealing the maid's face, squinting and suspicious. She huffed. 'It's you.'

'It is, mother,' I said politely.

'Alone, are you?'

'Aye.'

'No one followed you?'

'No.'

'Sure?'

230

Before I could answer, Sláine intervened. 'Let him in.'

The maid stepped sourly aside, and I entered. Sláine had shed her cloak. Her long red hair was tied back in a ponytail; her cream cheeks were a little flushed. A chain of colourful beads linked the silver brooch over each breast, and held in place her long blue dress, which despite its loose fit, managed to accentuate her figure. This would have been Sigtrygg's choice, I thought, his queen in Norse raiment from the start. She was a magnificent sight.

'My lady,' I said, and bowed.

'You came.' Her voice was breathy.

'I did.' I wanted to add that I was not going to stay, but fuelled by the beer I had drunk, my determination was soaking away, like rain on dry soil.

'I must thank you for finding Cú.'

The maid wasn't entirely mean-spirited, I decided. 'It was nothing.'

'I disagree. He could have strayed further, and I might never have seen him again.'

'I'm glad he was yours,' I said. 'By happy coincidence, my father once had a dog of the same name.'

'You must tell me about him.'

Sláine ordered the maid to keep watch outside the door, ignoring the under-the-breath tutting and disapproving looks. When she had obeyed, Sláine slid the bolt home. 'There. We are alone.'

This was no girl, I decided, but a woman who knew her mind. I steeled my resolve. 'I should go.'

She came close, placed a hand on my chest. 'But you have only just arrived.'

I looked down into her upturned face. Her expression was open, her lips a little apart. 'You are married,' I said, hoping this would act as discouragement.

'To a man I do not love!'

I had no answer to that.

Standing on tiptoes, she kissed me. Slowly, languorously.

A pulse beat in my throat.

'Did you like that, Finn Thorgilsson?' she whispered.

'I did.'

'Kiss me then.'

So I did.

CHAPTER TWENTY-FOUR

Midsummer was nigh, and Imr's leg was still not right. He had listened to Vekel's advice for the first month. Then, impatient to go to sea, he had overdone it and put himself back to where he'd initially been. Grumpier than ever and often drunk with it, he had himself carried to *Brimdýr* every day to oversee preparations for departure. Rotas were drawn up, tasks allotted, and woe betide the man who didn't turn up for his spell stitching holes in the sail, caulking the strakes or re-braiding ropes.

Imr didn't care who did what, and no one liked filthy tasks such as applying pitch to the timbers, so it was easy enough to swap out my jobs when they clashed with a time I was supposed to see Sláine. My intention not to get involved with her had died a death that first meeting, not least because of the enthusiasm with which she had taken me to bed. Each time we parted, I was already looking forward to the next.

Generally, we met in the middle of the day, when it was usual for Sigtrygg to be dealing with court business. It was always in The Brazen Head, and Orm, the smith's nephew, proved to be worth every piece of silver I handed over. A detailed report was given each time I arrived and left. Fortunately, the only indication that Sláine and her maid were being followed was the unexpected revelation that Lalo tracked my every visit. As one of the few blámenn in Dyflin, it was easy to deduce that it was he.

When I challenged him, Lalo wasn't the slightest bit embarrassed, and said that he was looking out for me. One day when Orm's uncle was gone to see a customer, and before Sláine arrived, I introduced the two to each other. Orm was astonished by Lalo's now fluent Norse, but when he heard that a blámaðr could not just be free, but my friend and also a crew member on *Brimdýr*, his eyes all but fell from his head.

Upon discovering that they both liked fishing in the Ruirthech, the pair began to plot a day's outing.

I left them to it, and hurried inside The Brazen Head. I had become obsessed with Sláine, who was not just a passionate lover. Intelligent, sharp-witted, and well-informed about the power struggle between her father, Máel Sechnaill and Sigtrygg, she possessed a good sense of humour. She never mocked my humble origins, nor my tales of childhood, instead wishing for the freedoms I had never given a second thought to. Curious-minded, she was forever asking questions about Vekel and seiðr, or Lalo, and where he came from. I had had to ask Imr for more details of Miklagard, so fascinated was she by my first description.

In turn, I learned about her family, in particular her famous father. Growing up, I'd known a few things about Brian Bóramha, but not the fine detail. Sláine, rightfully proud, enjoyed the telling. One of twelve brothers, he had lost both parents – in separate attacks – to Norsemen, which explained his determination to defeat them wherever they were in Ériu. He had grown up campaigning against the Norse, developing into a brave and capable leader. As the youngest royal scion, he ought never to have taken the kingship of Mumhan, yet some twenty-five years earlier when his older brother Mathgamhain was killed in battle, it was Brian who took his place. Defeating another claimant to the throne, he had begun a long-running, bitter war against the high king Máel Sechnaill. Brian suffered many setbacks during Máel's frequent invasions of Mumhan, but achieved as many successes by sailing his large fleet up the Sionainn to raid the western borders of Máel's kingdom; he had also taken Laighin.

Determination defined him; it applied to all aspects of life. Once he'd decided that she was to wed Sigtrygg, begging and pleading had made no difference. Sláine told me it would have been easier flying to the moon than to change his mind. A sad sigh had escaped her before she returned to the rivalry between Brian and Máel Sechnaill.

Peace had finally come four years before, when the two kings each recognised the other's sovereignty over the northern and southern parts of Ériu. The background to the savage battle at Gleann Máma had been Máel Mórda's rebellion against Brian's rule. This threatened not just Brian, but Máel Sechnaill, which is why they had briefly joined forces against Máel Mórda – and Sigtrygg. Their amity had not lasted,

Sláine continued. Her father had every intention of invading Midhe this year, and forcing Máel to recognise him as high king. This was not a surprise to me, because Sigtrygg had declared his support for Brian, and would send warriors to join the Mumhan-men.

I imagined being part of that army, and fighting Máel's host. The chance of meeting Cormac in battle was slim, but it was there. Why then, a voice in my head demanded, was I risking my position in Dyflin by bedding the king's wife? There was no sensible answer, and I wasn't willing to address the issue either, so I buried it deep, and slaked my lust instead.

Sláine loved recounting her fathers' campaigns; I often joked that she should have been a man. One day it opened a door; to my complete astonishment, she asked to join *Brimdýr*'s crew. As she forcefully put it, it was no kind of life staying in Dyflin, bearing children for Sigtrygg, possibly dying in the process. If Thorstein could be one of us, why not her? She could use a bow, she said, and would quickly learn to wield an axe or spear. Despite my infatuation, the suggestion was impossible. Imr might have stolen her away, risking Sigtrygg's eternal enmity, but he was not her lover. There was *no* chance he would do it for me.

Sláine's desire was one of the few things I would not give way to her on. She did not take it well. Sometimes she raged, saying I did not care about her, and at others, she stormed out of our encounters. There would be no communication for several days, during which I told myself that it was over, and then the sour-faced maid would appear with a fresh summons to The Brazen Head.

Vekel would roll his eyes, and say that women were never happy, but such was the attraction I felt for Sláine, and my anticipation of our lovemaking as we made up, I did not listen. She was as eager to see me, and our trysts began extending to early evening, which made her 'reason' for leaving the great hall to go shopping more suspect than it already was. Looking back, it was foolish behaviour, but at the time it was easy to believe Sláine's assertion that Sigtrygg paid her no attention save in their bedchamber, and that his days were spent plotting revenge on the Ulaidh, who had turned him away in his time of need.

A month passed. The weather, which had been changeable for much of the early summer, had finally grown dry and hot. The foul smells which filled Dyflin grew immeasurably worse. It was hard to decide which was most unpleasant. Decaying animal dung. The acrid tang of sun-drying urine. The stench of rotting offal. The stomach-turning reek of an unclaimed corpse in an alleyway. I had taken to wearing a cloth wrapped around my face when on the streets; it was worth the resultant sweating.

One particularly hot day, Sláine and I were to meet. I longed to take her for a swim in the Ruirthech, but it was impossible. The bathing spot upstream favoured by Dyflin's youngsters was thronged daily; she would be recognised within moments of our arrival. The Brazen Head would have to do. When I reached it, hot and ill-tempered, Orm was not in his usual spot. He had gone to cool off in the river, I decided. It didn't matter. Nor, I told myself, did the fact that Lalo had vanished with Vekel to the ship recently come in from Britain. If the stories were to be believed, it carried goods from Serkland and even further afield.

I entered. It was quiet, just a few customers seated in the gloom. None seemed noteworthy, and I made for the stairs. The need to tell the innkeeper that I was 'meeting an old friend' had long since been dispensed with. Up the stairs, two at a time I went, to the same room Sláine and I had first met in. The tiny window was open, letting in more of the stink I had breathed all the way from the Black Pool. I did not shut the door, hoping it might draw some air inside, foul though it was, but there was no breeze, so it made little difference.

I sat on a stool, now and again wiping away sweat with the arm of my tunic. When Sláine arrived, she was as warm and uncomfortable as I. It did not stop us wanting to do what we always did. I closed the door, leaving the maid to bake in the heat of the corridor, and we both took off our clothes.

Things took on a life of their own, and it was for this reason that I at first ignored the sound of voices outside the room. As the maid's tone rose, becoming even shriller than normal, however, I felt a tinge of concern. Sláine had also heard. We stopped kissing and listened.

'No, you cannot go in there! Get away, you dog!'

A man's voice replied, low and threatening.

Cold reality crashed in. Leaping away from Sláine, naked, I lunged for my belt. Seax in hand, I slid back the bolt and threw wide the door. Two astonished faces regarded me: the maid's, and a bearded warrior I vaguely recognised.

The latter's expression went from shock to delight, and I thought, he hoped to find me here. In the same moment, I recalled that he was one of Sigtrygg's household warriors. He turned, intent on pounding downstairs, and I knew with sickening certainty that he was going to tell the king. If he succeeded, Sláine might survive, but I would be a dead man.

I leaped past the maid. The warrior was already at the top step, calling out to someone below, his comrade, probably. I wrapped an arm around his neck, clamped fingers over his mouth and bodily heaved him back a short distance. The seax blade ran across his throat, neat as neat. Blood sprayed everywhere, he sagged into my grip, and the maid shrieked.

This was all going wrong, and fast. 'Innkeeper!' I roared.

'Aye?' He sounded wary.

'There's been an argument. Get up here.'

I hissed to the maid, 'Get your mistress dressed. Quickly!'

She had not lost her wits, and vanished into the room.

I dragged the dead warrior away from the stairs, and waited for the innkeeper to appear. He took in the body. 'Christ and all His saints,' he said.

'You've seen the like before,' I said harshly. 'Can you get rid of him?'

His expression sharpened, but when I retrieved my purse and he gauged its weight, he nodded. 'That can be done.'

'See that it is. And keep your lips sealed.'

'I will.'

I stuck my face into his. 'If I hear that you haven't, I will geld you.' I brought the seax up between us, letting him see the blood. 'You won't die, though, because I'll cauterise the wound. After that I will flay the skin from your back.'

He had gone a pasty shade of grey. 'I will not tell a soul – I swear it on the White Christ!'

I stared into his eyes until convinced he was utterly terrified, and then I ducked back into the room.

Sláine was almost dressed. The maid was helping.

'You must leave now,' I said. 'With your hood up, you understand?'

'Let me come with you.' Sláine's gaze was steady.

Images flashed through my mind. Fleeing the town, making a life together, I knew not where. I came to the swift and unpleasant conclusion that we would not get far. Under torture, for that is surely what would happen to the maid when she returned without Sláine, Sigtrygg would discover that we had eloped. Every warrior in Dyflin would be sent after us.

'Stay. We will work things out later,' I said. 'I am going after the other one.'

I was tugging on tunic, breeches and shoes, wiping my seax on the bedclothes and ramming it into its sheath.

'There were two?'

'At least.' I had a leg out of the window. 'I will get word to you soon.' I pulled the other leg after the first, and dropped into the narrow lane that ran between the inn and the next house. A pig rootling in the muck squealed in alarm and took off. In other circumstances it would have been funny. Now I just followed it to the street, praying to all the gods that my quarry hadn't put too much ground between us.

The pig emerged right in front of a large mastiff, which barked and set off in pursuit. To my delight, the racket attracted everyone's attention. My luck continued; no crowd was spilling out of The Brazen Head, and Orm was close to the door. I ran over.

'Anyone come out in a hurry?'

He scowled. 'Just now? A man all but knocked me over.'

Relief flooded my veins. One only. 'Do you think we can catch him?'

'Uncle,' Orm shouted, 'I've got to go!' He didn't wait for a reply, but sprinted off down the street.

I caught up fast. 'We have to reach him before the royal hall.' Or, I thought, I would be joining the ranks of aspiring einherjar outside Valhöll.

'Why?' Orm was ever direct.

'He's going to the king.'

'To tell him you've been ploughing his wife?'

'Eh?'

He slowed to sidle through the gap between an ox-cart and the fence of a house. Throwing me a sly glance, he broke into a run again. 'Think I didn't know?'

'Does anyone else?' I asked, horrified.

'I don't think so.'

That didn't help much. I ran, studying everyone in sight. Two women talking, one with a babe dandled on her hip, the other holding a basket of vegetables. A man sitting outside his house, whetting a knife. A group of youths, swaggering and blustering the way youths do. A bent-backed thrall carrying a sack of grain, and his master strolling behind. There was no one running, no sign of the man I sought, and my worries sharpened. 'Hurry!'

'We can still catch him. Six silver pennies, it'll be.'

'Done.' Orm might have been an opportunist, I decided, but he wasn't cynical. Either that, or he didn't fully appreciate the depth of the cesspit I teetered on the edge of.

Orm dodged right, into the lane between two houses. I followed. I leaped over the larger piles of turds, bucket-deposited by the residents on either side, but there was so much of it, I soon gave up trying. Shit-covered shoes were the least of my troubles.

'How do you know about me and Sláine?' I demanded, chest heaving.

'Simple.' Orm couldn't have sounded more smug. 'I followed her and her companion from The Brazen Head one afternoon. Straight to the royal hall they went. I did it another day, curious to know who she was. Her hood got blown back by a gust of wind, and I recognised her.'

'Did you tell anyone?' I demanded.

'I'm not stupid!'

We emerged onto another street, turned left, went a short distance and entered another laneway. I had lost my sense of direction; my fate was entirely in Orm's hands. I hoped the gamble was worth it.

'If you catch up to the man we're after, I'll give you twenty silver pennies. How's that?'

'Done. What are you going to do to him?'

I said nothing, but when he'd looked away, I touched the handle of my seax, making sure it hadn't fallen out.

We passed a stench-laden butcher's yard where crows clamoured over a pile of discarded bones and offal. Geese honked in a pen, unhappy at being confined in the heat. A mother working a loom outside her house used her foot to rock a cradle, singing a lullaby to her infant. Outside an inn, a boy watched two drunks engaged in a pissing competition.

There was still no sign of my quarry. My fear swelled. Fail to catch him, and I would have to leave Dyflin before nightfall, or face a lingering and unpleasant death. Even if we succeeded, my choices were grim. A man couldn't murder one of the king's warriors in broad daylight and expect to get away with it. I had been around the town long enough; someone would recognise me. I would have to flee regardless, I decided.

'Is that him?' Orm pointed. The man some distance ahead was clad no differently to most, but the scabbard slapping against his left leg as he ran denoted a warrior. Every now and again, he cast a backward look, which was also telling.

'It must be.' My mouth was dry.

'Stay close behind him. Don't do anything until you see me.'

I wanted Orm to explain, but he had disappeared into yet another laneway between houses. Cursing, thinking it was Loki-luck for my destiny to be in the hands of a child I barely knew, I kept after the warrior, moving in until perhaps twenty paces separated us. That kept a few people between us, far enough, I hoped, to prevent him realising that I was so close.

My wish was in vain. He turned, saw me, and put on a burst of speed.

He *was* the second warrior.

'Sir!' Orm had somehow materialised in front of him. 'A moment, sir!'

'Out of my way!'

Orm stuck out a foot, but the warrior had a neat sidestep.

It was not far to the royal hall. I had failed.

Beyond all hope, Vekel and Lalo.

Vekel and Lalo, right in the warrior's path. Vekel, his face painted white, rings of black around his eyes, looking entirely like a creature from another world. Lalo, teeth bared in his dark face, his fists clenched.

'I thrust from me *göndull's* breaths,' Vekel cried, pointing his staff.

The warrior came to a juddering halt. His hand went up in a warding gesture.

'One breath to bite you in the back, another to bite you in the breast,' Vekel intoned, 'and a third to turn harm and evil against you.'

People were staring, horrified. No one dared to intervene.

Vekel continued his chant.

The warrior quailed at first, but when nothing happened, he rallied. 'Move,' he grated. Out came his sword.

'Do not harm the vitki!' I roared.

The warrior's arm went back. Vekel didn't flinch. Lalo grabbed for his dagger, too late.

I shoulder charged the warrior from behind, sending him face-first to the street. He was lithe, though, and managed to cat-twist up onto his knees. Wrapping both arms around my thighs, he took me down. I slammed into the dirt, my head, shoulder and hip banging, one, two, three. Hurting, I didn't see the punch aimed at my jaw. Flashes of light burst across my vision, pain exploded in my skull. A voice shouted, Vekel's. So did another, piping in tone – Orm. I heard a blow landing, a solid connection of metal on bone, and a body landed close by.

A calmness fell. People asked questions, and I heard Vekel say that the warrior had taken against him after a prophecy he had paid for and not liked. Groggy, I sat up. The warrior lay beside me. Vekel had smacked him across the head with his staff, I decided, but only partly scrambled his wits. He was stirring, and groaning, and my fears re-surged. The moment he struggled to his feet, he would go to Sigtrygg, and I would be undone all over again.

Vekel hauled me up. 'Come on,' he said in my ear. 'Get across the river, and we can make for Linn Duachaill.'

'The king will send men after us – riders.'

'They will have to catch us. Unless you'd rather stay here?'

'Look out!' Orm's voice.

Movement at the corner of my eye. As the warrior lurched upright, a wicked skinning knife in his fist, I whipped out my seax and lunged. His momentum carried him forward onto the sharp steel. Slicing through tunic, skin, muscle, the tip hit bone – a rib – skidded up a fraction, and ran in to the hilt.

It brought us face to face, close as lovers, as intimate too, but in a deadly way. His eyes were pain-filled, shocked; mine, cold, hard, determined. I whispered in his ear, 'Never spy on a queen.'

When I tugged the seax free, he fell, dying, at my feet.

'You all saw,' Vekel shouted. 'He came at me with a knife!'

Orm joined in. 'He tried to kill a vitki!'

A man in a doorway made the sign against evil. Others averted their gaze. There were no challenges, no accusations of murder. No one appeared to know who the warrior was either.

There was time for swift consideration. When the king found out about this man's death, he would want an explanation, justifiable kill-ing or not. Even if no one remembered me, Vekel and Lalo would stick in most people's minds. That was enough reason to leave at once. I could not be sure about the owner of The Brazen Head either. If he identified me, willingly or not, Sigtrygg would definitely be out for blood.

My decision had been made, but I could not leave without getting word to Sláine, no matter how great the danger. I said this quickly to Vekel; my heart warmed that he accepted my decision without protest. He was ready to go. My seax cleaned, so was I. We walked into the crowd as if nothing had happened. Lalo, and Orm, amazingly calm considering what had just happened, were with us. No one stopped us, and within a hundred paces, we had left the chaos behind.

I asked Vekel for his purse, reassured him that yes, I would pay him back, and offered it to Orm.

His eyes widened; the bag was fat with silver.

'You've earned it. You could be a warrior one day, if you wanted.'

His chin rose. 'I'd like that.'

'I need one more thing from you.'

He lit up. 'Tell me.'

I whispered in his ear. He nodded. I spoke a few more words. 'I'll do it,' he said.

I clapped him on the shoulder, as I would with a comrade. 'I am grateful. Make yourself scarce now, eh? The fewer people who see you with us, the better it will be.'

There was a sadness in his eyes. 'You're leaving, after?'

'I have to.'

'Will you come back?'

'I don't know. Probably not. It'll be too dangerous.'

'Farewell, Stormcrow.'

I smiled as he slipped away, unsurprised that he also knew who I was.

The three of us returned to *Brimdýr*, told Imr that a message had come from my sister, and that I was returning to Linn Duachaill. He looked dubious, but wasn't about to call me, Vekel, *and* Lalo liars. It was agreed that when his leg healed, he would sail north. We made no mention of going next to The Thatch, which was done via a circuitous route; I waited down an alleyway until Thorstein, who had joined us, had procured the use of a building in the yard. Like a criminal hiding from a mob, I stayed there for the rest of the day.

I suffered Vekel, commenting and laughing, to dress me in the women's clothing Thorstein had gone and bought. I also wore one of his glass bead necklaces. I even had a Norsewoman's headdress, which helped conceal my too-short hair. Two rolled up balls of cloth served as my bosoms. It was fortunate I had no beard, else a shave would been necessary too. The only weapon I had was my seax, strapped high up on the inside of one thigh, in the Miklagard style mentioned a lifetime ago by Havard.

'Quite the looker, you are,' Vekel said, and tried to pinch my arse.

I punched him, and glared at Lalo, who was chortling with mirth. Thorstein held back, for which I was grateful.

Too readily identifiable, the pair stayed behind while Thorstein and I slipped back onto the streets. The sun had gone down, but the remaining light in the sky was enough for us to pick our way, again by less-used thoroughfares, towards the great hall. If Sigtrygg had sent out warriors to search for me, they were no longer about. Few other people were abroad; at this hour it was safer to stay inside one's house. If anyone stared, and few did, we looked like a warrior and his wife, going about their business. I was pig ugly for a wife, Thorstein told me – he could no longer resist – but now that we were together, he'd keep me. I told him where to go in no uncertain terms, which only amused him more.

To my great relief, the open space before the great hall was quiet; we skirted around its edge to reach our destination, the very door where I had rescued Sláine from Rognald. An immediate quandary presented itself. There was no sign of Sláine, and I had no idea if Orm had succeeded in his task: asking her to meet me outside between vespers and compline. I was familiar with monastery bells ringing at sunset, and again not that long after, but I'd had to ask Thorstein to find out what the Christ-worshippers called them. He had duly done so.

Various possibilities rolled around my head as I stood in the shadows, hoping that no one saw us, or worse still, demanded to know our business. Orm might have failed, and Sláine would not come. In that case we would leave a short time after vespers sounded. Or he might have succeeded, but Sláine was unable to leave her quarters. Given what had happened to Sigtrygg's men, sent to follow his wife, this was a distinct possibility. It was also feasible, and my greatest hope, that Orm's message had not just got through, but that Sláine would soon

242

emerge from the door and into my arms. It would be a bittersweet farewell, but better than nothing.

'I am a fool.'

'Do not be so hard on yourself.'

Startled – I had spoken out loud without realising – I shot a look at Thorstein. 'Why? I should never have got involved with Sláine.'

'Many men would say the same thing about me and Vekel.'

I had never thought of that.

'The heart is a strange organ, Finn, with its own purpose. Ignore its voice at your peril.'

From Thorstein, this was a speech, and a deep-meaning one. I was cheered by his words, and his loyalty, standing here with me when it was as likely that twenty of Sigtrygg's household warriors might come barrelling out the door rather than Sláine.

Time passed, and I began to think that we had come in vain. The compline bell would sound before long, and waiting on after that would be sheer lunacy. I wished now that I had told Orm to come and meet me here; that way at least I would know if he had failed or not. I paced up and down, fighting the urge to force the door open and enter the great hall.

A noise. Movement behind the door. I heard Thorstein's sword come free of its scabbard. Guts twisting, I reached under my dress and took out my seax. I would not die weaponless.

A whine, the scuffle of paws.

My heart sang.

A bolt moved; the door creaked. Cú emerged, straining on the leash, and after him . . . not Sláine, but her maid.

Fighting disappointment, I whispered, 'Where is the queen?'

A glower that would have made a child cry. 'In her quarters, under close guard.'

'Is she unharmed?'

'For the moment, yes. The king is suspicious – one of his men slain in the street, the other vanished – but he has no proof of any wrong-doing by her.'

Relief surged. Sláine had kept silent, and the proprietor of The Brazen Head had not played me false. Yet.

'Be quick! I was seen going outside.'

'Tell Sláine I love her. I will always love her.' The maid did not sneer, which encouraged me. 'Tell her that I have to leave, but I will return.'

'When?'

'I do not know. When it is safe.' The maid sniffed, and I knew well why. It would never be truly safe, not while Sigtrygg lived. I hesitated, unsure what to say that was not a lie, or trite.

There was movement at the end of the great hall. Thorstein stirred. 'Finn.'

'Go,' I said to the maid.

She nodded, the friendliest gesture I had ever seen her make. 'Christ be with you.'

Oðin guard you and Sláine, I thought.

CHAPTER TWENTY-FIVE

'*You bedded Sigtrygg's wife?*' Ashild could have been heard in Linn Duachaill, a good walk away.

'Her name is Sláine,' I muttered, wishing I had kept the reason for our arrival secret.

'Like the village?'

I had walked through Baile Shláine with Vekel what seemed like a lifetime ago, on our way to Loch Ainninn, but had never given a moment's thought to its name. 'Yes, I suppose.'

'No matter,' she said with a withering look. 'You are a fool, Finn Thorgilsson, a fool who thinks with his bod, not his mind!'

I reddened, and tried to ignore Vekel's broad grin, and Thorstein, watching in amused surprise. Lalo's eyes were huge to see me cut so roundly down to size. My sister's husband Diarmaid had gone outside, ostensibly to check the livestock, but more likely to save me further embarrassment. From his parting expression, I suspected it was more usual for him to be on the end of her acerbic tongue. I didn't envy him. I busied myself petting Madra and Niall, who were at my feet, demanding attention, and hoped she would be done soon.

'Am I wrong?' demanded Ashild.

'What was I to do? We fell in love.'

An exasperated sigh. 'In the eyes of God, she is a married woman. You broke the seventh commandment!'

I snorted. 'I don't believe in that nonsense.'

'I will ignore that blasphemy. God will have his justice on you one day.' She crossed herself. 'For the moment, it is Sigtrygg you need to be worried about.'

'Maybe not.'

Her hands went to her hips, just like our mother when she was angry. 'Why might that be?'

'The warriors who came to the inn where we used to meet' – I met Ashild's disapproving gaze, refusing to look away – 'are dead.'

'So you are also a murderer!'

'The second one tried to kill Vekel. I was protecting my friend.'

'And the first?'

'Disapprove of me, sister, think what you will, but if I hadn't slain him, he would have told Sigtrygg. It was the same for them both. Their corpses can't talk.'

'And Sláine?'

'She will keep her trap shut.'

'You cannot be certain of that.'

'No, but it will not be in her interest to admit to anything.' I hoped this would end my interrogation, but of course Ashild, wanting to examine every possibility, would not let it go. On and on her questions went.

In the end, I could take it no more. 'It's done. Over. We got out of Dyflin safely, and with a little luck, Sigtrygg has no idea about Sláine and me. Imr will soon be here in *Brimdýr*. We'll sail for Britain, and the king can kiss my arse goodbye.' I saw in her face what I had not thought of, and my heart skipped a beat.

'Suppose he does know about you and his wife! Having failed to catch you, what if he decides to seek out your family?' asked Ashild, her voice quiet. 'Me. Diarmaid. Our child.'

I wanted the floor to open up and swallow me.

Vekel intervened. 'That will not happen, Ashild.'

'How do you know?' She was a Christ-worshipper, but still used a softer tone than she had with me.

'I consulted the rune bones last night. You will come to no harm.'

She stared at him for a long time, and then she sighed. 'I hope you're right. It's not as if we can do anything about it. This is our home. We can't just jump on a longship and sail away, like some.'

'We shall leave,' I said, not wanting to place her or her family in any more danger than I had already. 'Stay close to the shore, and wait there for *Brimdýr*.'

'You'll do no such thing,' scolded Ashild. 'It's bucketing down outside, and you haven't eaten yet. You look half-starved, the lot of you.'

My eyes went to Thorstein, then Lalo. They appeared eager not to go out in the heavy rain. Even Vekel seemed content not to move.

'Thank you, sister,' I said.

'You can build a shelter in the morning. Diarmaid knows a good spot, protected from the weather, but close to the sea for keeping watch.'

I had to smile. There was always a sting in the tail with Ashild.

I didn't mind.

In the event, we had camped out for only a day when the gods intervened in the most unexpected way. Not that long after sunrise, Ashild came looking for us, her face stern.

She was coming to give out again, I decided. When I said as much, Vekel just raised an eyebrow.

'Is all well, sister?' I called.

She proffered a fresh loaf. 'I baked this for you.'

'That is kind.' I waited, because there was more.

'It was not just the bread. I have news.'

'I thought that. Go on.'

'I was out in the sheep pasture early this morning. I saw Cormac riding north.'

This I had not expected. Nor, from the momentary shock on his face, had Vekel. 'The high king's son?' I said.

'Yes.'

'Are you sure?'

'I think I would remember him.' Her tone was acid.

I coloured. 'Of course. How many men were with him?'

'Six. They were carrying bows and spears.'

A hunting party, and close by. Suddenly, my heart was racing as if I'd run up a hill in my mail shirt.

'We will need horses,' said Vekel.

How I loved him in that moment. No questions, no warnings, just an acceptance of what I had to do, and a willingness to be part of it.

'Who's Cormac?' asked Thorstein.

'The man who murdered our father,' said Ashild, and there was death in her eyes. 'Best leave soon to be sure of catching him.'

I nodded. 'Thank you, sister.'

'Make sure, Finn.'

'I will,' I swore.

Thorstein announced he was coming too; he made it sound as if we were going for a stroll. Lalo wouldn't be left behind either.

I grinned at Ashild.

Four against seven were odds that I could live with, especially when it gave me a chance to kill Cormac. I prayed that my sword was with him.

The horses we were loaned by Gunnkel and one of his neighbours were sturdy *gerráns*, but they weren't of the same quality as those of Cormac and his companions. If Máel's son had been riding somewhere in a hurry, we would never have caught them. But as it transpired, they were out for sport and taking all the time in the world.

We followed their trail at a decent pace, through the rolling countryside that was so familiar to me. The raths were large, the land being good. Sheep dotted the low hills. Cattle grazed the pastures, watched over by thralls. No one greeted us, instead wary of an armed group that included a vitki and a blámaðr. Word of our passage would spread fast, but it didn't matter. Our quarry was not that far ahead.

Sunset wasn't far off when Lalo pointed out smoke rising above oak trees in the middle distance. The grove would provide a good place to camp. It might not be Cormac, but their horses' hoofmarks led in that direction. I decided that the chance of it being anyone else was small. Tethering each gerrán with a *langpheitir*, a rope that ran from the hindlegs to the neck, we talked first. Get close enough to spy out Cormac and his party before the light went, it was agreed, and our attack could be in darkness, a real advantage.

Thorstein and I had prepared as we would for a raid. Lalo never wore armour, but he had a shield and a spear, as well as his seax. He was also adept with a bow, of which we had two, loaned by Gunnkel. Vekel, who normally didn't fight, said he would use the other. I hadn't seen him use a bow in years, but Thorstein and I were the only ones who could effectively charge our enemies. It made sense; I just hoped his aim was good.

We walked to the treeline, and then Lalo slipped away between the oaks and rowans like a dark wraith. He came back not long after, an impish look on his face.

'It is them.' He anticipated my question, and added, 'Seven men. Good horses. One has long fair hair, and the others defer to him.'

I licked my lips. 'That sounds like Cormac. What are they doing?'

'Lounging around a fire, roasting meat, drinking. There is lots of boastful talk.'

'Sentries?'

Lalo chuckled. 'No.'

It was perfect, I thought.

We waited until full dark before getting into position. Lalo, able to move silently to and fro, brought back word that most of the group were drunk, or well on the way to that state. Annoyingly, Cormac was being abstemious, the reason for which was not clear. Vekel's response was that Lalo should shoot him first, get the job done immediately. I would have none of it. The whole point of the ambush, I argued, was for me to avenge my father. It would not feel the same if Lalo had slain Cormac. My passion won the day.

We crept closer, placing our feet with incredible care in case of treading on fallen branches. Nothing could be done about the plentiful nettles, but lengths of bramble were held back not to whip the person behind. We paused often to listen. It was a pleasant, cool night, the sky partially clouded. An owl call, haunting and eerie, carried through the still air. Rustling in the undergrowth marked the passage of small creatures. A fox barked thrice, and was silent. From some distance away came the characteristic call of a nightjar. Voices became audible too, loud and beer-fuelled, relaxed. My stomach clenched. Since the disastrous events in Dyflin, I had given no thought to avenging my father. Now here I was, with Cormac about to be handed to me on a platter. If Loki was in a really good mood, the sword might be with him. I offered up thanks to the gods, adding, *I will not forget this.*

The last hundred paces were infinitesimally slow, crawling on hands and knees. I was with Vekel. Lalo and Thorstein were a little distance to our right. Attacking from opposite sides of the fire would have reduced the chance of escape, but the risk of a stray arrow was too great.

About half the distance remained when Cormac began to hold forth. I pricked my ears. He had been the one to take down the deer. It was the finest shot he had ever made, he claimed – and the longest too. 'A hundred and fifty paces it must have been.' I shook my head in disbelief. Any hunter who risked an arrow at that distance was a fool, or one chancing his arm. Cormac was exaggerating, and he had a captive audience. His men rained down praise, saying that they could not have done it, that Cormac was a truly skilled archer.

One was a real brownnose, claiming that the mythical warrior Cúchulainn himself could not have made the shot. An awkward silence met this comment, and I bit the inside of my cheek not to laugh. Kissarsery only went so far. When fawning was overdone, even half-wits realised. Cormac was many things, but he wasn't stupid. Right now, I wagered, he was glaring at the brownnose, who, embarrassed and scared, was wishing he had held his tongue.

Vekel snake-bellied in beside me. Even the darkness could not conceal his smile. He had heard too. We made no move until the conversation around the fire started up again. It wasn't a long wait; men like Cormac love the sound of their own voice. Was the meat ready yet, he demanded. He was famished. Almost, he was told. Not much longer. Cormac responded surlily that it better not be burnt.

'Beer,' he said.

'Here, lord.'

Cormac drank loudly, from a skin, I guessed, then belched. 'Maybe we'll get a boar tomorrow.'

'If we see one, lord, I am sure your spear will be first in its flesh,' said a voice.

I made a face at Vekel.

Cormac was then asked to recount the tale of his last boar kill, which had been the previous winter. He launched into a long, rambling story, pausing often to accept his companions' adulation. It was the perfect opportunity for Vekel and me, and I presumed, Lalo and Thorstein to close in.

Cormac's group had set up camp in a small clearing. When the trees began to thin, I stopped. Peering through the scant undergrowth, I made out seven men lounging around a large fire. Cormac was about a third of the way around the blaze, gesturing expansively as he described killing the boar. Three men had their backs to me, and the remainder faced in my direction. None were wearing armour, and I could see no shields. I judged the bows to be with the pile of spears a short distance from the fire, or perhaps lying by their owners' sides. Their horses, each hobbled with a langpheitir, stood quietly nearby.

'Ready?' I mouthed at Vekel, who was awkwardly nocking an arrow. He nodded.

I considered taking the bow from him, and putting a shaft in Cormac's back. At this range, it would be easy. No, I decided. I wanted him to know who had ended his miserable existence.

The agreed signal was an owl call, not something I was good at replicating. Lalo was, unsurprisingly, and Vekel was to reply.

We had lain there for fifty heartbeats before Lalo called out. It was so close it had to be him. Vekel waited, but there was no reaction from Cormac or his companions, so he copied the sound. It was a poor imitation of Lalo's, but that didn't matter. We were on our feet, and fifteen paces to our right, so were Lalo and Thorstein.

Lalo's bow sang, and one of the warriors facing in our direction was punched backwards, an arrow deep in his chest. Vekel loosed, and a man with his back to us roared as a shaft took him in the shoulder.

I charged, knowing Thorstein was too.

I ran towards the fire as if the dragon Niðhöggr was on my heels. The first warrior I met was still scrabbling for his dagger when my axe split open his chest. I managed to hit the next man with the backswing. The heavy axe head smashed his cheekbone and he reeled away. I whirled, looking for Cormac. With the dexterity of a hunted deer, he leaped the fire to get away.

A sudden thump in my midriff made me pause. I had been stabbed in the belly by one of Cormac's companions. There was pain, but the steel rings of my mail had held. He had not gutted me.

I broke his nose with my shield boss, and as he stumbled backwards, cut off his left arm with my axe. The dagger dropped from his other hand. He stared vacantly at the spraying stump, then the pain hit and he began to scream.

Panting, I looked for more enemies, but there were none. Thorstein was all right; Vekel was fumbling another arrow to the string, and Lalo had just loosed one over the fire. After Cormac, I realised, and hurdled it, my feet moving the instant I hit the ground.

'Did you hit him?' I roared.

'No,' came Lalo's disappointed reply.

I was a nithing. If I had shot Cormac, or agreed to let Lalo do so, I thought, he would be lying dead with his lickarse companions now, instead of running unhurt into the darkness. I chased twenty paces after him but my eyes had adjusted to the firelight, which meant I saw almost nothing. I cast about, hoping to see a branch still moving from his passage, or a footprint in the soft ground, yet found no trace. I was on the point of giving up when a crash resounded from the darkness. I sprinted towards it, barking my shins on a low-lying trunk. Brambles whipped one of my cheeks, but I did not care.

I was running so hard, barely able to discern a thing, that I didn't even see the dip in the ground. My feet went from under me, and I went down. My head banged off something hard – a fallen tree? – and stars clouded my vision. Dazed, my axe gone, I lolled back like a man blind-drunk at a feast.

Someone leaped on top of me.

Cormac, I thought dully. He had tumbled in the same hollow, but regained his footing before I'd arrived. My strength was gone. I could not stop his hands wrapping around my throat, choking the life out of me. My breath rasped, my lungs starved. I began to slip away, lose consciousness. The blackness was welcoming. I would see Father soon, I thought muzzily. Mother too.

A sneer. 'Like father, like son.'

My descent into the abyss slowed.

'I thought you'd have more fight in you, herring choker, but you're no better than your dog of a father. He didn't try to stop me burying the sword in his flesh, the coward. It's just a pity that I didn't plough your sister as well.'

A spark of white-hot rage birthed itself in my mind. Pulsing, it swelled in size, illuminating the dark corners and the soft, silent path to eternity. My father was no coward, I screamed silently. My sister had done nothing to you! The injustice of Cormac's actions fuelled the rage which grew, filling my skull. It gave me the desire to live, and with that came a desperate, furious strength.

My first, poor-aimed box barely connected with Cormac. It wasn't powerful either, but it startled. His grip on my throat weakened. The second hit his chin, snapping his head back, and he let go. A powerful squirm of my hips, and I had him off me. He fell one way, I rolled the other. We got on our knees and stood in the darkness, sensing where the other was through close proximity. There was time for a rasping inhalation, and then I threw myself at him. He punched me in the face; I caught him with a hook to the jaw. He kneed me in the balls, or tried to, but I twisted from the waist in time, and he banged off my hipbone instead.

Cormac was the smaller man, but I was half-strangled. We traded blows, neither able to knock down the other, both willing to take the hits. I attempted a headbutt, a favourite move, but he anticipated, and all I did was hurt my forehead on his cheekbone. He gouged at my eyes, but managed only to fingernail-rake some flesh from my face. I landed a punch; he did the same. It made no difference.

Shhhh. The sound of a knife being tugged from a sheath.

I felt sick. All I had were my bare hands.

Cormac padded nearer.

'Nithing.' I heard a voice, clear as day. 'Your seax.'

I had not remembered it until then. My hand went down, fingers closing on the familiar haft. Out it came, snugly fitting in my fist. I closed, uncaring of injury, interested only in burying it in him.

An impact in my midriff, a burst of dull pain following, an oath from Cormac.

I stabbed him in the guts. I buried the seax to the hilt, and he mewled like a pup ripped from the tit. Only when he fell away groundward, taking my seax with him, did my addled mind realise that I was not in the same way because my mail, *which I had forgotten I was wearing,* had stopped his blade.

Cormac was screaming now, sobbing for his mother.

I pulled out the seax, and he bawled even louder.

I did not care. In fact, I rejoiced. 'How do you like that, lord?' I asked.

He cried and sobbed, and said he was sorry.

'You are far too late.' I stabbed him in the chest, and he died. A great weight lifted from my shoulders. My father had been avenged, and Ashild's honour restored. When I bent and groped around his waist, and my fingers closed on a hilt, I felt as if I had found the greatest hoard in the world. After so long, the sword was to be mine again.

When I got back to the clearing, dragging Cormac's body, all his men were dead – the wounded dispatched by Thorstein. Vekel embraced me, and said I had done well. He admired the sword, and declared that Oðin was pleased to see it returned to its rightful owner. My father's shade would definitely rest easy now. My heart warmed to hear it. Together we dug a deep grave further into the woods, and piled the corpses into it, higgledy-piggledy. We covered them in earth, and walked the ground to tamp it down, before laying a massive pile of cut branches on top. Their horses we loosed and chased into the darkness. They would go their separate ways, and like as not, never be returned to Inis Cró or Dún na Sciath. Unless someone found the grave, which seemed unlikely, Ashild, Diarmaid and their child, not to mention Madra and Niall, were safe.

The sooner I left the area, however, the better. Máel might well send men to search for his son; if I was not there, I could not be suspected.

Imr's arrival in *Brimdýr* could not come too soon.

CHAPTER TWENTY-SIX

Our longship reached Linn Duachaill the afternoon of the second day after the ambush. I had spied its sail some time before, so we were waiting at the rivermouth as she came nosing in. Karli returned my wave; plenty of others, already at the oars, called out a greeting. I did not see Imr, and assumed he was lying down, resting his leg.

I was able to keep pace as the longship eased its way against the current to the mooring place where I had first clapped eyes on it, a lifetime before. 'Any news from Dyflin?' I asked casually.

'Sigtrygg is like a maddened bull. I was glad to be shot of the place,' said Karli.

I decided to be prudent. It was still possible that my involvement with Sláine was not generally known. 'Has Brian changed the terms of their treaty?' This was not outside the realms of possibility.

A snort, then a word to the oarsmen, who backed water, and he returned his attention to me. 'Nothing like that. The king took a notion that someone was ploughing his new wife, even though she swore blind it wasn't true.'

Sláine had kept her word, I thought, relieved. 'And them just married? It seems unlikely.'

'So you would think, eh, but stranger things have happened.' He stared. 'By all accounts, she and her lover met in The Brazen Head. There were witnesses.'

I did not panic. This was not recent information. Sigtrygg had been aware of it, which was why his two men had gone there to catch the cuckold.

Karli's attention moved on, but now Imr had appeared at the ship's side.

'D'you know the inn?'

'You're up and about,' I said, actually pleased, even though I was avoiding his question.

A grunt. 'It wasn't before time.'

'Are you back to normal?'

'Almost.'

'That's good,' I said, watching as the oars were shipped, and Twin-brows and Vali, ready at the prow, prepared to drop the anchor.

'So?' Imr demanded.

'What?' I adopted a curious expression, and hoped it was enough.

'Do you know the Brazen Head, you nithing?'

'I've walked past it. Never went in, though. The ale is expensive, they say.'

'It wasn't you bedding Sigtrygg's wife there? The customers talked of a tall Norseman with red hair.'

'Ara, that's one in every three men in Dyflin,' I said, scoffing.

Imr's eyes were slits. 'Not quite. Besides, half are too old or have no teeth, so that rules them out.'

'Would I be that stupid?'

'I'm not sure, Stormcrow. It's a little odd that you left Dyflin the same day two men sent by the king to find the culprit were killed.'

I gave him an it's-nothing-to-do-with-me shrug. 'I told you, a message came from Linn Duachaill. I had to go.'

'To see the sister you never visit,' he shot back.

'She needed me, or more, her husband did. Sheep had been rustled. He wanted help guarding the flock. We had time on our hands, so I went. It's not my fault that Sigtrygg's men were slain.' I could see the arcing spray of blood from my first victim, and the bulging eyes of the second as my seax filled his chest.

'And the sheep rustlers?'

'They were hunted down,' Vekel offered.

'We killed all seven,' added Thorstein.

'We got back yesterday,' said Vekel. Lalo was nodding too.

Imr glowered and muttered something under his breath, but wasn't up for more of an argument, not against a vitki, two of the best warriors in his crew, and Lalo, the finest archer now that Goat-Banki was gone. Not that there was any need to be, I thought, because he and *Brimdýr* were safely beyond Sigtrygg's reach.

Nonetheless, I struggled to put Sláine from my mind that evening, as we sat outside Gunnkel's longhouse, eating a fresh-roasted wether he'd sold to Imr. Sláine had been wonderful company, and in another life, I would have asked her father Brian for her hand. Whether my offer would have been accepted was another thing, but despondent about the manner in which our affair had ended, and certain it would never again be rekindled, I refused to consider that. I was leaving Ériu and I did not know when I would return. I had given Ashild a large portion of my riches, and buried the rest nearby.

The following day *Brimdýr*, with a brisk westerly snapping her mainsail and her prow aimed firmly at Britain, chopped her way through the waves and I set aside my issues of the heart. It was not hard after the previous night's fireside conversation. Imr had waxed lyrical about the weak English king, Æthelred, and his policy of giving silver to Norsemen instead of fighting them. *Gafol*, the English called the payments, and we were talking about thousands of pounds of it being handed over each year. This dwarfed any riches to be made in Ulaidh, Imr said, and we had slapped our thighs in agreement, and raised our beer mugs in anticipation of this great wealth. He had given no indication of how we might join the Norse fleets that threatened England, but that was for another day.

As for Sláine, I concluded, the threads of her life and mine had moved apart on the Norns' tapestry.

It seemed certain that they would never be joined again. Much as I did not want to admit it, that was probably a good thing.

The coastline of Bretland was not much different to that of Ériu. True, there was Inis Mon, an enormous island almost attached to the mainland, but as *Brimdýr* ran past that to the south, we could have been sailing from Linn Duachaill to Dyflin. Most of the beaches were rocky, but there were some of yellow-gold sand. The river mouths were small, and thanks to the onshore wind, the tree cover sparse. Hills were visible further inland.

My father had talked of monasteries on this coast, but they had long since been raided by Norsemen and afterwards abandoned. The same was true after we crossed a stretch of open water towards what was known as West-Bretland. One day Kar spotted the ruins of a monastic settlement; Imr declared it to be 'Saint Petroc's Stow', destroyed almost twenty years before.

Lalo spent even more time at the prow than I, wrapped in his cloak, deep in thought. More than once, I noticed a sad cast to his features. I asked once, to be told he was remembering Bláland, his home, and how it was still half a world away.

'I will never see it again, Stormcrow,' he said. 'Never see the river near my village sparkle in the sun, or the girls bathing there. Never hunt with my friends. Never dance under the stars to the beat of drums. Never find a woman of my tribe to wed, to have children with.'

'You don't know that for certain,' I said, trying to be cheery, but thinking the same about Linn Duachaill and my former life there, and Sláine too. I felt my mood sour.

'If you were to wager on it, Stormcrow, what odds would you give?'

I stared into the teeth of that question, and didn't like the answer.

'Well?' Lalo's voice had a rare harsh tone.

I did not want to lie to a friend. Nor did I want to seem a doom-monger. 'I would advise you to save your silver – for the journey home.'

'*Phhhh.*' Lalo retreated further into himself.

'Do not give up hope,' I said, as I had before. 'There is a chance you might return to your homeland one day, even if it is a small one.'

He did not reply, and I wondered if I should have lied, and told him he *would* see Bláland again. It was too late, however, so I awkwardly patted his shoulder and left him to it.

I nearly fell over Vekel, whom I had not noticed right behind us. He was on his haunches, rune bones covering the planking. He looked up.

'See anything?' I asked.

'Always.'

'Know-it-all,' I said, determined not to start worrying about Lalo, or myself. 'I meant about West-Bretland.'

'The pickings will be lean.'

'Anyone on *Brimdýr* could have told you that.' We hadn't seen a settlement worthy of the name village yet.

'There will still be danger. Bloodshed.'

Unease tickled my belly. We had gone ashore twice since crossing the sea from Ériu, and both times managed to find fresh water, and either hunt for deer or kill far-from-their-owners sheep. There had been no sign of local warriors, indeed we had hardly seen a soul on our voyage down the sparsely inhabited coast. All the talk had been of a quiet enough voyage to the south coast, where we would make contact with the Norse fleet, the leaders of which would welcome another long-ship into their midst. It was not clear on what terms, but Imr seemed confident. There seemed no good reason for Vekel's doom-mongering, I thought. And yet he was the vitki, not I.

'Why?' I asked.

A graceful up-down of his shoulders.

I wanted to shake Vekel, but he had always been this frustrating, and it amused him if I reacted to his reticence. I went instead to Kar and suggested a training session. A keen student, willing to take advice, he was coming along nicely. He accepted, as always, and soon, sweat-lathered and working hard to prevent myself being injured – even with a leather cover, an axe hit hard – I had forgotten about Lalo and Vekel.

I gave no thought to the matter later either, when Imr told Karli to take *Brimdýr* in towards the shore. Lalo, keen-eyed as ever, had spied a flock of grazing sheep.

Bow at the ready, he cast a glance at Imr. 'They are close. I see no shepherd.'

Imr's lips twisted, which was as close as he ever got to a smile. 'Go on then, Mandinka.'

Lalo laughed. 'One or two?'

'I'm famished,' said Vali. 'Two.'

'Two!' Thormod and Hrolf cried.

'Two it is,' said Imr.

'I'll go as well,' I said. Vali got ready also, and Thormod. Four of us could easily carry a pair of dead sheep.

'I want to come.' Kar had a bow in his hands; whose it was I had no idea.

'Have you any skill?' I asked.

'I'm a decent enough shot.'

I glanced at Imr, who said, 'Let the lad go if he wants. Be quick.'

He didn't need to add that we were vulnerable onshore, that at anchor, *Brimdýr* was too.

Karli guided us close in to a stony, seaweed-covered beach. The anchor plashed down, and seeing how shallow the water was, I followed after, leaving spear and shield behind. Chest-deep in the gentle swell, careful not to be hit by the prow, I reached up and accepted my weapons. Holding them above my head, I waded in. Vali and Thormod were next, and Lalo and Kar. Soon we were all safe ashore, dripping and already growing cold in the brisk breeze.

Lalo strung his bow and nocked an arrow. To Kar, he said, 'Ready?'

Kar nodded, his face eager, and the two went off, crouching down low.

Vali, Thormod and I remained where we were. Sheep were stupid creatures, but not so dim they would stay put if strangers approached. Lalo and Kar would keep out of sight until they were close enough to shoot. If that proved impossible due to lack of cover, they, or perhaps Lalo only, would try to walk into range.

So the plan went, and so it came to pass.

Not long after, Lalo's loud, whistled summons came. We found him in scrubby grass, gutting a fat ewe. Kar was a short distance away, doing the same with another. The rest of the flock were in the middle distance, running as fast their short legs would carry them. Vali and Thormod praised Lalo, who barely looked up. I was already anticipating the fresh meat we would eat that night at a mooring place far from here. Common sense dictated we avoid the chance of reprisals by the dead sheep's owners.

It was as if Loki heard me, and sniggered.

An angry shout.

My head went up.

A youth in a rough tunic and breeks was sprinting towards Kar. There was a spear in his hand. The shepherd, I thought, and cupped a hand to my mouth. 'Kar! Pick up that carcase and get over here. Now!'

He glanced at me, then followed the direction of my pointing arm. Rather than obey, though, he set down his knife and fitted an arrow to his bowstring.

The young shepherd did not slow a fraction, instead waiting until Kar let fly, when he threw himself onto his face. The shaft flew over his prone shape. He was up and running again in a flash. Kar's second arrow missed as well, and my belly knotted.

'Kar, you fool! Come back!' I roared.

Kar's third effort almost took down the shepherd. Almost. And then the youth was close enough to throw, launching his spear without slackening speed. It was an incredible shot, taking Kar smack bang in the middle of his chest. Death must have been instantaneous. He went down like a sack of grain, bow falling from slack fingers.

I didn't think. I charged. A hundred paces it might have been, and I covered it with valkyrja-given speed. The shepherd took one look and fled. I sprinted harder, breath sawing in my chest, past poor Kar and his sheep, closing the distance until my lungs burned and leg muscles screamed. I juddered to a halt, drew back my right arm, focused and threw. It was a good shot, arcing well, coming down fast, looking as if it would take the shepherd in the back.

It went into the heather two paces to his right. He jinked and kept running.

A bitter curse escaped me.

Then I realised Lalo was by my side, his bow bent, the arrow tip at an acute upward angle. He had one eye closed, and his lips were moving in prayer.

I joined in with one of my own.

The shaft went skyward.

Time stretched as it rose, becoming a tiny black sliver against the cloud. The shepherd ran on, never looking over his shoulder. My chest rose and fell as I regained my wind. Sweat stung my eyes. Lalo was muttering in his own tongue. I heard Vali and Thormod's pounding steps.

Down came the arrow. Down it came, like a bolt from the gods, vengeance in a slender length of wood and iron.

It hit the shepherd between the shoulder blades, the sweetest shot I had ever seen. He hit the ground face first and was still.

'Oðin's balls,' said Vali, his voice reverent.

'That was well done,' I said.

'It will not bring back Kar.' Lalo's face was bitter.

'No, it won't,' I said heavily, remembering Vekel's mention of bloodshed, and hoping that this was the limit of it. 'And we had best get back to *Brimdýr* in case that shepherd had any friends close by.'

We returned to the longship, carrying the carcases of two sheep and Kar as well. Cries of alarm and anger met us on the beach. Imr leaped into the shallows, demanding an explanation. Hearing the tale, he swore, and called Kar a stupid arsewipe. 'Should have listened to you, eh?'

'Yes,' I said, wondering if someone else would have been slain if Kar had not accompanied us. Lalo. Thormod. Vali – or me. Maybe, I decided, but it was also possible that Vekel's prediction had nothing to do with our scavenging expedition. Perhaps others would die in the coming days. I shoved these concerns aside. Trying to second-guess the gods hurt my head.

We heaved the sheep and Kar aboard, and rowed away from the wretched spot. Wary of the shepherd's kin tracking us along the coastline, Imr didn't let Karli bring *Brimdýr* in again until the evening was well on. It was a good spot, a little gorse-bound promontory with flat ground to camp on, and anchorage that protected from the wind. Fires were kindled and the sheep butchered and set to roasting, and Imr ordered a score of us to hack branches from the few trees. From these we fashioned wooden stakes. Not until a rough barricade ran across the neck of the promontory did he let up. Even then, he found several gaps, insisting more branches were cut to fill them.

Imr's next announcement, that sentries would have to watch the barricade all night, was not popular either, but a glance at Kar, stretched out by the edge of the camp, was enough reason not to argue.

When the sheep had been devoured, men began to drink in earnest. There was a dedicated fierceness to the way they went about it. I felt the same emotion. There was a tendency not to get close to new crew members, because when one died, the pain was worse than if he had been kept at arm's length. Kar had been different, though. For all his cocksureness, he had not been shy of asking for help when needed. There had also been a burning enthusiasm in him to learn how to row, navigate, fight with any weapon. Karli had taught him to rebraid snapped ropes, and even how to stitch torn sails. It was no surprise that he had been popular.

We drank to his shade entering Valhöll. He had been young but valiant, Thormod declared in the ponderous way of the drunk. Oðin would see him right, and accept him as an einherjar. Men liked that, and hoomed their appreciation. Sitting beside Vekel, I heard his quiet comment. 'If a sheep-rustler can get into Valhöll, there's hope for everyone.' I stared, and he said, 'I'm only telling the truth.'

I had not the heart to argue, because he was right.

It made Kar's death even more pointless, so I drank to forget. We finished one barrel of Dyflin ale, and started on another. That didn't last long; nor did the third. There was singing, and poetry, and toasts to Kar and all our lost comrades. I shed a few tears for Ulf, whom I had not been able to save either. I would later reflect that my dark mood might also have had something to do with the manner of my parting from Sláine, but at the time, determined to send myself into oblivion, I gave it no consideration.

Late on in the night Hrolf, owlishly drunk, told Lalo that he had never known of an arrow shot like it. 'To think a blámaðr could do such a thing,' he said, his face redder and blotchier than normal.

My mouth opened, ready to tear Hrolf a new arsehole, but Lalo got there first. 'Strange, is it?' he asked.

Hrolf nodded. 'Aye.'

'Why would that be?' Lalo's voice was quiet.

Hrolf took in Lalo's stony expression, and began to realise the quagmire he had just waded into. 'Well, you know how thralls are . . .'

'Tell me.'

Hrolf hesitated.

'TELL ME!'

Karli half-choked on a mouthful of beer. All conversation ended.

'They're not very bright. Clumsy too. You know what I mean, surely?' Hrolf stopped, as if he had realised what he'd said. 'Not meaning you are like that.'

Lalo's look would have withered a freshly opened flower. 'I thought you were stupid the first time I clapped eyes on you, Hrolf. I was wrong.'

Hrolf's initial scowl died away; the beginnings of a confused smile hovered on his lips. 'So it's clever you think I am?'

'No. You are thick as two short planks, skítkarl, and ignorant with it!' Lalo's seax was out and under Hrolf's chin.

Men shouted in alarm. Thormod drew a blade, but did not dare to rush to his brother's defence.

'Lalo,' I said. 'Do not be hasty.'

'Hasty?' He rolled the word around in his mouth. 'What does that mean, Stormcrow?'

'It means *think* before you open that nithing's throat,' said Vekel, sober. 'You cannot murder him in front of all of us.'

'Can I not?' Lalo chuckled, and put a little pressure on the seax. A bright red line of blood sprang out along its length, and Hrolf whimpered. 'Who says?' Lalo demanded.

'I say.' Imr was on his feet, and he was angry. 'I will not have my men killing each other over nothing.'

'*NOTHING?*' Lalo shouted. 'Have you been called thrall, Imr? Treated as less than human? Spat on? Laughed at? Compared to an animal? HAVE YOU?'

Imr scowled, but give him his credit, he did not lie. 'No.'

'Of course you haven't! I used to live with that abuse every day. Every cursed day, and I grew so sick of it, but I could never say a word, because I was a thrall. A blámaðr thrall. Then I joined *Brimdýr*, and Vekel freed me. After a while, I thought the shit-talking had ended. That I had been accepted for myself. I was wrong,' said Lalo, and he moved the blade to and fro under Hrolf's chin. 'The shot that killed the shepherd was no accident. I have been using a bow most of my life – d'you understand?'

Hrolf couldn't nod because of the seax. 'Aye,' he whispered.

'I speak fluent Irish and Norse as well as my own tongue, and a bit of Saxon and Frankish besides. I can read Latin too. How many languages do you know?'

'Norse, a little gioc-goc.'

A contemptuous snort. 'Can you read or write?'

Hrolf's cheeks flamed. 'No.'

'I can.'

This was a surprise to me, but looking at Vekel, I saw that he knew.

'Put away the knife,' Imr said.

Lalo completely ignored him. 'Am I still a stupid thrall?' he asked Hrolf.

'No.'

'Say it, nice and loud.'

'You are not a stupid thrall.' Hrolf was puce with embarrassment and shame now.

'Did everyone hear?' Lalo cried.

'I did,' I bellowed.

'And me,' said Thorstein.

'I heard as well.' Vekel pitched his voice loud enough to be heard in Dyflin.

'And I,' growled Imr. 'Now, enough of this nithing behaviour. Mandinka, sheathe your blade.' His tone brooked no refusal.

Lalo looked at Imr long and hard before obeying. He did it very slowly.

Hrolf spun, Lalo tensed, and I thought, blood will be shed yet, but that was not Hrolf's purpose.

'Holmgang,' he said. 'I challenge you to holmgang, Mandinka.'

'Agreed.'

No, I thought, no. Yet it was too late. The challenge had been issued and accepted. Imr was downright furious, but could not go against tradition. It would not happen now, he said in a cast-iron voice, or he would see them both dead. No, it could take place in the morning, when everyone had clearer heads.

The festivities had had a sombre note because of Kar; Hrolf's challenge poured ice-cold water on what remained. Before long, most men had rolled up in their blankets and were snoring to wake the dead. I had no desire to fall asleep, however. As I said to Vekel, Hrolf or Thormod, or both of them, might try and kill Lalo during the night.

'They won't,' he said confidently.

'Why not?'

'Where is he?'

I looked. To my surprise and delight, Lalo had vanished. 'Did you say something to him?' I asked.

'I didn't have to.'

It was good news, but as I lay down, I couldn't help chewing over the outcome of the holmgang. Neither seemed good. If Lalo was killed, I would lose a good friend. If he was victorious, Thormod would hold a massive grudge against him, and Lalo would need to be on constant lookout against a blade in the back, or being heaved overboard in rough weather.

I lay awake for a long time.

CHAPTER TWENTY-SEVEN

'Stormcrow!'

Lalo was shouting. I didn't know why. I paid no heed.

'Stormcrow, wake up!' A kick.

'Hey!' I was angry now, and opening my eyes, realised I had been asleep, and that Lalo was not. Standing over me, he was very real, and by his face, alarmed. 'What is it?'

'A fleet!' He was shaking Vekel, and stepping round the remnants of our fire to Imr. 'A fleet,' Lalo cried. 'WAKE UP!' Over and over he repeated this, moving between the prone shapes of *Brimdýr*'s crew.

I stood up, gummy-eyed, furry-tongued, and faced the sea. Cold dread filled me. Not a patch of water was without a ship. A great flotilla ran from left to right, all the way to the horizon. There were a few longships, but the majority were broader in the beam, shorter too. No Norse fleet this, I thought: it was English. What it was doing in this remote place I had no idea, but the chances of its crews being friendly seemed vanishingly small. Even as I watched, four vessels changed tack, heading towards our position. We had been seen.

Imr was up, cursing, and rousing men from slumber. 'To the ship,' he shouted. 'Move!'

'Take *Brimdýr* out there,' said Vekel, 'and we are all dead men.'

Imr turned on him, furious, but he was too wily a creature not to see what was in front of his face. 'Aye, aye. Why in Frigg's name is an English fleet sailing along this coastline?' he demanded.

'I have no idea,' Vekel answered. 'Of more importance is how we are going to escape.'

'There's only one thing we can do,' I said. 'Abandon *Brimdýr*. Go inland.'

Imr eyed the approaching ships and swore again. 'Stormcrow's right.' His gaze moved over the expectant, hungover faces. 'Don your war gear! Pack all the food you can carry. Quickly!'

'What about Kar?' Vali asked.

'Cover him in stones. That will have to do.'

Vali didn't argue. I and five others helped, piling enough rocks over Kar's corpse until it was safe from gulls and foxes. No one mentioned what the English might do to such an obvious, recent grave.

There is only so much speed that sore-headed, heavy-limbed men can reach. It isn't fast either. But with Imr literally kicking arses, and Lalo, clear-eyed and loud of voice, announcing the shrinking distance between the English craft and the shore, we outdid ourselves. They were still a good distance away when Imr and Karli, having poured a barrel of pitch along *Brimdýr*'s deck, lit pieces of hnjóskr and tossed them on board. She began to burn at once, the fire spreading with incredible speed.

There were tears in Karli's eyes as flames licked skywards. He had overseen her construction, I thought, and sailed her from the first day she was floated. His face was as resolute as Imr's, however, when he urged us away from the shore, and into West-Bretland.

Imr was full of energy, quite unlike someone who had spent half the night carousing. Despite the heavy cloth bundle on one shoulder, he paced up and down the ragged column, encouraging, urging, telling men all would be well. He gave particular praise to the two carrying his chest of hacksilver. He also wanted to know who had seen the English first.

Heads were shaken. Couldn't-says and not-sures were his only answer.

I suspected.

Imr reached me and Vekel, and beside us, Lalo. 'Any of you know?'

'It was I,' said Lalo. 'I woke early, before dawn. The sentries were all asleep, so I kept watch.'

'Hear that, lads?' Imr roared.

'What?' 'No!' 'Say it again!'

'It was Mandinka who raised the alarm – Mandinka!'

A ragged cheer. Given the general state, I decided, it amounted to a rousing one.

Lalo didn't seem to care either way; he was grinning.

Imr stuck out a hand.

267

They shook.

'You're as true a warrior as ever sailed in *Brimdýr*,' Imr declared.

Another cheer, more robust this time. I searched for Hrolf. He wasn't smiling, or joining in, but I put him from my mind. There were bigger fish to fry, the most urgent of which was to put some distance between us and the English.

Loki was behind the fleet coming upon us unseen, I decided, hoping that the tricksy bastard had had his fun. I also began to wonder if the bloodshed mentioned by Vekel had nothing to do with poor Kar.

As Imr sent Lalo and the four other bowmen to the rear – our best defence against pursuit – I put my head down, and concentrated on picking my way through the gorse and in the patches between, bugloss, wild cabbage and horsetail. There had been a brief discussion of which way to go, but no one knew the area. Away from the sea, it had been decided. Put enough distance between us and the fleet, and then we could work out what to do. Imr's chest of hacksilver, brutally heavy and impossible to carry fast, was not mentioned.

It was no kind of plan, but it was all we had.

The uselessness of it was soon clear.

Shouts and cries became audible from our rear, together with excited barking. The English were using dogs to track us. Not that they were needed, I thought sourly. Fifty plus warriors in full gear, moving fast with no attempt at concealment, left a path that a blind man could follow.

'We need somewhere to stand and fight,' I said to Thorstein. 'Lalo and the others will do their best, but the English will have come ashore in force.'

The rolling terrain, bare of trees, did not lend itself to ambush. The best we could come up with was a low hill, at the summit of which stood two giant pieces of stone topped by a third. Ancient, covered in lichen and moss, it was similar to structures in Ériu. No one knew who had built them, but often built over graves, they were regarded as sacred. It was a good place to set our backs against.

The gorse bushes grew thickly enough on the upward slopes to prevent a line of men attacking us, but there any advantage ended. Those who arrived first formed a rough circle around the stones, chests heaving, spitting, and wiping away sweat. A quick head count came to forty-five. Taking Lalo and his four companions into account, it meant that seven warriors had fallen behind.

Lalo appeared a short time later and confirmed our suspicions. The English war party was strong, at least a hundred and fifty warriors. He and the bowmen had accounted for ten, perhaps more, but the English had grown wise and were advancing with their shields up. How far behind were they, I asked.

'Close,' Lalo replied. 'Some of our men are slow.'

'There are seven?'

'Aye.'

'I'm going to get them,' I told Imr.

'Be careful, Stormcrow. I don't need to lose you in the first skirmish.'

Lalo and Thorstein came with me, but Vekel stayed behind to weave magic for the crew. We ran, and as the expectation of battle increased, I found my weariness falling away. It wouldn't last; I had drunk too much the previous night for that. But for the short term, I felt ready to fight. Ready to kill. Ready to send as many English as I could into the mud.

Karli was the first one I saw. He was blowing like a winded horse, and his broad face was an unpleasant shade of purple.

The causes, I decided, were his corpulence, and the large leather bag which held his loot.

'Stormcrow,' he wheezed.

'Get a move on,' I told him, 'unless you want the English to carve you into little slices.'

Karli was so out of breath he just nodded, but his pace picked up.

We came upon four others. They too responded to our dire warnings, managing to half walk, half run towards the hilltop. A droll part of me wondered if it was merely delaying their fate.

By this point, I could see the English, and scarily near, the other bowmen. The reason they were taking such risks lay between them and us. Hrolf and Thormod moved like a pair of arthritic greybeards. Now and again, Hrolf would stop and dry retch, with Thormod waiting until his brother was done. Unsurprisingly, the English were fast closing in.

As Lalo loped off to rejoin his fellow archers, I exchanged a grim look with Thorstein, and we pounded towards the laggards, trampling the dandelions and purple-flowered mallow.

'Are you blind?' I shouted at Thormod.

'I see the English, but Hrolf can't stop puking.'

'He'll have more to worry about than that if you don't get a move on!'

Thormod nodded, and Hrolf wiped his mouth. Pasty-faced, he looked like death warmed up, but they shuffled off together, noticeably faster than before.

'Shall we charge?' asked Thorstein. 'Make enough noise and the English will think there are men behind us.'

'Might cause a bit of panic,' I said, giving no thought to the risk.

Lalo heard. He trotted up the slope, and I saw he had only three arrows left. 'Is there no one else?' His voice was incredulous.

'We're going to attack,' I said.

'Drive the English back.' Thorstein was smiling.

'You're insane,' said Lalo. 'Do not throw your lives away!'

'We won't,' I said, but I was thinking, we are dead men. I was unwilling to let Hrolf and Thormod die, however, and it seemed the only way.

'Wait,' said Lalo, and summoned the other bowmen. None were hurt, but they too were down to their last shafts. Quickly, Lalo explained our plan, and as his comrades gave one another incredulous looks, he laid out a fresh strategy. It made sense, even if it wouldn't change our fate. We muttered our thanks, and Thorstein said, 'Ready?'

We moved to stand side by side, and hefted our broad axes. Prideful, I was wearing the sword too, although I had much to learn in its use. Perhaps a hundred paces separated us from the mass of English, who, thinking we were up to something, had slowed to a walk.

I brought my abiding memory of Ulf to mind, when he'd jumped into the Sionainn and tried to reach *Brimdýr*. Instant rage bubbled up. Then I made myself imagine the bowmen, including Lalo, as well as Hrolf, Thormod, Karli and the other stragglers, being butchered by the English before they could reach Imr at the hilltop. Red mist blurred my vision, a vein throbbed at my temple. I was hungry. Hungry to kill. I was careful, however, not to let the anger take control.

'*Brimdýr!*' I shouted, and broke into a run.

Thorstein caught up before I had gone ten strides.

We screamed and roared all the way to the English, while Lalo, keeping his promise, let out an ululating war cry that sounded like a bean sidhe and her five sisters combined. The other bowmen yelled as well. It was a fearful din.

It was also mad. Yes, we were in mail, while most of the English were not, but they numbered more than a hundred and we were just two. Fear is a strange thing, though, and to our enemies, it might have seemed we were the front-runners, that a short distance behind would come Imr and our crewmates.

The English stopped. Raised their shields. Glanced at each other. A few of the more clear-headed lobbed spears, but they were poorly aimed or fell short.

'O-ðin!' I screamed. 'O-ðin!'

Thorstein was yipping like a crazed dog.

Lalo's timing was perfect. Five arrows flighted in, aimed just so, hitting the enemy's front ranks. Two men died, and several were bawling in pain. Another volley arrived, inflicting similar damage. A third landed, and more men were slain, others injured. A degree of panic took hold; the English did not know that these were the last shafts Lalo and his companions had.

I saw an Englishman twist to look at the rear, and exultant, I changed the angle of my run, to reach him first. I roared again, and he flinched. I closed at full tilt, somehow avoiding the spearpoints aimed at me. My shield smashed into his, and he reeled back, making no attempt to fight. My axe split him from neck to mid-ribcage, and blood fountained. Over me, over my shield, but best of all, covering the man to his left. He wailed, and tried to turn, and I opened the back of his skull.

Close by, Thorstein was swearing and battering, battering and swearing. Englishmen yelled, shoved, even *argued* with each other. I slew a third one, and a fourth. The English ranks parted in front of me; men at the back were edging backwards. Would they actually break, I wondered, break and run?

Of course it was too good to be true.

A captain of some kind, in mail and a Norse-style helmet with protective eye rings, appeared, clattering men with the flat of his sword and issuing dire threats. The English closed up again, and men pressed forwards at me. I aimed at another, a clumsy sideswipe that almost missed. But the edge of my axeblade caught in his flesh, and that was sufficient. It carved a deep line across his neck, opening the major vessels. I think it cut his windpipe as well, because he made a horrible, frothy noise as he collapsed.

That made the nearest men pause, and I yelled, 'Thorstein!'

'Aye?'

'Have Hrolf and Thormod gone far enough?' I spoke in Irish. Some English knew Norse, but few indeed could understand my tongue.

'Who knows?' Thorstein laughed, a manic, devilish sound.

'The others need us.'

'Fighting retreat then?'

'Yes!'

I chopped off an Englishman's arm, and rammed the head of my axe into another's face, pulping his nose. I took a step back, and another. An Englishman launched himself at me, but the blood-slippery ground was treacherous, and he fell, obstructing two men behind. I edged another few paces, took a quick glance to see if Thorstein was there – he was – and continued to withdraw.

The English captain was bellowing. He had seen, knew this was a golden opportunity to swarm forward and kill the pair of us, but his men were wary. I had finished five, and disabled two. Thorstein would have done the same. The English had the numbers, but the first to reach either of us would die, and in all likelihood, the second would too. So they hesitated, and using their timidity, Thorstein and I increased our speed. A score and a half paces from them, an exchanged nod saw us turn and run.

Baying like hounds, the English came up the slope in pursuit. It is amazing how fast one can move with a horde of enemies on your tail. We gained some ground, and then a little more, but gradually the weight of our mail began to count. It was the beer too, although I hated to admit it.

Lalo and the others were running alongside the English, hurling rocks, but they were only heavy enough to distract, not cause real damage. The tale would have had a bad ending, but Imr arrived, unexpected, and more welcome than rain after a drought. He brought with him half our number, about twenty-odd warriors. Formed into a boar snout, with him at the front, they came past me and Thorstein and hit the enemy with a mighty crash.

It was a one-sided engagement. The English went from an easy pursuit of two warriors to facing an armoured formation of axe-wielding killers. Men screamed and died. They broke off and retreated down the slope, ignoring their captain's furious shouts.

We wouldn't have long before the English came back. There were still far more of them. Imr, wily, had the warriors walk backwards to our position. 'You took long enough, Stormcrow,' he said.

'I could say the same about you,' I replied. We laughed, a combination of relief and humour.

Spirits were high. Everyone had made it to the hilltop, even Hrolf and Thormod. The piss was mercilessly taken out of them and the other dawdlers, but they gave back as good as they got, throwing accusations of sitting on arses, doing nothing, while their poor, suffering oarmates were at risk of being massacred. As the good-natured laughter continued, men sat down to rest. Water was drunk, bread shared, and gear checked.

The hilltop offered a view back to the coast. A pall of smoke marked where we had camped, where the remnants of *Brimdýr* still burned. I counted four ships at anchor nearby, but the remainder of the enemy fleet was receding from view. It was something, and with the English war party content for the moment to stay put – licking their wounds, planning – the place was actually beautiful. Meadow brown butterflies flitted about. Bees were busy in the red heather, and not far off, a chough dug in loose soil for grubs, while keeping a beady eye on us, intruders in its domain. High overhead, a pair of falcons glided through the air.

'Four crews makes how many men?' Vekel asked.

'If it's similar to longships,' said Imr, 'two hundred to twelve score.'

'I counted about a hundred and fifty,' said Lalo.

Imr grunted. 'The rest must be guarding the ships.'

'Between arrows and our axe-work, you can cut that number by thirty, maybe thirty-five,' I said.

Imr liked that. 'You did well, all of you. Even more because you came back alive.' His gaze went to the English, and his expression hardened.

We had suffered no casualties thus far, I thought, but that was about to change. Our bowmen were out of arrows, and although we had the high ground, there weren't enough warriors to prevent the enemy reaching the hilltop. They would surround us, and by sheer weight of numbers, annihilate every last man.

'What in Hel's name is a fleet that size doing this far west?' Imr grumbled again.

The reason didn't matter, I thought. We were screwed.

Thorstein shrugged, Lalo too. Imr sucked his moustache, and said, 'Perhaps Æthelred isn't all about kissing arse and handing over silver.'

I thought of Brian Bóramha, and what he had done earlier in his life. 'You think he's scouring the land of Norse?'

'How do you get rid of fleas on a dog? Keep combing it day after day until you don't find any more.'

'I've been called worse things,' said Thorstein, amused.

'What is a flea?' asked Lalo, which lightened the mood.

I was grateful that Imr had not said we would have been better off staying in Dyflin. I had gone from the frying pan into the fire, but he and the rest of the crew could have safely remained and served Sigtrygg, rather than being butchered atop a hill in the middle of nowhere, West-Bretland.

'Well, vitki, now's the time for some magic,' said Imr.

'Do you want me to cast the rune bones as well?'

'No need,' Imr replied, his face deadpan.

I didn't want to know either; our future was blindingly obvious.

'I have an idea.'

This was unexpectedly quick. My attention sharpened.

'Spit it out,' said Imr.

'Push that down the hill.' Vekel pointed.

We all regarded the stones in bemusement.

'The top one does look a little unstable.' I hadn't noticed before.

'Because of that smaller stone,' Vekel replied.

The top stone was shaped like a lying-down triangle, and its narrow end was balanced on two rocks, the top one of which was about the same size as a cross section of a middling size tree trunk. It was tiny in comparison to the stone below, the two 'legs' and the 'roof', all four of which were vast.

What Vekel was suggesting would anger the shades of whoever had been interred here, but if the idea worked, I could live with it. Imr and Thorstein did not protest either, nor Lalo.

'Get the strongest men,' said Vekel, 'and push the top stone off the smaller one. It wouldn't have to move far to become unbalanced. It's quite rounded too.'

274

'Get it to the top of the slope . . .' said Imr, looking excited.

'Exactly,' said Vekel.

'We would have to stand in front of it, or the English would see,' I said. 'And the timing would have to be exact.'

'It's worth a try,' said Imr, invigorated. 'And we'll need to prepare.'

'There is another thing we could do,' said Lalo, looking sly. He explained, and I began to feel hope again. Just the slightest trace, but that sufficed. Judging by Imr's face, and Thorstein's, they liked it too. I couldn't tell with Vekel, but that was nothing new.

Time would tell.

CHAPTER TWENTY-EIGHT

The English prepared to attack just before midday. It was warm, and with the low cloud cover, humid. Beneath my mail, my tunic was sodden; sweat rolled from under my helmet, down my face. The air was still; clouds of midges plagued us. I was horrid thirsty as well, but I didn't drink. Water was in short supply, and I would want it even more after the fight began. Everyone was in the same boat except Lalo. It didn't rain in Bláland from one season to the next, he said, adding that this weather wasn't even hot.

Perhaps because of this, I shot furtive looks at his full waterskin. It didn't go unnoticed, because before leaving to carry out his plan, he entrusted it to me.

'Drink as much as you want, Stormcrow,' he declared. 'Just save some for Vekel and Thorstein.'

I nodded my thanks, and wished him luck. He grinned, and said his gods would help. Then he slipped away downhill, on a side unseen by our enemies, and left us to fend for ourselves.

The English captain – having watched for a time, he definitely seemed to be the main leader – organised his men into two groups, one to attack our front, the second our rear. By rights, they should have ascended at the same speed to hit us simultaneously, but unable to see each other, the first was a decent distance ahead of the second.

Imr leaped into action. This was our chance, he said.

'Our only chance,' someone commented dourly.

No one laughed, but there was plenty of energy in the way men formed lines one deep on both sides of the hilltop, in full sight of the English. Meanwhile a dozen of us, including Vali, myself and Thorstein, went about pushing the top stone off its 'legs'. We heaved until I thought my arm muscles would burst with the strain, and for what

276

seemed an age, it did not move. Imr, supervising from the side, though, swore that it had shifted. We took a breather, and tried again.

'Hold,' said Imr after a moment. 'Where are those English bastards?' he called.

'A good spear's throw away, no more,' came the clipped reply. 'Best get a move on.'

We pushed again, and this time, I felt stone grate against stone. Imr confirmed it. The English were now thirty paces from the top, we were told in an urgent tone. Vali counted us down, one, two, three, and once more we shoved.

'It's going to fall!' Imr shouted. 'Out of the way!' This was to the warriors in front of the slab.

Down it went with a thunderous crash. The earth beneath my feet actually shook. A great cloud of dust rose, and my heart sank. Our plan had failed. The stone had landed too far from the top of the slope.

Then, with ponderous slowness, it began to slide, and hope against hope, to roll. An awful scream shredded the air, and the stone vanished.

'Forward!' This was Imr, urging us into a line. We obeyed, eager to press home the advantage.

The shriek had come from one of our warriors. It was unclear why he hadn't jumped out of the stone's path in time. Both his legs were shattered. His screams came to an abrupt end when Vali, his heavy face set, knocked him on the head with an axe. It was a mercy; no one said a word.

The stone had done far worse to our enemies, leaving a trail of broken bodies in its wake. The survivors were reeling, their advance brought to a halt, men staring in dazed confusion at the red ruin of what, an instant before, had been their comrades.

'With me!' cried Imr, and led us down the slope.

The demoralised English put up little resistance, and we slew a dozen before they fled. No one followed; our oarmates on the other side of the hilltop needed us. Or so we thought. When we got there, they were cheering and hurling insults at the second group of English.

'They heard what was happening, and refused to come at us,' a delighted Karli revealed.

'Yellow-livered dogs,' said Imr, and spat.

Not necessarily, I thought. Only a nithing walks into certain death, and the English captain would soon realise that our tactic with the stone had been a once-off. If he was any kind of leader, he'd be telling his men that we were still outnumbered, and had no arrows. Sure enough, it wasn't long before our enemies came at us again. This time they were better organised, reaching the hilltop together.

It was a bitter struggle. With our survival at stake, we had more fire in our bellies, but the English had an almost three to one advantage in numbers, and their captain was a man who led from the front. A towering figure, he reminded me of Odd Coal-biter, who had died at Gleann Máma. He used an axe too, which along with his helmet, made me wonder if he had Norse blood. Whatever his ancestry, he carved a hole in our pitifully shallow line in the first assault, cutting down Thormod and another warrior. It might have been the end for us had not a grief-stricken Hrolf thrown himself at the captain, providing distraction long enough for Karli to sneak in behind. Mail and fighting skill count for nothing when your hamstring's been cut. The captain fell, and Hrolf, bawling like a child, opened his throat.

That took the wind out of the Englishmen's sails, and they retreated. Our dry-throated cheers came out cracked and discordant. In reality, there was not much to celebrate. Fifteen of *Brimdýr*'s crew would never leave the hilltop, and ten others were injured. Some of these could fight, but not many. Imr was hurt too, blood soaking through the arm of his tunic. He would not let Vekel look at it, brusquely ordering him to care for the rest of the wounded.

Just shy of a score and a half warriors were left to meet the next English attack.

I hoped that the death of their captain might cause a change of heart, and a withdrawal to their ships. It was not to be. Messengers were dispatched, and not long after, reinforcements arrived at the base of the hill. The party was not huge, about thirty men, but the odds, which had balanced out somewhat, were again massively skewed towards the English.

The one thing it did was decrease the number of men guarding the enemy's ships. I said this to Vekel, and he half smiled, that curious expression that always made me think he knew what was coming. I was desperate to ask if Lalo would succeed, but if the answer had been 'no', it would not have helped, so I stitched my lip, and focused on bolstering my comrades' morale. It was a crude tactic, but I'd seen old hands like Ulf and Coal-biter do it before.

'Ho, Vali,' I said. 'Didn't need our help to move that rock, did you?'

He knew instinctively what I was at. 'That's right, Stormcrow! I was sparing you girls' blushes.'

Roars of protest. 'Think you're strong, Vali?' Thorstein cried. 'When this is over, let's have an arm-wrestle. We'll soon see who is stronger!'

Hoots and cheers. 'I want to see that!' Vekel observed.

Vali snorted. 'I will be happy to win that contest.'

'Five pieces of hacksilver on Thorstein,' I said, thinking, if the bout ever happened and I saw it, we would all three have survived. Losing some silver was nothing in comparison to that fantasy.

'Is that the sum of my worth?' Thorstein challenged.

He was trying to get a rise out of me. I snorted. 'Ten pieces then, and you had better win.'

Men began betting with one another; the lightly wounded joined in. Nearly everyone wagered on Vali, whose upper arms were about as thick as Lalo's chest. To my amazement, Imr said he'd put his silver on Thorstein.

'It's all about tactics, eh?' he observed.

Vali was starting to get a little defensive. 'No one could beat me on Man!'

'Man's a small place,' Thorstein said dryly.

'Let's do it now!' Vali said, and a roar of appreciation went up.

I chuckled; it was insane to have an arm-wrestling contest during a break in a battle which we were bound to lose. Somehow that made it more appealing.

The lack of a table or any flat surface immediately became apparent. With some reluctance, Vali and Thorstein – who was most amused by his opponent's keenness – agreed to postpone the contest until another day.

The good-humoured atmosphere lasted until our sentries, positioned on each side of the hilltop, announced that the English were attacking again. Sensing that the tide had turned in their favour, our enemies sang during their ascent.

With the wounded propped up against the standing stones, or lying between them, we formed our pitifully weak circle. Imr was there too. He would have it no other way, even though his face was blanched. Vekel stayed behind us, but had picked up a spear, the first time I had seen him bear an actual weapon. It emphasised the grim reality of our situation.

The English halted a short distance away. They stared at us, and jeered. They did not attack. Yet.

My belly tensed; there had to be fifty of them. We were seventeen, including three wounded. Our oarmates at our backs were facing the same overwhelming numbers. This was our final battle. My final battle. I would make it a glorious end.

'Ho, Norsemen!' A mail-clad warrior in the front rank spoke.

'Aye?' Imr answered.

'You do not have to die today.' His Norse was poor, but understandable.

'That's right,' Imr shouted. 'We will leave here victorious, walking over the bodies of you and your comrades!'

We cheered, and I recalled a saying my father had been fond of. When death stares a man in the face, all he can do is stare back.

'Brave words, but you and I know that they are false,' said the warrior. 'I meant that you should lay down your arms. Surrender.'

I jeered. So did many. A number stayed silent, though. They could not help themselves; they wanted to know what was being offered.

'We would become thralls, eh?' demanded Imr.

'Correct,' said the warrior, 'but you would be alive.'

'I'll ask my comrades.' Imr's tone was mock-courteous. 'Well, boys, what you say? D'you fancy becoming this ragr Englishman's thralls?'

'No!' Even those had kept quiet joined in. Our roar startled a stonechat out of the gorse.

'There you have it,' said Imr, with an apologetic shrug. 'My warriors refuse your "offer", which I suspect was only made because your followers are spineless worms!'

The mail-clad warrior sucked in his cheeks. His men didn't like it either.

Vali chose this moment to set down axe and shield. He turned his back on the enemy, and quick as a flash, dropped his breeks and undergarment. It was perfect. We cackled uproariously as he waved his hairy, sweaty arse at the English, who hurled insults and spears in reply. One landed beside Vali. His response was to pitch it back downhill, and with a bit of Loki luck, he hit a warrior. Again we voiced our appreciation.

Vali gave a last arse waggle, and pulling up his garments, resumed his place in the line.

'You should have stayed put,' said Vekel. 'With that monstrous crack to face, the English wouldn't have come any further.'

'Give it a fondle if you like, vitki,' said Vali with a chuckle. 'Just know that when Hlif Horse-gelder hears, she might want a word with you. I'd mind your ballsack!'

Vekel bellowed with laughter. The sound of his mirth was so loud, and he so outlandish-looking with his black eyeliner and whitened face, that the English hesitated.

'Come on, you cowards,' I yelled, clattering axe head off shield boss. 'COW-ARDS!'

We called them that all the way up the slope. It was simple but effective, and I think if the mail-clad warrior and a couple of others in the front rank hadn't been there, the assault would have died before they came within reach. As it was, their attempt was half-hearted, especially after I smashed the mail-clad warrior's shield apart with the first blow of my axe, and beheaded him with the second.

We drove them back, but things were going badly for our oarmates. In the first moment we had to draw breath safely, mixed shouts of triumph and despair from the other side of the hilltop filled our ears. I intuited their meaning. Yelling for Thorstein, telling everyone else to stay where they were – or else the English on our side would swarm uphill like rats – I turned and leaped past the wounded, desperate to get to the far side of the standing stones.

Ten steps. It might as well have been the distance from that hilltop in West-Bretland to Linn Duachaill, or for that matter, Miklagard. Imr was still on his feet, screaming like a lunatic, so covered in blood that it was impossible to tell if it was his or his enemies', but the rest were down, wounded or dying, or fighting alone against several foes.

I was about to die, but an odd calm bathed me. I parried a spear thrust with my shield, and belly-punched its wielder with my axe head. His mouth made a shocked 'O', and I chopped low, removing his left leg at the knee. I caught a blur of movement towards my face, and jerked to one side. A spearhead whistled through the space. Carried forward by the momentum of his lunge, the Englishman had no defence against my axe, which cut away most of his lower jaw. A bubbling scream tore the air as he staggered back, but two comrades took his place and came at me with spears. From the corner of my eye, I sensed a third moving around to attack from behind, and I thought, this is it.

'Look!' Vekel, who had clambered on top of one the stone 'legs', was pointing. In Saxon, he cried, 'The ships! The ships are on fire!'

Lalo, I thought, and hammered a blow at one of the spearmen.

Over and over Vekel repeated himself. The English, like all sailors who are onshore, were alive to the danger of losing their means of travel and escape, stopped fighting, and looked.

And with space to breathe, so did I.

Four ships had landed. Two were now aflame, and I fancied I could see the frenzied figures of men running hither and thither. Loki, you faithless shit, I thought, keep Lalo safe. Oðin, strike down any enemies who come near him.

The sight of their burning vessels saw the Englishmen's desire to fight vanish. They broke away and retreated down the hill. Without a backward glance, they ran for the shore. I had not the energy even to cheer. Nor did anyone else.

Vekel was unhurt. He was chanting, and pointing his staff at the English, weaving magic against them. Thorstein had a shallow cut on his right arm, but seemed to be otherwise unhurt. Karli had escaped without injury, to my relief. Vali had survived too; he was tending to Hrolf, who had a wounded leg. Imr, however, was down, and his face had that near-to-death grey pallor I knew too well. I hurried to his side.

'S-Stormcrow.' Imr grimaced. 'Where are the English?'

'Gone,' I said, kneeling. 'Lalo set two ships ablaze.'

More of a smile. 'Ah, that blámaðr, he's a clever one. Vekel was wise to buy him, and even more to set him free.'

'I hope he's all right.'

'They won't have caught him. Me, though . . .' Imr closed his eyes.

'Imr.'

No response. I felt for a pulse at his neck. It was there, but weak and irregular. Then I lifted his arm. I wished I hadn't. By some unlucky chance, Imr had taken a novice's wound, in the armpit. It couldn't have gone in deep, because that was instantly mortal, but his tunic, crimson-sodden to his waist, told its own story. I wondered if he'd known when refusing treatment earlier.

'I'm done.' Imr's gaze, although distant, was level. 'There's no fixing it, Stormcrow. Not you, not Vekel, not even Oðin himself could.'

'He wouldn't help you anyway, because it would delay you joining his einherjar,' I said, voice thick. 'You will be in Valhöll soon.'

A low chuckle. 'I hope so.'

I glanced up at Vekel, who had stopped spell-casting. 'What are they doing?'

'Running about like headless chickens. There's time to get away.'

Vekel was right. We needed to go. The chance of pursuit was still there. I did not want to leave Imr, but nor could we carry him. Speed was of the essence.

'I will stay behind, Stormcrow.'

Ashamed that he had so easily read my mind, I coloured. 'No, Imr, we—'

'I will not have it any other way.' A liquid cough, another grimace. 'I am not long for this world.'

'Which way shall we go?' During the battle, sure of death, I had given it no consideration. Now, with escape possible, but *Brimdýr* burnt and gone, and Imr dying, I was at a loss.

'That is your decision, Stormcrow.'

I wondered if I had heard aright. 'What do you mean? Thorstein, Vekel, they—'

'A vitki cannot lead warriors, and Thorstein isn't the leader you are.'

'Karli—' I began.

'Is a good shipmaster, but he is not the chief of a warband.'

I thought of Twin-brows, Karli's right-hand man, and discounted him as well. The other survivors were brave enough, Vali and Hrolf and so on, but they were not warriors whom men would follow.

'You will do it?' Imr whispered.

'I will.' I bent my head so he would not see my grief.

'Take my silver, Stormcrow.'

My heart stilled. 'Imr—'

'I have no use for it . . .' The words were slurred.

I swallowed. 'Very well.'

Imr made no reply.

I looked down. His eyes were staring, his jaw a little open. He was gone.

Battening down my sorrow, for despite his wiliness, he had been a good leader, I announced it was time to leave, before the English returned. No one questioned the order. There were nine injured warriors, however. Five were reasonably mobile, but the remaining four could barely stand. I was matter-of-fact, asking what they wanted. Three asked to be put out of their misery; the last was unconscious. The thirteen able-bodied among us drew lots, using Karli's black and white stones. I could have opted out, but as the new leader, I felt it important to participate in everything.

Twin-brows drew the first white stone, and I the second.

I wished my two warriors, one a quiet man by the name of Boslof, the other a beer-swilling oaf called Ogmund, a swift passage to Valhöll, and after they shut their eyes, opened their throats with my seax. Twin-brows used his axe. I didn't look, but asked that those men also went to Oðin's great feasting hall.

Then it was time to go. I helped to pick up Imr's chest, and was amazed by its weight. I was adrift in a foreign land with little more than a dozen warriors, and with no real idea where to go, but I was a wealthy man. It was wryly amusing.

I had momentarily forgotten about Lalo; Vekel mentioned him, and we cast about, but could see no sign of him. He would find our trail, I declared. I hoped I was right, but crucially, no one questioned my order.

Not Thorstein, nor Karli. Not even Vekel.

Which told me Imr had been right.

CHAPTER TWENTY-NINE

There was a settlement a short way inland from the hilltop. When the eighteen of us arrived, it had just been abandoned. Smoke trickled from a few roofs, before being carried away by the brisk easterly wind. A collection of thatched, one roomed, wattle-and-daub huts, it was like a thousand others I had seen. Remembering Imr's stories, it was easy to surmise that the inhabitants were all too familiar with Norse raids, and had fled, taking their livestock and everything they could carry.

I posted sentries in case the English decided to follow us. The rest set about securing food and supplies. A few hens had been missed; these were swiftly caught and dispatched. A scrawny dog nosing a refuse heap barked furiously at me, and ran off. We went from house to house, moving fast. There wasn't much, but as Vekel said, something was better than nothing. Vali showed everyone his haul, a quiver of twenty arrows, and invaluable to Lalo and our bowmen. Thorstein found a pile of cabbages; not all were mouldy. Hrolf discovered a wooden bucket with two hands' depth of barley flour. I was luckiest, chancing upon a leg of ham in an outbuilding. Perhaps too heavy for its owners to carry, it had been hidden under a mound of sacking. Delighted, we took the latter as well, to serve as blankets.

The search was almost complete when Lalo appeared, grinning from ear to ear. I grabbed him in a bearhug. As Vekel seized him next, men gathered, pleased and relieved in equal measure.

'You did well,' I said.

A frown. 'I would have fired the four ships, but the English saw me. I had to run.'

'It was more than enough, Mandinka,' said Thorstein. 'You saved our lives.'

Lalo's gaze trailed from man to man. They dipped their chins, and muttered their thanks. If any had had a poor opinion of him before, I thought, it had changed.

'You still want a holmgang?' Lalo asked Hrolf.

'No!' A rueful look. 'I spoke in ignorance before, Mandinka. I am sorry. You have saved my life twice since, moreover – when climbing the hill, and now this. I am in your debt.'

'As are we all,' Vekel declared.

Hooms. Hands beating off shields. Ayes.

Lalo beamed.

'You look as pleased as a dog with two bods,' I said.

'A dog with what?' he asked as Thorstein creased with laughter.

'Two bods. Pricks.'

Lalo thought this was hilarious, but suddenly, his posture changed. 'Someone's there!' He shot towards a hovel at the edge of the settlement. Reaching the doorway, he leaped inside, spear at the ready.

I ran forward, sword in hand. I heard others behind me.

Lalo emerged with a girl of about twelve years, barefoot and in ragged clothing. Giving him terrified looks, but making no attempt to flee, she burst into tears. I couldn't help but smile.

'She has never seen a blámaðr,' said Lalo. It was acceptable if he said it.

'I would say you're right,' ventured Thorstein. 'No one will have in this shithole.'

'Do you understand me?' I asked in Irish.

A slight frown, a look as if she almost knew.

Imr had said that the language of West-Bretland was similar to Irish. I repeated myself, more slowly.

'I understand,' she said.

'We won't hurt you,' I told her.

Unsure, she half turned towards Lalo. 'And him? Is he a demon?'

'No,' I said, smiling again. 'He is from a land far, far away, where the sun always shines.'

'Everyone there has black skin,' said Lalo in Irish.

A look of wonder, and I thought, the child has probably never been further than the next hamlet, if that. Whatever my concept of the world was, hers was infinitely smaller. She was won over soon enough, however, after Lalo did some sleight of hand, pulling a silver penny from behind her ear, and making it disappear from his hand. When he

286

gave her the coin at the end, she gasped, and held it so tight I knew she had never possessed such a thing before.

I fed her a couple of slices of ham, which she wolfed down, eyeing the rest with such hunger that I cut her a larger chunk. I would have offered more, but men were staring. It wasn't unreasonable. We had eighteen mouths to feed, and enough rations to last perhaps three days.

According to the girl, the place was called Cambronn, which meant Crooked Hill. Her people were farmers and fishers, and their lord, to whom they paid rent, lived away to the east. She didn't how far, or how many warriors he had, other than it was a lot. More than us, I asked. A nod.

She had no awareness of the large fleet we had seen. Everyone had run away because of the battle on the hilltop, she said. She hadn't, hampered by her left ankle, red and swollen after an accident at the low cliffs nearby. She had been hunting for seabirds' eggs. You were lucky not to be killed, I told her, and received a cheeky grin.

'My parents are gone,' she said, 'but thanks to my grandfather, I know how to climb, and where the water is deep if you fall.'

Vekel shook his head. 'This one is feisty, eh?'

'She is,' I said, and gave her three more silver pennies. She clapped her hands in delight, and when I asked, willingly led us to a stream. I am not ashamed to say that I went down on all fours like a dog to slake my raging thirst. Only when my belly could hold no more did I fill my leather skin.

The girl was still examining the coins as we left a short while later.

I waited until she was out of sight before opening Imr's chest and divvying out as much of the silver as possible. We couldn't carry it all, but we made a good fist of it. The wealth was ours now, I told the warriors, and it would help to buy us a ship. What we could not carry was buried; the spot hidden by a large, odd-shaped boulder. Memorise the place, I told everyone. We will come back for it one day.

I hoped that that was the truth, that we didn't end up like Imr and the rest.

I did not linger, but headed eastward. I had no real idea where we were going, other than away from the English ships. Imr had talked of meeting the Norse fleet plaguing the southern coastline, but hadn't known where it was. As I said quietly to Vekel, he'd probably just been going to sail *Brimdýr* towards the sun until we found it. One location that held some promise was Wiht-land, a large isle that had been used as a base by the Norse of recent years. How far away it was and how we would reach it remained to be seen, as did finding a boat to carry us the final distance from the mainland.

Despite the day's brutal events and our uncertain future, I was in good spirits. The sword was mine again. I was rich, *and* I was leader of the warband. In my mind, these were surely signs of Oðin's favour. Vekel agreed. This was my time, he told me.

I was given little opportunity to bask in happiness.

The settlement was still visible to our rear when Lalo, who had offered to stay back, came loping in to say the English were approaching the hamlet. Groans met this unwelcome revelation, and I wondered if Loki, unhappy with Oðin's beneficence, had decided to level the field. It wasn't a total surprise. As Vekel said, the massive English fleet probably signified that King Æthelred *was* trying to rid Britain of the Norse, and that meant the warriors we had fought saw us as targets. There was to be no rest.

Tireless, Lalo again offered to act as a scout. Thorstein, whose reserves also seemed limitless, also went. I led the rest of the band east northeast, now searching for a suitable place to ambush our relentless enemies. I skirted around a gorse-covered hill, the top of which we might have held with *Brimdýr*'s full complement. Not with a third. When Twin-brows asked what we were going to do, I told him brusquely it would soon be apparent. He did not question me further, but I sensed the warriors' growing unease. I couldn't blame them. In my mind, I could imagine little but a second, unequal battle that would leave us all dead or enslaved.

'Got any ideas?' I muttered to Vekel.

'I do, as it happens.'

For once, his smugness failed to irritate. 'Spit it out.'

'The weather is changing.'

Intent on finding a location suitable for an ambush, I had been paying little heed to the sky. Dark clouds were piled atop one another to the east, and moving towards us at a decent clip. 'It's going to rain,' I said. 'How does that help, other than slowing down the English?'

'There's more than rain in those clouds.'

'Thunder and lightning?'

'Exactly. Thor is angry.'

'He might be,' I retorted, 'but that doesn't help us.'

'When the heavens open, the English will seek shelter and wait it out, because they will assume that is what we will also do.'

I began to see his purpose. 'You think we should attack during the downpour.'

His eyes were bright. 'Who would do that, only madmen?'

Or men with nothing to lose, I thought grimly. And the rain would have to be torrential to prevent us being seen.

Lalo returned not long after, reporting that about fifty warriors were on our trail. 'They don't look happy,' he said.

'Nor would I if I had lost a fight against some Norsemen, then had my ship fired, and straightaway been forced to chase after the very same Norsemen,' I said, grinning.

'It is good news,' declared Vekel.

'There are still three of them for every one of us,' said Hrolf.

'But the English do not have a god on their side!' I declared.

Vekel pointed at the threatening black clouds, and explained his plan.

Carried by a howling wind, the heavy rain drove in at an acute angle. The gale found a dozen ways beneath my cloak. To add to the unpleasantness, the garment was already letting in water. My trousers were wringing, and both boots also leaked.

It was a familiar and objectionable sensation. Getting drenched had been part of life in Linn Duachaill. It might have been a drier part of Ériu than Mumhan, say, but there had been dreich days aplenty. Booleying cattle, helping neighbours with their sheep, walking to a neighbour's or on occasion, Mainistir Bhuithe, all ran the risk of encountering a downpour.

I had not liked it as a boy, and I did not like it now.

The only thing to do was grit your teeth and carry on.

Nonetheless, I had a job to perform, one a great deal more important than physical discomfort. Half-stumbling into a gorse bush, I squinted into the gloom and tried to make sense of the darkened landscape. I had no idea where the Englishmen were. Lightning flashed, a bright white illumination that hurt my eyes. By the time they had adjusted, darkness had descended again. I swore, and trudged on. A few moments later, thunder rumbled overhead. The gaps between the two were shortening, a sign that the storm drew nearer.

'This way!' Lalo, invisible until five or six paces separated us, was jabbing a thumb in the direction from which he had come.

I peered over his shoulder, seeing nothing, baffled by his unerring sense of direction. 'You have seen them?'

'Yes! They are huddled together like a bunch of cattle in the corner of a field.'

'How far?'

'Maybe five hundred paces.'

'Sentries?'

Thunder rolled, making speech impossible. Rain sheeted in.

Lalo shook his head, no, his smile dazzling in the lightning.

'Bring us in close,' I said, determined to make the best of this insane situation. 'Nice and slow.'

A happy nod, and he led off again.

I filled in Thorstein, next in line, and he passed the information on.

I counted down the distance, sweating despite the chill in the moisture-laden air. At one point, I sank my left leg up to the knee in mud, and needed help to extricate myself. We continued.

At just over three hundred paces, Lalo again appeared out of the blackness. Lightning flashed. Brilliance illuminated us all, and I waited for a shout, the cry of a sentry.

Nothing.

We gathered in a huddle, and I studied my warriors' faces. Some, those of the wounded, were etched with pain, but to a man they looked determined. Resolute. There was even a trace of eagerness, which I felt myself. I had to prove my worth as leader, and winning this unequal contest would be a good start. *Loki, you trickster*, I thought, *do not play me false now. Thor and Oðin, help me.*

'We shall attack from two sides,' I said.

'Some will escape anyway,' said Thorstein.

'If they do, they do. Let them go,' I replied. 'And make plenty of noise. Scare the shit out of the English, and the battle's half won.'

Fierce, whispered ayes.

'Thor is with us,' Vekel added.

Even Christ-worshippers like Vali were pleased by this.

We separated, Lalo leading Thorstein and seven others in a semicircle around the Englishmen, while I remained in place with Vekel and the rest. Lalo had told me it was about four hundred paces to his position.

The count was the longest wait of my life.

I crouched down so as not to be seen in the lightning bursts, motioning my companions to do the same. My heart was racing, and every time the black turned to blinding white, I tensed, expecting a wave of Englishmen to crash into us. I reached one hundred, and it hadn't happened. Still my belly was knotted with tension. I kept counting, imagining Lalo leading the others through the foul weather. Two hundred came, and an eternity later, three. If things were going to plan, I thought, both groups now had one hundred paces until they reached the English.

I had opted for my bearded axe tonight. There would be enemies all around, and it needed little room to swing. I motioned, and Vali came to stand alongside me; the others filed in two by two, with Vekel at the rear. He would not take part unless, he had archly observed, we needed help.

We walked in the direction Lalo had indicated. I was as wet as if I'd jumped in the Sionainn, but I no longer cared.

Fifty paces, and we spread out into a line.

The rain had not let up, a gods-blessing, but the lightning had, another stroke of luck. It was as black as Hel, hard to see much beyond what I could touch. Gaze searching the ground, I tried to pick out anything human-shaped.

Two score paces. Thirty-five. I could still not see an Englishman, let alone a whole group of them. Worry gnawed my guts, and I wondered if I had headed entirely in the wrong direction.

Thirty.

Twenty-five.

Finally, a shape in the darkness that was not a gorse bush. My eyes had accustomed to the darkness. I peered, realised it was the English. They were bunched together just like Lalo had said, and incredibly, none appeared to be keeping watch. I checked again that my men were ready, and taking advantage of another thunder roll, threw myself forward.

I was very close when an Englishman turned his head and saw me. His cry was brought to an abrupt end by the bearded axe, which caved in his skull. His panicked companions pushed and shoved at one another as they tried to stand, to grasp weapons that were beneath cloaks, to fight back.

We took full advantage.

Even a praise-seeking, arse-licking skald could not have called what happened next a battle. It was wholesale slaughter, cutting, chopping, kicking men into the mud, stamping on their heads, ignoring pleas for mercy. I hacked and swung mechanically, over and again, as if I were chopping wood, not human flesh. The iron tang of blood was on my lips, and it was not mine. I liked the taste.

A pair of hands lifted towards me, fingers wrung together in a wordless plea. I sheared through them with my axe, lodging the blade in the man's face. A sudden sting in my side had me whirling to find an Englishman whose dagger had been thwarted by my mail. I cut at him, laughing when arm and dagger fell to the mud, and as he screamed, I stove in his ribs.

The massacre was over quickly, leaving the ground littered with corpses. There were some wounded, mud-thrashing men who bawled and cried for their mothers. We killed them. When there was no more noise – the storm had moved past, and the rain had also stopped – I did a headcount. Sixteen, two men fewer than had begun the attack. I could see Vekel, and Thorstein, and Lalo, and felt no guilt that I was glad they were among the unharmed.

Our casualties turned out to be two of the previously injured. Both were dead, but this loss did not diminish the magnitude of what we had done. A handful of our enemies had escaped in the confusion, but forty-four had been slain. The English warband had ceased to exist. As I jubilantly told my warriors, even if the few survivors reached their ships, the spine-chilling tale of the ambush made the chance of further pursuit vanishingly small.

'Stormcrow!'

The chant was taken up so fast, I didn't see who began it.

'Stormcrow!' my men roared, hammering bloodied weapons off shields.

Gooseskin dimpled my arms; the hairs on my neck were standing too.

Sure that Oðin was watching in approval, I drew the sword that I had taken from a beach-corpse so many years before, and held it aloft.

'STORMCROW!'

CHAPTER THIRTY

Near the coast of southern England

Ten days later, I did not feel so brash. We had gone east after the fight near Cambronn, sometimes southeast or south-southeast. I always kept the coastline, our only guide, to our right. Wiht-land would eventually appear, or so I kept telling myself. How we would see it through the murk was another matter.

The weather had been brutal, its dominant feature the rain. Light, heavy or torrential, the precipitation was often accompanied by violent wind. Always in the open, unable to light fires, we lived in a drenched, chilled state, weapons rusting and leather gear mildewing by the day. Hunting was impossible, all game having vanished, and keen to avoid being identified as Norse, we avoided human habitation.

For the first few days this was easy enough, the land being poor and sparsely populated. As the rough scrub and gorse gave way to rolling grassland and pasture, though, farms grew plentiful, forcing us to lay low in the day and move only at night. The pitiful existence was a constant sting to my pride, but it was the sensible choice. Fifteen warriors and a vitki was not a sufficiently strong force to march through hostile territory. We risked enough by sneaking into farm outbuildings at night and taking a few hens, or killing a sheep in a field far from any dwellings.

Norsemen, we were enemies to everyone in West-Bretland and after it, England. Not until an encounter with our own kind would there be a possibility of welcome. We had no guarantee of that either, however. With a fully-crewed *Brimdýr* and Imr, a well-known longship and captain, there had been a decent chance. No longer. Wolf packs accepted single individuals, as we had with Vali and Kar on Man, but large groups of shipless newcomers were a recipe for trouble. Allowing Hrolf and Thormod to join together had been an unusual exception. Staring round at my warriors, gaunt-cheeked, sunken-eyed, miserable-looking, it was hard to imagine anything other than a hostile reception. Or one where we had to join different ships' crews in twos and threes.

I told myself that Óðin would not grant the storm-victory over the English only to cast me aside immediately afterwards. That would mean the loss of *Brimdýr* and Imr's death, not to mention the others who had fallen, counted for nothing. I tried also not to think of Loki, who would have found it highly entertaining to subject us to such trials. This was a test of my mettle, I decided. Nothing more.

And so I endured, and I helped my warriors to endure. When Hrolf came down with a fever, I carried his gear and my own until he recovered. Karli, weakening from lack of food, got half my ration for several days. I ripped up my own garments to fashion new bandages for the wounded, lanced Vekel's blisters with a needle, took more sentry duties than anyone else. I went out setting snares with Lalo, and on the eleventh night, found two with rabbits in them. It was not much food compared to the size of our band, but we received a rapturous welcome in camp, and no one held back from eating raw meat on the bone.

When a raven alighted the next morning on one of the tossed-away carcasses, my spirits rose further. I sat and watched as the black bird pecked and tore, its scaled feet holding the rabbit steady, and thought, Óðin has not forsaken me. A second raven, its mate perhaps, landed to join in the feast, and it was hard not to think that these were Óðin's birds, sent as a divine sign.

I was not alone in drawing this conclusion.

'Friends of yours, Stormcrow?' Vali asked, his tone sincere.

'Indeed,' I said, plucking the raven amulet from under my tunic. 'I am never without one, see?'

With uncanny timing, the first raven swallowed a gobbet of red and turned a beady eye in our direction. *Krrruk.*

'It heard you.' Karli's tone was reverent.

I didn't have the arrogance to agree, but fortunately Vekel was there.

'Of course it did. Huninn, that one is. The other is Muginn. Óðin likes to watch over his chosen.'

Krrruk. The second raven spoke.

Fresh determination flowed through my veins. Even if we were damp, hungry, footsore and in foreign, unfriendly territory, the most powerful Norse god was with us. More blood might be required, it was true, but that was the warrior's way.

'It will not be long until we reach Wiht-land,' I said, loud and confident.

'And then?' Vali asked.

'There will be longships who need crew.'

'You will not be our leader.' This was Karli, sounding unhappy.

'We'll gather the rest of the silver for a ship soon enough.' I hoped it was true. 'Another *Brimdýr* will sail the seas. I shall captain her and you warriors will be foremost among her crew.'

They liked that enough not to want to discuss placing ourselves under another's command. Relieved, I sought out Vekel.

'That was well done,' he said.

'Aye, well. Our fortunes are going to take a turn for the better now.' They have to, I decided, or we will also be raven-food.

Things improved for a day or two. Creeping out of camp in the dark before dawn, Lalo came back bent double under the weight of a decent-sized hind. It was dangerous to light a fire in the daytime, but a vote resulted in an almost unanimous decision to risk it. Only Vekel and I, wary, voted against. Loki was in good humour with us, though; no one came. We were also helped by the gusting wind that dispersed the smoke as it rose above the trees.

Everyone was famished; we hovered around the fire, barely able to hold back as twig-skewers of venison sizzled in the flames. I doubt a single piece of meat cooked through before it was taken from the heat and devoured. The liver was finely sliced and handed round, raw and glistening. The heart came after; I had rarely eaten anything as delicious.

'A bit of salt, and it would be perfect,' said Karli, licking his lips.

'Tastes fine to me,' said Thorstein, expertly disarticulating a hindleg from the pelvis. Vali leaned in, dagger ready to slice, but Thorstein lifted it out of the way with a tut, tut shake of his head. He threaded a length of branch I had hacked into a skewer in and out of the hock, and through the meat at the back of the haunch. Then, balancing each end on a neat pile of stones built by Twin-brows, he suspended it over the flames. 'This needs time,' he said, smacking away hands that strayed towards the joint.

'I saw the coast from a high point while I was hunting,' Lalo said.

Belly growling, I continued studying the roasting venison. 'And?'

'There is a big island just off the coast.'

My eyes shot to him. 'You did not think to say this before?'

A Lalo-shrug. 'I am telling you now.'

Vekel thought this was amusing, even if I did not.

'How big exactly?' I demanded.

'It would take a day to walk across.'

'Wiht-land.' I was triumphant. 'It has to be.'

'We just need a way of reaching it,' said Vekel drolly.

He was immune to my glare, so I dunted him in the ribs.

'What was that for?' he squawked.

'Not being helpful.' I was frustrated that my happiness at passing safely through West-Bretland and southern Britain had been so short-lived. Now another mighty obstacle confronted us, the channel of water between us and the island.

I had no idea that my attention was soon to be focused entirely on land rather than sea.

The following day it was Gunnar's turn to come back with news of interest. The sentry position overlooked a track that led down to a fishing village on the shore. It was the nearest settlement to our position, and where we hoped to beg, borrow or steal a vessel. Gunnar had spied two wagons slowly working their way down to it from the chalk downs to the north.

'Probably a merchant or trader. Who cares?' said Karli. 'We can't sail to Wiht-land on wagons.'

Gunnar, not the brightest knife in the box, looked crestfallen, but then he said, 'Merchants don't have thirty guards – not for two wagons anyway.'

'Thirty? Are you sure?' I asked.

A resentful look. 'I can count.'

Cold certainty seized me. 'They're carrying silver. What else could it be? Thirty warriors is half a warband.' I turned to Gunnar. 'How long until they pass our position?'

'Not that long.'

'Have we time to fell a tree?'

'If we move now.'

'I see your mind,' said Twin-brows. 'You mean to take the silver for ourselves!'

Vekel was grinning; so was Lalo. Vali smiled back. But for the arrows I had found in the settlement, the mad plan I had in mind would have been inconceivable.

'It is risky,' said Thorstein. 'Sixteen of us against thirty?'

'We have faced worse odds and won through,' I replied.

'Aye, at night, in the midst of a storm.'

'Two wagonloads of silver will buy us a longship,' I said.

'I don't see too many for sale around here,' Thorstein retorted. 'And that's before we take into account the Norsemen the silver is intended for. They won't be very happy when it doesn't arrive. There'll be precious little chance of joining their number.'

'If no one gets away, the Norsemen will be none the wiser. We can join a different part of the fleet further down the coast,' I said confidently, aware that I was rolling the dice with all of our futures, and expecting to get two sixes. My gaze travelled. 'Well?'

They agreed, as I had hoped. So did the rest of the group when we put it to a vote. The prospect of vast treasure was too much to resist, even if it involved tremendous risk.

Having lived in our mail shirts since Cambronn, we had only to snatch up weapons and shields, and make our way to Gunnar's sentry point. Rising above the ash and beech trees, it was a rocky outcrop with a bird's eye view over the surrounding area. Thorstein, Vekel, Lalo and I accompanied Gunnar to the top while the others stayed out of sight. Crouching on the rocks' westward side, we viewed the rutted track as it wound from the chalk downs towards the coast.

'There.' Gunnar pointed.

The ox-drawn wagons stood out, the only traffic visible. The accompanying warriors constituted ten riders and twenty men on foot, evenly divided in front and behind the pair of wagons. Doubt flared bright in my mind. Given the value of the cargo they protected, these warriors would be no inexperienced youths, but seasoned fighters. They outnumbered us two to one, and a couple of my band were wounded to boot.

'Well?' I stared at Vekel.

'Fortune favours the brave.'

I waited, but he wasn't going to give me any more. My eyes moved to Thorstein, who shrugged. 'It's insane, but I'm with you.'

'It is vital that none of the riders escape,' I said to Lalo. 'If they do—'

'I understand.'

'We'd better move,' I said. 'Trees don't fell themselves.'

A tree across the road always suggests an ambush. I therefore chose a decent-sized beech just around a bend; it would not be seen until the last moment. Vali took charge, and with axe-wielding men working in pairs, both sides of the trunk, the beech was soon brought down. It blocked the track nicely, but we needed more. With Lalo running back and forth from the woodland's edge to keep us informed of the wagons' progress, we tackled another tree, this time an ash, a hundred paces to the north. A jay screeched protests at our presence. We worked differently this time, trunk-chopping the ash to the point where Vali could push it across the track, trapping the wagons and their protectors.

Preparations completed, and our prospective victims hopefully still unaware, I ordered Lalo and the two others with bows to choose the best shooting positions. Each had six or seven shafts; none could miss.

Vekel aside, there were twelve warriors to carry out the ambush. Vali would push over the ash, and then join me and four others as Lalo and his companions rained down arrows. When we attacked, Thorstein and his five men would charge in from the other side.

It was peaceful in the woods. The birds, silenced by our axes, were singing again. I heard the two-note call of a chiffchaff, and one of my favourites, a willow warbler. A blackcap started out hesitant and chattering, and followed with its long, beautiful sequence of notes.

My reverie didn't last. The magnitude of what lay before us was driven home as our quarry drew near. Several riders had mail shirts; I hoped Lalo saw this, and aimed at throats or the horses. The warriors around the wagons were tough-looking too, and some also wore mail. Fortune favours the brave, Vekel had said, but I couldn't put from my mind the saying that fools often rushed onto ground that wiser men were wary of treading on.

I considered retreat. Humiliation would be our only companion. An approach could be made instead to the recipients of the silver, soon to arrive at the fishing settlement. With no knowledge of our aborted attack on their riches, they might be well disposed to taking on fresh crew, in particular men who had come through the trials we had: the battle on the hilltop, the storm-ambush, our journey from West-Bretland.

We would be split up between different ships, though. That was hard to stomach. I also bridled at the thought of acknowledging another as my leader. I had commanded the warband for a short time only, but it felt good. Natural.

The attack would go ahead, I decided, wiping one sweaty palm, then the other on my breeks.

'Nervous?' whispered Vekel.

'A little.' I could say it to him.

The lead riders reached the bend.

My breath caught in my chest.

One of the horsemen reined in. His face twisted.

Now, Vali, I thought. NOW.

A loud, cracking noise, which dragged on, and ended with a heavy impact.

Arrows flew, blurred dark shafts. Men died, fell from their mounts. Horses reared, kicking, and collapsed on riders. Shouts filled the air. Orders. The warriors on foot formed a line on each side of the wagons, or tried to. More arrows came. I counted the horsemen, the ones who could most easily escape. Four of the five at the front were dead or dismounted. One only was still in the saddle, and he was rallying his men. At the back, two remained on their horses, but the arrow in the haunch of one meant it was unrideable, wheeling and turning in evident agony. The last rider spurred alongside the wagons. A warrior in his path collided with the horse, and was knocked down. I lost sight of him until he emerged beyond the lead wagon, and I knew he intended to jump the beech. If he succeeded, our hopes would be dashed.

Oðin be thanked, Lalo was tracking him too.

An arrow blurred in, taking the rider in the throat. It was the most extraordinary shot, even more skilful than the one which had slain the shepherd.

Now it was up to us.

Bellowing a war cry, I charged towards the track. There hadn't been time to count how many warriors remained, but they still outnumbered us by a considerable margin. We had to win fast.

My first opponent was tough, and wily with it. He lunged, and anticipated me ducking down. Angling low, his spear connected with my helmet, the top, fortunately. It screeched off, but the force sent waves of agony down my wrenched neck. In he came, *smack*, shield boss clattering into mine, and I staggered back. Back went his right arm for a second lunge. Completely unbalanced, I went down hard, arse first.

A howl of triumph, and the spear loomed above me, point aimed at my upward-looking, fear-filled eye. I hacked sideways, blind, with the bearded axe. One of the valkyrja must have been with me, because the blade bit deep. Into what, I didn't know, but the warrior screamed, and forgot all about spitting me like a pig for the roasting fire. It was his turn to stumble, which allowed me to get up, balls tight with the expectation of a different spear, or a sword ramming into my flesh. I made it to standing, however, and saw the ruin of the warrior's thigh. White bone gleamed amid the bleeding muscle – he was maimed. I put him out of his misery.

I killed another wounded man next, so busy trying to pull the arrow from his right arm that he didn't see the bearded axe sweeping in. Two warriors, one in mail, came at me together, and I had a hard time of it. But for my own mail shirt, I would have been badly hurt. They got cocky, though, and with it, sloppy. I pulled the mail-wearer's shield towards with me a flick of the axe's beard, and then, fast as a snake, cut downwards. I parted one of his shield straps, and damaged the other. With it sagging down, he was defenceless against the next blow, an angled swing that shattered his shield arm. Mouth agape, breath sawing, he was easy prey. Again the bearded axe drank deep.

The mail-wearer's companion attacked. His spear rammed clean through my shield, and the point hit my chest. Robbed of force, it did not penetrate. Its wielder gave an almighty tug. The spear did not come free, but he jerked me forward. Unable to disengage my arm from the straps, I hammered at him with the axe. He caught the first blow with his shield, and the second, but simultaneously trying to dislodge his spear, he didn't anticipate. I switched angles and came in from the side. The bearded axe hit just below the bottom of his ribcage, slicing through the abdominal wall, and lodging in his backbone. I let go and grabbed my seax.

I had to release my shield too, with the spear still in it. That left no protection but my mail, and what in effect was a large fish-gutting knife. All my enemies had either a spear or sword. A nearby warrior saw, and immediately came at me. Ashild would have been proud of my sideways skip, neat as she at dancing, and also how I converted that into a jump forward. A vigorous slash of the seax decorated his throat with a new, gaping mouth. Crimson gushed; his eyes bulged; he died.

In desperate need of a shield, expecting another opponent before I could find one, I realised with amazement that there were no warriors standing. None of my men appeared to be down either, and there was no sound of fighting from the other side of the wagons.

'Did any get away?' I shouted.

'Not from here,' Thorstein called.

'And from this side?' My struggle to survive had taken all of my attention.

'No.' Lalo came into view.

'Only the wagon drivers are left.' Vekel gestured. 'Lucky for us they didn't run, or the oxen might have stampeded off the track.'

That wouldn't save them, I thought, refusing to let any notions of mercy take root.

The one nearest me, a beardless youth, took the easy way out. Leaping down from his seat with a spear, he charged. Vali dodged and swung, and the sound of his axe was reminiscent of a butcher's cleaver hitting the block. That left the second wagon driver. Older and wiser, he raised his hands, and in stumbling Norse, said that he had a wife, a family. He would go home and never say a word of what had happened.

'As if he could do that,' said Vekel dryly. 'They would put his feet in a fire to discover what happened to the silver.'

'I know,' said Thorstein, and killed him.

My initial headcount had been wrong. One of my warriors was dead. He wasn't much loss. Wounded in the leg at the hilltop, he had kept up thanks to Vali, who had half-carried him much of the way. Remarkably, the only other casualty was Thorstein, who taken a cut to the face. It needed stitching; Vekel did that at once, tutting as Thorstein grimaced.

'Do not move, or it will scar.'

''Twill scar regardless.'

In a whisper, 'I'll still fancy you.'

Thorstein pretended not to have heard, as did I.

I went to the back of the first wagon and pulled aside the heavy canvas covering. I liked what I saw: two long timber chests, bound in strips of metal, each with a heavy padlock.

The enormity of what we'd done sank home, and as the next obstacle presented itself in my head, I began to laugh.

'What's wrong?' Karli's blood-spattered face appeared beside mine. He looked in. 'That's silver, or I'm a three-legged dog. Why are you laughing?'

'We don't have enough men to go wandering about the countryside with a fortune in silver.'

'It's a bit late for that, Stormcrow.'

He was right of course, but it didn't help a jot.

I had been rash, I realised, rash and proud. My throw of the dice had given me two sixes, but the Norns had not taken the thread of my life away from danger. No, the bitches, they had kept the two entwined, snug as me and Sláine wrapped up in each other's embrace.

As I saw it, we had several choices.

One was to bury the silver, and try to enlist with the Norsemen who would soon be arriving. It would not be without risk, given the non-appearance of the silver. Some form of suspicion was bound to fall on us, even if we appeared penniless – and that was assuming they didn't send men up the road to look for it. A blind man could find the ambush site. Succeed in passing that trial, however, and we would be split up among different ships' crews. I would also not be my warriors' leader. It was potentially very risky, but was no longer completely unpalatable.

A second option was to journey east through Wessex, in the hope of finding a Norse fleet. I did not like this prospect either; fourteen warriors and a vitki provided far too little protection for our newly acquired riches. Travel at night was dangerous with wagons; hiding our tracks nigh-on impossible. Someone would notice our passage. Someone would see our party. Any ealdorman worth his salt who heard would put two and two together, and send a warband to investigate. My toes curled at the thought.

The third option was only appealing because the first two were so unpleasant.

I gathered everyone in and laid it out.

Vekel laughed, but did not argue against my suggestion. None of the others liked it. Hrolf suggested returning to Man or Dyflin with the silver – that aroused a lot of interest – but the longer voyage around the West-Bretland coast and over the sea to Ériu, not to mention the perils of meeting the English fleet again, meant that it soon died a death.

We went back to discussing my third option. An age it took, back and forth, without agreement. In the end, frustrated, rolling the dice yet again, I declared we would take a vote on all the options: my three and Hrolf's.

To my surprise, Vali chose the first option. No one opted for the second. Hrolf was alone in voting for his plan, which meant that I carried the day.

CHAPTER THIRTY-ONE

The rest of the afternoon passed without incident, that is to say the track saw no other traffic, and the sea remained clear of longships. Mightily relieved, because either could have been our ruination, I gave permission for two oxen to be butchered when darkness fell. We lit a massive fire deep within the trees and set to roasting. There was such a quantity of meat that in the end even Vali, by everyone's admission possessor of the largest appetite, declared himself defeated. Good, I told him, because we needed the rest, or as much as could be carried, for supplies. The remaining kine I ordered set free. Some farmer would round them up eventually, thanking his lucky stars at the unexpected gift.

It was well after midnight when we skulked towards the fishing village. I say village, it was more of a hamlet, perhaps a dozen cottages straggling along the moonlit, pebbly shore. There was no harbour; the inhabitants' boats were simply dragged up out of the water. All this had been evident from the rocky outcrop. What was less clear was whether any of the craft were large enough to take fifteen men and four chests full of silver. According to Lalo, who had crept in not long before us, one was. It looked to be in use too, he said, with nets piled at the prow.

We were going to sail along the southern coast of Wessex. Our silver could have bought a dozen vessels and crew, yet we could not go throwing our weight around, lest a leader with more warriors than us simply take it. With most of the treasure safely hidden before encountering any Norsemen, therefore, we would somehow establish cordial relations. How this would be established was unclear, but again my desperate men had not argued. After a few months of campaigning, I told them, there were bound to be longships short of oarsmen. I had reconciled myself to the idea of not being captain. A second chance would come sooner or later.

We skirted around the backs of the houses, keen not to be discovered. The fisherfolk here would be no match for us, but the darkness and their familiarity with the surroundings, not to mention most of us being needed to carry the chests, considerably shortened the odds in their favour. If we could get the boat in the water and away before anyone realised, so much the better.

My main concern was dogs, and their acute hearing. One had barked a few times while Lalo was scouting, but it had fallen abruptly silent. Of course he had cut its throat, and when its owner came outside to investigate, he suffered the same fate. The man must have lived alone, Lalo told us, because no one else appeared. He had managed to reach the shoreline without any further problems.

Let there not be any near us, I thought. I would kill dogs if I had to, and their owners, but there was no battle joy to be gained from either.

A dog did start up inside a house, but was soon told to be quiet. I was reassured, because it meant that the previous noise had gone unnoticed. I relieved Karli from one of the chests, and got a grateful look. He was getting long in the tooth; I had noticed his stiffness in the mornings, and how long it took him to limber up. He wasn't a complainer, though, not like Vekel, who had given up trying to help after a few steps.

If it had been anyone else, even me, there would have been fierce abuse, pisstaking and the rest, but no one uttered a word against the vitki. It helped, I decided, that after we had finished gorging ourselves on beef, Vekel had thrown the rune bones and read our future. The outlook was good, he'd announced. The boat would take us and the silver, and we would sail it right to the Norse fleet. Would there be danger, Karli had asked. Vekel had snorted, and asked if there was ever a time without perils. Of course it would be dangerous, he said, and there would be fighting, but we would win through.

He hadn't said how many of us.

I had seen this exact question in men's eyes, but no one asked it.

Nor had I. With *Brimdýr*'s loss, and the deaths of Kar, Thormod, Imr and so many others weighing like millstones round my neck, I didn't want to know.

I folded away my worries at the back of my mind. I was nearing the boat, which looked a decent size. Lalo gestured, excited, and my heart lifted. We *would* get away from this place without having to murder half its inhabitants, and before the rightful owners of the silver came to claim it.

Standing over the boat, I saw that it had been made for eight men, perhaps ten. It would be more of a squeeze than I'd first thought, but I refused to let any doubt creep in. We were committed; it was this craft or nothing.

'The chests go in first,' I whispered.

We got safely away from the hamlet, eight men at the oars pulling us into deeper water. The sail was unfurled, and a light wind bore us eastward. It was quiet on the water, and peaceful, yet my nerves were stretched taut. There were Norsemen on Wiht-land, over to starboard, and although they were probably wrapped in their blankets, I did not relax until the island had been left well behind, and the open sea stretched before us.

Morale was high. There were jokes about what the boat's owners would say when they found it gone, and also much anticipation about spending silver on ale, mead and women. We were rich, Vali said, and we deserved it. Men hoomed at that; I grinned at Vekel.

'It does feel good,' I said, tapping the chest under my arse.

'Money does not buy you happiness.'

'Goes a long way towards it.' I thought of Sláine, thinking that I would give up my share of the silver in the blink of an eye to bring us together again.

'Does it, Stormcrow?' Even in the darkness, his gaze weighed heavy.

'She is married to a king,' I said quietly. 'What can I do?'

'For the moment, nothing, but your time may come.'

'May?'

'The future is rarely certain.'

'Aye, and in the meantime, I'll rely on silver.'

Vekel lidded his black-rimmed eyes, and I busied myself with watching the distant horizon. I had enough on my mind without mooning over Sláine.

It was several days' sail to the mouth of the great river that came from Lundenwic, an English town often attacked by the Norse. Pickings were rich along the coastline too. We would meet longships at some point. The skill – I corrected myself – no, the gamble, was to decide where to go ashore and bury the silver. In truth, I had not the faintest idea when that might be, and I suspected Vekel and Thorstein knew that. Neither had offered an opinion. As for the others, I had their trust, for the moment at least. It weighed heavy on my shoulders.

The morning passed without incident. We saw a couple of fishing craft, but they were distant enough to be of no concern. Late in the afternoon, with the wind still at our backs, Twin-brows spotted a little bay. Down came the sail. We rowed in, eyes peeled for trouble. In Wessex, that didn't just mean longships, it was anyone at all. Even a shepherd might carry word of our presence. Luckily, there wasn't a soul about. I still insisted on sentries. We spent a quiet night close to the water's edge and were gone before dawn, slipping away on the blue-green sea with only seabirds as witnesses.

Our luck began to change halfway through the second morning when the wind picked up. It changed direction too, becoming a gusty, squally brute from the south that left the sail flapping and empty. We had to take it down, lest it be torn to flitters. Before I could even give the order, men took up the oars and began to row. Heavy-loaded, our progress was imperceptible. The sea was also against us now. Choppy waves, tall as a man, rolled in from starboard. Each vigorous slap against the hull threatened to unbalance the boat, which was keelless. We were soon drenched, but that was the least of our worries. Water was pooling between our feet, lifting a scum of debris – fish scales, untwined pieces of rope, and gods-know-what.

'Bail,' I cried. 'Use your helmets!'

The order did not need repeating.

Not everyone could stoop and fill, empty over the side, so I searched for a place to bring us ashore. My stomach tightened. There was no-where suitable, only tall white cliffs undulating off into the sea-mirk.

Another wave crashed in, heeling the boat over to port. Water slopped over the side, undoing all the bailers' efforts. I roared, calling them flabby-armed nithings.

'Do you *want* to drown?' I asked.

They redoubled their efforts, as did the men at the oars. We made a little distance, and I could see the planking again. There was still no visible landing place, but we could keep on like this, bailing and rowing, until one came into sight. So I told myself.

Then a big wave hit. It had the water lapping my ankles. I felt a tickle of fear, but refused to let it show. Lalo's face was grey, however, and he was muttering in his own tongue. Karli, the best seaman on board, was swearing. Thorstein and the other rowers bent their backs, rowing with a strength born of desperation. It was not enough, and never could have been. The boat might have been a decent craft with eight or ten fishermen aboard, but carrying fifteen of us and four silver chests turned it into a sluggish, wallowing pig of a thing.

The solution was as obvious as the nose on the end of my face. Nonetheless, I did not act. Instead I asked the sea-goddess Rán to help. The only answer was more seawater, dashed over us. I waited, praying harder.

The level at my feet rose further.

'Stormcrow.'

I met Karli's gaze.

'We are going to sink.'

Men glanced at one another. Stared at me. Vekel and Thorstein were the only ones whose faces were calm.

I could no longer ignore harsh reality. Curse it, I thought. 'Throw one of the chests overboard.'

Hrolf protested, but Twin-brows offered to heave him in as well, and he shut his trap. Vali and Twin-brows got up, standing wide legged in the bottom of the boat. They needed no telling that even resting a chest on the narrow-edged side would tip us over. The throw also had to be done in the interval between waves.

Veins on their necks standing out, they lifted a chest straight up. Gentle as a mother with a babe, they swung a little to the left, then to the right. Again they did it, increasing the angle, and a third time. The boat swayed to and fro, and water came spilling over the starboard side.

'Quickly,' I said.

They let go. For an instant the chest floated in the air, and then it dropped straight into the sea, right beside us. A fountain of spray erupted, the force sending the boat sideways. A wave hit from the other side, and a torrent poured in.

My request that Rán accept the offering dying on my lips, I stared at my feet. We were no better off. I could still see nowhere to come ashore. The sea, so welcoming the day before, was an ugly, froth-capped vicious beast that seemed hungry to drown us all, and the wind was its hissing companion.

'Get rid of another one,' I grated.

This time no one protested.

They didn't argue when I ordered the third chest pitched over the side either.

The boat lifted, easier in the water, and Karli grinned.

One chest was sufficient, I declared. We would none of us be poor.

At these words, I sensed Vekel's seiðr-gaze, and my skin itched. Clearly, the danger was not over yet. I did not look at him again, nor ask any questions, as if that would prevent whatever it was that he saw from happening. I might as well have stuck my head in the sand.

Intercede with Rán, Oðin, I prayed. Let us keep one chest. That is not greedy. She already has three.

It seemed he had granted my wish, because we made a little headway along the coast. With more room to bail, the water level went down. Men changed places at the oars; the newcomers' energy had the boat forging through the sea. Conditions grew a little calmer, and I dared to hope that the worst of our ordeal was over.

'Is that a longship?'

My despairing eyes followed Thorstein's outstretched arm.

Off to starboard, perhaps fifty spear casts away, a square shape had appeared. It was unmistakeably a sail, and with its coloured stripes, on the mast of a Norse vessel.

'Yes,' I said, adding the faint possibility, 'Maybe they won't see us.'

There followed a time when all eyes were on the longship, hoping against hope that its crew were laggards, not watching the seas around. Even if they did notice us, I told myself, perhaps they wouldn't bother with a few fishermen.

It was not to be.

'The whoresons are coming this way,' said Vali.

I swore I heard the Norns cackling, then realised a pair of gulls were screeching overhead. Bitches they are, I thought, the Norns. Miserable bitches.

'What are we to do, Stormcrow?' Vekel asked.

'A beach!' This was Lalo, looking off to port.

He was right. It was a shingle-lined strip, not all of which was backed by cliffs.

'We can reach it before the longship,' said Gunnar, eager as a leashed hound with the scent of deer in its nostrils.

'And go where? We can't outrun its warriors carrying the chest,' I snarled.

Gunnar looked crestfallen.

'We can bargain with the captain,' I said, not at all sure that this was the case. 'Buy our way on board.'

'The price will be the entire chest.' Vali's face was thunderous.

'That's better than nothing, isn't it?' It could work, I thought.

But the Norns weren't finished their malevolent weaving.

'It's *Sea-stallion*, or I'm a dung-shovelling Mumhan man,' said Thorstein. 'The figurehead has a notch in its neck.'

I looked, and acid rose to my gullet. Thorstein was right. Not only would we lose what remained of the silver, but Asgeir would take it. Think like Loki, I told myself. Be wily. Devious. I studied *Sea-stallion*, and inspiration hit with the force of a strike from Mjölnir, Thor's hammer.

'To the beach,' I ordered. 'Row, you dogs, because your lives depend on it!'

'What are you going to do?' Thorstein asked.

Everyone was looking at me. Even Vekel looked curious, and I took satisfaction from the fact that he hadn't already anticipated my intention.

'I thought you said we couldn't escape with the chest,' said Vali.

'I did.'

Vali wasn't happy. 'Are we going to fly away then?'

'No.' And I explained.

CHAPTER THIRTY-TWO

Sea-stallion almost cut us off from the beach, but not quite. Our oarsmen put in a heroic effort, and helped by the incoming tide, our boat could almost have been a nimble two-man faering. *Sea-stallion* was left in our wake. Reaching the shallows, Vali, Thorstein, Karli and I leaped in and hauled her out of the water. The chest was lifted up – we took it, and went a few steps before the weight had us set it down. Everyone tumbled out of the boat, and as I'd ordered, formed a circle, with Vekel, Lalo and the chest at our backs. Vekel was no face-to-face fighter, however he might argue, and Lalo was better with a bow than a spear. Thirteen of us there were in our little shieldwall, and a fine one it was too, I declared.

There were no cheers, only a few half-hearted hooms, but when I looked around, I knew my men would fight if I ordered. The silver helped, stiffening their backbones.

Sea-stallion's shipmaster beached her on the shingle. It was sufficient purchase for Asgeir's needs. We weren't running, so the warriors aboard took their time. In twos and threes they leaped off, and came ashore, cocky as you like. They were all clad in mail, with shields – ready for a fight.

'They've been in the wars! Mark how few there are,' I said. 'I count thirty-eight.'

'There's Asgeir, last of all, the arrogant skítkarl,' said Vekel.

'Thirty-nine then,' I replied.

'They outnumber us three to one,' said Hrolf.

'And if it comes to a fight,' I retorted, 'we will kill how many? One warrior each?'

My warriors didn't like that, which was precisely my intention.

'Two men each!' Gunnar cried.

Vali snorted. 'Three!'

311

'I will not enter Valhöll unless I have put down five at least,' Thorstein declared.

'Asgeir won't have a crew left by the time we're finished,' I shouted.

Now they cheered, pride stirring, and the blood thrummed in my veins. Part of me wanted to fight then, just to prove how many warriors we could take with us. If Thorstein was set on five, I thought, I had to kill six. More if I could.

Our high spirits shocked Asgeir's men. Their approach continued, but slower and warier. Vekel began to chant, and pointed his iron staff in their direction, which visibly increased their unease.

Asgeir was a snake, but he was a clever one. Stalking in front of his men, fancy helmet obscuring most of his face, he came almost within spear range.

'Asgeir,' I said.

Surprise, then, 'If it isn't little Stormcrow, with a fine sword on his belt.' He was as suave as a moneylender about to close a deal. 'And the vitki, I forget his name . . . oh, and the blámaðr too!'

I heard Lalo's bowstring tauten. 'Easy,' I said from the side of my mouth. 'Not unless I say.'

Lalo obeyed, but he was muttering curses in Irish, Norse and his own tongue.

'Funny meeting you here,' I said.

Asgeir's eyes were on the chest – like his crew, he would have seen it being unloaded from our boat. 'Where's Imr?'

'Dead.'

'*Brimdýr* is at the bottom of the sea too?'

'No.' I wasn't going to explain anything.

'There's silver in that chest, or I'm a monk.'

'A decent quantity.'

'We'll be taking it,' said Asgeir, and his men laughed and smiled. I thought I spied Rognald, the man who had assaulted Sláine, in their midst.

'Will you now?'

'Aye.'

'Come on then, and welcome,' I taunted. 'More than half your warriors will die, and where will you be then, eh? *Sea-stallion* needs at least thirty, better, forty men as crew.'

Asgeir sneered, but didn't give the order to attack.

We stared at each other. I let him stew, wonder what I had up my sleeve.

'You can't get away,' he said.

'We're happy to stay here,' I said, 'eh, lads?'

They cheered, loud and lusty, and Asgeir's scowl deepened.

'Have you a proposition, Stormcrow?'

'I do. Half the contents of the chest are yours.'

'And the other half is yours?'

'Yes. There is more.'

His eyes were slits. 'Go on.'

'You will take us on as crew.'

A surprised chuckle. 'Have you taken leave of your wits? Your men and mine hate each other's guts.'

'We know why that is, don't we?' Thorstein, normally reserved, couldn't help himself. 'It's because you abandoned us at Cluan Mhic Nóis!'

'Left at the opportune time, I would call it.' Asgeir's grin was greasy.

'What's done is done.' The memory of Ulf drowning burned bright in my mind, but I kept my tone placatory. 'The past is best forgotten. What's needed here is a way to prevent bloodshed.'

'You just want to save your skins,' said Asgeir, his lip curled.

'And you need enough crew to sail *Sea-stallion*. Come at us with shield and axe, and by Oðin, twenty warriors and more of yours will never leave this beach.'

Thorstein hammered his shield boss, and every man copied him. They made a fearful racket, throwing insults and threats. Asgeir's crew shouted their own war cries, but for the number of them, it didn't drown out my men's shouts.

The tumult died down, and I stared at Asgeir.

'What's it to be?'

Asgeir withdrew a short distance to consider his options. I called out that there was no point leaving us on the beach, and hoping to attack our boat in open water. We wouldn't be leaving anytime soon, I shouted, and we'd do so after burying the silver, which he would never find.

His warriors did not look happy. Who would, I said to Vekel, when the choice was between free silver and a good chance of dying.

'We'll be sleeping every night with our seaxes in our fists,' Hrolf grumbled.

'If you have a better way out of this, tell us,' I said.

He chewed on his moustache instead.

'A man can only play the tafl moves on the board,' I said. 'We need to get on a longship. I'd rather a different one than *Sea-stallion*, but the gods sent her.'

'And Asgeir too, the skítkarl,' said Thorstein.

'He'll try to do us out of more silver.' We had talked about this briefly.

'No more than two-thirds,' said Vali to a rumble of agreement.

I nodded. 'Here he comes.' There was a man with him, his shipmaster, I assumed. Dour of face, thin, he looked in need of a satisfying shit.

There was no preamble. 'We need more silver,' Asgeir said.

I *hmph*ed.

'Two-thirds of the chest's contents.'

'Done.' I stuck out my hand.

'I am the leader on *Sea-stallion*, not you, or anyone else. You follow my orders.'

'As long as you give the same commands to your warriors,' I shot back.

'Aye.'

Asgeir's grip was limp, like his prick. I trusted it not one tiny bit.

Vekel appeared beside us. His staff rose high. 'Swear on the gods, both of you.'

Asgeir's lips twisted.

'Take the oath,' I said, 'or our agreement counts for nothing.'

'You shook my hand.'

'And you mine, but that would not prevent your warriors knifing me and my men in the middle of the night.'

A snicker.

'Am I wrong?'

The rings in his beard braids tinkled as his head shook. 'You are not.'

'Swear not to harm each other while you are on *Sea-stallion*,' Vekel said.

Asgeir obeyed. So did I, thinking, when we are not on the longship, we can murder one another to our hearts' content. Knowing Vekel, that had been his intention. Asgeir would have noticed too, I had no doubt about that.

'Let Oðin, the All-Father, own you both,' Vekel said, loud and authoritative. 'Let the thunder god Thor receive you both!'

We bent our heads as he made the divinities witnesses to our oath. I would not break this sacred vow; it was unlikely Asgeir would either, for all his snake-wiliness. Vekel was not done. Not until every warrior present had made the same promise did he let up. Finished, he bestowed a beatific smile on me and Asgeir.

'There. We are all friends now,' he said, like a mother who has just forced two squabbling brats to make peace.

'Open the chest,' said Asgeir, making clear where his main interest lay.

I stood back, letting Thorstein watch over Asgeir as the contents were tallied up and divvied out. It was strange, but I no longer cared about this silver, nor that which had gone into the sea. My high hopes of buying a longship had come to nothing, but that did not take away from my achievements. Against all odds, I had led my men – and whatever our oath said, they were *my* men – across a vast swathe of enemy territory without many casualties. There was some silver in our purses, and we were crew on a longship. Not the vessel we would have chosen, but a longship, nonetheless. It was not our own – my gaze went to Asgeir and then Rognald, both of whom I could not trust. We were alive, and free, however, and Oðin still held me in some regard. I felt sure of it.

Vekel didn't look happy, though, which was unsettling. I followed his gaze out to sea, and saw rolling banks of dark clouds, presaging more bad weather. 'Will there be a storm? Should we stay ashore?'

His dark eyes met mine. 'More than that, Stormcrow. The greatest danger of all awaits.'

My skin crawled. 'When?'

'Soon. You will need the sword. Danger will come from the most unexpected place.' He saw me glance at Asgeir and Rognald, whom I had mentioned. 'Not them.'

It was bad then, I decided. 'Where then?'

'I do not know.' Vekel's normally calm expression was absent. 'We must be on our guard.'

I clutched my sword hilt, and asked the gods for guidance.

None came.

AUTHOR'S NOTE

I had my first serious thoughts about writing in 2001/2. My initial plan was either to set a story in the Viking Age or Roman times. Growing up in Ireland, loving history, it was impossible not to be influenced by the huge historical impact of the Norsemen. Thanks to Asterix and books like *The Eagle of the Ninth*, however, I also had a great interest in the Romans.

Seeing Bernard Cornwell's first Uhtred book in the window of Waterstones in Newcastle-upon-Tyne made the decision for me. I literally cursed him. In my ignorance I thought that when an author of his stature started writing about Norsemen, it meant that I couldn't. In fact the opposite is true, but I went with the Romans. Things didn't work out too badly and nineteen books later, I have come back full circle. It feels good.

The early and middle medieval period left scant written detail of Ireland's history. Frustratingly, the same can be said of Norsemen, whenever and wherever they lived. Thus gaping holes exist in our knowledge about the Irish, the Norse and the Hiberno-Norse. For the historical novelist, it is both blessing and curse. I can make things up to my heart's content, but this approach only works if reasonable assumptions are made rather than wild supposition. Good common sense also helps.

It's worth noting that the medieval Irish didn't make hay, rather grazing their livestock outside all year long. This worked except when severe winters occurred. Massive cattle mortality is recorded for those years. Interestingly, the longest Irish measurement of distance was a spear-cast. It makes sense, though. The world of most medieval people was very small. It was rare to go more than a few miles from where one was born, lived and died. That's why there is no mention of quarter miles, half miles or miles, etc. in this book.

The same principle applies to the measurement of time. In the medieval period people would have had far broader parameters than today, with its atomic clocks and automatically updated smartphones and computers. There was sunrise, morning, afternoon, sunset, evening, night and little more than that. If one didn't live close to a monastery, where bells sounded up to eight times a day, there was no way to tell the time except the position of the sun in the sky. If it was cloudy . . . you do the maths. I'm sorry that I didn't use this approach to time much earlier in my career, so please forgive my heroes doing something 'half an hour later' in many of my Roman novels.

I spend a lot of time researching, but I am time-constrained; one novel a year, or my kids don't eat. I joke, but it's also true. To try and avoid potential mistakes caused by insufficient research, I consult academics before my books go to print. With *Stormcrow*, I am deeply indebted to Professor Neil Price of Uppsala University in Sweden, who generously gave of his time to read the manuscript. He liked it too! It must be mentioned that his two superlative texts, *The Viking Way* and *Children of Ash and Elm: A History of the Vikings*, had an enormous impact on this book. Thank you, Neil. I have to mention my late friend Robert Low here too. His Oathsworn novels are quite simply the best Viking novels I have ever read; I like to think he would look kindly on this book. Giles Kristian's work is brilliant as well. On the subject of Norsemen, the letter 'ð' in their language is not pronounced as a 'd', but as a 'th'. So Oðin would have been pronounced something like 'Owe-thinn'.

Growing up near the sea in County Louth, Ireland, I had no idea that there had been a large Norse settlement just a few miles away, in Annagassan. The moment I heard about Linn Duachaill, that was where my hero had to come from – it seemed written in the stars! It wasn't until 2005 that the site – known in the medieval period as Linn Duachaill – was identified by Micheál McKeown, a local historian, along with two others. I am greatly indebted to Micheál, who generously shared archaeological information and his remarkable drawings of the site. Sadly, he died in late 2023 after a short illness. I am sure Micheál is in Valhöll, from where I hope he looks kindly on this story. The Brazen Head is the oldest pub in Dublin, reputedly open since 1198. Although it may not have existed when Finn and Vekel were in Dyflin, I felt it deserved to be included. I wonder if that will get me a free pint! Maybe I'll go in there one day with a copy of the book and see . . .

All the kings, queens and rulers mentioned in the book were historical figures, except for Cormac, Máel's son. I used his real son Flann for a time, but potential confusion with Finn, and the unappealing names of his other sons meant I decided to invent Cormac. The rivalry between Brian Bóramha and Máel Sechnaill was very real, so too the duplicitousness of Sigtrygg, known nowadays as Sitric Silkbeard. The battle at Gleann Máma took place on New Year's Eve AD 999, and Sigtrygg's ignominious flight, ending up on the Isle of Man, comes from the texts. So does the double royal marriage to seal the peace, although it was my invention to have Sláine fall in love with Finn. Lalo is a fictional character, but his tribe, the Mandinka, are a real people in modern-day Mali. The name is also a nod to the late, great Sinéad O'Connor.

An incomplete list of texts in my library includes Neil Price's books above, and also: *Ireland in the Medieval World* by Edel Bhreathnach; *The Vikings in Britain and Ireland* by Carroll, Harrison and Williams; *Early Irish Law Series Volume 1: Bechbretha*, edited by Charles-Edwards and Kelly; *Dublin and the Viking World* by Clarke, Dooley and Johnson; *Ireland and Scandinavia in the Early Viking Age* by Clarke, Ní Mhaonaigh and Ó Floinn; *Medieval Ireland* by Clare Downham; *A Regional History of England (The South-East to AD 1000)* by Drewett, Rudling and Gardiner; *Viking Longship* by Keith Durham; *The Archaeology of Early Medieval Ireland* by Nancy Edwards; *The Vikings* by Ian Heath; *Viking Age Dublin* by Ruth Johnson; *Marriage Disputes, A Fragmentary Old Irish Law-Text*, edited by Fergus Kelly; *Early Irish Farming*, edited by Fergus Kelly; *The Vikings in Britain* by H.R. Loyn; *National Geographic*, March 2017 issue, *Chronicles of the Vikings* by R.I. Page; *Viking Age England* by Julian Richards; *The Viking Age: Ireland and the West, Proceedings of the Fifteenth Viking Congress*, edited by Sheehan and Ó Corráin; and *Cogadh Gaedhel Re Gallaibh, (The Invasion of Ireland by the Danes and other Norsemen)*, translated by James Henthorn Todd.

Read all my published novels and wanting more? Seek out my Kickstarter-funded digital novellas *The March* (a follow-on from *The Forgotten Legion*), *Eagle in the Wilderness*, *Eagles in the East* and *Io, Saturnalia!* (all three feature Centurion Tullus of the *Eagles of Rome* trilogy). There is also a stand-alone novella, *Centurion of the First*, set on Hadrian's Wall in second century AD Britain. Don't own an e-reader? Simply download the free Kindle app from Amazon and read the stories on a phone, tablet or computer. If you don't read e-books, all but the last two are available in print and as an audiobook, *Sands of the Arena*.

Enjoy cycling? Google Ride and Seek (rideandseek.com); this company runs epic cycling trips (Hannibal, Napoleon, Marco Polo) that I am involved with as an historical guide.

I am a long-term fundraiser for Combat Stress, which helps British veterans with PTSD, and Médecins Sans Frontières (MSF), responsible for sending medical staff into disaster and war zones worldwide. I have walked Hadrian's Wall in full Roman armour twice to raise money for these causes. I once marched with two friends from Capua to the Colosseum in Rome. The result, the 'Romani walk', is on YouTube, narrated by Sir Ian McKellen – Gandalf! Link: tinyurl.com/h4n8h6g

I also raise money for Park in the Past (parkinthepast.org.uk), a community-interest company which is building a Roman marching fort near Chester in north-west England. The partly constructed fort is already open to the public.

Big thanks to my amazing editor Sam Eades and to the ever-enthusiastic Paul Stark in Audio, and to the rest of the fantastic team at Orion. You all work so hard to make my books the successes they are, and I appreciate it.

And now to you, my amazing readers. I love your emails and comments/messages on social media. Please keep them coming! I often give away signed books and goodies and auction for charity – stay tuned on these media. Sadly, historical fiction is still a shrinking market. A short review or just a rating of this book, left on Amazon, Goodreads, Google, iTunes or Waterstones.com, would be a real help. Gratitude!

Thank you to my children Ferdia and Pippa, whom I love to the moon and back.

There is one other thank you as well. Always.

Ways to get in touch:

Email: ben@benkane.net

Facebook: facebook.com/benkanebooks

Twitter: @BenKaneAuthor

Instagram: benkanewrites

My website: benkane.net

Soundcloud (podcasts): soundcloud.com/user-803260618

YouTube (short documentary-style videos): tinyurl.com/y7chqhgo

GLOSSARY

a chara – *kha-ra* (the kh is guttural). Means 'my friend'.

Aédh – *A as in 'pay'*.

amadán – *ama-dawn*. A fool.

Araboo – Arabs.

Baile Shláine – *Boll-yeh Hloy-neh*. Slane, County Meath.

Bealtaine – *Byalth-a-neh* (the th is guttural). Festival at the start of May, celebrating the first day of summer.

bean sidhe – *ban-shee*. Fairy woman.

Bifröst – mythical bridge to Asgard, realm of the gods.

blackleg – a Norse insult.

Bláland – the northern part of Africa and beyond.

bod – *bud*. Means 'prick'.

bod salach – *bud sal-ach* (the ch is guttural). Means 'dirty prick'.

Bóinn – *Bo-inn*. The River Boyne.

Breandán – *Brendawn*. Modern-day Brendan.

Bretland – Wales.

Brian Bóramha – *Bree-an Boh-rah-va*. In today's language, Brian Boru.

Breifne – *Breff-neh*. A medieval Irish kingdom.

Buite – *Bwee-cheh*.

Cairlinn – *Car-lynn*. Modern-day Carlingford, Co. Louth.

Cambronn – Camborne, Cornwall.

Casán – *Ka-sawn*. River Glyde, Co. Louth.

Cenél nEóghain – *Ken-ale No-en*.

Cerball – *Kar-ool*.

Clann Cholmáin – *Clann Khul-moyne* (the kh is guttural).

Cluain Fearta – *Cloo-an Fer-theh* (the th is guttural) Modern-day Clonfert, Co. Galway.

Cluain Mhic Nóis – Clonmacnoise, County Offaly.

Cnogba – *Kuh-nog-ba*. Knowth, County Meath, situated less than 2 km from Newgrange as the crow flies.

Conchobar – *Kon-koor*.

Congalach – *Kunga-lah-ch* (the ch is guttural).

Connachta – *Kona-ch-ta* (the ch is guttural). Connacht, today one of the four provinces of Ireland.

crannóg – *krann-ogue*.

Cú – *Koo*, meaning hound.

Cúchulainn – *Koo Chul-an* (the ch is guttural). An ancient Irish mythical warrior.

Dál Fiatach – *Dawl Fee-a-tack*h (the kh is guttural).

Dearbháil – *Dar-voyle*.

Domhnaill/Domnall – *Dough-nul*.

Donnchadha – *Du-na-kha* (the kh is guttural).

Dubhlinn – *Duve-lyn* ('u' as in 'pull'), Black Pool. Dublin.

Dún Corcaighe – *Doon cur-kee*. Modern-day Cork city.

Dún na Sciath – *Doon na Shkee*. Site on Lough Ennell, County Westmeath.

Dyflin – Norse for Dublin, derived from Dubhlinn.

Eochaidh mac Ardgail – *Yok-y Mack Ardal*.

Ériu – *Air-ee-oo*. The island of Ireland.

fear gorm – *far gu-rum*, literally, 'blue man'. A person of colour.

Fionn mac Cumhaill – *F-yun Makool*.

gerrán – *ge-rawn*. Small horse, gelding.

gioc-goc – *g-yok gok*, pidgin Irish spoken by Norsemen.

Gleann Máma – *Glown Mawma* (the ow is pronounced 'ow', as in an exclamation of pain).

Gormlaith – *Guh-rum-la*.

gouger – an aggressive lowlife.

Hjaltland – Shetland.

herring chokers – an insult from Galway city in the twentieth century, referring to those who lived closest to the sea.

Inis Cathaig – *Inish Kath-ayg*. An island in the Shannon which was part of Norse Limerick.

Inis Cró – *Inish Crow*. Site on Lough Ennell, County Westmeath.

Inis Mon – the island of Anglesey.

Jorvik – York.

Jórsalaland – the Holy Land.

Jórsalir – Jerusalem.

Laighin – *Lie-in*. Leinster, today one of the four provinces of Ireland.

langpheitir – *lang-fetter*. Derived from Norse, a type of hobble.

Leth Cuinn – *Leh Kwin*.

Leth Moga – *Leh Muga*.

Liath Macha – *Lee-ah Mock-a*. One of Cúchulainn's two chariot horses.

Linn Duachaill – *Lyn Doo-ach-ull* (the ach is guttural), Duachaill's Pool, Annagassan, County Louth.

Loch Ainninn – *Loch Ann-inn* (the ch is guttural). Lough Ennell, County Westmeath.

Lochlann – *Loch-lan* (the ch is guttural). Modern-day Scandinavia, esp. Norway.

Lughnasadh – *Loo-na-sa*. A midsummer festival, celebrating the beginning of harvest.

Luimnech – *Lim-nech* (the ch is guttural). Modern-day Limerick city.

Lundenwic – London.

Máel – *Male*.

Máel-mórda – *Male more-ga*.

Mainistir Bhuithe – *Man-ish-teer Vwee-huh*. Monasterboice, County Louth.

Mandé – an area of West Africa including parts of modern-day Mali and Guinea.

Mandinka – a tribe in Mali.

Mathgamhain – *Mah-ga-won*.

Miklagard – the Great City, Constantinople, modern-day Istanbul.

Midhe – *Mee*. Meath, today an Irish county.

Mumhan – *Moo-an*. Munster, today one of the four provinces of Ireland.

Orm – a tribute to my late friend Robert Low, this was the name of the main character in his outstanding Oathsworn series.

Osraighe – *Us-ri-uh*. Medieval Irish kingdom.

Ruirthech – *Roor-hech* (the ch is guttural). The medieval name for the River Liffey.

Saint Petroc's Stowe – Padstow.

Samhain – *Sow-un*. Celebrated on 1 November, an ancient Irish festival marking the end of harvest and beginning of winter, and a time when the boundaries between this world and the next blurred, meaning contact with the spirits was more likely. Also the Irish word for November.

Seal Islands – Orkney Islands.

Sechnaill – *Shek-nal* (the k is guttural).

Serkland – a vast area, which may have referred to the territories of the Abbasid Caliphate, in the modern Middle East.

Sí an Bhrú – *She on Vroo*. Fairy Hill. The UNESCO World Heritage Site of Newgrange, County Louth.

Sionainn – *Shun-an*. The River Shannon, largest of Ireland's waterways.

Siúr – *Sure*. The River Suir, which flows through modern-day Waterford city.

Sláine – *Slaw-nye*.

'tafl – short for hnefatafl, a board game.

Teamhair na Rí – *Tower na Ree*. The Hill of Tara, County Meath.

Uí Chonaing – *Ee Kh-onang* (the kh is guttural).

Uí Dunchadha – *Ee Duna-kha* (the kh is guttural).

Uí Faeláin clan – *Ee Fay-loyne*.

Uí Néills – *Ee Nails*.

Ulaidh – *Ull-ah*. Ulster, today one of the four provinces of Ireland.

Ulfreksfjord – *Ull-freks-fiord*. Modern-day Larne, County Antrim, Northern Ireland.

Valland – an area spanning much of modern-day France.

Vedrarfjord – *Vedr-are-fiord*. Modern-day Waterford city.

Groenland – Greenland.

Waesfjord – *Vays-fiord*. Modern-day Wexford town.

West African tribal names: Mandinka, Soninke, Ligbi, Vai, Bissa.

West-Bretland – Cornwall.

Wiht-land – the Isle of Wight.

young wans – young ones, young females.

CREDITS

Ben Kane and Orion Fiction would like to thank everyone at Orion who worked on the publication of *Stormcrow* in the UK.

Editorial
Sam Eades
Snigdha Koirala

Copy editor
Sally Partington

Proofreader
Kati Nicholl

Audio
Paul Stark

Contracts
Dan Herron
Ellie Bowker
Oliver Chacón

Design
Tomás Almeida
Joanna Ridley

Editorial Management
Charlie Panayiotou
Jane Hughes
Bartley Shaw

Finance
Jasdip Nandra
Nick Gibson
Sue Baker

Marketing
Ellie Nightingale

Publicity
Frankie Banks

Production
Ruth Sharvell

Sales
Catherine Worsley
Esther Waters
Victoria Laws
Karin Burnik
Toluwalope Ayo-Ajala
Rachael Hum
Georgina Cutler

Operations
Jo Jacobs

THE
LIONHEART
SERIES

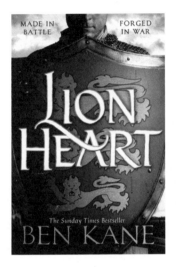
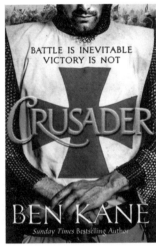
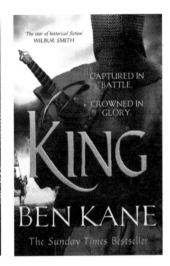

MADE IN BATTLE. FORGED IN WAR.

'A rip-roaring epic, filled with arrows and spattered with blood'
Paul Finch

'Deeply authoritative'
Simon Scarrow

THE
CLASH OF EMPIRES
SERIES

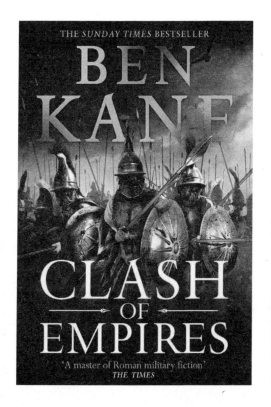

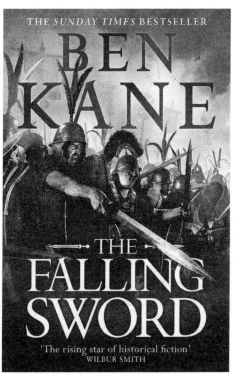

Can Greece resist the might of Rome?

The final showdown between two great civilisations begins . . .

'A triumph!'
Harry Sidebottom

'Fans of battle-heavy historical fiction will, justly, adore Clash of Empires'
The Times

SANDS
of the
ARENA
And Other Stories

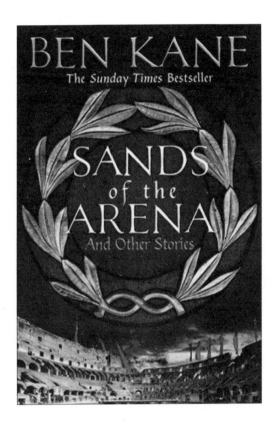

THE EPIC SHORT STORY COLLECTION

Available to buy now